Clash by ✦ Night

THE CROW ™

Clash by Night

CHET WILLIAMSON

INSPIRED BY THE SERIES CREATED BY
JAMES O'BARR

HarperPrism
A Division of HarperCollinsPublishers

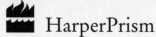 HarperPrism
A Division of HarperCollins*Publishers*
10 East 53rd Street, New York, NY 10022-5299

ISBN 0-06-105826-2

HarperCollins®, 🏭®, and HarperPrism®
are trademarks of HarperCollins Publishers, Inc.

The Crow™ is a trademark of Edward R. Pressman Film Corporation

HarperPrism books may be purchased for educational, business, or sales promotional use. For information, please write: Special Markets Department, HarperCollins Publishers, Inc. 10 East 53rd Street, New York, NY 10022-5299.

Cover illustration © 1998 by Cliff Nielson

Designed by Lisa Pifher

First printing: July 1998

Printed in the United States of America

Library of Congress Cataloging-in-Publication Data

Williamson, Chet.
  Clash by night / Chet Williamson.
    p. cm — (The Crow)
  ISBN 0-06-105826-2 (trade pbk.)
  I. Title II. Series: Crow (Series)
PS3573.I456238C58 1998
813'.54—dc21   98-2618

Visit HarperPrism on the World Wide Web at
http://www.harperprism.com

98 99 00 01 02 ❖ 10 9 8 7 6 5 4 3 2 1

To Mac and Robin—
Don't let the music and the dancing ever stop . . .

acknowledgments

For their kind assistance in realizing the Crow's present incarnation in these pages, the author wishes to thank John Douglas, Rich Miller, Jimmy Vines, Jeff Conner, and Edward R. Pressman.

And we are here as on a darkling plain
Swept with confused alarms of struggle and flight,
Where ignorant armies clash by night.

—Matthew Arnold, "Dover Beach"

PART ONE

Ah, love, let us be true
To one another! . . .

—Matthew Arnold, "Dover Beach"

one

"It's payback time, friends. Time to make the wrong things right."

Everywhere you looked in the room there was trash and there were guns. The trash included empty pizza boxes, the sauce long dried into patches of a far brighter red than blood, the cheese hardened like burned and crusted flesh. Empty beer cans and throwaway bottles sat on tables, imparting a thick, yeasty smell to the room. The occupants viewed the scene through a haze of cigarette smoke, as though with eyes clouded by cataracts. The light of the two floor lamps, caparisoned with tattered shades, cast soft shadows into the crags and pockets of the men's faces, some gaunt, others full and doughy.

Cigarette ends glowed red like eyes in the jungle night, then dimmed as more smoke clouded the air and the ashtrays, already filled, mounded higher with the powdery fragments of dead breath.

"Payback for Waco . . ."

Piles of magazines with titles like *The Christian Patriot, White Pride, American Times*, and the quasi-Shakespearean *Arms Against Troubles* sat on two small tables.

"Payback for Ruby Ridge . . ."

There was a small bookcase with several dozen tired and tattered volumes, among them *The Turner Diaries, Mein Kampf,* and a number of books on guns and ammunition. On one shelf sat a collection of manuals from a small publisher on how to make bombs and perform assassinations, as well as a series entitled *How to Kill*, and another called *The Poor Man's James Bond*.

"Payback for Tim McVeigh . . ."

There was music playing in the background, just loud enough for a listener to make out the lyrics over the solid country-western beat:

> *The Jews'll be gone, and the black folk too—*
> *We'll have an America for me and you.*
> *Yeah, we'll get those mongrels on the run*
> *When each American stands up pointin' his gun . . .*

"And we're gonna start that payback with Senator Robert King."

But what caught the eye most readily in the smoky, warm room were the guns. The precision of their storage and presentation was in sharp contrast to the slovenliness of the rest of the room. Many were leaning neatly in racks, their dark metal shining, while others were secured to the expanse of pegboard fastened to the wall on either side of a large American flag. White outlines had been painted around each weapon as if to show their users where to replace them, leaving ghosts of themselves to whisper silently while their corporeal selves spoke aloud.

"That Jew-marrying, nigger-loving, patriot-hating, mother-poking sonovabitch liberal . . ."

Some of the weapons were legal, but many, capable of full automatic fire, were not. Among them were several AK–47s, two Finnish Jati-Matics, a pair of Ingrams, an obsolete but still functional Wilkinson Linda, a KG–9, and two MK Arms 70 submachine guns. All were cleaned and oiled, and loaded clips rested on small shelves or hung from hooks next to their prospective weapons. These were only the weapons for immediate use in the event of an incursion. The others were in the powder magazine in far greater numbers.

"And we'll get him when he comes to Hobie." Virgil Withers, known to his fellow Sons of a Free America as Rip, leaned back and smiled. His teeth shone whitely between thin lips. The rest of his face was far from thin. It was pouchy and wrinkled, lined with hate and fattened with a diet of beef and cheese and plenty of carbohydrates. But Rip stayed active and so was stocky rather than fat.

"King's coming here?" The words rushed from Junior Feeley's mouth on a carpet of cigarette smoke. Junior was what anyone would have called fat—but not to his face since he was also six feet, eight inches tall and an awful lot of his three hundred and twenty pounds was solid muscle. The Sons of a Free America had elected Junior Feeley treasurer since they figured that no one would ever dare to steal money from him, and he was too stupid to steal it himself.

"Damn right King's coming," Rip said. "Chip cracked into their website on the Internet . . ."

"It's hacked, not cracked, and I didn't have to hack into it," Chip Porter said, waving his bottle of beer in protest. "I just, hell, *found* it."

"Whatever. Anyway, we know he's gonna be in town, we know when, and we know where. Read them the itinerary, Chip."

Chip read from a printout. "Tuesday, April thirtieth, he arrives in Hobie at nine A.M., meets with the mayor at city hall. At ten, he tours the flood site . . ."

"That bastard gave our tax money away so those damn river rats could rebuild," said Sonny Armitage, "and now he's coming here to take the credit, get more damn votes for his damn presidential race."

"Your uncle's gonna rebuild his house with that money, Sonny," Ace Ludwig reminded him.

"Well, my uncle was a horse's ass to buy a house there in the first place, the damn senator was another horse's ass to give him money for being that stupid, and my uncle's a horse's ass three times over to take that money and build right in the same damn spot where it's gonna flood all over again in another year or two."

"Amen to that," said Junior Feeley. "Why you stickin' up for King, Ace?"

"I'm not sticking up for him, he's a damn traitor and I'd blow his brains out as fast as I'd blow out Reno's or Billary's or Teddy Kennedy's. I was just stating a *fact*, that Sonny's uncle got money from the prick and his damn senate bill."

"All *right*," Rip said. "Now just shut up and let Chip read this thing. Go ahead."

"Okay, so the senator will do photo ops there for a couple of hours, then at noon they eat at Barney's Diner, he presses the flesh, meets the little people."

"Maybe we could get Barney to poison the prick," Ace Ludwig suggested, and the others laughed.

"After that he speaks to the chamber of commerce at one thirty, answers questions and bullshits till three thirty, then he starts visiting small businesses in the area."

"Five'll get you ten," Sonny Armitage said, "he doesn't go to Peters' Gun Shop. Hell, I bet we could get Jimmy Peters to give him a 'Death to the King' bumper sticker free."

They laughed again, even Chip, who continued reading with a smile. "Okay, now these visits aren't firmed up yet—we don't know what stores or offices he's gonna go to when, but we know what the last one's gonna be before he flies out of here at nine. It's the one closest to the airport, on the outskirts of Hobie."

"You gonna make us guess?" said Sonny Armitage, filling the pause.

"It's a day-care place," Chip said. "The Making Friends Child Care Center, it's called."

"Chip checked it out good," Rip Withers said. "Been open about six months, two women run it, got another one who helps. It's our best bet. The other places are like computer stores, electronics stores, and they got security systems up the ass or offices in buildings with even tighter security. But this place has nothing."

"Why not?" asked Will Standish.

"'Cause they don't have anything worth stealing," Rip said. "Probably a couple VCRs, maybe a computer or two for the kids to play with. Other than that, toys, right? And best of all, it's in the suburbs, mostly houses around, on a nice quiet block with hardly any traffic after ten at night. Yessir, brothers, it's the perfect place to bomb a bastard."

Amy Carlisle hung up the telephone and looked around the room, almost dizzy from the news. Then to center herself, she pictured the room as it was just hours earlier and as it would be hours from now, filled with bright, happy children who she only wanted to make brighter and happier.

True, every one of the fifty-three children that she and Nancy and Judy watched over at different times during their six-day week may not have had genius IQs, but they all had something going for them, from the one year olds just starting to form their words to the first and second graders who were dropped off before school started or who spent an hour or two after school before their parents picked them up on their way home from work. Each of them had something different to offer and each of them was special.

Amy knew all of their names and all of their likes and dislikes. She knew, most importantly, what made them smile. When their little faces lit up, the younger ones at the sight of a brightly colored mobile or a noisy toy, the older children at a glimpse of art supplies or a well-loved book that Amy was about to read, she knew she was doing more than earning her money.

She had never wanted to be a mere baby-sitter but had wanted a true learning center, where the children would do more than just pass the time. They would learn new concepts and skills and how to interact with others and make friends. They would leave knowing more than when they came in. They were in her charge and she felt they had become *her* children, every single one.

What made them even more precious was that Amy would never have a child of her own. When she had turned twenty-seven, she and Rick had decided the time had come to have a baby, maybe more than one, and she stopped taking her pills. But after a year of trying, her gynecologist's examination proved that the problem was hers, not Rick's. They had looked into adoption, but the waiting list was long and they didn't want to be new parents at thirty-five or forty.

That was when the idea of a day-care center came into Amy's head. She had a degree in elementary education and had taught school the year after she and Rick had graduated from college. But although she loved her interactions with the children, she had quickly become frustrated by the inability of the system to deal with the problems she saw. When a child was having trouble, be it in hearing, speech, vision, or learning, it took months to schedule proper testing and longer still to get the student into a special program once the diagnosis was made.

There were other concerns as well. Amy had had several students who she was certain were victims of abuse, but drawing aside the bureaucratic curtain on such suspicions made the testing delays look insignificant. Children were sad and suffering and there was little she could do to change that. Though she tried to remain upbeat, she could not, and gradually grew depressed. This depression, along with the vast amounts of out-of-school time that she spent planning and preparing for class, drove her a few steps short of a breakdown, and she gave her notice at the end of the year, to Rick's great relief.

Through some contacts at the architectural firm where he worked, she found an administrative position at an educational supply company. There she learned about running a small business from the ground up and she remained for seven years. During that time she had mused about opening a day-care facility but it wasn't until she learned she couldn't have children of her own that she began to get serious.

She had the training but the money was slower in coming. She had been stockpiling her salary for several years, thinking that it would allow her to be a stay-at-home mom after their baby was born. When it became apparent that wasn't going to happen, it was another year before she could make a down payment on an abandoned health club a half mile from their house. A bank loan secured the rest, with enough left over to turn the ex-gym into a day-care center.

It had taken another six months to make the renovations and get the proper certification, but at last the Making Friends Child Care Center had opened. It had been in operation now for six months and was, by every standard except the financial, a huge success. But Amy was making enough to break even, and with the news she had just received, even that situation might improve.

"Last little mite gone?"

Amy turned and saw Nancy Fowler standing in the doorway to the infant and toddler area. "Yeah," she said. "Megan just left."

"And you're still standing here?"

"I was on the phone." Amy smiled, trying hard not to let the secret show, wanting to have some fun first. "Nancy, I was just thinking. You know what would be great for this place? If we were to appear on TV—really heavy local coverage and even some national coverage. Don't you think that would help get enrollment up to where we want it?"

"Uh, yeah," Nancy said. "What are you saying, you think we ought to take out a hundred thousand dollar loan and buy a few minutes of airtime on ABC?"

"All four networks, including Fox," Amy said, looking up at the ceiling as though plotting the strategy in her head. "Six thirty news shows would be perfect, I think . . . Parents back from work, watching before or after dinner . . . and saturation on the Hobie station, both at six and eleven o'clock, with coverage statewide, heavy in the Twin Cities . . ."

"Amy, what the hell—you'll forgive my language in these sacred halls—are you talking about?"

Amy grinned. "The phone call. You know any senators who are polishing up their presidential images for the next race?"

"King? Senator King?"

"None other. He's coming here to survey the flood damage from last month, *and* he's going to visit some small businesses in the area, probably to get some backing for his Business 2000 bill that's coming up for a vote . . . And guess what one of those new small businesses is?"

"Oh no . . . you're kidding?"

"One of his press people just asked me if I minded—can you believe that, if I *minded*—if he stopped here and they shot some footage!"

"Oh my God, oh my *God, when?*" Amy wasn't at all disappointed in Nancy's reaction. She did everything but jump up and down.

"Four days. Next Tuesday. It'll be around eight at night, they're going to get us on their way to the airport. Novak, the press guy, was real honest about it, said they wanted to get some shots of Senator King with kids *and* with small business owners, and that Making Friends was a perfect combination."

A frown creased Nancy's face. "Eight at night? The kids are all gone by seven."

"Maybe not," said Amy, the gears turning. "Not if we give the parents a free hour and a half, maybe to go out to dinner alone or to . . ." She wiggled her eyebrows up and down. "Well, do something else they can't when the kiddies are around."

"Ah, the old bribe of solitude, huh?"

"You got it. Oh, we'll tell them what it's for and everything, but I bet most of them would be happy to see their kids on TV with the senator. And we'd only need ten or a dozen. The parents could come around eight thirty for the kids, maybe even see the senator themselves."

"Sounds fantastic. But look," Nancy said, glancing at her watch, "I gotta pick up Karin at my mom's. Give me a call at home and we can talk about who can call which parents, okay?"

As Nancy swept out the door, Amy felt a little sorry for her. Nancy had her own daughter and there never was a sweeter third grader than Karin, but what she didn't have was a husband.

John Fowler had been, to all appearances, a friendly man, devoted to his wife and daughter. But the problem was, Nancy finally realized after denying it for several years, that John was a little *too* friendly, or as Nancy put it to Amy when she finally filed for divorce, "The son of a bitch would stick it in anything with a hole that moved." Nancy had never made clear whether she meant that the hole or its bearer moved, and Amy had never asked for details. But Nancy's lawyers had come up with

so i   that Amy realized Nancy was probably
not ex

Her   ten a good financial settlement and cus-
tody of Kar   in only allowed visitation one weekend a
month. But Nanc   d been divorced for over a year now and
still had not had one date. She had plenty of offers, including
some from the few single fathers who brought their children to
Making Friends. But she always politely declined and explained
why to Amy.

"These guys are all divorced. The only guy I know who's
divorced is John and I'm damned if I want to get involved with
another John." The only way she'd go out with a divorced man,
she said, was if she knew he had been cheated on by his wife
rather than the other way around, and even then that wouldn't
say much for his ability to keep a woman happy.

No, she had said more than once, the only good men were the
happily married husbands, like Amy's Rick, and the only way to
get one of those was to grab one out of the gate (for which it was
too late), to steal one (which meant that he could then be stolen
from you), or to catch one as a widower, and she wasn't about to
start checking the obituary pages for prospective mates.

Maybe Amy wasn't lucky enough to have a child, but she
considered herself very lucky indeed to have a husband like
Rick. Through twelve years of marriage, they had never had a
disagreement that wasn't cleared up by the time they went to
bed. He had been faithful to her and she to him, and he had
never given her any cause to doubt his love for her. It had been
one of those love-at-first-sight things that had proven to be love
now and forever.

So she was lucky after all, and maybe with this visit from
Senator King, her luck would get even better. The exposure
would mean more customers, and that meant that she could
expand and hire more staff and maybe turn a healthy profit
besides doing what she felt she had always been meant to do.

For the life of her, she couldn't see a downside to this visit
no matter how hard she tried.

two

"Now wait a minute," said Will Standish, who was the official historian of Sons of a Free America. "Rip, are you saying that we're going to bomb a day-care center with kids in it? Because if you are, I've got to lodge a protest here. I'm not for that, no way. I mean, look at how killing all those kids made McVeigh look. That's not good, Rip, not good at all."

"Relax, Will," Rip Withers said. He considered Will Standish his pet in a way. Will was the oldest of the Sons and definitely the mildest of the council that made the decisions. He was the best spoken of them all and could write better than anyone else, which was why he was appointed historian, a title they preferred over secretary, which sounded too feminine for their tastes. "All the kids are out of the building by seven or so. The only people there are gonna be the ones who run the place, Senator Quisling and his ass kissers, and a bunch of lefty reporters and photographers."

Will shook his head. "Uh-uh. They'll have kids there, Rip, you know they will. What's the point in King going to a day-care center if he can't get a photo op with kids?"

"So what do you think, Will?" Sonny Armitage said. "They're gonna rent kids just for that night?"

"Besides, Will, what if a few kids *are* there?" Rip said. "There could be a few anywhere we try to hit him."

13

"I'll tell you *so what*, Rip. What's the one single image people remember most from Oklahoma City? And I don't mean us patriots, I mean most of the American public." No one answered and Will went on. "You're not saying because you know. It's that fireman holding that dead kid in his arms. You get one image like that, it sets our cause back twenty years. Hell, man, even if no kids get killed, we still bombed a day-care center, for pete's sake. What kind of image is that?"

"Maybe you're after images, Willie," Sonny said, "but I'm after results and the result of a dead Robert King would be one helluva coup to count. It'd be a warning of the highest caliber to every one of those sonsabitches. Look, there are civilian casualties in every single war that was ever fought, and when you're fighting a guerrilla war like we are, they're inevitable. And it's not just our side that kills innocents—remember a little boy up on Ruby Ridge?"

"Up to me," said Ace Ludwig, "I'd as soon take him out with a single bullet—and I could do it too."

"We've been through this, Ace," said Rip wearily, "and it's too big a risk. To give you a clean escape, you'd have to be at a greater distance than we'd have for an unobserved shot. Besides, you can't get him from the side. He's flanked too heavy. It'd have to be from above and there's no buildings higher than three stories around this day-care center."

"Let's take him in town then."

"Dammit, Ace, you got witnesses up the ass in town. Now I know you want to shoot and you'll get your chance soon enough, but not on this one. This one's Powder's."

Ace looked over at a thin, pale, dog-faced man sitting near the corner of the room and sneered. Ralph "Powder" Burns was leaning over, his scarred hands dangling between the bony knees revealed by his khaki shorts. "You mean fumble fingers there?" Ace said. "He's never blown up a damn thing but barrels."

Powder looked up at Ace through his wire-rimmed glasses, his face expressionless. "Never had to before. But you don't have to worry. I can take care of this just fine." His voice sounded like razor-legged spiders scuttling over glass.

"Oh yeah," Ace replied. "All them burns and scars show us just what good hands we're in."

"Explosives," Powder hissed, "is a learning process. It's like as if the first time you ever picked up a rifle, you had to experiment with making your own loads first. Wouldn't know you had too much powder in a casing till it blowed up on you. You think *you* wouldn't have a few scars and burns after a while?"

Ace made a disgusted noise. "So what you gonna do with your shit bomb, Powder? Rent a U-Haul van and park it outside the center? That ain't gonna look suspicious, hell, no . . ."

"Ain't gonna use no fertilizer bomb," Powder said. "You're right for once, Ace. Too big. Too unwieldly."

"Un*wieldy*," Will Standish corrected, barely loud enough to be heard.

"So what the hell you gonna use then? Dynamite sticks take up a fair amount of room too, y'know."

"Let's let the master-at-arms explain that," Rip said, nodding toward Sonny Armitage.

"We've been stockpiling plastic for the past year," Sonny said. "Storing it inside the powder magazine."

"Plastic?" asked Ace. "Plastic explosives?"

"That's right. We've got a helluva stash now. More than enough for the two bombs."

"Two?" Junior Feeley said. "Who else we bombing?"

"Just King," said Sonny. "But there are two major units of the center, for different age groups. They're divided by a hallway down the middle of the building. We don't know where our target will be so we figure if we plant a device in each location, we can't go wrong."

"How big would these bombs be?" asked Will Standish.

Powder shrugged his knobby shoulders. "Small. Could look like a couple of wrapped books."

"And how would you detonate them?"

"Two timers, set to go simultaneous."

"What's that?" asked Junior Feeley.

"At the same time," said Powder.

"Could it be done remotely?" asked Will.

"Not as dependable."

"All right," Will went on, "for the sake of argument, couldn't you hook them up to a timer but have a remote that could stop the detonation if we learned the visit was canceled or something? You know, so if King doesn't get there for one reason or another, or shows up early or late, we could call it off? I mean, after all, our target's King, right? No point in blowing the place up if he doesn't show, right?"

Rip Withers nodded and looked at Powder. "Can you do that?"

"Yep. Have to be kinda close though. Two hundred yards, maybe, that's the range. But I don't wanna set it off with no remote. Might not work."

"Then," said Will, "a remote might not work to abort it."

"Might not," Powder agreed. "But my main concern is that it goes bang when it's supposed to, not that it doesn't. You can depend on a timer but not on a remote."

"Then you couldn't depend on a remote to stop it."

"Look, you want odds, your timer'll work ninety-nine times out of a hundred. A remote'll work nine times outta ten."

"Besides, Will," Rip said, "we're not gonna have to stop this thing. King'll be there. Now let's put your mind at rest. Powder'll hook up a remote, okay? Just in case. The bombs'll still be on timers, but ones that can be stopped by the remote, that make you happy?"

"Well, I just don't see any point in setting off bombs if our target's not there," said Will.

"And neither do the rest of us. Okay, Powder, you go ahead and set 'em up. I wanta get in there tomorrow night to plant 'em. Don't know how early they send in their secret service teams but the sooner we get 'em in the easier it'll be. Okay? That's it then. Powder, I wanta see you and Sonny in ten minutes in my cabin. And have somebody clean this shit up in here. This is supposed to be a meeting room, not a pigsty."

The men dispersed, leaving through the outside door. A dozen or so militiamen were leaning against trees or sitting on the white resin chairs around the heavy wooden picnic tables where mess was sometimes served. There were twenty men living full-time in the compound and another ten who still lived with their families but spent their weekends and many evenings at the compound. They could not be in the council, though they were sworn to secrecy just the same. The penalty for breaking their vow was instantaneous death.

There had been a few who had broken their vows in the past, and they had paid the price. But as Rip Withers walked past his current corps, he felt he could trust them all. They were one hundred percent dedicated to the freedom that their ancestors had bought for them with blood.

Rip considered himself a Jeffersonian, though he would have been hard pressed to explain exactly what that meant. The words he clung to, however, were the words of Jefferson that had been found on Timothy McVeigh's shirt, about the tree of liberty having to be watered from time to time with the blood of tyrants. Rip knew that was God's own truth.

But the problem was that it wasn't the tyrants' blood that was being shed, it was the people's. And it wasn't just Waco and Ruby Ridge. Hell, the normal guy was getting bled drop by drop, day by day in little ways they hardly noticed, until they were just zombies, doing whatever the government told them.

Yeah, the government was getting into every nook and cranny of people's lives. The schools taught your kids not just how to think but what to think with all their "values" training, teaching the kids how to be good little liberals and save the goddam rain forests while forgetting to teach them the basics of the three R's. TV and movies had become cesspools, with faggots and lesbians looking just like everybody else, but religious folks looking like backward idiots.

And as for just being able to make a decent wage so that you could feed and clothe and house your family, shit, forget that flat out—half your pisspot salary was going to feed niggers on crack or pump medicine into homos with AIDS who were gonna die anyway or get put back into the pockets of the rich sonsabitches who paid you in the first place.

Politics didn't mean jackshit. Every single politician in Washington was a buttboy for somebody. The Democrats wanted to take your money and give it to the junkies and wetbacks and welfare bitches, and the Republicans wanted to give your money to the rich bastards who paid you with one hand and snatched it back with the other. They were all pricks, and Rip Withers would've gladly put a gun to all their heads and splashed their brains all over until the Capitol dome looked like a big, bloody tit. Those assholes weren't Americans, none of them. They'd forgotten the meaning of the word.

But Rip Withers hadn't and neither had his brother, Ray, and neither would his son, Karl. Ray wasn't the brightest guy in the world but he was Rip's brother and Rip loved him and he knew damn well that Ray's heart was in the right place. Besides, he wasn't dumb the way Junior Feeley was dumb, with a kind of meanness that just dared you to laugh at him.

No, Ray was slow and he knew it, and it was okay if you knew it too. There wasn't a mean bone in his brother's body, and that was why he had made Ray vice president of the Sons. The vice president didn't really have to *do* anything, just take care of things if the president wasn't there, and Rip was always there and always would be. If he died or something, Ray wouldn't take over automatically. There would be an election and Rip felt sure that Sonny Armitage would win. That would be okay. Sonny was strong in a lot of ways and he wouldn't fuck up.

In a few more years, if they survived that long and weren't wiped out by Clinton's fire troops, Rip hoped that his son, Karl, would be fit for leadership. The boy had turned into a real good patriot once Rip had gotten him away from his mother, the bitch. She'd wanted him to go to one of those goddam liberal state colleges where he'd have been sure to become either a tree-hugging moron or, more likely, a young Republican Ralph Reed clone. And if he ever picked up a gun again, it would have been because some nigger burglarizing his house dropped it: *"Here you go, my black brother, you dropped this . . ."* Shit.

Not anymore though. Karl was eighteen and that bitch had no more hold over him, even if she *did* still have a hold on Rip's bank account after that divorce. No-good Jew lawyer made it real sweet for her, probably taking his share of more than the money too, with his little hebe circumcised pecker.

Well, he was welcome to her. All women were good for

anyway was to procreate the race and dress up tool catalogs, and he pitied the poor dumbass who thought of them as anything more than wet holes in a dry bed.

No sir, there were no women in Sons of a Free America and no camp followers either. If somebody wanted a piece of ass, they went into Hobie or to the Twin Cities and got their nuts off, and they better damn well use a condom since anything worse than crabs meant they were dishonorably discharged, and that meant a discharge with extreme prejudice. The married or otherwise attached men who didn't live full-time in the compound got their nookie at home, but the longer they were in the Sons, the more likely it became that they'd break up with their women eventually. Patriotism, as Rip liked to say, was a jealous mistress.

Rip noted with pride that not one of the cadre standing outside asked any of the council what the meeting had been about. Sure, they were curious, but they were good soldiers who knew as much as they needed to know. When the time came they would be informed so that they could share in the joy of the strike. But until then loose lips sank ships, and things could come out accidentally, especially once you got talking in bed. That was another reason to stay the hell away from women.

Rip's cabin was just a ten-by-ten room with a cot, a couple of chairs, a foot locker, a stand with a basin, and a phone. He showered, shaved, and shat with his men in the community latrine. But the phone was there because he needed a private line, and there were times he had to talk to just a few of his comrades. That was what the folding chairs against the wall were for. He unfolded two of them now, then sat on his wooden, straight-backed chair and prayed.

He didn't do enough praying and that was ungrateful. It was Yahweh who had brought him to this point, same as he had brought Randy Weaver and his family to Ruby Ridge in Idaho. True, Vicki and their son, Samuel, had been shot by the damn government troops but Yahweh worked in mysterious ways. Those deaths had been the spark that ignited the patriot movement and Waco had been the flame that lit the fuse that blew up the federal building in Oklahoma City. It was all linked, all part of God's plan.

No, he thought, *Yahweh's* plan. The name God was nothing, *dog* spelled backwards. That's why they could say goddammit, but if anyone said Yahweh damn it, well, he just might lose his tongue. Of course, *Yahweh dammit* didn't roll right off the tongue either.

There was a knock on the cabin door and Rip called for the boys to come in. Sonny Armitage and Powder Burns sat in the folding chairs, Sonny straddling his and crossing his arms on the back. "It's you two I want to do this work," said Rip without preamble. "Now we got three days till King shows and a day and a night before we plant them so you start building now, Powder, and I'll give you all the help you want."

"Don't want no help. People don't know what they're doin', make a crater outta this forest. I can get 'er done by tomorrow night."

"Okay. If the remotes are a problem, fuck 'em."

"I can do the remotes too. But like I said, no guarantees they'll work."

"Long as you guarantee the bombs'll work."

"Damn right."

"All right then, let's keep Will happy and give him his remotes. Now tomorrow night, the two of you go in and place them. You're gonna have to put them where they won't be found on a sweep but where they'll do maximum damage. And you've gotta get in and out without a trace."

"No problem," Sonny said with a confidence born of dozens of previously successful missions. It was Sonny's midnight visits to the Twin Cities that had a lot to do with keeping the Sons supplied with food and ammo. Sonny was ex-special services and could get inside a mom-and-pop or a corner drug store undetected, disarm an alarm system, pop a safe, and be off with several thousand dollars on a lucky night.

True, the Sons got most of their financing through labyrinthine channels from a pair of St. Paul businessmen, but it was Sonny's icing on their patrons' cake that enabled them to have an armory that would have been the envy of nearly every other militia group, had anyone outside of the Sons known about it. And that was damned unlikely since nobody outside the group even knew about the Sons at all.

"All right then. Set them to blow at eight ten. King prides himself on being punctual. No reason he ought to change now."

three

"HEY, MONKEY," SAID RICK CARLISLE AS HIS WIFE WALKED IN THE door. He was sitting at the breakfast nook, a half-full cup of coffee and the evening newspaper in front of him. Amy leaned over and gave him a kiss, which he returned in full, holding his cheek against her own before they broke the embrace.

"The monkey needs a banana," Amy said. "I'm starving."

"Well, there are three slices of pizza left—warming up in the oven."

"Three left . . . ? That means you ate five." Amy shook her head in mock exasperation. "Monkey and piggie."

"Why so late?" Rick asked, getting up and sliding the pizza out of the oven.

Taking a slice, she set him down in the chair, sat on his lap, and told him as calmly as possible about the phone call and the upcoming visit of Senator King.

"My God, honey," he responded, "that's *great!* Amazing publicity for the center—you couldn't *buy* stuff like that."

"I know . . . but I was thinking about it on the way home and I feel a little funny *staging* something and asking the parents to . . . well, *use* their kids, you know? It seems too commercial somehow."

"Hey, I know you get involved with the kids on a very pure level but this is a business first and foremost, right? And the parents love you. I'm sure they won't mind you commercializing their kiddies for an hour or so. I mean, how often does a chance like this come along? Once in a lifetime, maybe. And as hard as you've worked to get to this point, you deserve it . . ."

On Sunday Amy and Nancy made the telephone calls, asking for permission to keep certain children after eight the following Tuesday evening. When they were told why, every parent agreed, and by the end of the day Amy was getting calls from parents *asking* if their children could stay to be part of the senatorial visit. Amy happily agreed and by the day's end she realized that she was going to have ten children in preschool and another dozen in the kindergarten/primary section, with every parent promising to pick up their child by nine.

She didn't know how things could get much better.

"Shut the fuck *up*, for shit's sake!" Sonny Armitage hissed. He loved doing this kind of work on his own but he hated doing it with someone else, especially when that someone was as big a stumblebum as Powder Burns.

Christ, it was a wonder the guy hadn't blown up himself and the compound long ago. If there was anything on the floor, Powder's size-fourteen shoes would seek it out and trip over it. At least Sonny was carrying the bombs, both of them, each wrapped in brown paper. The weight of them made them feel like books of death in his knapsack. It had been years since he worked with plastique and that shit had been about as stable as a college boy draftee under fire for the first time.

But Powder was using the real stuff, as good as it got, and it had a solidity and heft that he somehow admired, though he found it hard to believe that such a small amount could do as much damage as Powder said. He hoped he was right.

Getting into the center had been as easy as talking a Vietnamese whore into a blow job. He had picked the lock so sweet and clean that he doubted he had left a scratch in the tumblers, let alone on the face. And all the blinds had been conveniently pulled down so they could have used standard flashlights instead of their infrared goggles. Still, the goggles gave them an unlimited range of vision and a guarantee that no stray beam would work its way around the edge of a blind to alert a passing cop, although this particular neighborhood seemed barren of life at this time of night. They had parked six blocks away and hadn't seen a single lit-up house, passing car, or living person anywhere. The peace and quiet of the suburbs.

A peace and quiet that would be loudly disturbed in forty-eight hours.

The center's front door opened into a building-wide lobby area ten feet deep. There were coat racks and benches as well as rest rooms on either side of the hall that went down the middle of the building.

To the left was obviously the preschool, infant, and toddler area. There were a dozen mesh-sided cribs, beanbag furniture, and numerous small plastic chairs and tables. Toys were everywhere, as Powder's feet quickly learned. Pegboards with hooks showed where the kids hung their things. Sonny read the names: *Brendan Adams, Tyler Greer, Jacob Goldberg, Virginia Cash, Charlie Tran, MacKenzie Feldman, Luis Ruiz, Yolanda Jefferson* . . . The whole damn spectrum, he thought. Jews, spics, blacks, gooks.

On the other side of the building was the primary area, with toys and games oriented toward older children. Each area had its own pair of rest rooms and a kitchen area at the back with a refrigerator, double sink, and microwave oven. There was also a sink and a diaper changing counter in the preschool area. The names on the primary room pegboard showed the same kind of racial and religious intermixing.

"Any ideas?" Sonny asked Powder.

The bomb man scratched his scruffy chin, then walked back toward the sinks, opened the door to the storage area beneath, and stuck his hand up into the darkness. "How about under the sinks, in the space between the two. Tape 'em up in here."

"And somebody fills up the sink with hot water and the tape melts. Package goes clunk, kid says, 'Hey teacher, what's this?' I don't think so, Powder."

Powder turned back, looking for all the world in his goggles like some big bug trying to find a mate. "Well, how about under here," he said, slapping the side of the refrigerator. "Underneath at the back."

"Wouldn't the refrigerator sorta cut down on the impact? I mean, it's pretty heavy and—"

Sonny shut up. Even behind the thick goggles, Powder's face registered unmistakable amusement. "Sonny," he said, "that bomb goes off, that refrigerator might just as well not even be there."

They secured the first bomb packet high up within the coils but not touching them to avoid any tell-tale sound of vibration. The spot where it rested was warm but not hot.

"You gotta set it?" asked Sonny.

"Set it last night. Digital timer. Could set it for a month from now. Them 24-hour alarm clock days are long gone, man."

They set the second bomb in the other refrigerator with even more ease. "You got them synchronized?" Sonny asked.

"Close as I can. They may not be perfect, lose or gain a few seconds in forty-eight hours. But odds are the first one'll set off the other."

"Boom, boom," Sonny said.

"Yeah . . . the Boom-Boom Room." Powder chuckled at his weak joke. Sonny didn't.

As they walked down the hall to the front door Sonny asked Powder, "It bother you knowing you might be blowing up kids? I mean, even if it's an accident."

"Nope. Don't bother me a bit. You seen the names . . . Some of 'em probably niggers, some Jews, that Tran—that's gotta be Vietnamese. Got your other non-white, non-Christians too. Now I wouldn't bomb a Christian school or day-care, but this place . . . it's full of mongrels. And as for the white Christian kids, why aren't their mothers takin' care of them at home? Why they gotta bring their little babies here?"

"Because they don't know any better." By that time they

had reached the front door and the conversation paused until they were safely out, the door locked behind them, and in Sonny's pickup on the way back to the compound.

"All the dumb shits know," Sonny continued, lighting a cigarette, "is that they gotta work harder and harder to pay the federal government's taxes so mom and dad both go to work and they dump the poor kids in some liberal day orphanage where they learn that the little colored boy and Jew boy and gook boy are their brothers and that being a Christian don't count for shit."

Sonny exhaled deeply, the yellow smoke adding another thin layer to the coating on the inside of the windshield. "Hell, Powder, now I think about it, blow up all those goddam places. Nothing but breedin' grounds for the enemy." He flicked on the radio and country-western came twanging out. "Find Wilson," he ordered Powder, who turned the dial until a soft but intense voice spoke from the twin speakers.

"But, friends, don't take my word for it," the voice said. "Listen to your neighbors, your friends, the people you work with, you go to church with. They're going to tell you, because they know firsthand, just like you and me, that this government is the most intrusive in our history.

"And if you don't do what they want you to, they'll arrange it so that they can *kill* you, my friends, kill you without fear of *legal* reprisal. Oh yes, they'll kill you the way they did Gordon Kahl and Vicki Weaver and Robert Mathews and the men, women, and children of Waco and all the other modern martyrs to freedom.

"But though the killers may not suffer a legal penalty . . . since they're the ones, my friends, who make the laws in the Jewish-run courtrooms, they can still suffer the penalties of the Lord and of those who act in his holy name. There are good Christian people out there—patriots each and every one—and the time is coming when the murderers and thieves of our freedom will pay, when Christian patriots will make the streets run red with unsanctified blood."

"Damn, you *tell* 'em, Wilson!" Powder muttered.

"I know you good people are listening and I'm not exhorting

27

you to violence, make no mistake, you watchdogs of the FCC and the other government rabble who listen and watch our every move, desperate to take away our constitutional rights. And you know what Constitution I mean—the one our founding fathers set up, the Bill of Rights. Not all that junk that came later, once the Jews got their greedy hands into it. You're not going to get me on your sedition charges, oh no.

"But you can't stop me from making a prediction, just like your godless, New Age seers do. I predict a war in this country. A war of patriots against the Jew banker–controlled government, with their dark-skinned lapdogs and soldiers. It'll be a war of faith and a war of race, and when it's all over, the white Christians, *true* Christians, will lead this country once again.

"And then woe to the Jew, woe to the black man, woe to the Hispanic, to the homosexual, to the woman who disobeys the biblical injunction to be subservient to man, to . . ."

The list went on and Powder Burns sat back in the truck and smiled beatifically. "Man, is Hobie ever lucky to have Wilson Barnes on the radio . . ."

four

THE NIGHT BEFORE SENATOR KING'S VISIT, AMY CARLISLE HAD trouble sleeping, even long past midnight. She had gotten up quietly, trying not to wake Rick, and went to the kitchen to make a cup of herbal tea. She turned on the radio but the only station that came in clearly at that time of night was the small, twenty-four-hour "nut station," as Nancy always called it, that carried Wilson Barnes from midnight to six A.M. Even at a low volume the hate monger's voice seemed to fill the kitchen, and Amy made a face and turned it off.

She was barely a few sips into her tea when Rick appeared in the doorway, his bathrobe thrown crookedly over his nude body. "Whassa matter?" he said, then held up a hand. "No, don't tell me. Let me use my psychic abilities. You're, uh, concerned about something. I see a white-haired man in a dark suit, surrounded by other men in dark suits . . . This man looks vaguely, um, yes, *senatorial*."

"Gee, is it that obvious?"

"Why don't you come back to bed?" Rick said, standing behind her and putting a hand under her pajama top to massage her shoulders. "I could relax you . . ."

"In that very special way you have?"

"Me and my little friend."

She felt something pressing against her back. "Your little friend's getting bigger."

"And promises to grow bigger yet, shown the proper appreciation and enthusiasm." Rick leaned down and kissed her at the soft place just in front of her ear lobe. "I love you, Amy. All kidding aside, I do love you. Don't worry about tomorrow. Come to bed, huh?"

She did and they made love, sweetly and gently at first, her desire increasing as her body relaxed, until she reached the point where the tension of the day had been forgotten, transformed into the tension of the night, the sensation of being pushed toward a vast cliff, teetering on the edge of the abyss, and then, finally, falling over the edge, the tension broken, surrendering to the moment, and letting the red blood rush into every part of you, filling your hips and belly and breasts, rolling up, up to your shoulders and into your face, across your arms until the burning blood sprouts from you, forming red wings that bear you up out of the abyss, up and up from the blackness of the chasm to the deep and blacker velvet of the sky, soaring into sleep . . .

And Amy Carlisle, sated by sex that, to her sorrow, planted only pleasure and not seed in the barren soil of her womb, slept and dreamed of flying, still flying, but as a bird. She could feel the wind as it whispered through her beating feathers and kissed her black eyes, eyes as shiny and unfeeling as onyx, open against the rush of air. Her wings were strong, bearing her at great speed through the night sky.

Above, pinpricks of stars glinted, fixed and constant lights, vast and eternal. Below, the artificial and puny illuminations of men, fleeting as their lives, blurred as she rushed past, vanishing as quickly as they were seen, born and dying in a moment, flaming into existence so fast, and darkening in a single breath of eternity.

And it was with eternity that she felt at one. She was a fixed and constant black star, moving in an orbit of her own around the world, seeing the sad and sullen lights shine below, watching for the ones that flared and sparked and were extinguished, but that continued to glow a dim but angry red. These were the ones to whom she could speak, to whom her raucous cry would tell volumes. These red souls, refusing to die, needed her wisdom, her power.

Yes . . . There was one, far below, like a cigarette tip winking in some dangerous alleyway. She folded her wings slightly and started to drop down, down toward that eye of redness.

But as she neared it, the air seemed to thicken, become dense and gray, as though she were sinking through airborne ash that clung to her feathers, weighing them down. The currents of air she had been riding vanished, and she fell now instead of drifting. She spread her wings wide, tried to flap them, tried to rise to seek the thermals once more, but the gray dust, the heavy ash on her feathers would not permit it.

And she fell.

She fell toward the red dot, still visible to her coal black eyes through the dead gray air. She fell, and as she neared the ground and the red soul that refused to die, the red blotch sharpened, became a figure whose face looked up at her, a dead face coated with pale ash, through which had cut tears of rage and hate and refusal to accept its fate, tears flowing out of the being's eyes and down its cheeks and over its lips so that it looked like a white mask, eyes and mouth rimmed with black.

And just before she fell directly into that face, just before she struck it with enough force and terror to end the dream and bring her, sweating and terrified, back to wakefulness, she saw that the face was her own.

By morning Amy had nearly forgotten the dream and would not remember it again until much later, both in terms of time and of events. There was too much to do today to think about dreams.

Amy worked with Nancy Fowler and Judy Croft in the preschool area for most of the day, occasionally sneaking over to the elementary room to supervise the cleaners there, making the center spick-and-span for the senator's visit. In the afternoon when the elementary kids started coming in and many of the working mothers picked up their infants and toddlers, the cleaners switched over to the preschool room while Judy fussed around, making sure that nothing the cleaners did endangered the remaining children in any way.

Judy was a gem and Amy had been lucky to find her. She was in her early sixties, had already raised four children of her own, and had been a registered nurse for twenty years. Though she claimed to be retired, she still put in as many hours at Making Friends as she ever did when she worked for Doc Garber, who had retired himself five years earlier. Though they had never had a medical emergency at the center, it was reassuring to know that there was someone to take care of things should any occur.

By four the majority of the remaining children were school age. Round, matronly Judy stayed with the younger children while Amy and Nancy took charge of the older ones. Amy was playing a game of Button Button with Ashley Corcoran, DeMarole White, Polly Phelps, and Pete Grissom while several of the boys were taking turns on the new Pocket Gameboy one of them had just gotten.

Brenda Tran was working on the computer, her younger brother Charlie looking over her shoulder, waiting his turn, his dark eyes staring intently at the screen. Such smart kids, Amy thought with a touch of pride. They owed their intelligence to the genes of their parents, native Vietnamese who had made a great success with a string of software stores that had started in Hobie and were now expanding into the Twin Cities area.

Still, Amy felt she had done a lot to expand the Tran children's world. Strangely enough, they didn't have a computer at home but they both took to Amy's old 386 like a duck to water. Brenda navigated both DOS and Windows with the ease of an MIT grad, and Charlie changed CONFIG.SYS files like hats. Amy was tempted to see if they could fix the constant crashes of the Pentium computer on which she kept the center's records but decided that she couldn't bear the feeling of computing inferiority if they were successful.

As she looked around the room she realized that she could find something special and wonderful about all her children. For an hour, or two, or six every day, she was a mother, raising, teaching, caring for her children, taking care of them, guarding them against harm. She was proud of them all. She loved them all.

At five thirty the pizzas came and the kids gathered for a party. All but a few were staying past their usual pickup time, yet none of them were impatient. On the contrary, it seemed special, even festive, and the pizza made it more so. Amy just hoped that tomato sauce and pepperoni didn't get thoroughly ground into the freshly cleaned rugs.

After they ate they played some more games, but at six the phone rang. It was an aide of Senator King. "Mrs. Carlisle," he said, "I'm terribly sorry to call you so late but something unforeseen has occurred."

Amy could feel her heart start to pound. She knew what the man was going to say as soon as he had identified himself. "Senator King won't be able to get out to your center tonight. A bill came up unexpectedly and he has to fly back to Washington immediately to vote on it. The vote's predicted to be close and it's one the senator's very concerned about, and . . . well, every vote counts. He asked me to please extend his regrets and he'll call you tomorrow personally to apologize."

"Oh, that's all right," Amy said. "I understand." And she did, but that didn't help ease the disappointment.

"I assure you," the aide said, "the next time the senator returns to the Hobie area—and I promise you he will—your center will be the first place he visits. I'm sorry to rush off now but I've got a dozen other calls to make. I do want you to know, though, that we've contacted all the media people so you won't have any mobile units or reporters banging on your door."

"Thank you. I appreciate that," Amy said, thinking that she had *wanted* reporters and TV crews banging down her door. "And I appreciate the call and the, what, the rain check?"

The aide chuckled. "Yes, consider it a rain check. Thanks for your understanding, Mrs. Carlisle. Sorry it didn't work out."

"That's quite all right. Well, good-bye."

"Till next time."

The children, with Nancy at the front of the room, knew there was something wrong when they saw Amy's vacant expression. "Amy . . . ?" Nancy said.

Amy brightened, forcing a smile. "Well," she said, "the good news is we won't have to share any of our dessert with reporters."

The kids' faces fell and they gave out with a heartfelt, "Awwwww . . ."

"The setter's not gonna come?" asked Mary Alice Shearer, a normally shy kindergartner who had gotten unaccountably excited about the visit.

"No, honey," Amy said, "the senator had to go back to Washington, D.C. He had to vote on a bill."

"Like a money?" Mary Alice asked.

"No, it's a different kind of bill."

"Like a law," Brenda Tran said. "They pass bills and then they're law." Brenda went on to explain the workings of the Congress while Amy went into the other area to tell Judy Croft about the cancellation.

"Well, I'm sorry," Judy said, "but I can't say I'm surprised. With politicians, I never believe *anything* until it happens. Are you going to call the parents?"

"I don't see how I can. I'm sure a lot of them made other plans."

"Maybe they'll hear about the senator going back early on the news," Judy said.

That was what happened with several of the parents, who heard the news on the sole Minneapolis station that ran it. The others apparently did not know. Neither did any of the members of Sons of a Free America.

five

AT SEVEN THIRTY THAT EVENING POWDER BURNS, SONNY ARMI-
tage, Will Standish, and Rip Withers drove into Hobie in Rip's
1989 dark green Plymouth Acclaim, a car that had been chosen
for its nondescript quality. Under certain lights the dark green
appeared deep blue, and in bright sunlight it looked black. The
generic styling was indistinguishable from dozens of other
models. And that suited Rip just fine.

Will had come along because he felt he should at least be
nearby. "I agreed to this," he explained. "It's on my hands as
well. And it'll be an event worth preserving in words." He made
certain too that Powder had brought along the remote control
in case the senator's visit was canceled.

When they arrived in Hobie they planned to park several
blocks from the day-care center and wait for the explosion, but
first Rip wanted to drive past to make sure that the visit was
proceeding according to plan. When they did and saw only
three cars and no limos or mobile television trucks, they knew
that something was wrong.

"You got the right day?" Powder asked from the backseat as
Rip pulled over and stopped against the curb.

"Of *course*, I got the right day," Rip said. "Don't be so fucking stupid."

"Well, *somebody* got their wires crossed," Will said, and Rip
could hear his voice shake.

"Or somebody found the bombs," Will said, "and canceled the visit. My God, maybe they're watching us right now! Maybe they set a trap . . ."

"Godamighty," said Sonny, "if they'd set a trap, there'd be more cars there. There's nobody on the fucking street but us! No, they canceled," said Sonny. "I can't believe this . . . That *prick*, that goddam fuckin' homo shithead *coward!*"

"All right," said Will, "what are we going to do? Rip, we've got to stop this thing. Look at those cars—there are people in there, maybe kids."

"No sweat, Will," Rip said, trying to stay calm. It wasn't the prospect of the bombs still going off that upset him. It was the fact that they had missed their target and it could be months before King came back to the area, *years* before they had as sweet a shot at him. "Hell," he said, thinking aloud, "I should've let Ace take a shot at the bastard this afternoon."

"Rip," Will said, "forget about it—that's for the future, this is *now*. We've got to get those bombs shut off. Come on, Powder, get that remote out."

"Okay, okay, I got it here, no problem." From somewhere inside his coat he pulled out what looked like an old TV remote with a telescoping antenna.

"Are we close enough?" Will asked.

"Sure, sure . . ." Powder yanked the antenna open to its full four-foot length. "Just lemme stick it out the window. It'll shut off the contact points and we can come back and get them whenever the hell we want."

He pushed the button, then frowned. "Shit."

"What?" said Will. "What is it?"

"Well, that little red light, I think, is supposed to light up."

"Supposed to? Don't you *know?*"

"Yeah, I *know*—it's *supposed* to."

"Well, what's it mean if it *doesn't?*"

"Means it didn't work . . ." Powder shook his head in puzzlement, then pushed the antenna closed and turned the unit over. "Maybe the batteries are bad."

Will made an exasperated noise deep in his throat. "The batteries? Didn't you put in new batteries?"

"They were new, yeah, but I had 'em for a while."

"You—"

"I had 'em but I didn't ever use 'em. Batteries go bad on their own, y'know, Will."

"Oh, for God's sake . . . Well, can we get some new batteries?"

Rip pulled the car onto the street and turned around. "There was a SuperAmerica back a few blocks," he said wearily. "They'll have batteries. Now relax, Will. They're set for eight ten and that's twenty-five minutes from now, plenty of time to get batteries and a bunch of fuckin' Slushies to boot."

Powder bought four double A's, but no Slushies, and loaded two of them into the remote.

"Does it work now?" Will asked.

"I don't know," said Powder peevishly. "We're not in *range* now. Even if I pushed it and it worked, I wouldn't *know* that it worked."

"Well, let's go *back* then," said Will, gesturing to the road ahead. "Come *on!*"

Rip turned to Will and slowly set one arm on the steering wheel and the other on the back of the seat. "Will, let me tell you something. I don't enjoy being told what to do, not by you, not by any of my men. I am your superior officer and you will address me with the dignity befitting my rank."

Will swallowed and nodded several times. "Okay, I'm sorry, Rip, uh, Colonel, I'm sorry."

"Now I've told you that we are going to be back in plenty of time to successfully abort this mission, and as a soldier, you will obey your commanding officer, who now orders you to maintain silence except to respond to direct question with yessir or nosir until we are clear and away from Hobie." He raised an eyebrow. "Is that clear?"

"Yessir," Will said. Even the two syllables sounded upset and scared. Rip put his hands on the wheel and drove.

They stopped again near the school. "Okay," Rip said. "Ten minutes. Time to spare. Go ahead, Powder."

Powder once more slipped the antenna through the window, once more pushed the button, and once more muttered, "Shit . . ."

"Hell, now what?" said Sonny.

"Wasn't nothin' wrong with the batteries," Powder said. "I just figured it out."

"What?" Rip asked for Will, who looked like he was about to shit himself.

"The signal. It's gettin' through the windows okay, but it's the refrigerators that's the problem. We stuck 'em up in there and there's too much metal for the signal to get through."

"Oh Christ!" Will said, in spite of the silence imposed on him. Rip didn't reprimand him for the blasphemy, under the circumstances.

Rip looked through the window at the Making Friends Child Care Center and chewed on his lower lip. Eight minutes. And with Powder's imprecise timers, maybe less than that.

Then at the window, Rip saw a blind pulled aside and a face looking out. It was a woman, and behind her Rip could see small, moving figures, and he knew he was looking at a woman and children who were already dead.

Eight minutes. Just time enough to clear the area.

He looked away from the woman. Let her see him, he thought. Let her see them all. Let her see the car, get the license plate. In another eight minutes it wouldn't matter at all.

"What are you doing?" Will said, disobeying orders again. It didn't matter. In another eight minutes Rip would have enough on Will to make sure of his silence forever. They would all be bound by the shedding of blood. Like it or not, the Sons of a Free America was about to make its first strike.

Amy let the blind fall back against the glass as the car pulled away. She thought it might have been a parent coming to pick up a child, but instead it looked like four men who had gotten themselves lost.

She had become observant concerning cars around the center. There was always the possibility of kidnapping, if not for ransom, then for darker reasons that Amy didn't like to think about. But she kept the possibility in the back of her mind, as did Judy and Nancy. There were strict procedures to follow whenever anyone who wasn't a parent came to pick up a child.

Amy was startled from her reverie by a tap on the shoulder. "You want to keep an eye on things?" Nancy said. "I've got to run and pick up Karin from swimming practice."

Amy smiled and nodded. Hobie Community Center was only ten blocks away. Nancy would be there and back in as many minutes. "Be careful," Amy said. "There was a car outside with four men—probably just lost, and they took off pretty fast when they saw me—but keep an eye out anyway."

Nancy nodded and waved as she went out the door. Amy didn't worry too much about her friend. They had taken a self-defense course together and Nancy carried a can of pepper spray in her huge purse. But the training and the spray wouldn't be much use against four strong men. Still, she would probably be okay.

Amy turned her attention to the children. There were only six left in the room—Brenda and Charlie Tran, who had turned their attention back to the computer, Mary Alice Shearer, who was dozing in a beanbag chair, Pete Grissom and Ashley Corcoran, who were playing Chutes and Ladders, and DeMarole White, who was puttering around the toy kitchen, shoving pots and pans into the wooden oven and adjusting clickable dials with such panache that her plastic bracelets clattered. *I'm gonna be a chef—that's what my dad does*, she had told Amy innumerable times. Amy and Rick often ate at the hotel restaurant where Micah White was the head chef and he never failed to present them with a special dessert at the meal's end.

"Whatcha making?" Amy asked DeMarole.

"Booly-baze," she replied, her bright teeth splitting her dark face in a grin. "Dad makes that a lot. I forget what all's in it, but it's neat to say. I *know* it's got fish heads."

"Okay, let me know when it's finished," Amy said. For a moment she thought about checking on Judy, but she didn't like to leave her charges alone and figured Judy was fine anyway.

She had four children there now. Two were babies, Mark Dreyfus and Shannon Pierce, who seemed struck from the

39

same mold. They slept well and were a delight when awake. Frank Boone was a two-year-old who always nodded out promptly at six and remained sleeping until his mother picked him up at seven. Three-year-old Annabel Jorgensen, however, was a terror, or had been, until Judy got ahold of her.

Amy believed it was Judy's age that impressed Annabel, whose parents were in their early twenties. All it took was a look from Judy and Annabel would immediately cease running or screaming or flailing her arms or whatever combination of the three she was engaged in. The response amazed young Mrs. Jorgensen, who had only half-jokingly suggested that Judy become Annabel's live-in nanny.

Since all her own children seemed happily occupied, Amy decided to give Rick a call at his office. She seldom disturbed him but he had been working late on a project for several weeks and had told her that hearing her voice in his dismal office was an interruption he looked forward to. They were lucky, she thought once again, to still be so much in love after twelve years of marriage.

"Hey, it's me," she said when he answered.

"Ah, so how goes the media blitz?"

"The media blitz was a dud—you didn't hear?" She told him about the cancellation and he clucked sympathetically.

"I'm sorry, baby. Damn, that really would've lit a fuse under the business . . ."

"What are you doing?" Will Standish asked. "Rip, what are you *doing*?"

"I'm driving away. Believe me, you don't want to be around when those bombs go off."

"Amen and hallelujah to that," Powder said.

Will felt as if his heart was going to burst out of his chest. "We can't let this happen . . . There are *kids* in there!"

"Yeah," Rip said. "I saw them too. But it's too late now."

"It's not, it's *not!* Let's find a phone, call them . . . tell them to get out quick!"

"Will, when those babies go off, there are going to be cops and ambulances and fire trucks swarming through these streets. And if we're seen fleeing the area, we are going to be under suspicion. Now I'm prepared to be a martyr, like every last man here, but not if we don't accomplish something by our martyrdom. And blowing up that building isn't much of an accomplishment."

"A *building?*" Will said. "That isn't just a building—we're blowing up kids, little *kids!*"

"Little nigger kids," Powder said. "Little gook kids. Fuckin' place is a mini-UN."

"Pull over, Rip," said Will, trying not to sound as scared as he felt. "I want to call them."

"There's no phone booth around, Will. Now you just get a handle on yourself."

"I'm going to jump out of the goddamned car, Rip, if you don't stop." Will grabbed the door handle.

The rack of a slide jamming a shell into a chamber was deafeningly loud. Will winced at the sound and then felt a cold weight pressed against his neck under his right ear.

"You try it, Will," Sonny Armitage said, "and you'll hit the pavement a dead man."

Will knew Sonny well enough to know that he wasn't bullshitting. His voice was as flat and as dead as Will knew he would be if he pulled back on the door handle. He let it go and put his hands on his lap, wishing his fingers weren't shaking so much.

"All right," he said as gently as he could. "All right, I'm not going anywhere. Put the gun away, all right, Sonny?"

With relief he heard the sound of the hammer slowly coming to rest on the firing pin. "All right, Will," Sonny said.

"It's a done deal, Will," Rip told him. "I know you're upset but you're gonna have to live with it. We tried to stop it, we couldn't. Now we'll just deal with it."

They drove a few blocks before Rip spoke again. "There's one thing though. After this, they'll know that we're serious. They'll know we'll stop at nothing. No one's safe. No one."

A minute later they heard, far behind them, the explosion.

Will's stomach cramped and he felt his bowels pushing down. Jesus Christ, *no*, he wasn't going to shit himself. He tightened his ass, held it back, tried to hold back the thoughts, tried not to see what was happening back there, tried to think about anything except what they had done.

But he failed. He saw it all in his mind, and wondered if the others did too, or if they had come so far on their dark path that they saw nothing and felt nothing but grim satisfaction.

The first explosion occurred in the infant and toddler care area. Amy was talking to Rick on the phone when there was a deafening blast and the wall separating her room from the hall shattered like glass, throwing large and small pieces of itself toward her and the children. It was, for an instant, like being in a tornado, with a wind so strong that nothing could stand against it.

Amy was hurled backward, toward the far wall, striking it hard enough to make her black out for a moment. Still, she felt the debris slamming into her. The pain brought her back to consciousness instantly.

She could barely see through the cloud of dust and smoke but as she looked toward the source of the blast she thought she saw a distant street light where the wall should have been. That meant that not only the wall between her and the hall was gone, but *all* the walls.

The entire preschool area was gone. Judy. The babies.

Amy looked around frantically for her own children and crawled over the wreckage, crying, *"Kids! Kids! Where are you!?"* over and over. She heard someone moaning, someone else crying and stumbled toward the sounds. Then she saw an arm sticking out of a pile of rubble, a dark arm with plastic bracelets around the wrist. DeMarole.

Amy grasped the hand, and the arm followed, too loosely. There was no weight attached to it. The bracelets rattled up the arm and fell into deeper darkness.

A cry ripped up through Amy's throat, a wordless, mindless

keening sung for eons. *My children,* it said. *What has happened to my children . . .*

She hauled herself to her feet and stumbled toward the answering cries. There was Brenda Tran, bleeding badly in a dozen places but alive. She grasped the girl, trying to ignore her cries of pain. Amy didn't even think about the dangers of moving her. All she knew was that this was a bad place, a place that had harmed her children and she had to find them, find them all and get them out.

Now she followed the sobbing she heard near the back of the room. Half dragging, half carrying Brenda with her right arm, Amy held her left out before her, feeling for the boy amid the ruins of her dream. Finally her ringing ears heard the screams become words. *"Mommy . . . Mommy . . ."*

I'm coming, she thought. Mommy's coming . . .

She found him pinned under what had been part of the inner wall. She set down Brenda as gently as possible and pulled away the metal panels from over Pete Grissom's body with a strength born of desperation, rage, and motherly love. In Amy's shattered mind, these children were her children that never were, and nothing would take them away from her again.

Both Pete's legs were broken, and Amy positioned him over her shoulder as gently as she could, then raised up Brenda, and looked through the dust and the darkness. There at the back of the room was the emergency exit. The path was relatively clear and once there, all she had to do was push on the bar and they would be outside and away from this bad place. Then she could set the children down and go back to look for the others.

She staggered toward the door, carrying and dragging the children and paused for a moment, to gather strength for the final push to freedom. She paused just for a second, right next to the refrigerator.

At that instant the second bomb's timer, delayed through the imperfection of Powder Burns's skill and its own inexactness, reached 8:10:00 and triggered the cap.

The bomb exploded with more force than the first one. Amy never heard the sound of her own death, never had time to feel more pain than what she already felt. She died feeling only the pain of loss, the pain of love destroyed.

She, and the children she held, disintegrated, became a wet red cloud that dried to dust in the same instant. What had been left of the building after the first explosion was gone.

What had been left of Amy was gone.

six

Rick had not heard the first explosion over the tele-phone, which went dead. But he did hear the sound of it, five miles away.

In his office he could not tell the direction it had come from, but the fact that it *had* come at the instant he was talking to Amy stiffened him like a statue as he listened to the dead telephone. In a few seconds the busy signal started and he hung up and dialed again, only to receive a rising three-tone beep and a taped message telling him that the number he had dialed was out of order.

Then he heard the second explosion.

He grabbed his coat and bounded down the stairwell, ignoring the elevator, ran to his car in the parking lot, and headed for the center. The sirens started before he had gone a mile.

Officer David Levinson was the first policeman to arrive on the scene. He had been patrolling a half mile away when he heard the first explosion and saw the flash. He immediately turned the prowler around, hit his bubbletop and siren, and tore toward the area.

He was a block from the day-care center when he thought he was able to make out some moving figures in the dust of the shattered building. But then the second explosion occurred and its flash blinded him, the noise pounded at his ears, and debris clattered on his roof. He stopped his car dead on the street until his sight came back.

A mass of smoke and dust drifted skyward and Levinson got out of the car and walked toward the building. Irrationally, as he realized later, he had no fear of further explosions. There seemed nothing left to blow up. His first thought was of the people that he thought he had seen moving. But the closer he got to the site, the less of a possibility that seemed.

The building was leveled. Nothing remained but dust and rubble and a few smoldering fires, flickering weakly as if disappointed at not finding enough fuel to burn. This, he realized, had been the Making Friends Child Care Center, which he drove past three times a day. He lived in the same neighborhood as Amy Carlisle and her husband, had seen them at street fairs and in downtown Hobie. And here was Amy's place, destroyed, as close to vaporized as you could get. God, what had happened?

Levinson ran back to the prowler and started to call in an APB, but he already heard sirens and saw the lights of incoming emergency vehicles. They lit up the sky before they lit the ruined center, and when he looked at the rising cloud of dust and smoke, it seemed to shift oddly, thinning and thickening in places, spreading outward until it made a rough shape in the sky.

It was the shape of a bird, its wings spread.

For a moment, Levinson couldn't breathe. He could only watch the shadow of the huge black bird drifting higher into the sky, remembering the story his grandmother had told him, and fearfully wondering . . .

But then a gust of wind made the shadowy cloud shimmer and shiver and break apart, and Levinson was uncertain whether he had seen it at all. Maybe he had imagined it, the way people see animals in clouds against a blue sky. He hoped so.

The first fire truck pulled up then and the chief ran up to him, bulky in his rubber coat, and asked if anyone had been inside.

"I don't know," said Levinson. "I thought I saw something moving in that area there . . ." He pointed. "But then the second blast hit, and . . . and there *wasn't* any area there," he finished apologetically.

The chief turned to his men as more police cars came driving up, followed by an ambulance. "Crew One, search that area for survivors. Two and Three, get the hoses on those fires."

"You, uh, think it could've been a gas line or something?" Levinson asked the chief.

The man made a face. "You smell any gas?" Levinson shook his head. "Me neither. Uh-uh, this wasn't gas."

Levinson got out of the way while the firemen tramped into the rubble. Then he told the other officers everything he had seen except for the shadowy form rising above the site.

Dan Trotter, an older detective who had worked on the LAPD bomb squad before coming to Minnesota, shook his head. "This wasn't any accident. Two blasts, coming two minutes apart . . . and you know what was supposed to happen here tonight?"

Levinson knew, along with the rest of the force. "Senator King," he said. "But that got canceled."

"Too bad somebody didn't cancel this too," said Trotter. "Or maybe they just thought what the hell. This is your beat, isn't it, Dave?" Levinson nodded. "You know if people were usually in here this late?"

Levinson didn't think he remembered seeing cars in the small lot on his eight-thirty run. "Not usually, that I recall. But cars are here tonight." He pointed to the lot, where two vehicles lay, overturned and crushed by the force of the blast.

Suddenly a woman came running up to them. Her face was pale in the artificial lights, and her voice sounded like she was struggling to hold it under control. "Where's Amy?" she said. "And Judy . . . Where are the *kids*?"

"Amy . . ." Levinson said. "Amy Carlisle was in there?"

"Oh Jesus . . ." the woman said and then broke down, crying

in soft, dangerous sobs that threatened to break into hysteria. "Oh my God, there were *ten* of them in there."

"Ten children?" asked the fire chief, who had come over as soon as he saw the woman. "Or ten altogether?"

"Ten *children.*" The word rasped out like a curse. "Babies . . . and Amy . . . and Judy."

"Ma'am," said the fire chief gently. "Who are you, please?"

Then things really became chaotic. Three cars pulled up, nearly at the same time, with parents who were picking up their children, followed by more just a few minutes later. Though the emergency medical technicians had no injury victims to care for, they were kept more than busy with the grief-stricken and, in some cases, hysterical parents who had to be physically restrained from running into the rubble and digging for their missing children.

"This was plastic explosive," Trotter remarked to David Levinson. "And a lot of it."

"What do you mean, a lot?" Levinson, who knew little of explosives, asked. "I mean, I don't even know how this stuff is packaged."

"Different ways," Trotter said. "Sometimes in canisters, so you can shape it—it's got the consistency of Play-Doh—or in small blocks of one pound each. But you'd need about twenty pounds of plastic to do this kind of damage, say ten pounds per bomb."

Levinson looked at the firemen picking through the ruins. "Are they going to find anything? Bodies . . . parts?"

"Maybe some but it's doubtful. Hell, you can see what it did to steel and wood and glass. Flesh and bone's a lot more vulnerable. Only chance is if somebody, or *pieces* of somebody, got thrown under a section of wall or something from the first explosion. In that case, they might not have been totally wasted. As far as surviving, though, forget it. And if their bodies didn't get buried by the first blast, they're gone. The power of that stuff is incredible. It goes off, a human being gets vaporized." Trotter shook his head. "One thing you can say for it is that it's fast. I doubt anyone suffered."

"So . . . we can't even recover the bodies?"

"Pick up a scoop of dust and put it in an urn," Trotter said in a voice that blended grief and anger into bitterness. "That's as close as you can get to—"

Trotter broke off and looked with concern over Levinson's shoulder. Levinson turned and saw a man getting out of a car behind him. His mouth was hanging partly open and his arms were dangling at his sides. He looked as if he had just been poleaxed. Levinson recognized him as Rick Carlisle.

"Rick," he said, moving toward the man. Rick started to shake his head and his arms came up as if pleading with Levinson to tell him that there was some mistake. Levinson didn't know what to say. The bare, blasted space before them was all too tragically eloquent.

"Rick . . ." said Levinson again. "I'm sorry. I'm so sorry."

Rick Carlisle scarcely heard the words the policeman said to him. The blood was roaring too loudly in his ears. Somewhere in the back of his mind was the realization that he knew this man but it wasn't important now. Nothing was important except absences. The absence of the building. The absence of Amy. Where was she? She could not, would not, be in the building because the building was not there, and if the building was gone, then Amy was gone and she couldn't be gone, that was not possible.

But then where was she?

He felt someone grip his arm and the sudden pain focused him. He looked at the face that was looking up at him and knew that it was Nancy, Nancy Fowler. Then he thought that everything would be all right after all because if Nancy was there, then Amy would be there as well.

He looked at Nancy and asked her, with the simplicity of a child, "Where's Amy?"

Nancy didn't say anything right away. Her face was wet with tears but maybe that was because of the building, Amy's dream that had vanished. But that was all right. Buildings could be rebuilt. And if Nancy was here, then Amy was too and Rick looked over her shoulder to see if Amy was behind her but she wasn't. "Nancy, where's Amy," he asked again.

Nancy didn't respond in words. Her face seemed to shimmer, melt, almost fall apart, as huge, wracking sobs escaped her small frame and she shook her head, back and forth, back and forth. *No*, the movement said. *No*.

No Amy. No Amy ever again.

Then the heart and the spirit went out of him, and the knowledge crushed him, and his legs gave way and he fell to his knees on the asphalt, looking at the ruin in front of him—ruined building, ruined lives, absent forever.

seven

AT ELEVEN DAVID LEVINSON'S WORKDAY WAS OVER. HE HAD stayed at the site, helping as much as he could. There had been a lot to do. The grieving parents and relatives had been the biggest problem but the media had made things far worse.

By nine, mobile TV trucks and vans had descended on the formerly quiet Hobie suburb like crows on a piece of roadkill. While the cameramen's lights pinned the grieving, reporters shoved microphones into their faces and asked them how they felt. Uncertain of what to do, some waved them away while others actually tried to cooperate, attempting to put their loss and horror into words.

It sickened Levinson. He finally had enough when a testosterone-charged, lacquer-haired reporter kept pursuing an Asian woman who had made it clear she did not want to speak. The man still came after her, beckoning his cameraman and yammering at the woman, "Ma'am, please wait, we want to talk to you, won't you share your feelings with us . . . Hey, don't you speak English?"

He followed her beyond the plastic yellow police line, at last cornering her between three cars. "Please, ma'am, tell us how you feel."

The bastard was in Levinson's territory now and he walked up to the man, pressed his palm over the camera, and snatched the microphone away, yanking it from the power cord. "How the hell do you think she feels? Now you get your stupid ass on the other side of that line before I arrest you."

"Hey, pal, I'm just doing my job!"

"I'm not your pal and I'm just doing mine. Now *move*."

He did, and Levinson sat the woman inside a police car and held her for a few minutes while she cried some more. "Both my children," she said and Levinson's stomach and throat turned to ice. What could you say, what could you do to respond to such pain, to loss that would always be felt, even in the midst of happiness. A fist had wrapped itself around this woman's heart and would squeeze until the day she died.

By ten thirty, federal investigators had arrived, since there was no doubt that the destruction had been caused by bombs. The small fires had long been extinguished and the firemen had searched diligently through the wreckage, but found no survivors. As Trotter had predicted, they found no body parts either.

In another half hour the relatives had either gone home or been taken to hospitals for the night, where they were kept under sedation. Levinson had heard that the husband of Judy Croft, one of the two missing adults, had suffered a heart attack and was in critical condition.

Now Levinson just watched as the investigators searched through the rubble, taking small samples of the debris and dust as they went, and using tape measures for what Levinson assumed was finding ground zero. Huge lights made the area as bright as a sunny day and hundreds of curious citizens crowded behind the police lines, looking at where a building had been and where twelve lives, by best reckoning, had been lost.

"Shift done?" asked Dan Trotter, coming up to him. Levinson nodded. "Any orders to stay?" He shook his head. "Why don't you go home then?"

"I don't know," Levinson said, although he did. The emptiness of his house would only make him think about the emptiness of this dreadful place.

"Want to get a cup of coffee? Maybe a roll or something?"

"Yeah. I'd like that."

They took Levinson's prowler and drove several miles to an all-night diner where the waitresses were friendly but never overly curious. Tonight would test their mettle, Levinson thought.

But they just smiled and nodded at the two policemen, took their orders, and asked no questions. Levinson sat back in the booth and took a long sip of coffee.

"Know why I left L.A.?" Trotter asked. "It was getting too violent. Every time I turned around some asshole was planting a bomb at some bank or some government office, hell, even schools. So I said to my wife, fuck it, let's get out of here before you're a widow. And I got two kids and it was getting to be a shitty place to bring them up in.

"So I came to Hobie, got a promotion, and ironically took a big cut in pay but the difference in cost of living made it a wash. I was a detective and I was happy and things were a lot less violent here than they were in La-La Land." He shrugged, spreading his fingers wide. "And now this." He pulled a note pad out of his pocket and looked at it. "Two women, four babies, six little kids. Gone in a flash. Worst thing I've ever experienced. Most hateful, sick, twisted, disgusting crime I've ever seen committed. And I don't know if we'll ever find the motherfuckers who did it." He closed his eyes and shook his head.

"I left Detroit for the same reason," Levinson said. "All the killing got to be too much after a while. That smell . . . it gets in your nose, you can't get rid of it. It's like a fisherman smelling fish or a farmer smelling shit all the time. I smelled the bodies, you know? Got to me, started affecting, well, my personal life."

He and his wife had started to pull apart as a result. Levinson had hated the gap that had started to come between them. He wanted a perfect relationship with Carol and it wasn't happening in Detroit. She seemed happy to go with him to Hobie and he hoped for the best, but by that time things were too far gone. She left him three months after they arrived and went back to Detroit, the same damned place whose crimes had torn them apart. But that wasn't something he wanted to tell Trotter about.

"So they tried to kill Senator King," Trotter said, looking out the window, "and they didn't care if they killed a bunch of kids in the process." He looked sharply at Levinson. "You know who they are?"

Now it was Levinson's turn to shrug. "Not specifically. But I know the mind-set. I know how they think." He smiled thinly. "I know who they hate."

"Who?"

"They hate me. They hate Jews. But they also hate blacks and Chicanos and Vietnamese and Japanese and anybody whose skin or religion isn't the same as theirs. They hate what's different."

The waitress came and Trotter took a bite of his coffee cake, chewed ruminatively, and swallowed before he asked the question. "You been getting any shit on the force?" Levinson didn't answer and Trotter went on. "Just between us. I heard a few things. Just want to know if they're true."

"There are a few fellow officers," Levinson said slowly, "who, I get the feeling, don't care for Jews very much."

Trotter snorted. "Don't know why they don't quit the force and join one of these damn militias." He grinned. "My wife's maiden name is Rachel Rabinowitz. She goes to synagogue, I don't. But I still catch it from some of the boys. So . . ." His tone grew more serious. "You think it's a militia thing?"

"The bombing? Probably. We've got enough of them around here."

"They do seem to love the north woods, don't they? Only thing is, they've been as quiet as church mice. I know of nearly a dozen different militia chapters within a hundred-mile radius of Hobie and all they do is train and recruit and stockpile arms. But the sons of bitches do it legally as far as we can tell."

"Even if they don't," said Levinson, "after Ruby Ridge and Waco all the authorities from locals to the feds are thinking twice before going into one of those armed camps and making arrests."

"You bet. The militia nuts *like* it when things escalate. Another damn chance to be martyrs to the cause of white Christian brotherhood. Hell, with all that training and all that propaganda bullshit they get fed, they'll jump at the chance to fight us storm troopers of the *guvmint*."

"You think it was a militia did this then?"

"Well, I'll tell you—I don't know of any private citizen who would have access to the amount of plastic explosive you'd need to level a building like that. No, this thing was planted in that building early by somebody who knew about breaking and entering. And they knew that the secret service would do a sweep of the building before King went in so they had to hide it well. The whole operation shows some professionalism. All except the part where they miss their target and blow up a bunch of children instead. That was a little stupid."

"So do you think the feds will investigate the local militias then?"

"No, I don't. I don't think they'll have the guts to because they're not going to want another incident. If they had absolute proof that a militia was involved, then yeah, they'd go in. But to ask questions? Poke around? Examine armories? Uh-uh, it won't happen. In fact, unless something breaks our way, I'd be surprised if this bombing is ever attributed to anyone but 'person or persons unknown.'"

"I heard her die," Rick Carlisle said. "On the phone, when the line went dead, that's when she died."

He and Nancy Fowler were sitting in Nancy's living room. It was two in the morning. Once it had become clear to Rick that Amy had been killed in the explosion, he had grown more calm and had buried his pain and agony by cooperating in every way possible with the authorities.

He and Nancy had sat in the back of a police van and answered questions for a half hour, first with Hobie's chief of detectives and then with a federal investigator. Nancy had been able to give the names of the children who had been in the center when it had exploded and Rick had told about the final telephone call and the sound of the explosion that followed the line going dead.

That was all they could tell, that and the fact that Amy had seen a car with four men in it outside the building a few minutes before Nancy had left. No, they had no idea that anything had been placed in the building . . . No, they hadn't seen any sign of a break-in . . . No, there was nothing strange that occurred at all . . . No . . . no . . . no . . .

For a moment Rick felt that the federal investigator suspected Nancy herself of having planted the bombs and then leaving before they went off, but he was too weary to speak to the contrary. Let him think that if he liked. That was one theory that would quickly go up in smoke.

Up in smoke.

When the questions were finished and they were left alone, Nancy had said that she had to take Karin home. The little girl had been with a policewoman ever since Nancy had arrived. "Listen," she told Rick simply, "if you don't want to go back to your place tonight, why don't you stay in our guest room."

She didn't say that she wanted the company or suggest that Rick would find it unbearable to be in the house that he had shared with Amy, both of which he suspected were true. She just made the offer and Rick had nodded a weary acceptance.

And now they sat over cups of tea, the events of the night almost like a dream. How, Rick thought, can such a cataclysm occur in your life and hours later you're calmly drinking tea as though it never happened?

Still, it was all they could think about or talk about. They quickly came to the conclusion that the target had been Senator King. "They'll find who did it," Nancy said. "They found Timothy McVeigh, they'll find these guys." She closed her eyes, frowning. "Amy probably *saw* them," she said. "I wish I had asked her more about them—what they looked like, what they were driving. I just wish . . ."

She left it unfinished. There was so much, Rick thought, that he would have wished for. But wishing couldn't change things. It couldn't bring anything back.

"If they don't find her," he said softly, "it's almost like she didn't die but just went away somewhere, and maybe someday she'll be back." He looked at Nancy and saw surprise and pity on her face. "Oh, I know she won't. I'm not crazy, I know what happened. But this way, with no . . . body, it's like she's still out there somewhere, still . . . alive in a sense, though I know she's gone."

They were silent for a while and then he said, "You know what I hope? I just hope it was fast. I hope she didn't know anything. Because if she knew . . . if she knew about the children . . . I don't know how she could have died knowing that.

"I don't think she *could* have died. Knowing that."

I want . . . I want to come back . . .

Wait.

No . . . it wasn't right . . . I have to make it right again. They can't rest until I make it right.

Not yet. Wait.

I can't wait! It hurts too much to wait! It hurts me—hurts them . . . Oh God, the sound of their screams . . .

Wait, Amy, wait.

The crying . . . the crying for mommy . . .

Soon.

Soon.

eight

"MY FRIENDS, WELCOME BACK TO THE SECOND HOUR OF THE
Wilson Barnes Show. If you've been listening, you know what
I've been talking about tonight. And that's the explosions that
have rocked the home of the Wilson Barnes Show itself—beautiful Hobie, Minnesota. A day-care center, my friends. Yes,
that's right, a day-care center has been destroyed. Two adults
and ten little children have lost their lives, have been blown to
bits, my friends, their bodies unrecoverable.

"Federal authorities are already on the scene—and I say
already with a bit of irony, for in a very possible scenario, some
clear-thinking folks might say that they were there *before*. Let's
look at the facts . . .

"Senator Robert King, ultra-liberal god, was scheduled to
appear at that day-care center at eight o'clock this evening. But
the senator never arrived—instead he went back to his cesspool
known as Washington, D.C. At ten minutes after eight, my
friends, two bombs went off in that day-care center. Now
what's the average person supposed to think? What does the
media *want* you to think?

"They want you to think that some big bad right-wing, conservative kooks, maybe even one of those awful *militias*, my
friends, was responsible. These people are so nefarious, so terrible
that they'll blow up *babies* to assassinate one of their political

enemies! Well, let's hunt these monsters down! And let's not rest until every one of these diabolical right-wing fanatical organizations is destroyed, their dangerous weapons and bombs taken away from them, and their leaders in prison where they belong!

"That's what they *want* you to believe, my friends. But we're Americans, we don't buy all that bull, do we? Now let's look at the facts . . .

"If this was a plot to kill Senator King, it sure was a lousy one. There were dozens of opportunities to do so today. The quisling senator was out in the open in half a dozen neighborhoods. Bombs could have been planted anywhere or a sniper could have easily executed the senator—not that I'm saying that would have been a good thing now.

"But where do these terrible right-wing kooks put a bomb? In a day-care center with little children, on the very last stop of the day, the stop that is *most likely* to be canceled! And when the bomb goes off, King isn't even there! They say it's because he had to go back for a vote, but is that true, my friends?

"Or did he know all along that there was a bomb planted there?

"Did he know who did the planting?

"Was he even part of a conspiracy to smear the right-wing, conservative, and militia movements in this country so badly that they could never hope to rise from the dust of the Making Friends Child Care Center?

"Did he aid in the *staging* of an assassination attempt by the government purely intended to discredit the right, sacrificing ten innocent children in the process? Is the government capable of doing such a thing?

"Well, they were capable of shooting Vicki Weaver in the face while the only thing she held in her arms was her baby . . . They were capable of creating a firestorm at Waco in which over *twenty* children died, children they claimed they were acting in the best interests of . . . Hell, what's ten more?

"You tell me what Bill Clinton and Teddy Kennedy and Janet Reno and Robert King *aren't* capable of, my friends!

"And add to all this the fact that this wasn't any homemade fertilizer bomb, oh no. This bomb, claim experts who have seen the destruction, was plastic explosive. The *same* kind of plastic explosive, I might add, that the United States military has in abundance.

"And the children? It was a rainbow coalition, my friends. Jews, gentiles, Orientals, Negroes—almost as if it was *planned* that way, as if these children were sacrificed so the liberal Jew media would be certain of having everybody in the United States hating the people responsible for this dreadful act.

"It was a dreadful act indeed, and in deeper ways than just the killing of innocent children. Am I making accusations, my friends? No, I'm asking questions. You're going to see *plenty* of accusations from the government and the Jew liberal media in the next few weeks. And when you do, don't forget the very real possibility of government involvement, of people so hungry for power that they will sacrifice anything, even the lives of little babies, to achieve their nefarious ends . . ."

At six that morning, after Wilson Barnes left the radio station, he went back to the downtown apartment house that he owned, and rode the elevator to the penthouse where he lived alone. He poured himself three fingers of Tennessee whiskey and sipped it as he dialed a familiar number.

"Yeah?" said a sleepy voice.

"It's me," said Barnes. "You were sleeping. You heard earlier?"

"I heard."

"Worth something?"

"Yeah."

"You bet it was. I'll keep on it, too—pass the line to the brethren on the air. And I'll expect a show of appreciation?"

"The usual place."

"Pleasure doing business," Wilson Barnes said, and hung up before Rip Withers could say anymore.

nine

THE FOLLOWING DAY WAS ONE FOR MORE SPEECHES AND RHEToric. News of the explosion led every national TV broadcast, and by the time the morning anchors were ready to tell the public what had happened to the Making Friends Child Care Center, federal investigators reported finding traces of cyclonite, the active ingredient in C–4 plastic explosive.

This seemed to indicate, according to the carefully worded report, that one or more explosive devices had been planted in the building. The fact that Senator Robert King had been scheduled to visit there only added more fuel to the conspiratorial fire.

The mainstream media and press quickly came to the conclusion that the explosion had been a tragically botched assassination attempt by a right-wing extremist individual or group. In a midmorning statement, the President promised to use the full force of every federal law enforcement agency to find the perpetrators of "this heartless and terrible attack." Media pundits, however, were not as certain, echoing Dan Trotter's remarks to David Levinson concerning the reluctance of the government to enter the armed camps that comprised most militia groups.

The ultra-conservative media took another tack, the same one suggested by Wilson Barnes. The less extreme radio show hosts with the largest audiences urged their listeners not to jump to conclusions, that this might indeed have been a conspiracy, but a conspiracy of the left. That the government itself was involved *seemed*, they said, unlikely but possible. But there were "left-wing wackos" as well as so-called "right-wing kooks" out there, and the left-wingers were more dangerous because they worked alone. Theodore Kaczynski's name was frequently mentioned in that regard. It was altogether possible that one of these "lone wolf left-ies," with advance information of Senator King's agenda, might try to discredit the right by staging such an assassination attempt.

The more extreme commentators went with Wilson Barnes the whole way, suggesting in no uncertain terms that Hobie was just another Oklahoma City, a terrorist act staged by the government in their efforts to destroy their strongest enemy, the patriots of the white Christian militias. This theory was bolstered later that afternoon when the news came out that one of the victims had claimed to see a car with four men inside, who were immediately transformed by the radical commentators into the federal government's dreaded "men in black."

But in all the United States it was only inside the compound of the Sons of a Free America that one could hear the truth.

At one o'clock, just after noon mess had been finished, Rip Withers had all the members of the Sons come to the indoor drill building, in which training sessions were held, mock combats were fought for prizes, and speeches were given. It was this last activity that Rip engaged in now.

"By now you've heard the news on the radio. For all I know, you might have heard more. But I'm here to tell you the truth." He looked at his men, hard and faithful soldiers all, who were sitting on the backless wooden benches, listening intently.

"The truth is what makes us different from them," Rip went on. "They lie to the people, they lie to each other—they lie *with* each other too but that's something else entirely." He was rewarded with a knowing chuckle from the men.

"I'm not going to lie to you. I'm going to tell you the truth.

Your council of commanders made the decision to terminate with extreme prejudice the life of an un-American traitor, Robert King. Our intelligence told us that there was little chance any children would be harmed in the attack. But as you all know, intelligence is not always correct. There were children present and, what was equally harmful to our cause, our primary target was not."

The reaction was what he had expected but not what he hoped. While most of the men listened without emotion, some of them seemed disturbed, a few even shocked.

"It was tragic, yes, but it sent a message. No one is safe. In our struggle, we have to be as ruthless as the government that gunned down and firebombed innocent children. And if the only way to show that we are is by something like what happened last night, then so be it.

"I wish it hadn't happened. I wish we could take it back but we can't. It's finished, it's over and now we not only live with it but we must figure out how to use it to our advantage. If you heard Wilson Barnes last night, he showed us one way.

"Now if there are any men here who can't live with what happened, you let me know right now, and . . . we'll work something out." Rip looked at Will Standish, who sat near the back, his head down, eyes fixed on the dusty ground. Then Rip looked at the other men who had been uncomfortable with the news, but they too seemed reluctant to speak.

"All right then," he said. "You know the regulations. If any man betrays his brothers by word or deed, death is the only penalty. We have another secret now that we have to share the way we share our convictions and our commitment. Be true. Be loyal. And our day of victory will come, praise Yahweh."

There were a few shouts of Amen, then a few more, and soon they all were standing and giving the salute of white Christian patriots. Even Will Standish was standing and saluting, though Rip saw little enthusiasm in the gesture. At least there would be no protest, no breach in their carefully constructed bulwark of command and obedience.

Finally Rip Withers smiled and saluted them back with pride.

• • •

When Rip gathered the council later that day, he did not hesitate to invite the historian, Will Standish, as usual. Before the meeting, however, he drew Sonny Armitage aside privately and told him to keep a watch on Will. Sonny nodded, and Rip knew that was all he had to say. If Will had second thoughts about his loyalty to the Sons, he would be quickly taken care of.

At the meeting he told the others that they would be lying low for a time, taking no risks, until they were able to gauge the government's reaction. In the meantime they would continue to drill, train, and stockpile for the inevitable confrontation.

This they did and as the days became weeks, no government troops invaded their territory, and no investigators came with warrants to search the "White Oak Hunting Camp," the cover name for the Sons' compound. Had that occurred, the Sons would not have allowed it. They would have resisted, whatever it took, at the last blowing up the powder magazine and the compound itself before they would allow themselves to be captured.

The government knew this all too well, Rip exhorted his troops. They were not willing, not *yet*, to have another bloodbath. That was why they had not bothered *any* of the known militia in the area. And even if they had, the Sons were a covert militia, known only to its members.

Still another reason, however, was that the federal investigators had no physical evidence, aside from quantities of C–4 residue. The explosion had been so violent, the destruction so complete, that the only remaining traces of the bomb were microscopic. As for the sighting of men in a car, no witnesses had noticed any strange vehicle leaving the area just before the explosions. This added fuel to the "men in black" theory since once these contemporary phantoms were sighted, they did not appear again.

There had been a number of crank calls taking credit for the bombing, but since the primary victims had been children, there were not as many as usual for a terrorist act. None of these calls produced any tangible results.

In short, the investigators had no leads whatsoever, short of searching for an unaccounted-for supply of plastic explosive in government facilities, a search that continued and was made nightmarish by the reluctance of each agency to fully open its operations to another. The media was all too aware of the investigation's impotence and, naturally, so was every militia group in the country, including the Sons of a Free America.

As the weeks and months passed and absolutely nothing happened, the Sons' apparent success in the bombing of the Making Friends Child Care Center led Rip Withers to believe that Yahweh was truly with them, and that their continuing freedom was a sign from Him that the time had come for something else.

The time had come for another explosion, one that would shake this godless, traitorous government to its core.

PART TWO

Ah, love, let us be true
To one another! for the world, which seems
To lie before us like a land of dreams,
So various, so beautiful, so new,
Hath really neither joy, nor love, nor light,
Nor certitude, nor peace, nor help for pain; . . .

—Matthew Arnold, "Dover Beach"

ten

ALL THE WHILE, THE DUST REMAINED.

When the investigators had taken their last samples, when the searchers had finished gathering the few bits of human remains that were larger than the particles in which they lay, when the media had taken their photographs and videotapes of what had been a child care center, the dust remained, a variegated relief map of a village lost.

In some places it lay gray as ash, in others the ivory pallor of bone, and in still others brown as rust or long-dried blood. Fine as powder, coarse as gravel, the place and the people had intermingled, become one, in a thick sheet of dead lives and dead dreams. The plastic ribbons that marked the police lines still remained. Where once they had been a yellow as bright as the balls and toys the children had played with, now they were tattered and rotting, bleached by sunlight into the shade of jaundiced flesh.

At once cemetery, memorial, and place of execution, the site seemed to call out to people. Even after nearly six months had passed, they still brought flowers and teddy bears. They prayed, they cried, they stood and looked at the dust.

Some knelt and picked up a handful, letting fall between their fingers what had been both a place of love and the beloved ones who had occupied it. The voices that had laughed, the legs that had run, the faces that had smiled, the hands that had cared were now all dust, dust that clung like memories to the fingers and made its way thoughtfully to the lips, entering the worshipper like an unblessed host.

But for all the dust that departed on fingers and lips and soles of shoes, for all that the wind blew away, mingling with the dust of the playgrounds and yards where the children once played, an infinity of that dust remained and would remain for as long as anyone could guess. The property, still in the names of Richard and Amy Carlisle, had gone into receivership until the class action suit of the victims' parents against the Making Friends Child Care Center had been resolved, which would not occur until the government investigation into the cause of the explosions was complete.

It seemed unlikely that such a day would ever come. But when and if it did, the dust would still remain.

No one remembered, except for Rick Carlisle, that that particular night in late October was the anniversary of the founding of the center. The memory came to Rick in spite of himself, for he had been trying to forget about the center, about the explosion.

He had been trying, with all his heart, to forget about Amy. But his heart was where he held her.

On that Halloween night the children were trick-or-treating. But those who lived near where the Making Friends Center had once stood stayed away from the site and traveled several blocks to avoid passing it. Every child knew that it was haunted by the ghosts of those who had died there, and the hauntings would be far worse around Halloween.

Police patrols had been doubled during the two nights of trick-or-treating and David Levinson had volunteered for double shifts on those nights. He didn't mind the extra pay and it gave some of the second-shift officers a chance to go out with their kids.

He had finished the evening shift, feeling like a good spirit watching over all the little kids dressed up like vampires and clowns and whatever cartoon and adventure characters were hot that year. But by ten they were all off the street and safe at home, probably in their bedrooms surreptitiously stuffing their faces.

God, he thought as he cruised toward the diner for his break, what a difference from Detroit. Devil's Night was a whole lot more active than a Hobie Halloween. The toughest thing he had had to do tonight was to warn an older kid who was swiping some of the younger kids' stashes. Not a single burning car, rape victim, or homicide.

But there was darkness and evil everywhere, he thought as he drove slowly past what he had begun to think of as the Blasted Heath. He wished that damn lot full of dust and debris would get paved over as soon as possible. Or a couple of houses would be dandy, with happy, shouting kids and a couple of big, dopey, friendly dogs. Anything but that block-wide Death Valley. Halloween was creepy enough without having that hell-hole around.

This was far from Levinson's favorite time of year anyway. When he was a kid he had always hated Halloween. It usually coincided with his father's biggest trade show, which was held in Florida. His mother went along for a vacation and that meant that David and his brother had to spend five days and four nights with Grandfather and Grandmother Levensohn.

Grandfather had refused to change the spelling of his name from the traditional Russian, claiming a family tie to the Russian Hebrew writer Michal Levensohn. He and Grandmother had both come over from Russia and spoke Yiddish to each other, a habit David had found weird and creepy. He hadn't liked not understanding what someone else was saying while knowing that they could understand you. It seemed an unfair and selfishly adult thing to do.

But what creeped him out most about his grandparents were the stories they would tell of the old country. It wasn't so much the anti-Semitism of the czar's troops and the cossacks that frightened him. After all, he was used to that in his own life, even if the Jew haters at his school and in his neighborhood didn't come at him with sabers. It was the tale of Abraham Levensohn, his grandfather's uncle, and the crow that guided him.

Even now Levinson shuddered at the memory of it. There were things that should not happen in life. Some, like prejudice, were wrong, but you lived with them and tried to change them. Others, like the recent bombing, were abominations, atrocious and dreadful. These things you fought with all your might.

But others were unthinkable, like a dead man coming back to life, no matter what the reason.

Or was that really true? Were there some abominations even more unthinkable than the dead rising to life again to kill? And what if the dead rose to avenge those abominations, the way Uncle Abraham had?

Levinson hissed air out hard through his teeth and shook his head jerkily. Forget about that, he told himself. That damned story came back to him every Halloween, and it was probably no more true than the other tales Grandmother Levensohn had told, the ones that he had found later in books of Jewish folklore.

But he had never found the one about the crow, and it was that one that she had told more convincingly than all of the rest.

He saw the lights of the diner ahead. For the fifteen minutes he was allowed to sit on his ass without a steering wheel in his gut, maybe a good cup of coffee and a nice piece of pie would get rid of Grandmother's old stories. He didn't have to be on his way again until midnight.

And still the dust remained.

It waited, the street lamps turning all its undulations a uniform gray, like a sea on a cloudy, windless day. But as the clocks of men tolled and told that it was midnight, that the night was at the center of its darkness, the pendulum between the extremes of dusk and dawn hanging straight down, something black fell from the blackness of the sky, drifting and turning as it neared the earth, neared the dust that remained, waiting for its coming.

It slowed its descent, seeming to hang for a moment in the air, and from beneath its dark body, its feathers shining as if lacquered or sculpted in jet, two feet emerged, seeking a perch. They found one on a wooden stake holding the tattered police line ribbon, and the obsidian daggers of its fore claws dug into the wood while the hind claws of each foot gripped and balanced.

The crow sat unmoving, a gentle wind that stirred the ragged ribbon having no effect upon its feathers. The crow watched with eyes of glittering coal, watched that same wind dance in the gray dust, whirling and eddying, making the waves of that dry sea roll and shift as if creatures swam darkly beneath its surface.

Then the wind passed over the sea of waiting dust and left it, moving on to shake dead leaves, rattle loose windowpanes. Over the dust, the air stopped, died.

But the dust continued to move.

It was as if the wind, though none could be felt, continued to blow, but from all sides, in toward the center of the ocean of dust. And that dust began to mound, to grow in a shape that first suggested, and then reflected, humanity. A head, arms, a trunk, legs, all rose slowly from the dust as if they had been there all along, just waiting for the moment to rise and be recognized by the creature that sat above it, watching the recumbent woman being shaped by its dark will, or by the will of the soul that still occupied it. The shape formed as, in the old tale, God may have formed Adam from the dust of the ground.

But this was no Adam, and no creator-god blew the breath of life into its nostrils. Instead, breath burst from it in a scream of birth or rebirth, as its dust became flesh and muscle. Ash became bone and blood that surged like fire, bringing the being to life with a jolt of pain, a burst of agony, and memory of how it had died, and why it now returned.

eleven

AND WHILE THE BODY OF AMY CARLISLE REINTEGRATED ITSELF from its own particles and its own desire, Rick Carlisle dreamed of that reformation, his soul, still one with hers, witnessing her bursting from her womb of dust.

He saw her face coming up out of the debris of the empty lot like a woman rising from being buried in the sand. He saw her mouth filled with dust, and saw that dust explode from between her lips in an ashy cloud, saw her eyes open wide in pain and terror, and thought that he was seeing her in the instant before her own life ended, in the moment of realization that she and, most importantly, all her children would die.

Rick's eyes opened and he sat bolt upright in his bed, still seeing Amy in the darkness of the walls and ceiling. He was awake, he *knew* he was awake but Amy was still there in front of him, the dust and the ashes falling away from her, showing unmarked flesh, pink, bare skin, her shoulders and breasts untouched by the blast that had torn her apart.

She was whole, though her face was still alive with the anguish she must have felt in her last moments. *How could this happen?* it seemed to say. *How could I have* let *this happen?*

And then he saw her turn, put her hands on the dust that remained, and push herself up, up from the dust like a new creation. She stood naked against the wall of his bedroom, looking down at her body, as sweet and full and strong as he had ever seen it, then all around her, and finally at him.

She stopped and looked directly at him, her violet eyes, those eyes that had seared and crisped and vanished, staring into his own . . .

"No . . ." he whispered, then said again more strongly, *"no!"*

This was a dream, a vision, a torture of the mind born from his desire to have her alive again. There was nothing of reality in this. It was merely a dream child of his wish, and he closed his eyes, pressing them shut tightly, and opened them again.

But she was not gone. She was still there, only fainter, farther, receding as he watched until, in a few more seconds, her form was gone and only darkness remained.

If he had seen her body, he thought, it would have been better. If there had been something to prove that she was dead, he could have believed it fully. As cruel as it would have been to see her crushed and shattered body, it would not have been this cruel.

But never having seen evidence of her passing beyond the flattened building she had loved, he could never be sure. Though his conscious mind told him that she was dead, he would never *truly* believe it without proof.

And even then, perhaps not. Love never died. And if his love for her never would, then why should hers for him?

But why would her love torment him this way, with visions of her rising from the dust with which her body was mingled? It was a cruel and cunning torment, which gave hope where there was none.

No. She was gone. He would always love her, but she was gone, and he knew that she would have wanted him to try to love again. He would. He would do what she wanted, whatever she wanted.

But he would not go to where she had died in the feeble misapprehension that she had somehow returned. He was not a fool. Life, and the "person or persons unknown" who had planted their packages of hate in Amy's heart, had taught him that. There was no coming back in a world that murdered love.

Something moved in the bed next to him.

He lay back down slowly on his side and put his arm around his wife, pressing against her so that they were lying like a pair of spoons. "Are you all right?" she asked sleepily.

"Yes . . . a dream," he whispered into her fragrant hair.

"Mmm." She took his hand in her own, tucking it warmly against her breast. "It's all right . . . Go back to sleep. I love you."

He closed his eyes, trying not to cry, trying to make the words the truth. ". . . I love you, Nancy . . ."

For a moment she had seen him, Rick, looking into her eyes, and then he was gone and she was alone, feeling more pain than she ever had in her life, more pain than when she had died.

For then the physical pain had been nothing. A flare of light, a moment of severance from the earth, from life, from thought, from her body itself.

But not from pain, not from the pain of knowing what had happened, what she had lost. That pain alone survived, and maybe something deeper was mixed in. Maybe love was there.

But now, standing there in the dust, she felt not only the agony of knowledge, the torture of loss, but the greatest physical pain that she had ever experienced. Every atom of her body wrenched and twisted and jerked. She had pushed herself to her feet, thinking that the cool night air might prove a soothing balm. She could not believe her flesh appeared unmarked, while her senses screamed that her skin was torn from her, her body an open sore, oozing pus like a burst blister.

Yet as she stood and trembled and endured, having no other choice, the pain slowly began to pass, as if evaporating in the night air. And at last she breathed and there was no pain. She moved, touched herself, and it was gone.

But what remained? She was alive, but how had that happened? There had been a bomb . . . Had the blast blown off her clothing and left her otherwise untouched? But then where had the pain come from? And the children, they had died . . .

The thought stabbed a blade of anguish through her soul. Oh God, if God there were, all of them were dead, dead and gone. Had they been taken away or were they mixed with this dust?

She looked around, saw all her dreams, the things she had loved, reduced to dust and ash. Yet here she stood, naked and alive. Why? What had happened? Who had done this?

Then she saw the bird, huge and black, sitting on the post. The beads of its eyes were fixed on her, and its head cocked first to one side then to the other, as if it were waiting for her to speak, to ask a question, to cry, to rage, to wonder aloud if she were in heaven or hell.

And she stood and watched the crow, not understanding, lost in the ruins of her first life, and in the madness of her second.

It was shortly after midnight when David Levinson received the radio message. He had just fortified himself with several cups of black coffee and a slice of blueberry pie when the report came to him of a naked woman seen in the vicinity of North Spruce and Oak Streets. An elderly woman who had been walking her dog called it in, and Levinson was the closest officer to the vicinity.

North Spruce and Oak. God, he thought. That was the site of the Making Friends Child Care Center. All he needed to make his night was some mother pushed over the edge by grief, returning to the scene of her child's death—a naked woman rending her garments and searching among the ashes. The image made Levinson think of the passage from the book of Jeremiah, of Rachel weeping for her children because they were no more. Ah well, he had a blanket in the trunk, and handcuffs if they became necessary.

If only something had been done, if the feds had caught the unspeakable bastards who had bombed a dozen people to ashes, maybe the town could have put it to rest, and the wounds could have begun to heal. But this way, with the gutless government, his own local branch included, afraid to investigate for fear of stirring up a hornet's nest of self-proclaimed patriots, hell, it was no wonder the relatives might go crazy. The most frustrating thing in the world had to be knowing what kind of group was responsible for the death of your child, but knowing too that no one was even investigating. A sure recipe for madness.

"Shit . . ." he whispered to himself as he crossed North Spruce Street. The report hadn't been a Halloween trick. He saw the woman all right, standing smack-dab in the middle of the Blasted Heath. He couldn't see her face but she was standing, legs slightly apart, arms at her side.

There seemed an electric tension in the slim, supple body. At least she wasn't carrying a gun or knife, and a concealed weapon was out of the question.

He pulled the prowler over to the curb, deciding to approach her on foot. If she saw the police car, she might run, and he didn't want to chase a naked woman through the sleepy streets of Hobie. Levinson got out of the car and took a heavy brown blanket from the trunk. Then he started walking toward the woman from behind, treading softly in the dust.

When he was a few yards behind her, he saw the crow. The bird was sitting on a post, twenty yards from the woman. Yet in spite of the distance between her and the crow, it appeared to Levinson that they were somehow communicating, as absurd as that seemed. The woman's long dark hair hid her face from Levinson's view, and for a moment he wondered what he would do if she turned around and showed him a Halloween face of a skull, obscene in her nudity.

Then he dismissed the fancy and, stopping a few feet from her, said softly, "Ma'am?" and held out the blanket toward her.

What warily turned and looked at him was worse than a skull face. It was the face of Amy Carlisle. Gray dust lightly coated her face and body, but her violet eyes were clear.

Suddenly the blanket felt so heavy in his hands that he could hardly hold it. But he feared that if it dropped, the delicate balance of stillness between himself and Amy Carlisle and the crow sitting on the post would dissolve. It was as if they made a tableau formed in a dream. This can't be real, he told himself, and if the composition wavered, if the line joining the three of them broke, he did not know what stranger, more terrible dream might replace this one.

But then Amy Carlisle opened her mouth and spoke to him in Amy Carlisle's voice. "What . . . is this?"

She sounded frightened and helpless and lost, and he became a policeman again instead of a scared child dreaming, and went to her and wrapped the blanket gently around her. Then he looked at the crow again, sitting quietly, but watching with an intensity that bespoke more than mere sentience, and he thought he realized what had happened and what would happen still.

He recalled all too well Grandmother Levensohn's story about old Uncle Abraham and the crow.

twelve

"WHAT'S HAPPENING TO ME?" AMY CARLISLE ASKED. "I DON'T ...
I don't understand."

"Tell me your name," said the policeman who was holding
her. She thought she recognized him, but her mind . . . everything was so confused that she didn't know if she could remember her *own* name.

"I'm . . ." She looked at the man's searching face, then at
the crow sitting on the post and held its gaze as she answered.
"I'm Amy Carlisle." Then she looked back at the policeman.
"And this place is mine—or was." She shook her head, remembering. "They killed my children. And they tried to kill me. But
they didn't . . . I don't know how . . ."

"Amy," said the policeman, "tell me something. Tell me the
last thing that you recall."

She looked into the darkness and tried to remember. "It
was—just tonight. There was a terrible explosion . . . The wall
caved in and the lights went off and the children were crying."
She remembered DeMarole's arm then, that little arm attached
to nothing else, and bit into her lip, biting back the memory,
hard enough to draw blood though she could not taste it.

"I found two of them. And I was trying to get them out and
I saw some lights, far away, and then . . . I don't remember."

"Amy, my name is David Levinson. I've met you before. I'm

83

a policeman. Will you come with me? We'll go somewhere, get you some clothing, something to eat."

"All right." She nodded her head although she didn't want anything to eat. She wasn't hungry. "And then you'll help me find them, won't you?"

David Levinson's face looked even sadder than before. "Come on," he said, and with his arm still around her, he guided her to the police car. She sat in the front seat and he got in the driver's side and started the car. "I want to take you to my house," he said. "Away from here."

"You'll help me find them?" she said again.

"Amy, I can't. The children are gone . . . They're dead. All of them."

"I know that. I mean, find *them*. I survived, you see. I was the only one, the *only* one. So I have to . . . make things right."

She looked in the rearview mirror and saw the crow following them, flapping its wings slowly, yet easily keeping up with the speeding car. "I think I should go home," Amy said. "I think I need to . . . My husband, Rick, needs to know I'm . . . okay."

"We'll take care of that later."

They drove for a few blocks and Levinson turned on his radio. "Jean, on that report," he said, "it was just a prank. Some kids with an inflatable doll. I chased them off." Someone at the other end said something Amy didn't understand and Levinson spoke again.

"Jean, there's another problem. I've got some real—gastric distress. Been stopping every ten minutes or so and it's really wasting me. Is there another car could double for me till six? I'll make it up to them." Jean said something again and Levinson said, "Great, thanks. I'm heading home then."

He put the unit back in place and kept driving until he came to a row of houses in a cul-de-sac in a quiet neighborhood.

He pulled into a driveway, pressed a button on a remote, and a garage door opened up. Amy turned and saw the crow settle down to perch on a darkened wrought iron lamppost. Then the garage doors closed and she saw it no more.

Levinson led the way out of the garage, across a screened porch, and then into a kitchen, where he pulled down the shades before turning on lights. "Let's find you some clothes," he said, and led her down a short hall to a bedroom, where he once more pulled the shades before he dug into the back of a closet.

"These were my wife's," he said, taking out a blouse, a sweater, and a pair of jeans. "They should fit you. There's a bathroom through there if you want to wash off the dust first. Take your time, get changed, and then come out. We have to talk."

After he left, Amy dropped the blanket and stepped into the small bathroom, where she took a shower. The water didn't feel hot or cold. It barely felt wet, but she could see the dust washing away, swirling down the drain. Then she dried herself and slipped on the clothes.

She couldn't say whether they were comfortable or not. She could scarcely feel the weight on her skin, which almost seemed to belong to someone else, just the way the clothes did. In the mirror, however, they seemed to fit.

Then Amy looked more closely at herself, studying her face and her hair. If she looked hard, she thought she could make out a thin, pale network of lines in her face, even on her cheeks and forehead, which had never before had a wrinkle. Her skin looked like the underside of leaves, a patchwork of small cells stitched together so delicately that it appeared smooth until viewed at extremely close range.

Then she noticed that the surfaces of her eyes possessed the pattern as well, and when she examined the other parts of her body, so did her nails and the smooth skin of her inner arms and thighs. The nearly invisible markings were everywhere.

When she joined David Levinson in the living room, he had a tray of sandwiches, cookies, and fresh fruit and a pot of tea. "Something to eat?" he offered, but she shook her head.

"No, thank you. I'm not really hungry. Not for food, anyway. But for answers, yes." She sat next to him on the sofa, folded her hands so tightly together that her fingers whitened, and leaned toward him so demandingly that he drew back.

"What happened? How did I survive? Why did they all die and why am I alive? Can you tell me that, David Levinson?"

He looked for a moment as though he didn't know what to say. Then he shook his head uncomfortably and looked away, closing his eyes. When he looked back at her, his eyes were colder, his mouth a stern line. "I can tell you some things, Amy Carlisle. I can tell you things that aren't going to make matters any clearer, that may puzzle us more than we already are. But as to why you're alive? Amy . . . I'm sorry . . . but you're *not* alive. You've been dead for six months."

What in God's name was he saying. "Six . . . *months?*"

"Yes. And you're dead now. Moving, thinking, yes, but not . . . not truly alive. You've been brought back for a purpose."

She wanted to argue with him, to hit him, to tell him that he was a fool, but instead it seemed that she was hearing a confirmation of knowledge buried deep within her, knowledge that had been given to her in silence and in secret, by something dark and hidden.

The crow. The crow had something to do with this.

"I know you're anxious," Levinson said. "I know that you want to know what happened and who was responsible and all the rest. But first, I beg you, sit here and listen, and let me tell you a story that my grandmother told to me. And after it's finished I think it might help you to know who you are.

"And what you have to do."

thirteen

"MY FAMILY, THE LEVENSOHNS," DAVID LEVINSON BEGAN, "LIVED in Kishinev in Moldavia, under Russian rule. The beginning of this century was a terrible time for Russian Jews. We had few rights compared to non-Jews, and though there was no sanctioned government program against us, the officials did little, if anything, to prevent the pogroms from taking place.

"These pogroms were attacks on Jews by angry mobs. Everybody hated us. Since a lot of Jews were in business, the lower classes thought we were all capitalists, and since some Jews were political radicals, the bureaucrats thought we were all socialists. If there was a reason to hate, they found it.

"My grandfather was a boy at the time of the Kishinev pogrom in 1903. A mob attacked the Jewish community and savaged it for two whole days. It was the local leaders who egged on the mob, and the czar's soldiers did nothing to stop it. Many Jews were killed, many more wounded. The Levensohn family was one of the unlucky ones, and my grandfather's Uncle Abraham perhaps the most unlucky of all.

"He lost his wife and three of his children, my grandfather's cousins. My grandfather wasn't harmed—his mother hid him in a latrine for two days. He'd climb up and look through the cracks in the walls from time to time, so he saw everything and lived to tell about it.

"Uncle Abraham was a big man in his early fifties, who had started working as a tallow melter and had worked his way up until he owned a successful tallow business. He was a fierce competitor, energetic and tireless. He also had a dissident streak in him. When the riots began, his non-Jewish competitors saw it as a chance to end his success—and his life.

"They beat him and stabbed him, but Abraham survived, though badly wounded. At last the soldiers and police came out to disperse the rioters, and at last my grandfather came out of the latrine and saw what happened next. Uncle Abraham was probably dying already, but was perceptive enough to see the truth about what had happened. He grabbed the bridle of a cossack captain and accused him and his men of collusion with the rioters by their inaction. 'You killed my family as much as these stupid and greedy bastards,' he said. 'Yours is the greater guilt.'

"Well, it was the truth, but the cossack didn't want to hear it, especially not from a bruised and bleeding Jew. So he drew his saber and brought it down at the side of Uncle Abraham's neck, nearly severing his head. Uncle Abraham fell dead to the ground. The cossack said to all those watching that they had seen the crazy Jew attacking him—he had no choice but to defend himself. And no one said or did anything about it. Who wanted still another pogrom?

"So they buried Uncle Abraham and his family in the Jewish cemetery in the lower town, on the banks of the Byk River. His competitors took control of the tallow trade, and the soldiers and police and cossacks waited for the next pogrom when they would turn their faces away and let more Jews die. But that was not what happened.

"The cemetery was a very busy place for the weeks after the pogrom. People came to pay their respect to their loved ones, but after a while the mourners were content saying Kaddish in the synagogue. My grandfather, however, continued to visit the cemetery frequently, often at night, which was the only opportunity he had after his work was done. His mother, who had hidden him so safely, had been killed in the riots, and he sat next to her grave almost every night, until he grew sleepy and returned home to his father.

"One evening he was sitting by his mother's grave when he heard a loud cry from overhead and looked up to see a giant crow drifting down toward him. It landed on his Uncle Abraham's grave marker, a few plots away. Then my grandfather saw the earth over Uncle Abraham's grave start to shake and break apart, and Uncle Abraham rose up through the ground, dressed in his grave clothes, which were partially torn from him as he arose. My grandfather could see the wound that had killed him, but it seemed to be healed, with just a white scar showing where the saber had cut.

"Naturally my grandfather was terrified, but he remained frozen to the spot, unable to run. Uncle Abraham looked at the crow, and the crow looked at him for a long time. Then the resurrected man saw my grandfather and smiled. My grandfather said that he was sure the purpose of the smile was to reassure him, but it was so terrible that my grandfather admitted to having peed his pants instantly.

"Then the crow rose and flapped slowly away toward the upper town, on crags high above the river, where the Russians lived and where the soldiers' and policemen's barracks were. Uncle Abraham followed, his grave clothes trailing behind him. My grandfather had to see what was going to happen, so he followed them.

"As Uncle Abraham walked through the streets, plenty of people saw him. After all, Kishinev had more than a hundred thousand people in it. All the Jews ran screaming, shutting themselves inside their houses and praying until dawn. But they had nothing to fear from Uncle Abraham or from the crow.

"The bird led the dead man and the boy to the house of the tallow merchant who, along with his sons, had beaten and stabbed my uncle and helped to kill his family. There my grandfather watched as the crow sat on the edge of the roof while Uncle Abraham kicked in the door and went inside. There were screams and the sound of a pistol firing, and other sounds that my grandfather only described as *wet*.

"After a while the police arrived and went inside, and there were more cries and sounds of struggle. Several of the police ran outside and kept running. One man, my grandfather saw, had part of his face ripped away.

"Then all was silent inside, and Uncle Abraham came out, his grave clothes sodden with blood and gray pieces of flesh that clung to them, his face terrible. Some policemen who had been stationed outside fired at him with rifles. The bullets struck him but he did not fall, and was scarcely slowed by them.

"One young soldier attacked him with a saber, and although the blade struck nearly the same spot where the cossack captain's killing blow had gone, Uncle Abraham did not fall. He wrenched the saber away, and in a single backswing severed the young policeman's head from his body. Then the crow took to the air again, toward the soldiers' barracks, and Uncle Abraham followed.

"Someone must have warned the soldiers for they were all out in force, with a line of riflemen. The cossack captain was on horseback commanding them, and when Uncle Abraham walked toward them, holding the saber ahead of him, the cossack waited until he was scarcely twenty feet away and then ordered the men to fire.

"Two dozen bullets tore into Uncle Abraham, and he staggered for a moment but did not fall. Then the riflemen threw down their guns and ran, and although he could not see Uncle Abraham's face, my grandfather said he thought it was because Uncle Abraham smiled at them.

"The cossack captain had not run, though, and neither had his horsemen. They all drew their sabers now, and the cossack captain galloped down on Uncle Abraham, his saber raised. But when he brought it down, the dead man grabbed the blade and yanked the captain from his saddle. Then he stamped a foot on the cossack to hold him on the ground, and with the two sabers he now held, he plunged the points into both the man's eyes, killing him.

"The horsemen attacked then, and Uncle Abraham turned into a mad dervish of destruction, slashing the horses' legs so that they fell crippled, then hacking at the riders, lopping off heads and arms and legs with every swing of his sword, taking many wounds, but never a one that made him pause in his slaughter.

"In only minutes the horsemen were all dead, the street was empty. No one else dared to challenge this dead man in grave clothes. Uncle Abraham then severed the cossack captain's head, stuck it on the end of the soldier's own saber, and walked through the wide and empty streets to the cathedral, the seat of the archbishop of Bessarabia. There Uncle Abraham plunged the saber, the cossack's head still adorning it, into the wooden door of the cathedral, leaving an unmistakable message for the archbishop and the czar.

"The crow flew back toward the old town again and Uncle Abraham—and my amazed grandfather—turned and walked back to the cemetery on the river bank. And there the dead man lay down on his grave. My grandfather saw the ground part, and his uncle sink into the earth out of sight. Then the crow cried once, and flew away across the river."

fourteen

"MY GRANDFATHER TOLD THAT STORY TO MY GRANDMOTHER,"
David Levinson said. "He never would tell it to us himself but
my grandmother told it plenty of times, maybe at first with
pride, but finally, I think, to scare us."

"It's . . . just a story," said Amy Carlisle, hoping she spoke
the truth.

"That's what I thought too, at first. But whenever my
brother or I would ask our grandfather about it, he became . . .
different. Unlike himself. As if he had stared into an abyss and
didn't want to be forced to think about it again. That was when
I knew it was true."

"And you think what? That the crow we saw brought me
back from the dead? That's ridiculous. It couldn't happen."

"Then why are you here?"

"Because I'm alive!" she flared. "I never died to begin with.
I . . . I lost consciousness, didn't know who I was, wandered
away from the explosion . . ."

"Wandered away for six months and nobody noticed you
when your picture was all over the newspapers and TV. And
then you wandered back stark naked, covered in the dust of the
child care center. With a crow who just happens to accompany
you everywhere you go . . ."

Levinson yanked the cord so that the front drapes flew open, revealing the black bird still sitting on the lamppost. He flicked a light switch and the outside lamp went on, illuminating the bird's feathers, turning the black to a deep violet tinged with blue.

Levinson sat down next to her again, took her hand and turned it palm up so that he could see the skin of her arm. "Look at yourself," he said. "You see these?" He pointed to the tiny new lines in her flesh, the thousands of individual bits that made up the expanse of her skin. "They're *pieces*, Amy. They're the pieces of you that came apart and then came back together again. The pieces that came together tonight, from out of the dust, when that crow appeared."

Amy pushed Levinson away with such strength that his back hit the arm of the sofa and he grunted with the pain. "No!" she said. "No, it's not true . . ."

"How strong are you, Amy?" Levinson said, rubbing his back. "You were fit but never really buffed, were you? Couldn't hope to fight off a guy as big and strong as me, could you? A guy who saw you naked and got turned on and maybe wanted to get some cheap action . . ."

He went for her then, his arms coming around her, burying his face in her neck. And without thinking she reacted, using not leverage but pure force, tossing him away from her, over the coffee table and onto the floor. The force of the impact knocked the wind from him. Then before she knew it she was on top of him, her left forearm crushing his neck, her right fist raised to strike. Only the panic in his eyes stopped her from slamming his nose flat against his face.

Amy sat back then, lowering her arms while Levinson coughed and choked, then waved a hand as if in surrender. "I'm sorry . . . sorry," he said tightly. "That wasn't very gentlemanly but I wanted to prove my point. You're strong, stronger than you've ever been before. And you said you weren't hungry. Why would you be? You're dead."

"I'm not dead," said Amy, her head swimming.

"No, Amy, I'm sure you are," he said, walking to the other end of the room. "In fact, I'm so sure that I'm going to do something that will destroy my life if I'm wrong. That's how sure I am. And then there won't be any more arguments about it."

In one movement he whirled around toward her, jerked the pistol from his holster, cocked the hammer, and pulled the trigger.

Amy started to move toward Levinson and had actually halved the gap between them when she felt the bullet hit her in the chest. Its impact slowed her only for a moment and then she was on him, yanking the gun from his hand and pushing him back. His head struck the wall, the pupils of his eyes rolled up, and he slid to the floor unconscious, his back against the wall.

She looked at the smoking gun in her hand, then dropped it noiselessly on the carpet as she brought both hands to her chest to touch the place where she had been shot. It had felt hot for an instant, and then cold, and then she felt nothing at all and wondered if she was in shock. She saw the hole in the flannel shirt she wore, blackened around the edges. As she unbuttoned it, she felt as though she were dreaming. She had been shot in the chest and felt no pain. Then she drew back the front of her shirt.

The wound was still closing, a circle becoming smaller until it vanished altogether, leaving only a pale circle, a slight indentation, like the imprint of a lover's fingers, which faded even as she watched. She had been shot, shot over the heart, and she was still alive.

Or dead.

Then the truth overwhelmed her, the truth that she had suspected, but now knew for certain. It built up within her as thickly as the dust that had burst from her reborn lungs, until she felt that she would burst again, that the millions of fragments that had coalesced would once again disperse in a silent explosion born of her own terrible self-knowledge.

The sensation took what seemed an eon to pass, but then she regained control. Her eyes were open: it wasn't a question of *what* she was, but a new understanding of *why* she was.

She was a child of death come back to give birth, not to life through her still dead womb, but to *more* death through the strength of her hands. She had never been able to be a mother before but she would be one now—the Mother of Vengeance.

The only children she could ever think of as her own had died, and she had died with them. But her heart had survived, her savage mother's heart, a heart that knew that the deepest grief, the saddest story ever told, is that of parents outliving their children. A story sad and unnatural. An act too foul for breath to tell.

Who would do such a thing? Who could be so heartless as to bring it to pass? She would find out and she would visit a mother's vengeance upon them. The story of the old Jew had shown her the way. The Crow had brought him back for vengeance.

No. For *justice*. To put the wrong things right. And was there ever a deed more wrong than this?

But the old Jew had known the killers of his children, his wife, himself. That was an advantage she did not have. He could stalk through the streets, knowing where to go, whom to seek, but she could not. First she would have to learn the names of the monsters who had killed her babies. Maybe this policeman could help her.

She knelt next to Levinson and heard his regular breathing. There was a lump on the back of his head, but no blood ran from it, and his face looked peaceful.

It reminded her of Rick's face as he lay in bed next to her in the early morning when it was just bright enough to make out his features. Rick. Oh God, what could she do about Rick, with Rick, for Rick? If she was truly dead, there could be no place for her in his life, or for him in hers. Still, she loved him as she always had, and would, beyond death, forever.

But Rick was not why she had returned. She had returned for her children—and the people who had killed them.

"Wake up," she said, gently shaking Levinson's shoulder. He stirred and mumbled something, and then his eyes opened and he looked at her.

"Wow," he whispered. "You are *fast* . . ." He looked down at her half-open shirt, at the bullet hole in the cloth. "And alive." A smile creased his features. "Which proves that . . ." He raised his eyebrows as though wanting her to finish it, and she did.

"I'm dead. Yes, you're right, I know that now. The Crow

brought me back, out of the ashes. Because there's payment to be made. Justice for my children."

Levinson nodded, then winced and rubbed the back of his head. "And I have no doubt you'll get it. As fast and as strong as you are . . . impervious to bullets, a militia's nightmare."

"Militia?" she asked. "What do you mean?"

"I mean that it looks like a militia—or somebody involved with one—planted two bombs as an attempted hit on Senator King. He never made it, but you were there. You and the other woman and all the children." Levinson kept talking as he got slowly to his feet. "I think I saw you that night after the first bomb had gone off. I was driving up and I saw several people moving inside. I think it was you trying to get the children out. Then the second one went off." He looked down and chewed on his upper lip.

"And I died."

"Yeah. You died."

"Will you help me to find them? The ones who did it?"

"I don't know how I can. I mean, I'm a cop, I can't go outside the law, can't bend it to fit my view of justice."

"But I can." She tried a smile. It didn't feel natural to her. She felt strange and scary smiling, and imagined she knew what those Russian riflemen had seen. "I'll need a place to stay." She touched the bullet hole. "And some more clothes."

"And a way to get around too. There's a lot you need."

Her anger broke through then. "You say it's been six months and they still don't have these bastards? Don't you want to see them pay for what they did? I can make that happen, Levinson! But you've got to help me!"

He thought for a moment, then nodded. "All right, I will. But you don't say anything to anybody about me. And I want it understood that if I, or any other law enforcement official, get to these fuckers first, they're mine. The law and the courts take your vengeance then. I won't give that up—that's the code *I* live by."

She pursed her lips and nodded slowly. "It's a race then."

"If that's how you want to look at it."

"I do."

"Okay. This place has a spare bedroom, I'll hole up there—do you sleep?"

She thought for a moment, trying to assess her body and its needs. "I don't know. I'm not tired now."

"Well, you can take my bedroom anyway. All the clothes that my ex-wife left behind are in that closet."

"What about transportation?" Amy asked. "The Crow may fly but I don't think I can."

"Let me show you." He led her back to the garage. Before, in the darkness, Amy hadn't noticed the long, low covered shape in the second bay. But now Levinson turned on the hanging light and whipped off the cover, revealing the sleek black lines of a hardtop sports car. The styling made the hood appear twice as long as the passenger area. A single pair of headlights stared from a solid, grill-less front like a pair of owl's eyes.

"This," he intoned, "is a Studebaker Avanti, circa 1964. I've worked on this baby for several years and just finished it a week ago. I don't even have it registered yet. It's a phantom car. Now if you were to steal an old set of plates somewhere, you'd be riding high." He gestured to several old Minnesota license plates that had been nailed to the garage wall. "Well, well, look what the previous owner left."

"God," said Amy, still looking at the car. "It's beautiful. Thank—"

"It *also*," he interrupted her, as he took a three-year-old plate from the wall and affixed it to the Avanti's holder with a screwdriver, "is a classic car. It is a gem, my baby, pretty much all *I* have to live for and if you let anything bad happen to it, I will . . ." He paused.

"You were going to say 'kill you,' weren't you?" He looked embarrassed. "Well, that would be redundant. Don't worry. I won't let it get hurt."

Levinson shook his head. "Do with it what you need to do. Maybe this is why I've spent all those years on it—so it would be here for you when you needed it."

"You believe in synchronicity?" she asked with as friendly a smile as she knew how to give.

"Lady, after tonight I believe in a whole lot more than I

used to. Come back inside. There's something else I need to show you."

Levinson led the way to a large, semi-finished basement room lined with shelves. Labeled boxes sat on the floor and three four-drawer filing cabinets stood at one end. "My own little fortress of solitude," he said. "One of my hobbies is tracking these anti-Semitic groups and that includes a lot of militia groups." He chuckled. "Maybe I'll write a book someday. There's tons of raw data here, but it's stuff that I haven't had much time to correlate or do much with except collect."

He lovingly patted a computer that sat on a big desk near the filing cabinets. "This is a 300-megahertz Pentium 2. Top of the line when I bought it and still pretty damn powerful. Got a 57.6 modem in it and access to a number of sites that I really shouldn't have at home." He grinned. "Don't tell anyone. But you might find it useful. You know your way around computers?"

"To a degree. I always caught on pretty fast."

"Well, don't let the speed and power bother you. Works the same as the slow and clunky ones—just better and faster."

"Frankly," Amy said, "I don't think I want to spend my time sitting at a computer. For one thing, I don't know how long I have. And for another . . . I feel like I have to move. So tell me, if you were me, where would you start?"

Levinson had barely opened his mouth to speak when a tap sounded at the painted-over basement window. The tap sounded again. "I think there's someone else who can answer that question," Levinson said. "Maybe you won't need my files after all." He reached in his pocket and took out a pair of keys. "Maybe you'd better change before you hit the road," he said. "That bullet hole's a little suspicious looking."

Alone in Levinson's bedroom, Amy looked through the clothes in the closet, searching for something dark and unobtrusive that would let her move in and out of the shadows unseen. Near the back she found an outfit that would be perfect. Levinson's wife must have gone through a bleak period before the divorce, Amy thought. A plastic bag covered a pair of black denim slacks and a black long-sleeved top made of some stretchable synthetic material with not a· trace of sheen.

Amy threw off the bullet-riddled shirt and blue jeans and pulled on the black top. It felt like a second skin, holding her small, high breasts comfortably, but giving her plenty of room to move. Then she slipped on the black slacks, which fit perfectly.

A pair of low black boots finished the ensemble, and she left the bedroom and went back to the living room. Levinson's eyes widened when he saw her and he glanced at her chest once, then looked quickly back at her face. "I think you need . . . a jacket or something."

He went to the front closet and removed a black leather jacket. "This'll . . . keep you warmer," he said lamely, handing it to her.

"Thanks," she said, feeling oddly pleased that she was still able to arouse a man, if arousal was what Levinson was feeling, but thinking at the same time that her pride was perverse. She was, after all, dead. Wasn't she just dressing up a corpse? And wasn't what Levinson feeling an unprecedented form of necrophilia?

She put on the jacket but didn't zip it up.

"Now what?" Levinson asked.

"Now I go."

"You'll need something, something to . . . defend yourself with. I can't give you a gun but maybe you can use this." He handed her a knife in an ankle sheath. She withdrew it to reveal a six-inch slightly curved blade. The handle had separate finger holes, like brass knuckles. "A survival knife," Levinson said. "Though I don't have much doubt of *your* survival."

"Thank you," she said, strapping it to her leg and fitting her pants leg down over it. Then she turned and went through the kitchen and into the garage, where she lifted the garage door and got into the Avanti. She started it and backed out.

She had expected the engine to roar, but it purred gently and she wondered if one could hear it ten yards away. That was good. Stealth would have to be one of her tools.

The Crow still sat on the lamppost, but now it faced her

and stretched its wings, lifted one leg, then another, as though it were ready and anxious to fly. Amy sat there in the softly idling car, watching it. "Go ahead," she said. "I'm ready too."

The great bird spread its wings then and took to the night sky, flying above the street out of the cul-de-sac. Amy followed.

Jesus, Levinson thought, mentally swearing by the name of the non-divine prophet, what the hell have I done? What have I let loose on the world?

He was terribly frightened but also relieved, relieved that he had been right and that the returned Amy Carlisle was indeed what he had thought she was, a supernatural creature brought back to life by still another such creature. If she hadn't been, Levinson would have been sitting in his living room with a dead woman and either an awful lot of explaining or an awful lot of digging to do.

It had been a lot to wager on an old wives' tale and if he had been using pure logic, he might not have taken the risk. But there was something about the situation with Amy Carlisle that went beyond rational thought. After all, if he had been thinking rationally, he never would have entrusted this woman with a weapon, his car, and his home as a base of operations.

But what if he had done the rational thing and assumed she was a living woman, taken her to the hospital, had the doctors examine her, and say, *Sorry, no pulse, no lung function, no nuthin', nada, she's dead.* Amy Carlisle would have wound up in some secret government lab for the rest of her un-life, which could be immortal, for all Levinson knew. And if Amy chose *not* to be imprisoned, well, there could have been a lot of messed-up doctors before she got free.

The question was, what would she do now? If she followed old Uncle Abraham's game plan, she'd kick major ass and then go back to the arms of Mother Death. He just hoped she wouldn't leave too obvious a trail of destruction along the way. Or anything that anyone could trace to him.

And of course there was always the possibility that

Levinson would get there first. That was unlikely though. With all the goddamned militia groups in this area, it was like looking for a needle in a haystack when all the haystacks were behind rows of armed guards. That frustration was why he had turned her loose. If the cops wouldn't do it and the government didn't have the guts, then maybe Amy Carlisle and the Crow could take care of the job.

He hoped so, and though his Jewish faith had lapsed, he had seen enough tonight to almost make him pray for it.

fifteen

THE CROW SOARED OVER THE FLATNESS OF HOBIE, IGNORING the houses below, its black eyes fixed on a red light before it, like the red glow that had been the spirit of the woman mingled with the dust, the red glow that had caught the eye of the Crow. Flying high over the earth, the Crow was searching, always searching for the burning souls that could not rest, for the ones who needed justice before they could move on, into the country of Death.

But the glow the Crow sought now was not the radiance of a soul in torment, but a manmade glow, the topmost red light in a series of lights that climbed a radio tower, ascending like the words of hate that crept up the webwork of metal and then exploded outward, like lava from a volcano, spewing hot venom into the air that spread to wherever machines could catch the waves and translate them back into words.

The wings beat on, slowly, steadily, ever approaching the building that housed the station and the transmitter that brought Wilson Barnes's message to a hateful nation, to minds ready for hate.

". . . the time has come to rise, to speak out, speak up, and if words won't do the trick, won't convince those who need to be convinced, then there are other ways of speaking, my friends, other ways of making yourself heard, of shouting in a voice of *thunder* at this evil, oppressive, Jew-controlled, liberal-minded, godless government and the men who run it, both the puppets in the White House and the Congress and the shadow rulers who pull the strings behind the scenes.

"But do they pull these strings for white Christian Americans? Goodness no! You're the forgotten men, the ones they tax and tax and tax so that they can take your money away and give it to the black junkies and welfare mothers and the Mexicans who sneak across the border to take your jobs and the Vietnamese who ruined their own country and now want to ruin ours! Well, it's time to stop these traitors to America, these traitors to Christianity, and I believe you know how to do it!

"I've *seen* you do it! I know who you are and I know what you believe and it's what we *all* should believe in. Jefferson himself said it—you have to water the tree of liberty with the blood of tyrants. And you have to be merciless when you do it.

"Now, my friends, when you care for your gardens—and I know an awful lot of my listeners have their own gardens, live off their own land, keep the government out of it—you try to root out the bad influences on your crop. And sometimes when you spray to kill the pests, you can kill good insects too that do no harm. But if your vegetables are infiltrated with cutworms, do you say, 'Oh, I'd better let them live because I might accidentally spray a beautiful butterfly or an innocent ladybug or the earthworms that till the soil?'

"Of course not—you kill the interlopers, you root out what has to be destroyed, and if you kill a few innocents, that's the price you have to pay to ensure a good crop! Now you can read into this what you want, my friends—I'm sure you see what I mean, what I'm *really* talking about—and I know you're willing to make that sacrifice, because I know your hearts and souls . . . I know who you are, you true patriots, and you have my support and my prayers . . ."

• • •

I know who you are . . .

Amy Carlisle listened to the voice of Wilson Barnes and watched the Crow fly. Above the rising buildings she saw the red lights of the radio tower and she knew where the Crow was taking her. She felt the pressure of the knife sheath against her ankle and hoped that its metallic shine would soon be replaced by a darker shine, a red, wet luster.

The hands of the dashboard clock read two forty-five. Wilson Barnes was halfway through his show. He had found his groove and was riffing on his listeners' favorite themes. Well, Amy thought, there would be a new theme tonight. If the audience wanted blood, they would get it.

Of course, Wilson Barnes would know about the militias and might even know which one was responsible for the bombing. He was their hero. It would be natural for one or more of them to brag to him, to let him know how his words had inspired these patriots to action.

Against children. Babies. Her babies.

The Crow alighted atop a marquee over the building's front door. On it were the station's call letters and the words *Home of the Wilson Barnes Show*. Amy drove past the door and parked her car a block away, then walked back on the deserted street.

She looked through the glass doors and saw, twenty feet inside, a U-shaped security station and a beefy armed guard sitting behind it, reading a newspaper. Amy pressed the buzzer and the guard looked up, wary at first. But when he saw her he smiled, nodded, and pressed a button on his console. There was a buzz and she pushed the door open and walked in.

"Howya doin'?" the guard, whose name tag identified him as Donald, asked. "A little early, huh?"

She looked at him curiously.

"You know," Donald went on, leering at her with his fleshy face. "Wanna warm up with me first? The boss got another ten minutes before the network feed kicks in with the news." He gestured to the portable radio beside him, from which the voice of Wilson Barnes continued to spout invective.

Now she got it. He had thought she was one of Barnes's

whores. Apparently the man of the people gave little Wilson some exercise midway through the night. "Sure," Amy said, "I'll be happy to warm up with you."

As she came around behind the desk, Donald's eyes widened. "Holy shit," he said. "One of you finally said yes. Hell, I can't believe it. Thank God for the new girl." He laughed and wiggled in his chair, fumbling with his zipper. "Don't tell Mr. Barnes though, huh?"

"My lips are sealed . . . or will be. Hey, let me take care of that," she went on, kneeling in front of him.

Her hand snaked to her ankle, found the grip of the survival knife, and brought it up quickly across the fat man's face. The heavy brass knuckles collided with his temple and Amy heard a crack. He collapsed like a dead fish, sliding out of the chair onto Amy, who easily disentangled herself from the layers of flesh.

She slipped the knife back into the sheath and hauled Donald back to a sitting position as easily as if he had been a willowy girl. Not yet used to her strength, she had hit him a lot harder than she had thought, but whether he was unconscious or dying she neither knew nor cared. She arranged him so that he looked like he was sleeping and then consulted the floor directory posted near the elevators.

Meeting rooms were on the first floor, offices on the second, and the studio was on the third. She took the stairs, not wanting to let them know she was coming.

The stairs opened onto a long hall dimly lit by recessed ceiling bulbs. Bright light spilled from windows set into the wall on the left. Amy stepped slowly toward the nearest one until she could see Wilson Barnes.

He was sitting in front of a table covered in black velvet. A single standing floor lamp strongly illuminated his work area. Another table, loaded with newspapers, magazines, and books, was to his left. A microphone hung from a boom directly in front of his face and a thick pair of headphones covered his ears. His back was partially toward her and he was facing another, higher window with a row of colored lights visible through it. She assumed it was the engineer's room.

Amy had never seen Wilson Barnes or even his picture, so

his appearance startled her. She had expected a robust, Limbaughesque figure in his midforties, but instead Barnes was thin and wiry, almost emaciated, and he might have been any-where from forty to sixty. It seemed a freak of nature that such a round, full voice could come out of so spindly a frame. Maybe hate had eaten him away, Amy thought. He seemed well dressed, however, with a white collar peeking up from beneath a tailored gray suit coat.

His voice droned on from the inset speakers in the hall. There was no escaping from Wilson Barnes here. And there would be no escape *for* Barnes either.

Amy waited until the large analog clock above the engi-neer's window read two fifty-nine and Barnes was only a minute away from the news. Fat Donald downstairs had called it a network feed. That meant it would be coming in from out-side the station, so Barnes and whoever was in the control room were probably the only ones here tonight.

Amy crouched and duck-walked past the window below Barnes's field of vision. The next window showed her the con-trol room and had probably been placed there so that people touring the station could see the activity without disturbing the bigots at work. She wondered how many ignorant, easily mis-led, poor white assholes had come through here, wearing their mesh baseball caps and their faded T-shirts with "Where's Lee Harvey Oswald When You Need Him?" imprinted on them. Like a tour of the Reichstag, only jollier.

Only one man sat behind the controls. He was somewhere between Barnes and Donald in size but Amy didn't care. She felt invincible. When Barnes finished talking and the engineer switched to the network feed, she pushed open the door and stepped into the control room.

The engineer turned and looked at her in surprise. "New girl? Where the hell is Marie?" he asked angrily. "Look, you're *supposed* to be down *there*, bitch, so haul it. You got five min-utes so do it fast and sweet, okay?"

Ignoring him, Amy leaned over the console and looked through the glass into the studio. Wilson Barnes was looking up at her. At first, he seemed unsure of what he was looking at but then something happened to his face that hideously split it in two. Amy thought it was his idea of a smile. He turned off his microphone, took off his headphones, and stood up from behind the table.

Amy was shocked, then immediately amused, to see that he was wearing no pants or underwear. A small penis was standing at attention, though feebly. He grabbed it with his right hand, and with his left gestured at her to come down.

She wouldn't disappoint him.

Amy turned back to the engineer. "Would he mind if you went first?" she said. Without waiting for an answer, she grabbed the hair at the back of his head and slammed his face down onto the console, once, twice, three times, until his body went limp and slid into the darkness beneath.

When she looked back at Barnes, he was staring at her slack-jawed, his poor excuse for a cock drooping to half-mast as if in honor of his fallen comrade. In one swift move, Amy reached down for her knife, brought it up, and with a fist of brass she smashed through the double-paned glass that separated her from the man.

Barnes gave a startled cry but hesitated only a moment as Amy climbed through the opening, pushing the jagged edges of glass aside with her bare hands. He leaped to the table at his left, swept aside some papers, and jerked up a .357 magnum, which he grasped in both hands and began to fire at her.

She had to give him credit. He held that pistol steady as a rock as it exploded in his spidery hands. She felt the bullets slam into her, one after another, hitting her in the chest and pushing her back.

But she took two steps forward for every backward step that a magnum load cost her, and now she grabbed the gun by the barrel and ripped it from Barnes's fists. For a moment they stood there staring at each other and then Amy jabbed the barrel into her waistband. "You got any more bullets?" she asked. "I'm going to need them."

His mouth dropped open even further and he turned to run toward the door, but she grabbed his neck like a fleeing chicken's, grimacing at the way her fingers sank into the stringy wattles of his throat. With one arm, she turned him toward her and dragged him kicking and choking, his little cock flapping like a popped balloon, back to the velvet-covered table.

There she slammed him down on his back, still holding him by the throat, her other hand brandishing the shining blade of the knife, turning it slowly in front of his eyes. "You see this?" she said. "It could be the last thing you see, Wilson Barnes. But not because I'm going to kill you. No. Because if you don't tell me what I think you know, I'll take your eyes.

"I'll ask you one time. And if you don't answer me, I'm going to cut you, just cut you once." She moved the knife down to Barnes's testicles and pressed the point against them. He gasped and froze.

"That's right. There. Not badly. Just enough to hurt. And if you don't tell me the second time, I'll cut out your tongue, Wilson Barnes, so that you'll never speak those words again, those lying words that make people kill."

Barnes gave a little yelp of fright and humiliation, and when she looked down she saw urine trickling from his cock. "The third time, I'll take your fingers, all of them, so that you can't write your lies. The fourth your eyes, so that you can't see words and letters to respond to anyone. And finally your eardrums so that no one can tell you, thump once with your stump for yes, twice for no.

"I'll cut you off for good, Wilson Barnes. I won't kill you but I'll banish you from the land of the living so that you'll never communicate again. But if you position yourself just right, maybe you can rub your dick against something. At least you'll have that much."

She put her face so close to his that their lips nearly met. His breath smelled like shit covered with mint. "That's more than my children ever got, Wilson Barnes. Remember them? *Remember?*"

"Wh . . . who?" Barnes husked out, his oratorical voice dried up by fear.

"My children. Remember the innocent ones? The ones that sometimes just have to die if you're going to purge the garden of pests? I want to know who did the purging, Wilson Barnes. I want to know who killed the children with those bombs."

"I . . . I don't know, really I don't, I swear on the Bible, I swear by Jesus Christ almighty . . ."

Amy felt her face grow as hard as her resolve, and she pressed the flat of the blade against Barnes's scrotum until he squealed. Then she turned it so that the sharp blade just barely sliced into the puckered flesh.

The squeal turned into a scream that drowned out the far-away sound of the network news on the speaker in the control room. Barnes's body writhed and trembled, but he did not jerk about for fear that the knife would do worse than it already had.

As the scream died away, a cheery voice over the speaker intoned, "And that's the news . . ." A musical theme played briefly and then there was nothing but dead air and the labored breathing of Wilson Barnes.

"What's it going to be?" Amy asked. "If I have to cut apart an innocent man to get what I want, I'll do it." She held the knife, bright with his blood, in front of his eyes and he pressed them shut and clenched his teeth. Amy reached up with the point of the knife and quietly turned on the microphone.

"Who was it, Wilson Barnes?" she asked. "Your tongue. I promise you."

The skinny man moaned and whimpered, his eyes still tightly shut. Then Amy touched his lips with the point of the knife, pushing it slowly and gently into his mouth, so that he could taste his own blood.

Wilson Barnes's eyes shot open and he nearly shouted his reply. "The *Sons!*" he said. "Sons of a Free America! Please . . . please don't hurt me . . . It's the truth!"

Amy had heard the faint echoes of his voice from the control room. She held the knife in front of his eyes again, bringing it toward them, and he pressed them shut once more. Then she moved the microphone so that it was directly over Wilson Barnes's cringing face, and rested the flat of the blade over the man's closed eyes.

"Who? Tell me again. Tell me who the bastards are."

"The Sons . . . of a Free . . . America," he panted. "It's the truth. They're the ones, they're the ones, I swear . . . It was them, it was them . . ."

He continued to babble as she took the knife away from his eyes and released his throat. At last he stopped talking and began breathing more deeply. And then he opened his eyes and saw the microphone less than six inches from his lips, the switch in the ON position.

"This confession brought to you by Wilson Barnes," Amy said formally.

Barnes grabbed the mike and switched it off. He looked about panicked, too scared to be concerned about his half nakedness or the piss running down his skinny thighs. "You . . . you turned it *on*," he said accusingly, some of the old fire back.

"Yes. And you'd better not leave it off for long. If there's anything listeners hate, it's dead air. That and an informer. I have a hunch, Mr. Barnes, that you'll be hearing a lot more dead air soon." She rummaged through the items on the desk and came up with a box of .357 cartridges. "I knew a man like you would be properly equipped," she said with a smile, glancing at his groin, which he embarrassedly covered with his hands.

"Thanks for the information, Mr. Barnes. Now if I were you, I think I'd try and mend some bridges . . . with *your friends.*"

She turned and walked out of the studio, down the hall, down the stairs, and out of the building past the still unconscious Donald. All the way, she heard Wilson Barnes's shaky but persuasive voice over the speakers that pocked the building's walls:

"And that's what could happen, my friends, if this government continues on its ruthless path. As this dramatization shows, government agents—even female ones, inspired by pro-abortion feminists—could burst into a radio studio—or even your very own *homes!*—and torture you into giving up . . . into telling things that you didn't want revealed, such as the names of any groups that you were associated with, like this, uh, fictitious organization that the character I was portraying was forced into telling the name of . . . It could happen here, my friends, so be sure to preserve your freedoms, and . . ."

Amy had to hand it to him, the man sure had a way of covering his skanky ass. But she didn't think the bullshit would do much to soothe the ruffled feathers of the Sons of a Free America, whoever they were.

As she opened the outside door a skinny redhead with large breasts tried to push her way in. Amy grabbed a handful of red vinyl coat and forced the woman back outside with her, pressing the door shut until it clicked. "Forget it," she told the woman. "Believe me, you're the last person in the world Wilson Barnes wants to see right now." Then she thought about the Sons of a Free America and smiled a smile that made the hooker back up several steps.

"Okay," Amy corrected herself, "maybe the *next* to last person."

The Crow was perched on the parking meter next to the Avanti and Amy nodded at it. "Got a name," she said. "Now I just need the people to go with it . . ."

sixteen

IT HAD BEEN JUNIOR FEELEY'S TURN TO PULL NIGHT GUARD duty. He hated night guard. There were a thousand and one weird noises in the woods that surrounded the compound, not to mention an assortment of land mines positioned just inside the perimeter. If anyone was able to get over the ten-foot-high chain link fence topped with razor wire, they'd have to cope with Powder Burns's little surprises.

Junior didn't know how many of them there were, though he figured near a hundred. However, he wasn't about to go and count, since he had seen what had happened to a deer that had stepped on one. At least, they *thought* it was a deer. It looked more like deer jelly afterward.

Still, several deer remained within the compound, which encompassed thirty acres. The Sons, under a dummy corporation, also owned, or used at the pleasure of the businessmen who financed them, a surrounding four square miles of woodland. Junior didn't have to pace the whole perimeter of the compound and would not have if ordered, for fear of the mines. But because of the thickness of the woods, the only place that Rip Withers was constantly concerned with was the main entrance, reached by a narrow dirt road that was in turn accessed only from a little-used state road known primarily to hunters.

So now Junior stood by the gate and watched the dirt road, guarding the compound that no one had ever attempted to infiltrate. So that he had something else to listen to besides the sounds that alarmed him, he carried a small transistor radio in his pocket and listened at low volume. He had been listening to Wilson Barnes when something really weird happened. The news ended and then there was just silence and Junior thought maybe the batteries had gone dead. But then he heard a woman say something about a tongue and that made him perk up.

But then all of a sudden Barnes yelled out the name of the Sons of a Free America and Junior had nearly shit himself. That name was a *secret*, goddammit, *nobody* was supposed to hear that name except the ones that the council approved of. Hell, they were the White Oak Hunting Camp—that was what the sign said if anybody drove in far enough to see it. And here was Wilson Barnes, with thousands and thousands of listeners, *yelling* about them, the asshole.

Then the woman said something about bastards, and be damned if Wilson Barnes didn't say the name again and say how it was them, it was them that did something or other. And then the woman says it's a *confession*. Junior Feeley didn't know what the hell was going on here but he knew damn well that Rip and the others needed to know about it, even if they did give him shit for listening to the radio on duty.

So he abandoned his post long enough to run to Rip's cabin and knock on the door. But Rip didn't open it, his brother, Ray, did. And inside were Rip and Will and Sonny Armitage all gathered around Rip's radio, listening to Wilson Barnes's show. Ray raised a finger to silence Junior.

Shit, this was great. They were already listening, so now he was going to get into trouble for nothing. Unless he could come up with something else. The thing was, they didn't seem all that interested in what he had to tell them. They were staring at the radio and every now and then at each other.

Wilson Barnes was still talking but now he sounded like his usual self. It didn't look like Rip and Will and Sonny were all that pleased with what they were hearing though. Rip and

Sonny looked madder than hell and Will looked kind of scared. Ray just looked like Ray always looked. Then there was a pause and a commercial came on and they started talking.

"That chicken fucker," Sonny said. "Goddam him, Rip, he ratted on us."

"He sure did," Rip said. "That lousy little shit."

"But who *was* that?" asked Will. "Who was that woman?"

"I don't know—we'll find that bitch soon enough. But we're gonna take care of Barnes right now."

"What are you talking about, Rip?" Will sounded scared again. "You mean—?"

"You bet I do." Rip shook his head, gritting his teeth. "And then trying to cover it up like that—fictitious organization, my ass! Ray, you go get Ace. Tell him we got a job for him. That oughta brighten him up considerably." Then Rip finally seemed to notice Junior Feeley. "What the hell's with you, Junior?"

"I, uh . . ." Junior thought quickly. "I heard something, thought I oughta report it."

"Heard what?"

"Uh, somebody walkin' around . . . outside the fence."

"What!" Rip leaped to his feet. "Jesus, man, why didn't you fire your gun?"

"Well, I . . . I didn't want to scare 'em away, so I came to get somebody."

"Let's go!" Rip said, grabbing a weapon from the wall, and the others followed him. Shit, Junior thought. Here they were going out to look for nothing, just because he was too afraid to tell them he was listening to the radio during his watch. Hell, he was the fucking *treasurer*, he ought to be able to listen to the radio whenever he wanted to. And on top of that, he would have been able to pound any three of these guys into horse meat.

The fact of the matter was that Junior Feeley was a coward. Though he had been in a lot of fights, beaten up a multitude of men, and even killed a couple with his hands, he didn't like the possibility of getting hurt. He was big and he was strong, and because of that size and that strength there were always people who would challenge him. But he hated pain, although he liked inflicting it.

That was why he liked hurting women, because he wasn't afraid of them. It was the only time he could get rough with somebody and not have to worry about being hurt in return. Only thing was, there were no women in the Sons. *Hell*, Rip had laughed lots of times, *then we'd be the Sons and Daughters, and that sounds like shit*. He knew Rip was right, but that didn't stop him from getting horny as a hoot owl in heat.

He'd have a chance in a few weeks. He and Sonny were going to man a table at a gun show, and there was always a lot of hot pussy either cruising the tables or demonstrating the weapons, holding them up and rubbing them like they'd like to stick them somewhere where the sun don't shine.

But now he had to worry about Rip getting mad at him and it didn't seem far away. All the search lights were on, covering the small open area in front of their gate, and Rip was up in the guard tower holding his AK and glaring into the brush. "Open the gate and send out a search team!" he yelled down.

Junior opened the gate while Sonny went to the barracks and rousted half a dozen men, who ran out through the gate with their weapons and scattered as they had been trained to do. But after ten minutes they returned, shaking their heads and looking dubiously at Junior.

"There's nobody out there, Junior," Sonny said. "You hearing things again?"

"I heard *something*," Junior insisted. "Must've been a deer."

"Shit," said Rip, "as if we don't have enough to be concerned about with that weasel Barnes. Use your fucking head next time, Junior—shine a fucking flashlight, okay?"

Damn Junior anyway, Rip thought. For such a big boy, he sure was jumpy. And now he had woken up the whole camp. The lights and noise had brought most of the men out of their cabins and barracks and they stood around shivering in the cold night air, wondering what was happening. They didn't look as if they had been sleeping and Rip suspected that a few may have been listening to Barnes and then spread the word.

"False alarm," Rip told them. "Unless you've been listening to Wilson Barnes." From the looks on the men's faces, he knew they had been. They seemed angry and concerned. "We heard it all," he told them. "And we're going to do something about it. You don't betray the Sons of a Free America and get away with it. Now you all just go back to bed and don't worry about it. Though you might want to listen to Wilson Barnes finish his show. It's his last."

Most of the men nodded and smiled as they went back to their cabins. But none smiled more broadly than Ace Ludwig, who walked up to Rip. "Ray said you wanted me."

"You know what for?" said Rip.

"I'd guess a little rat extermination. A skinny little rat who talks too much. Even has his own rat show."

Rip nodded. "If you want to make him hurt, feel free."

Wilson Barnes wondered if he would be able to make it to his car. It wasn't the pain in his testicles that bothered him, although they still ached and the small cut stung. But his legs were shaking so hard that he wondered if he'd be able to walk the whole way.

Christ, tonight had been a nightmare. That crazy woman had been bad enough, but talking for another three hours until the show was over was a nightmare. Thank God Phil, his engineer, had come to. He had a broken nose and possibly a concussion but he had finished the show along with Barnes, jamming his nose with cotton until it stopped bleeding. Barnes had packed his own crotch with cotton but the slight cut hardly bled at all.

Donald, the apparently inept security guard, had come up to the studio at five o'clock with a bruise and contusions on his fat face and Barnes fired him during the news. The man threatened to tell people about the female visitors to the studio, but Barnes told him that would be a bad idea and that Barnes had many friends of a violent nature who would not take kindly to an insider making false accusations. Donald, not surprisingly, changed his mind. Barnes didn't, and Donald remained fired.

After the show was over Barnes stressed to Phil the importance of remaining silent and Phil, happy with his job and salary, agreed to do so. His doctor would be told that he had been mugged by an unseen assailant.

So now Wilson Barnes walked on unsteady legs toward the front door of the building, past the unmanned security desk, wondering who in hell that woman was. Not a cop but maybe a government agent, just like he had said. Who else would have been so well trained in interrogation techniques? He would have to talk to Withers, of course, convince him that no harm was done, that merely knowing the name of an organization doesn't mean that anything bad would—

And in the middle of that thought, just as he was about to open his car door, the first round caught him, punching him in the back, straight through his right kidney and out a hole in the front, spraying a shower of blood and piss onto Wilson Barnes's shiny Buick. He stood there for a minute, uncertain of what was happening, and then he felt the second bullet hit him in the shoulder and spin him around so that he slammed against the car door and slid down it until he was sitting on the blacktop of the parking lot.

He saw the man then, leaning out the passenger side of the window of a dark green van a hundred yards away. He was holding a rifle, aiming it at Wilson Barnes, who could do absolutely nothing about it except shake his head and whisper words that the man could never hear.

The man shot again and Barnes felt his stomach explode. The pain the woman had caused him was now totally forgotten, as Barnes feebly moved his fingers, trying to keep looking at the man, to tell him with his eyes that he shouldn't be doing this.

But then the man raised his head from the rifle's telescopic sight and smiled at him. He spoke one word, but loudly enough for Barnes to hear:

"Bigmouth . . ."

In between the moment when Barnes processed that word and the rifleman aimed again, Barnes concluded that he would not be able to explain anything to Rip Withers, that Withers had already made his decision.

Wilson Barnes did not hear the shot that killed him, nor see the bullet that hit him right between the eyes.

seventeen

AMY CARLISLE HAD NOT YET RETURNED TO DAVID LEVINSON'S
home. After she left the radio studio she had driven to the site
where the Making Friends Child Care Center had once stood,
and watched there until dawn lit the sky and the dust and ashes
turned from black to gray.

She never got out of the car. She felt that if she did, she
might somehow be taken back again, made one with the dust
before her work was done, and that could not happen. Surely
whatever force had birthed her from the rubble in agony and
love would not take her back so soon.

Still, she did not open the door or even the window, until
a wind began to blow from the east, as though carried on the
rays of the rising sun, and stirred the dust, carrying it up and
into the air. Though Amy could see no dust blowing to where
she sat across the street, she knew that the breeze contained
fragments of it, and she opened the window and breathed it
in, thinking that she breathed in the atoms and the essence of
her children.

Fill me. Be with me. Come deep inside me and never leave.
Make me strong.

They were within her now, one with her, the children she
had never had, the children who could never grow up. On her
tongue was the bitter taste of their pain and their love and their

loss, the husbands and wives and fathers and mothers who would never be, the lives that would never be lived.

Because of them. Because of the Sons of a Free America, who proclaimed their freedom by killing children, by stealing not only years but generations to come.

She lowered her head and cried, but no tears came. Maybe, she thought, she was made too much of the dust. And maybe whatever had made her knew that it was not tears that were needed now, but blood.

She had shed it and she would shed far more before she could finally rest. But before she started to track them down, there was one thing she had to do first. She knew she should not, but she could no more stop herself than she could make the bright yellow ball of the sun sink back down in the east.

Rick Carlisle loved the house that he had built with Amy.

Nestled in a half acre of trees, it was only minutes from the heart of town but seemed isolated, so that you could leave the curtains open and walk around naked and no one would see except the water meter reader. Its single story sprawled under the trees and when they had sat together on the small deck out back, it was like they were living in the middle of a forest.

But although Rick had built the house with Amy, he didn't live in it with her anymore. He lived with his second wife now, with Nancy, who had been Amy's friend, and her daughter, Karin.

Sometimes it felt strange, as though he were cheating on Amy, but both he and Nancy had needed someone after the loss, and it had been only natural that they had comforted each other.

At first Rick wanted to sell the house and move. Everywhere he looked he thought of Amy. Her belongings, her influence, her *presence* was everywhere. But Nancy had talked him out of it. "It's not the physical things," she had said, "as much as the mental. You have to face it, Rick, Amy will be with you always. The loss is always going to be there—it just won't hurt as much with time."

He knew she was right and decided to try and stay in the house. But he did, on one painful night, purge it of Amy's things. Those that they had gotten together, some paintings and prints, knickknacks and books, stayed in their places. But he removed the things that he closely identified with her, such as those books he had bought as presents for her with no intention of reading himself; the photographs of her parents, who had died five years before in a plane crash; and the original half-sheet poster of one of her favorite movies, *An Affair to Remember*, that hung framed in the basement rec room.

So Anne Tyler and Louise Erdrich fled his shelves and Deborah Kerr his walls. But Amy remained nonetheless in the closets and on top of the dressers and in dozens more places. These Rick tried to make vanish as well, giving her clothing to charity and sending her jewelry to Amy's sister, Fran.

He kept all their photographs and the videos that they had taken of each other, though he put these away in a box and stored them in the back of the bedroom closet. However, he ceremoniously placed one photograph of Amy on a bookcase in the living room, around a partition where it was not easily seen from the rest of the room. There, he decided, it would stay, no matter what happened.

After his marriage to Nancy, she had said nothing about the picture, except for the fact that she had always liked that particular portrait of her friend. Rick was glad she hadn't protested. He needed a piece of Amy to remember. He had placed a small stone in a nicely kept memorial park outside of town, but he knew that there was nothing of Amy beneath it. It read "Amy Carlisle—Beloved Wife," along with the years of her birth and death, but he knew she was not there.

In a way, the disposal of her remains was what Amy would have wanted. Though they had never made arrangements, they had discussed it and both of them wanted cremation, finding the thought of their bodies rotting in the ground unpleasant to the point of being horrifying. Interment of ashes in a columbarium or grave was what they had preferred. It allowed the grieving to come and stand in a place that held the departed's remains in a form that bore thinking about.

But that wasn't possible now. Rick had thought about taking an urn full of the dust and ashes from the site, but odds were that there would be nothing of Amy within. So he settled for the stone, which he had visited only once. His heart would be her memorial.

At last the alarm went off, sparing him more memories of her. He kissed Nancy as she awoke and together they prepared for the day, getting Karin ready for school. Rick was planning to work at home that day, but he made coffee and cooked oatmeal and got what had become his family off to school and work with warm bellies and a kiss.

Left alone in the house, he sat back in the breakfast nook with his coffee and thought about the last time he had sat there with Amy. They had both been so excited about the visit of the senator, but a day hadn't gone by since when Rick hadn't cursed the man. If only he hadn't canceled, the security people might have gone in first and found the bombs. But his cancellation, no matter how valid the reason, had broken Amy's heart and ended her life.

He knew he should blame the people who had set the bombs, but how could you hate people with no names and no faces? Rick tried to keep the thoughts of those men, the four Amy had seen in the car, far away. When he thought about them, anger and frustration built up inside him like tons of water behind the wall of a cracked dam. He shoved the thought away, letting Amy's face come back into his mind.

Then he thought about her gentleness, her kindness, and how much she had loved him. And as so often happened when his thoughts went to her, he found himself crying softly, not sobbing, but feeling tears run down over his cheeks and into the corners of his mouth so that he could taste them.

He had to see her then, had to look at and hold what remained of her in this house, and he got up and walked into the living room, around the partition, and picked up the framed picture. Amy, standing in the sunlight, her dark brown hair glowing like strands of gold, her violet eyes half closed from the sun, her smile just for him.

His tears blurred his vision and he looked away from the picture toward the window.

The image remained. Amy's face, no longer in sunlight but in shadow, looked in at him through the glass.

A chill gripped his heart and he blinked savagely to clear his vision. His eyes caught movement but whatever had stood gazing in was no longer there. He dashed to the window and looked out, but saw nothing except perhaps a hint of motion in the green of the deep brush that hid his house from the road.

Rick ran to the front door, yanked it open, and ran outside, but he saw only a large, black crow riding the wind between the trees, drifting toward the road. Rick opened his mouth to call Amy's name, then hesitated and closed it again.

Amy was dead. What he had seen had only been a negative afterimage of the photograph on the light source of the window. Of course. That had to be it. The face that had been in sunlight was in shadow, and the white clothes in the portrait had turned to black.

But he had seen her eyes. Even through the tears that veiled his own, her deep violet eyes had fixed him with love and longing and something else. No, it had not been an afterimage, no optical trick. He had seen Amy standing outside his window. Or her ghost.

Maybe that was the explanation, for he could think of no other that made sense. What had her look asked of him? There was something deeper there, some emotion other than sadness.

Then he knew. What did ghosts come back for? Because of an unhappiness that would not let them rest. Because of injustice unavenged. Because of a murder that had not been solved. He had seen *Hamlet* innumerable times, he had read ghost stories, he knew how these things worked. He just hadn't believed them before.

Now he did.

The police and the government had been totally ineffective in finding the crew who had blown up the center and killed Rick's wife and her children. And Amy's ghost had returned to tell him that it had to be done for her to rest. If the police couldn't do it, then he would have to.

He would have to, for Amy.

• • •

She drove away too fast but she couldn't help herself, just as she couldn't help going to the house and seeing Rick again.

Now Amy wished she hadn't. She wished that she didn't know he had gotten remarried to Nancy and had a family again and this time a child to love.

It wasn't that she didn't wish Rick happiness. She loved him and always would, and wanted only the best life for him. But there was still enough selfishness alive in her to feel hurt, more hurt on top of the pain that she already carried like a heavy sack, the pain that she had come back to assuage.

But slowly as she looked in window after window of the house, the truths had come to her. First was the shock at seeing Rick in bed with Nancy, then the deeper yet ironically reassuring shock of the rings on their fingers, Rick's narrow gold one replacing the broad one she had slipped on his hand a lifetime ago. Amy should have left then but trapped, helpless, she could not look away.

She watched with a dull numbness as they got up, a family, and had breakfast together, Karin hugging Rick as she left for school, Nancy kissing him warmly, lovingly when she went out the door. She watched Rick alone with his coffee and wished that she could knock on the door and put her arms around him when he opened it.

But then she watched as he started to cry and she knew what the tears were for. She followed him around the side of the house and watched as he picked up her picture, and then she knew what she had always known, that he still loved her and would love her always. This one truth, the joy and the sorrow that she felt, held her, even when he looked up and saw her standing there.

She had frozen for a moment and then run, hoping against hope that he hadn't seen her face. The thick brush tore at her as she ran through it, but she felt no pain from the slapping twigs or the buffeting branches. All was eclipsed by the hole in her heart.

Now as she drove swiftly through the streets, she knew that she had to put Rick out of her mind. He was not her husband, he was her widower, and now the widower had gotten married again and to a woman Amy had loved as a sister. Over time his hurts would heal. He had a family that loved him and he would be all right.

She headed back toward David Levinson's house in the black Avanti and saw no cars coming out of the cul-de-sac as she drove in. She parked the car in the garage and went into the kitchen. Levinson was sitting there in a bathrobe, holding a mug of coffee. "Give me your hands," he said.

She held them out and he sniffed her fingers. "Good. No cordite. I take it then that you're not the one who shot Wilson Barnes."

She tried to show no surprise. "Who's Wilson Barnes?" she asked coolly.

"That's what I like to hear," Levinson said. "I see nothing, I know nothing. I harbor . . . what, a fugitive?"

She nodded. "From death. I need to use your computer."

Levinson pointed toward the basement door.

Within a half hour of searching, she had found a lead. *Sons of a Free America* had drawn no hits, but *Free America* had taken her to a Usenet message from alt.militia.freedomfight, posted by a W. J. Standish. It read in part:

> Too many times our freedoms and, in some cases, our precious lives have been taken away by this present government. We should all pledge ourselves to a Free America once again, and be Sons of that Free America, even if the payment is in our own blood.

Standish's address was wstandish@rangenet.com. After some more searching, Amy discovered that Rangenet was a Grand Rapids–based Internet carrier that served north and central Minnesota. Now it was time to locate Standish.

She sent an e-mail disguised as a spam, concerning a Chevrolet truck sale in St. Cloud, to see if the address was current. It was not, as a "Mail undeliverable" message informed her a minute later. Then she made a phone book search and found a William J. Standish in Hobie. But when she dialed the number she received a recorded message telling her that the number was not in service.

There was one other Standish listed in the Hobie area, a Dorothy J. in Kilton, a small town five miles north of Hobie. Amy called the number but there was no answer. She decided to go to Kilton that evening.

For the rest of the day she busied herself among Levinson's files. Though his holdings on militias and their members were extensive, she came across no other mention of William Standish, except for a few letters to the editor that he had written to several "patriot" magazines.

The contents were similar to what he had posted on the Internet, but different from the other published letters in that they were far more eloquent and not nearly as rabid. The address on each of them was simply Hobie, MN, and the most recent letter had been published over a year before.

It was nearly dark by five o'clock and Amy left for Kilton without seeing Levinson, who she assumed had gone out on patrol. He had not bothered her the whole day except to ask her if she wanted any lunch. She had declined.

As Amy drove the Crow flew ahead of her as though guiding her. Although she knew where she was headed, she found its presence reassuring. The tie between them was something that she didn't begin to understand but she knew it was there for her, that somehow it was the avatar of whatever power had brought her back to life. She felt the same comfort in its presence that as a Christian she had felt in the cross.

Dorothy Standish lived in a mobile home set on a small corner lot. The back of the trailer faced thick woods and there was a small stone driveway into which Amy pulled the Avanti. As she walked to the door at the end of the structure, she saw that the pale green and white metal was rusting in dozens of places. The corrugated metal skirt that covered the bottom of the trailer was actually rusted through in spots.

Even before she knocked on the door, she saw the old woman looking at her through its opaque glass window. The crazed surface made her face look fragmented and monstrous, until Amy remembered that *she* was the monster. The door opened a crack and Amy stared into a room hazy with cigarette smoke. In a low, grating voice, the woman asked Amy who she was.

"I'm Margaret Evans from Publishers' Clearance," she said. "I'm looking for William Standish. Is he related to you?"

"What do you want him for?" she asked, her thin lips barely moving, more interested in retaining the cigarette clenched between them than in being understood.

"He won a prize in one of our sweepstakes, but we haven't been able to find him at the address we have."

The old woman's face brightened just a bit. "What'd he win?"

"Well," Amy said hesitantly, "in order to reveal that, I'd have to either talk with Mr. Standish or his appointed representative."

"I'm his mother," Dorothy Standish said, finally removing the cigarette from her mouth. "Isn't that good enough?"

"I'm sorry, Mrs. Standish, but I can only deal with a third party if Mr. Standish presents us with a written authorization. Now do you know where I might be able to find him?"

"He's not around right now. You can't reach him. What'd he win?" Amy smiled in spite of the woman's countenance. Her chin was wreathed with thin white whiskers and her teeth, or dentures, were uniformly brown. Her breath reeked of tobacco and garlic and decay.

"As I said, I can't reveal that. Perhaps he could contact us. Do you expect to see him soon?"

She nodded. "Tomorrow. He's coming to see me tomorrow."

"Well then, if I gave you my phone number, maybe he could give me a call and we could make the arrangements for him to claim his prize."

"Look, you tell me what it is first. How do I know this isn't one of them things where you win a condo in Florida or something, but then you got to pay for it, one of them tricks or something?" She moved her right hand in circles as she talked, so that the ash from her cigarette jerked in every direction like tiny bugs.

Amy nodded and smiled as if she'd been bested. "I see there's no getting around you, Mrs. Standish. All right, your son has won five hundred dollars."

"Five hundred?" Her face was a mixture of greed and annoyance. "I thought you people gave away ten million dollars. That's what your ads say."

"Oh, that's the one Ed McMahon's with. We're a much smaller company. But our grand prize was fifty thousand—a woman in St. Paul won that."

"Wait here," Mrs. Standish said, closing the door on Amy. When she came back she had a pencil and paper and a new cigarette and wrote down the name and number Amy gave her. Then without another word, she shut the door again, this time, Amy suspected, for good.

Amy had made the number up, along with the name. If Standish called it, he would assume that his mother had gotten the number wrong. But by that time Amy would have him. And then she would get the information she wanted, the names and location of the rest of the killers, these Sons of a Free America. And then she would see to it that the only freedom they had was deciding whether or not to scream when they died.

eighteen

THE NEXT MORNING AMY CARLISLE DROVE BACK TO KILTON AT eight o'clock and parked her car four blocks from Mrs. Standish's trailer. She went through a vacant lot and into the woods, coming around behind the old woman's trailer until she could see the stone driveway and the door from the cover of the trees. Then she waited.

Amy had never been very good at waiting but now she seemed one with patience, made of black stone. She sat on a fallen tree several yards within the relative darkness of the woods and the Crow sat next to her, stolid and unmoving, on a branch that bent and twisted like the arm of a drowning man. Its concentration fueled her own and she tried to emulate its stillness and implacability, to conserve the energy for when it was truly needed.

Now was the time to rest, though she didn't know if she even needed rest. She had no idea what her body was capable of, but since she had not had a bite to eat nor a second of sleep since her resurrection, she suspected that her powers were formidable. And if her seeming invulnerability, as terrifyingly demonstrated by Levinson, and the ease with which she had taken control of the radio studio were further indications, there would be few situations with which she could not cope.

She sat there as the day brightened and the sun reached its

zenith and then fell into darkness again. It was not until six that evening that a car pulled into the driveway and someone got out. Amy saw him clearly, a tall, thin, almost cadaverous man, who walked with his head bowed down, as though he carried a great sin upon his soul. Oh yes, thought Amy. If he was who she suspected, he did indeed.

She moved across the grass with the lightness of wind and crouched beneath the picture window. The murmur of voices inside was indistinguishable at first but as she attuned her ears to the rhythms, she found that she could easily make out what the son and the mother were saying.

When she raised her head above the window she saw them sitting in a smoky room filled with clutter. Antimacassars covered every arm of every piece of furniture, piles of magazines and romance paperbacks were scattered across the floor, and cheap china figurines littered every tabletop and the huge console television. Ashtrays were everywhere, most of them filled, and several opened packs of Pall Malls were scattered about so that a smoke was never more than an arm's length away.

Mrs. Standish was sitting in an overstuffed chair that faced the TV. Her eyes were on a strand of faux pearls being sold on a home shopping channel, though the sound was turned down. Her son, who Amy guessed was in his midforties, was pacing back and forth, quite a trick in the crowded room, and talking quickly, like a teacher with an urgent need to stuff his students' heads before the bell rang.

"I can't stay, not after this," William Standish was saying to his mother. "I mean, the bombs were bad enough but then they go out and shoot Barnes in broad daylight? And that's nothing compared to what they're planning next. I just can't be a part of it, Mother, I just can't."

William Standish sounded close to tears but the old lady kept her eyes fixed on the screen. It was as if she didn't hear her son's words at all.

"I mean, I believe in what I've said and written in the past, but this way . . . I hadn't imagined how it would be, all those children dead, and for nothing . . ."

If Amy's dead blood had ever run hot since her return, it

ran ice cold now. This was one of the men, these Sons of a Free America, who had killed her children. His own words condemned him. Amy felt triumph and rage and hate. She wanted to burst through the window and break the man's neck. But she would wait. It wasn't revenge she needed now, but knowledge.

"I've got to get out. I know the Sons will try and kill me but maybe I can get away. If I tell what I know, they'll protect me."

"*Who'll* protect you?" Mrs. Standish finally asked.

"The . . . the government," said William Standish in a voice so low that Amy barely heard it. "Or the press—I could tell what I know and they'll turn me over to the government. That way the whole truth will get out and they won't go back there . . . do what they did at Ruby Ridge and Waco . . . A lot of good boys back there in the compound, can't help what their leaders do . . . Oh *God*, Mother, I don't know, I just don't know . . ."

The man started crying then but his mother said nothing to comfort him. Instead she looked away from the TV screen at her sobbing son. "Do you know what it means to be a Standish? To have the blood of patriots run in your veins?"

He rubbed tears from his eyes and looked at her. "I know, Mother. I know . . ." Then he ran to the door and flung it open. Amy started toward him but it was too late. As she rounded the corner of the trailer, she saw that he was already in his car, backing out of the stone drive. The only way to follow would be in the Avanti.

She did not return to her car through the woods. The darkness of night provided enough cover and she ran through the streets, amazed at how fast she could go and how tireless she was. She was not even panting when she reached the Avanti. She threw the car into gear and headed in the direction Standish had driven.

There were several ways out of town but she didn't have to guess Standish's route. The Crow flew above, always in sight, the flat plane of its wings tilting on the turns. It seemed to fly without effort, as Amy had run, and she thought dreamily that there was ease in death.

She picked up Standish's car, a dusty white Ford Tempo, within a few blocks. There was a pickup truck behind the

Tempo but she made no attempt to pass, thinking the truck would provide cover for her.

Amy decided not to try cutting Standish off. After all, she couldn't lose anything by following him. For all she knew, he might be returning to the compound, and then she could confront the killers all at once. On the other hand, if he decided to carry out his threat and go to the press, she would have to stop him. This was to be her vengeance, not that of the police. Her law, not the state's.

They headed back toward Hobie and Amy kept the pickup between her and Standish. As they got on the four-lane that would take them into town, she noticed that the truck followed Standish whenever he passed a car, then fell back into line behind him. After this happened several times she concluded that the driver of the truck was following Standish too.

Who was it, she wondered. A cop? Or could the Sons of a Free America mistrust one of their own enough to put a tail on him? That seemed more likely. The bumper bore an "Impeach Clinton" sticker, and NRA and American flag decals were stuck on the back window. Maybe William Standish had his own personal tail. She would find out soon enough.

Once off the four-lane they headed into the heart of town. The city was sleeping now. At six o'clock most of the stores and offices closed and the streets were nearly deserted. Even the parking garages used an honor system after eight.

A green light changed to yellow and Amy got ready to floor the Avanti if Standish tried to slip through. But he stopped, as did the truck behind him, and the glare of the halogen street light shone directly down into the cab of the pickup so that Amy could see the top half of the driver's face in his rearview mirror.

He was looking straight ahead but she recognized the face anyway and felt her own face harden, her teeth clench, her lips draw back in a snarl. It was one of the faces that had looked at her from the windows of the dark car outside the center, one of the four men who had been there that fatal night.

Amy fought back the urge to plow the Avanti right into the back of the truck and watch the man's head snap. There was no rush, she told herself. She had two of them now. One of them would talk and then both of them would die.

The light changed and they started moving again. The *Hobie Sentinel* building towered ahead, an eleven-story structure that was the downtown's tallest building. The newspaper's business was conducted on the fourth through eighth floors while the presses occupied the first three. Amy had taken the older children there on a field trip the year before.

A parking garage adjoined the building and William Standish pulled his car into its narrow entrance. That meant only one thing, that he was going to make good on his threat to tell the newspapers everything. And that meant that Amy had to get to him first.

The pickup truck slowed at the entrance to the garage, as if the driver didn't want Standish to see him come in on his tail. Amy waited impatiently for the man, who finally drove into the entrance, through what Amy had always thought of as the cattle chute, with high concrete walls on either side.

But instead of driving straight through, the pickup truck stopped dead just as it was about to come out into the garage area itself. The passenger door opened, and the driver jumped out and ran around the corner out of sight.

The son of a bitch had boxed her in. The sides were so close to the Avanti that she couldn't even open the door far enough to slip through. Quickly, with fury building inside her, she lowered the window and began to crawl out.

That got her, Sonny Armitage thought as he trotted toward the elevator. He didn't know who the hell the bitch was who had tailed him ever since he came into the city. Maybe just some broad on the night shift at the paper. But with what he was going to do now, he didn't want a witness, and the truck was expendable, stolen earlier that night. He had hated to rip off a fellow NRA member, and a Clinton hater to boot, but he had to take what was available.

He heard the rumble of Will Standish's old Tempo as it

pulled into a space somewhere up out of sight, and he ran down the incline to the elevator. Will would get on at floor three and come down to the main entrance on one. But someone else would get on at two with a big surprise for Will Standish, Traitor.

As Sonny pushed the down button, he thought that Rip had been right to mistrust the prick, especially after the way he'd gone belly up that night they blew up the center. They should have killed him then and saved themselves a lot of hassle. Once a man showed signs of weakness, you had to cut him loose and the only way to cut loose a man who knew as much as Will Standish did was with extreme prejudice.

Sonny Armitage loved those words. That was what it was all about, wasn't it? Extreme prejudice, toward Jews, niggers, beaners, gooks, and all the liberal lowlifes who thought they were all brothers under the fucking sun. No, Sonny had had enough of *that* crap, fuck you very much.

He had fought in Vietnam alongside those "black brothers," goddam street punks more interested in where their next jays were coming from than in killing the enemy. They were animals, subhumans, and so were the gooks. If the niggers were apes, the gooks were monkeys, little slanty-eyed monkeys that darted through the jungle like ghosts. Sonny never admitted it but they had scared the shit out of him. If they had fought like men, out in the open, instead of hiding in the leaves or in their narrow rat tunnels, he might have had a little respect for them.

Then when he finally came home, the little bastards *followed* him. It seemed like the gooks loved killing Americans so much that they thought they'd just come over and kill their economy too. So they worked hours you wouldn't expect a dog to work, took just enough salary to buy rice for their little gook litters, killed rats and dogs to add some meat, and put the vets out of work, like with those shrimp boats down in Galveston.

And what little money you *were* able to make, the government took most of it to give to the nigger junkies or the AIDS faggots or the schools to teach the wetback kids who weren't even here legally. The rest of it went to the Jews, who ran the whole damn thing. Then they had the guts to accuse the real patriots of conspiracy.

The whole thing stunk to high heaven and Sonny thanked Yahweh every day that he had been able to find other people who thought the way he did, who saw what needed to be done, and weren't afraid to do it, the way this pussy Will Standish was. Probably a faggot on top of it.

Finally Sonny heard a ding and the elevator doors slid open. There was Will Standish in all his gutless glory, looking up at Sonny as if he'd taken a wrong turn somewhere and didn't know where in the hell he was, like the whole world had gone butt-side-up on him, and it had. Boy, how it had.

"Hey, Will," said Sonny, both his teeth and his knife smiling brightly, "goin' to buy a newspaper?"

Will tried to get past him but Sonny easily shoved him back against the wall of the car. The doors slid shut and Sonny pulled the lock knob. Then he slid the blade of the long knife smoothly between Will Standish's ribs.

"You fuckin' chickenshit quisling liberal pinko faggot traitor pussy," Sonny said softly into Will's ear, holding him up so that he would not fall to the floor, and drawing the knife across until it clicked against Will's rib cage, then sliding it out again. He felt blood fall warmly across his knuckles and thought that it felt good. It was a traitor's blood, a traitor who kissed the ass and sucked the cocks of tyrants and it made Sonny feel strong to have it pouring across his hand.

"Traitors shouldn't die easy," he told Will and then stuck the knife in again, right into Will's guts, and moved it around in small circles. Will was too shocked to scream, although his mouth worked at something. Sonny smelled Will's piss and shit escaping him and laughed. "Mama's gonna have to wash your panties, Will," he said, then pushed the lock knob in and hit the button for six, the top floor of the garage. He would leave Will there. No one would find him until morning.

Sonny chuckled softly as the elevator climbed. "Slow ride, Will," he said, "but getting there's half the fun, huh?" He twisted the knife again, joying in Will's unbelieving grimace, and pulled it out just as the door opened on the sixth floor.

"Does not play well with others."

The soft, feminine voice spun Sonny around and he found himself staring through the door at a woman, the sports car driver he thought he had boxed in. She was dressed all in black and her violet eyes were narrowed ferally, but she was smiling with white, even teeth. Her pale, long-fingered hands hung empty at her side.

Sonny didn't know what the hell she was smiling about. He was the one with the knife. He held it up, blood dripping from the end, uncertain what to do next.

The woman looked at it and shook her head. "Runs with scissors," she said, and the smile winked out like a candle flame. "And kills babies. That's three infractions. You need to be punished."

"Fuck you too," Sonny snarled and lunged at her with the knife, but she was fast, faster than he could have imagined, and sidestepped him so that the force of his blow made him stumble and fall onto the concrete.

The air went out of him as she kicked him in the side. It hurt bad, far worse than he had ever been kicked in any fight before, and he had been in a lot of them. Enough of this shit, he thought, as he winced in pain and rolled over, reaching behind him for the pistol he kept at the small of his back, thinking no bullshit, she's too fucking fast, just shoot, shoot quick, shoot now.

He fired from the ground, three shots in rapid succession, moving his shooting hand up as he fired, and was rewarded with the sight of them slamming into her, pushing her back— one in the gut, one in the chest, and one in the soft spot under her chin.

But she didn't fall. She kept standing, looking dazed for a moment. The bullet holes were in her clothes, so Sonny knew that he had hit her, but the spot where the bullet had gone in under her chin—and he had *seen* it, goddammit!—was no longer there. It had closed up like a finger hole in pudding.

The second of shock at the sight was long enough for her to pluck the gun from his hand as if he were a baby. She threw it into the darkness and it skittered for a long time across the concrete. Then she took the survival knife from its ankle sheath, slipped the brass knuckles over her fingers, and crouched down next to Sonny.

"Look at me," she said. "Do you know who I am?"

"Yeah," Sonny said, scared as hell but more scared to show it. "You're a fucking whore."

She raised her fist and hit him in the stomach so hard that he heard a rib snap and he gagged at the pain. "No." She shook her head. "Look close. Remember me? You've probably seen my picture in the newspaper."

Then Sonny Armitage got even more scared as he recalled the newspaper stories he had devoured after the explosion and the photos of the victims. Jesus fucking Christ, it couldn't be. But it was.

"You're . . . her," he said. "The one we . . ."

"The one you killed," she finished. "But not the only one you killed. You killed my children too. I was supposed to take care of them and you killed them. You and the others." She spat the words in his face. "The Sons of a Free America. Now I want to know who the rest of them are and *where* they are."

"I don't believe this," Sonny said, his mind swimming. "This ain't true, it ain't happening. I'm dreaming or something or it's a trick."

"Well, if it's not happening," the woman said, "if you're dreaming, then it won't matter if you tell me or not and . . ." She hit him again, this time across the jaw, so that his teeth snapped together. After the first flash of pain subsided, he could feel that several teeth had been loosened in their sockets. ". . . And you'll save your dream self a lot of pain."

"If it's a dream," Sonny said, swallowing blood, "then fuck you. You might as well kill me. Then I'll wake up. And you know what I'll do then? I'll find me some more nigger kids and gook kids and Jew kids and I'll shoot out their little pig eyes and fuck the—"

He didn't finish the sentence. The survival knife came down, not the knuckles but the blade, straight into his open, bleeding, cursing mouth.

nineteen

"WAKE UP THEN," AMY WHISPERED. "WAKE UP IN HELL."

In her rage, she had slammed down the blade so hard that it had driven through the man's neck bones and into the concrete beneath. She wrenched it out and stood up.

William Standish was still breathing, his eyes wide, his hands, wet with his blood, clamped over his dreadful wounds. Amy went back into the elevator and pulled out the lock knob so the car would not descend, then looked hard into his eyes. "You're dying," she said. "But you have a chance to help put things right. I know you want to do that. So tell me—where are they?"

He couldn't tell her although he wanted to. To list the route numbers, tell where the county road was, describe the place where the dirt road left the county road, all these things were far beyond Will Standish's ability. He tried to show her with his eyes how much he wanted to help and hoped that she read them correctly.

She said something else now and he could barely hear her for the rushing of the blood in his ears. It was as though he were hearing his life running out of him. Then the woman positioned herself directly in front of his gaze and her lips formed an O. And though he could not hear her, he knew she was saying *Who?* Maybe he could get that much out. Maybe he could tell the names.

He tried to remember who was in the car with him that night, then performed the mental gymnastics necessary to form the words. He barely had any air, for his lungs had been punctured, but he breathed out the first name that came to his dying mind: "Ruh . . . Ruhp . . . Withuhs."

"Withers? Rip Withers?" she repeated, and he tried to nod, then went on. In all, he was able to communicate only three more names and she repeated every one to make sure that she had heard them correctly. He couldn't remember who was in the car that night so he told her all the names he could think of. Junior Feeley. Powder Burns. Yes, he knew that Powder had been there but he wasn't sure about Junior. The only other name he could think of was Chip Porter and he managed to get that out as well before the cells that held that part of his memory were turned off by the lack of blood.

There was only one more thing that he wanted to tell this woman and he was able to reach out his left hand to her to make her know how important it was. Though it took several minutes Will Standish was finally able to say the words "Forgive me" and "Tell Mother I tried."

To which Amy Carlisle replied, "Yes . . . I forgive you" and "I will." She held William Standish's bloody hand for another minute until his breathing stopped and his eyes no longer moved. Then she dragged him off the elevator onto the dirty concrete floor and lay him on his back, his hands at his side.

She walked over to the other dead man, took the money from his wallet, and spat into his upturned face. Then she ran down the stairs to the street.

The Avanti was still there and she slipped in through the window, started the car, and backed it down the chute. It was indicative of the somnolence of nighttime Hobie that no one had even noticed that the parking garage entrance was blocked. Amy headed the car back to Kilton to fulfill William Standish's last wish.

It was near midnight when she parked the car several blocks away from Mrs. Standish's trailer. She covered the remaining distance quickly and was glad to see that the flickering light of the television set was still on. She went to the door and knocked gently. Then the television went silent, as though the old woman had hit the mute button, and Amy knocked again.

She heard slippered feet shuffling toward the door and the porch light over her head went on. Mrs. Standish's face appeared behind the glass, cracked and aged even further by its textures. Then the door opened a few inches and Amy smelled the reek of the smoke and the woman's breath.

"You again? What you comin' so late for? I told him about your money and he didn't care, had other things on his mind."

"I know," Amy said.

Mrs. Standish eyed her warily. "You *know*?"

"I think you'd better let me in, Mrs. Standish. Your son is dead."

The woman's face went soft for a moment and Amy thought that at last she glimpsed motherly concern. She pushed past Mrs. Standish and walked inside, pulling the door closed behind her. The only lights were from a small table lamp, the TV set, and the red glow of an electric space heater, whose grill guard had long since fallen off.

"Sit down, ma'am," Amy said, and stood waiting until Mrs. Standish sat in a small easy chair and fumbled for a cigarette, lighting it and taking in deep breaths of smoke. "William died bravely," Amy said. "Honorably. He wanted me to tell you that he tried."

"You ain't from no Publishers' Clearing."

"No."

"How'd he get killed?"

"He was going to tell the truth. To the papers. But a man stopped him. Killed him. Before he died, he told me where to find the other killers, the ones who . . . who blew up that child care center."

For a long while the old woman said nothing. Then her face twisted slowly into an expression of profound disgust and she shook her head angrily. "That little homo," she said in tones so bitter that they burned Amy's brain. "That damned little nancy boy, I should've killed him in the womb. I knew, I *knew* that he'd mess up whatever he got involved with. Little *coward* . . ."

Amy's mouth tasted of blood and metal. "He died trying to tell the truth," she said dully.

"He died betraying *patriots*," she said. "He was gonna turn 'em all in, wasn't he? All those good boys! His own father, God rest his soul, woulda killed him, he'da known that!"

"You're with them . . ." Amy said. "You *support* them . . ."

"Well, where the hell you think Will got it from in the first place, the TV? You're damn right—his daddy got him into the Sons. His daddy was a Klansman and his daddy before him and there wasn't a one of us wasn't proud of that." The old woman jammed her cigarette in an ashtray and pushed herself to her feet. "And you think you're gonna tell what he told you? Hell you are, not while there's a breath in *my* body . . ."

Mrs. Standish reached to her right side, down between the cushion and the chair, and came up holding a small revolver with a large bore. But just as she pulled the trigger, Amy cupped the pistol in her hands.

The sound of the shot was loud and it felt as if someone had pounded Amy's hands with a sledgehammer, but she took the pistol away and dropped it on the floor. Then she held out her hands so the woman could see them.

There was a hole and a black powder burn in her left palm, but in a matter of seconds it had closed up before Mrs. Standish's eyes and the burn had faded into white flesh. Mrs. Standish looked at Amy's hand in awe, then up at her face. "You're the *devil*," she whispered.

Amy took her hands and put them on either side of Mrs. Standish's face, cupping her gaunt and stubbly cheeks. "Yes," Amy said. "I'm a devil. And an angel. I came back from the dead for my children—now you go *to* the dead to beg mercy from your own."

And with her hands she snapped the old woman's head

backward until the brain stem kinked and the neck bones cracked and her eyes rolled up in their sockets. Her face became as empty and hollow as her heart and Amy knew she was in the country to which her son had preceded her, the dark country from which Amy had returned to bring death to such as she.

Amy spread her arms apart, letting the lifeless head fall to the side and carry the body to the floor, where it struck with a heavy thud, echoing in the blackness under the trailer. Amy stood still for a moment, listening to hear if there was any response to the shot. But there was none and she ransacked the trailer, opening drawers, reading letters and papers to see if there was anything that would help her find the Sons of a Free America.

After a twenty-minute search Amy came to the conclusion that this supporter of the Sons covered her tracks carefully. There was not a single mention of any of the names that Will Standish had given her, not even in the small second bedroom that housed a chilling collection of Klan memorabilia and a small library of racist books and pamphlets. In the back of the closet were two boxes of boys' books, among them the Hardy Boys and Tom Swift, which proved to her that the Standish family had lived here for many years.

This trailer, Amy thought, had been a breeding ground that had taken a young boy who liked adventure books and turned him into a man trained to hate, and who had only stopped when he saw what that hatred had done. Will Standish, Amy thought, might have been an intelligent man. The skill of his writings proved that. But he had not been wise enough to see the lies through the veils of revelation. Maybe he joined the militia to prove his own manhood, to deny to himself and the world that he was gay, if indeed he was, as his mother had suggested.

To this sick and twisted slice of humanity that used the lying label of patriots, anyone who believed other than they did was a queer, a liberal, a nigger lover, gook lover, Jew lover. Amy would be all of those and more. They hated these things because they feared them, and Amy would give them one more thing to fear. Death.

Already two of them were dead, along with the old woman. That would make them afraid. And soon she would destroy them all, would burn out this viper's brood.

The thought of fire reminded her of the space heater she had seen. It would be a good way to start the purge. This den, at least, would breed no more monsters.

She moved the heater over to the side of the couch, on whose arm hung an assortment of afghans and antimacassars. Then she tipped it over and watched as the glowing red coils met the filaments of cloth. In a few seconds the arm of the couch was smoldering. In a few minutes it would be ablaze.

Amy walked out of the trailer, closing the door securely behind her. Let it become a furnace, she thought. Let it punch out the windows and fling wide the doors. Let the reign of fire and death begin.

Let the fire devour. And let the fear come down.

twenty

A FEW MINUTES AFTER AMY RETURNED TO DAVID LEVINSON'S house at three A.M., he came out of the guest bedroom in a bathrobe. "Well, at least I got a few hours sleep this time," he said, then glanced down at her hands. "There's blood on your hands. Care to tell me where it came from?"

"Not really. What would be the point?"

"If I find that there have been any unsolved murders committed tonight, I'm going to be very suspicious."

"And if you are," she said, "what can you do about it? Are you going to arrest a dead woman? Tell your superiors that Amy Carlisle, who was blown to bits, committed these crimes?"

"Amy Carlisle exists. Therefore she wasn't blown up. She escaped the blast and now she's getting her revenge. *That's* what I tell them."

"You don't believe that. You could have believed that at the start, when you first saw me, but you didn't."

"No. Because of the Crow and because of, well, I just knew. And I was right. But what if you're traced here?"

"I won't be. Except for you, not a living soul knows I exist."

"A *living* soul, huh? I can't wait to read the police reports tomorrow."

"Levinson," said Amy, "either you're with me or you're

against me. If you're against me, then tell me right now and I'll leave and you'll never see me again. I'll find somewhere else to go. But if you're for me, then leave me be. Let me do what I came back to do, what you *know* I must do. You know that I came back for blood, for vengeance. That's my job. Are you going to let me do it?"

Levinson was silent for a moment, then he nodded his head. "Just try to see to it that it's only the bad guys that get hurt."

"It will be. And it *has* been."

"That's what I was afraid of. By the way, maybe not a living soul knows you exist but there are a hell of a lot of people who've heard your voice today."

"What do you mean?"

"I mean the Wilson Barnes show. The news media has been playing the tape every half hour. I have it memorized: 'Who was it, Wilson Barnes? Your tongue, I promise you.' And then she says, 'Tell me who the bastards are,' and finally, 'This confession brought to you by Wilson Barnes.' Barnes tried to bluff it out but apparently the Sons of a Free America didn't take it lightly. I—and the world—suspect that they're the ones who popped him."

"Who are the Sons of a Free America?" Amy asked, not letting any emotion show. She had known something like this would happen.

"That's what nobody knows. There isn't a trace or a whisper of this group anywhere. They sound like a militia but who knows? This state's got so many woods on private land that you could train an army and nobody'd be the wiser. And even if the police or the FBI could find out where they were, so what? They're not tied to anything in particular—except maybe the death of Wilson Barnes. No, only somebody with no official attachments could actually *do* anything about these people." Levinson cocked his head. "Sound like anyone we know?"

Amy didn't answer. "I'll be in the basement," she said.

• • •

She was scary as hell, thought David Levinson. Her eyes were cold when she spoke to him and it was easy to believe that there was actually no life in them.

But while he was afraid of her, he reveled in knowing that there was an avenger out there, resolute and invulnerable. And as he watched Amy go through the basement door, down into her lair, he was glad that she was there, glad that someone could treat this anti-Semitic garbage the way they treated his people when they got the chance.

He would have liked to have found them, have given Amy Carlisle the run for her money that she, and justice, deserved. But she had the passion and the motive and the power to try these men outside of the courts and execute them without going through the process of appeals. Appeals to Amy Carlisle would have been futile.

And what if the worst scenario happened and Amy got linked to him? He didn't think that she would let that happen, but if she did? Well, fuck it. He just didn't know and he didn't really care. He had had enough in Detroit of seeing scum walk free to kill again and he had tried to escape it. But sometimes you just had to stop and make a stand.

Sheltering Amy Carlisle wasn't especially proactive; in fact, it was downright passive. But it was the best he could do for now and he would keep on doing it until all the scumbags were dead or somebody stopped him.

Amy's first attempt at finding one of the names Will Standish had given her was a huge success. Chip Porter had his own website and by the time Amy finished examining its contents, she knew she had the right man.

Chip's Internet carrier was Rangenet and his site included a photo of Porter that showed a young man with close-cropped hair and a long, thin face. There were several strange pale spots on the jpeg's skin tone and Amy thought Porter might have digitally removed his pimples. If every one of the spots was a blemish, this guy was a real pus-face.

It made sense, though, considering that his brain was probably a mass of pus as well. The website's contents were hateful in every way, with short essays written by Porter about the virtues of white supremacy, the usual bullshit about Jews controlling the government, and dozens of links to other anti-Semitic and white supremacist sites.

But Porter, she discovered, wasn't just a bigot, he was a cyberbigot. Apparently he knew his computers and had devoted one area of his site to pranks to play on your on-line enemies, be they government sites or people whose names ended with "stein." Spamming, sending endless faxes, e-mailing false messages, locking up networks of liberal, Jewish, or black organizations—the list went on and on, always with a disclaimer that you *could* do these things but the webmaster wasn't *promoting* them.

Porter's passion for trickery was matched only by his love of skinhead music. There was a large section with profiles of skinhead "artists," and reviews of CDs apparently available only by mail or at special shows. It was doubtful, Amy thought, that Sam Goody was going to stock *Burn 'Em Up* by the Yidkickers or the Krazy Klanboyz's *Black Ain't Beautiful.*

Then she got a real surprise. Though she had as yet come across little information of a personal nature about Chip Porter, she discovered that he was in a white power band called Shoktrupz, pronounced *shock troops*, she assumed. She found it amusing how many of these anti-black groups used the "z" plural made popular by the "niggaz" and "homeboyz" they hated so much.

Though Porter's band had no album out, he had posted the lyrics of their best-known song, "White the Power," and they were as inept and ignorant as Amy had thought they might be. There was also a picture of Shoktrupz, good little leather-clad, skinheaded Aryans all, and the band's itinerary, such as it was, was listed. There was only one gig in November, none in December, and another in January.

The November date, however, was the following Sunday, a "White Christian Brotherhood" festival held at a fairground just north of Eau Claire, Wisconsin, a short drive southeast of the

Twin Cities. There would be nationally known speakers, bands on two stages, vendors, and food in two different buildings. Everyone who "hates Jews, mongrels, and all anti-Christians is invited."

How, Amy thought, could she refuse an invitation like that? But that was two days away. Amy couldn't just sit on her hands so she searched for the next name on her mental list, Junior Feeley. That one sounded like an intellectual giant.

She searched for "Feeley, Jr." and hit pay dirt, finding the name, Clarence Feeley, Jr., on a list of registered arms traffickers. A little more searching and she came up with a gun show that would be held Saturday at the Holiday Inn in Hobie.

The show was held every three months and there was a contact address posted. Amy decided to wait until morning, only a few hours away, to call the number.

In the meantime, she searched for Rip Withers and Powder Burns, both of whose first names she assumed were nicknames. Her search turned up nothing. Burns was a common name and there were dozens of Witherses in a hundred square mile area.

When she was finished, she called the contact number for the gun show. "My husband asked me to call," she said to the man who answered. She spoke quickly, trying to sound like a mother in a hurry, sloppy in her speech. "He wondered if Junior was gonna have a stand at the show tomorrow?"

"Junior," the man said thoughtfully.

"Yeah, Junior something? He told me the last name, but I just remember Junior. Is there a Junior sells guns?"

"Maybe Junior Feeley?"

"*That's* it! Oh yes, thank you, that was the name. Yeah, is he gonna be there, my husband wanted to know?"

"Yeah, I think Junior has a table. He usually does."

"Oh thank you, I mean it, thank you very much. I just *couldn't* remember his name and my husband woulda been so mad 'cause he was gonna take off work to get over there if this Junior was there, and if you wouldn'ta known, well, he woulda been fit to be tied at me. He says I can't remember nothin' and I guess he's right."

"Okay, was there anything else?" the man said impatiently.

"Oh no, no, thank you, that's all."

The man hung up without saying good-bye, probably thinking that he just saved some stupid bitch from getting smacked around by her husband. Dandy. Let him feel good while he could because his little gun show was going to make quite a bang tomorrow.

It was a date between her and Junior Feeley. She had the place and the time. Now she just had to figure out what to wear.

twenty-one

HE HAD TO LOOK THE PART IF HE WANTED TO BE ACCEPTED. OR was "accepted" the word? Maybe tolerated could be the most he could hope for at the beginning.

Rick felt certain that these people would be among the most distrustful he had ever met, and with good reason. The books he had read in his crash course on the militia movement indicated that government agents were quietly infiltrating many militia to gather information and evidence that could be used against them. So his cover had to be solid and unbreakable. And he might have to prove himself in some way that he would find distasteful. But he would do what he had to, short of killing.

Rick had told his partners in the firm that he wanted to take a couple of weeks off and they readily agreed. He had continued to work after Amy's death to keep his mind occupied and had only taken a weekend for a cursory honeymoon after he had married Nancy.

Nancy was not as agreeable. She was his wife now and he felt that he had to be honest with her. So he told her what he had not told his partners, that he wanted to take some time to see what he could learn about the bombing. But he did not tell her about seeing Amy at the window. That he kept to himself.

"You can't be serious," Nancy had said in disbelief. "Rick,

these monsters took my best friend and the children we both loved. I don't want them to take you too. God, please don't do this."

"It's not . . . much," he said. "I'm just going to some of these meetings, places and functions where they might gather, just to see if I can hear anything. If I do, I'll go straight to the police."

"Why not let them handle the whole thing? The only good that came out of all this was *us*. We picked up the pieces together. Don't throw that away."

"I'm not throwing anything away. I'm not throwing *us* away, Nancy, don't worry. I'm not going to be in any danger."

"Why are you doing this?"

"I'm doing it for Amy."

"But Amy's gone, you can't help her."

"I think I can. And I have to help myself too. I'm doing it for me."

Nancy got angry then and walked out of the room but Rick didn't go after her, although he wanted to. He knew that if he did, if he weakened for a moment, he might allow her to talk him out of this and he didn't want her to.

He knew he had made the right decision an hour later when he was coming back from buying clothes at a local thrift shop and heard Amy's voice on the radio. It had been recorded in the studio the morning that Wilson Barnes had been killed and when he heard it, he became one of only a few people who knew what it was all about. The Sons of a Free America knew it was about the bombing, but only he and Amy and David Levinson knew who the mysterious woman really was.

The sound of her voice shocked him so much that he pulled the car off the road and sat there trembling while he listened to the rest of the story. What the hell did it mean?

It was Amy's voice all right, there was no doubt of it. Had she appeared somewhere else—in that radio studio—in the flesh? But why? So that he would know, that the *world* would know, who was responsible for the bombing?

But the world didn't know, did they? They didn't know what the hell Wilson Barnes was confessing to. Only he knew because only he recognized Amy's voice and made the association. Only he had seen her and knew why her spirit had returned.

The realization put steel into him and he got back into the car and drove on, preparing to disguise himself, to change his looks, his attitude, his desires, to hate this oppressive government and anyone who worked for it. He would become one of them, and then he would find the ones who killed her.

"They killed Sonny," Junior Feeley said. He sounded close to tears.

Rip Withers looked up from his lunch. "What?"

"Sonny's dead," said Junior in a loud, upset voice that made the rest of the men in the mess hall put up their heads and listen.

Rip's belly went hot and he felt blood surge to his face. "The cops?" he asked.

"No . . . they don't know. I heard it on the radio, they . . ."

The mess hall door slammed open and Chip Porter walked in with a sheet of paper in his hand. "Off the local news service," he said and handed it to Rip, who quickly read it, then read it again more slowly before he spoke again, addressing the two dozen men who sat at the tables.

"Weird . . . shit went down last night, men. Let me tell you first of all that there was a traitor in our midst. Our brother Will Standish wasn't our brother at all. He turned on us. He went to the newspapers." There was a sudden uproar and Rip raised his hand for silence.

"No need to worry," he continued. "He never made it. We saw what was happening and Sonny Armitage was assigned to follow him. If Standish showed any signs of capitulation to the enemy, Sonny had orders to terminate him immediately. And when Standish drove to the *Sentinel* building, that's what Sonny did.

"But then something went wrong. Sonny was killed, stabbed to death. They don't say by who. But both Standish and Sonny are dead. I think we can safely assume that Sonny sacrificed his life for the Sons of a Free America." He looked every man there in the face. "Let's not forget him and let's not forget that any one of us may have to make that same sacrifice for our freedoms. This is a dangerous time and now that our activities are increasing, now that our attempts to bring down this godless, evil government are touching these villains so close to home, we need Yahweh's help more than ever to keep our courage up and our hearts on fire for Him. Let's all pray."

Rip Withers prayed aloud for Sonny Armitage's soul and when he was finished, everyone said amen and put their right fists over their hearts. Then Rip called Ray and Junior and Powder Burns and Chip Porter together and they went to Rip's cabin.

"All right," Rip said. "One thing that I didn't say because it wouldn't mean a lot to the men, and frankly, I'm not sure what it means myself, is that old Mrs. Standish is dead too." The men's faces registered surprise and Rip nodded. "I know," he said. "She was one helluva good old woman. Sent us twenty dollars a month for the cause. I met her a couple of times and I never knew how a woman that feisty could have given birth to a mama's boy like Will Standish."

"He was a good writer," said Ray.

It wasn't worth a reply, Rip thought. "They found Mrs. Standish in her trailer. It had burned up, pretty much destroyed everything inside, but there was enough of her left that the papers reported her neck was broken. That doesn't happen in a fire. The papers didn't have any theory yet about how it all happened—probably they want to get their stories cooked up so it looks as bad for the patriot movement as possible. But as far as I can see it, there are a couple different possibilities. The first is that Sonny stabbed Will and then Will stabbed him."

"That's a crock," Junior Feeley said. "Sonny'd never let Will get the drop on him that way, especially after Sonny stuck him. Hell, you know Will, he got hurt, he'd whimper like a goddam puppy and wait to die."

"You're right, Junior," Rip said. "And that's why I don't think that scenario's any too likely. I think probably what happened is that there was somebody else there. Sonny kills Will and this other guy kills Sonny."

"But then," said Ray slowly, "who killed Will's mama? Sonny?"

"Hell no," said Powder. "He was followin' Will, right? So why would he take the time to kill the old lady and then go after Will? Especially if he had orders to keep on Will's ass? And why the hell would he kill Will's mama anyway? She was a fine old lady, even if her boy was a shit."

"What if," Chip Porter said, "that third person you're talking about, Rip—what if *he* went out and killed Will's mama?"

"Why?" Junior said, struggling to follow the logic. "If he killed Sonny, it was because Sonny killed Will. So that means this guy *liked* Will. If he liked him, why would he kill his mama?" He shook his head, "Shit, this is confusing."

"Unless," Rip said, thinking it through, "this guy liked Will betraying us and knew that his mama was *for* us." Then Rip remembered the voice of the woman from Wilson Barnes's final show. "Or maybe not this guy—maybe this *girl*."

"What?" several of the men said.

"Look, what about that woman who was on with Barnes the other night—who got him to say our name?"

"You sayin' some *woman* stuck Sonny Armitage?" Powder asked in disbelief.

"I'm just saying it's a possibility," Rip answered. "You don't rule anything out if you wanta stay alive."

Junior snickered. "Day you catch me lookin' over my shoulder 'cause I'm afraid of a woman—"

"—Will be the day you're a whole lot smarter than you are, Junior," Rip finished. "Makes more sense to be scared of a.crazy woman than it does a little deer trotting through the woods. I'm just saying let's be on our toes. This could be anybody, we don't know. Maybe some mother went ballistic and decides to start hunting down people she thinks had something to do with the bombing."

"Wait a minute, Rip," said Powder. "A *mommy* goes wacko, breaks into Wilson Barnes's studio, past his guard, gets him to give our name over the air, then knifes Sonny, breaks Will's mother's neck, and torches her place. We talkin' Wonder Woman here?"

"All *right*, you assholes!" Rip shouted. There was too much bullshit smartmouthing here. It was time to retake command. "I'm saying don't take a fucking *thing* for granted, okay? It could be a man, a woman, a bunch of kids, your fucking *grandmother*, all right? It could be the last man you drank with, the last woman you fucked, the last Salvation Army lady you gave a nickel to, that's what I'm saying and that's *all* I'm saying! So don't give me any shit about it unless you know exactly who it is! Do I make myself *clear*, gentlemen?"

Muttered yeahs and a yessir from Junior Feeley filled the room for a few seconds and then they were all quiet again.

"This isn't going to change a thing," Rip said. "When it comes to the big strike, we're going to do exactly what we've been planning, and on our schedule. As far as everything else . . . Junior, you're still going to the gun show tomorrow."

"I need somebody else to help me," Junior whined. "I can't carry in all that stuff alone."

"And you'll have somebody. I'm sending Karl along with you."

"Karl? Jeez, Rip, I know he's your boy and all but can he handle—"

"He can damn well handle anything you can, Junior. He'll tote those gun cases just fine. And I'll look on it as a personal favor if you take good care of him."

Junior Feeley nodded and tried to smile but it didn't work too well. Damn, he was going to miss Sonny Armitage. He and Sonny were buds. And Sonny was so great at getting the customers talking real easy, and about more than just guns.

Sonny would find out what they thought of the government's gun control laws and then he'd lead that into other directions and find out about them personally, if they hated Clinton, hated Jews, hated niggers, and if they were willing to do anything about it; in short, if they were prospective members of the Sons.

Hell, it didn't make much difference whether they sold any guns or not, though Junior personally got a cut of the profits when they did. The main reason they had a table was to recruit members. They did it slow and carefully, maybe talking to a guy three or four times before finally inviting him to a private meeting with Rip. Sometimes it worked out, sometimes it didn't. But they never told so much that anybody they had read wrong would go running to the cops and the feds. When they got turndowns, most of the time it was along the lines of: *Well, this sounds like a great organization, but I'm afraid it's just not for me. More time than I could manage, with my job and the wife and kids—I'd just miss that too much. But hey, I think it's really great what you're doing and I'd like to make a contribution, you know? I'll pray for you too, I promise you that.*

No, by the time they got to that point, they knew they were good people. Not once had anybody even tried to rat on them. And maybe one time out of four you'd get a new member, someone who *was* willing to give up more than some money, someone dedicated to the work and to God and the White Race. And Sonny had been an expert at landing those big fish.

Another reason Junior was going to miss Sonny was that Sonny understood Junior's little quirks, the things he liked to do with the bimbos at the gun shows when he and Sonny could talk them into going out with them after the show closed.

He had let Sonny do the smooth stuff, telling them come on, it'll be fun, a few drinks, a few laughs, because Sonny was a pretty good-looking guy, and really well built. Junior was husky, and even though a lot of it was muscle, he looked fat, there was no use denying it.

And he farted a lot too, especially when he got excited, and the bimbos didn't like *that* at *all*. But generally by the time Junior got excited and started farting, he didn't give much of a shit what they liked or didn't like. One time when one of the bitches had started calling him names, he had done a whole lot worse than fart in her face. Call him a fucking pig and he'd damn well live up to it.

But now here he was stuck with Rip's kid, a skinny, eighteen year old who looked like he'd piss himself if you so much as yelled boo, let alone *"federal troops outside the compound!"* Well, Junior would just have to make of it what he could. Maybe he could dump the kid somewhere after the show, stick him in the game room or something, and go to one of the bimbo's rooms. He might have to pay one this time and the thought of it pissed him off since he never had to pay with Sonny. Dammit, he *missed* Sonny.

Of course, there was always the chance the kid might be ready for some action. Still waters ran deep and a man had to be a man, that was something that everybody in the Sons agreed on. Women were men's helpmeets, just like the Bible said, and they were supposed to be subservient to men, and as far as Junior was concerned, that meant they fucked when you wanted to fuck and if they gave you any shit, then they deserved it if things got rough.

The more he thought about it, Junior kind of liked the idea of holding one of those little gun-honeys down for the kid. In fact, he got a big ticket to Bonerville as he imagined it in more detail. Sure, let Rip's kid have first crack at it, get the bitch wet and warmed up for him and then Junior would have his fun. It might be a pretty damn good gun show after all.

Of course, he'd still miss Sonny. He was his bud.

twenty-two

"ARNIE, I GOT A FAVOR TO ASK."

Arnie Bailey made his *Christ, what now?* face and looked at Cyndi with his head cocked over almost onto his shoulder. "What?"

"I'm not feelin' so good," Cyndi said. "I think I swallowed some bad fish last night at dinner."

You swallowed some bad something after dinner was what Arnie wanted to say but he didn't. Instead he abruptly beckoned Cyndi into his room. "So what are you saying, we come all the way up from St. Paul and now you don't wanta do what you came to do? I already paid you half your money, Cyndi, *and* your hotel room *and* the per diem. So now I'm supposed to have only one girl holding up the guns?"

"Hell, no, I wouldn't do that to Tracy. I got another girl."

"What, come up from the agency? This morning already?"

"No, she's from here in Hobie. Name's Arlene. I met her last night, she was saying that she'd like to model sometime, and she was pretty good-looking, maybe a little older, like thirty or so. But a really good body, Arnie, honest. Flat stomach, never had a baby, y'know? So I gave her a call this morning and she said she'd *love* to do it. I can pay her out of my own pocket, from what you pay me."

"Yeah, well, that's between you two. What *I* want is a woman looks good in a two-piece, nice tits, nice ass."

161

"Oh, she's got good breasts, not *huge*, but good. Good butt too."

"You let me be the judge of that. Where is this Arlene?"

"Down in my room."

"Get her up here. Christ, the show starts in a half hour."

Amy Carlisle was looking at herself in the mirror in Cyndi Rose's room when Cyndi called her from Arnie's. Amy didn't particularly like what she was seeing.

In the high-rise red shorts and the silver halter top that covered the tips of her breasts, more of Amy's flesh was exposed than had ever been seen in public. But it wasn't the exposure that bothered Amy as much as the flesh itself.

The tiny, veined lines were there if one looked closely enough and although they were not nearly as deep as the wrinkles of age, Amy felt they gave her away, told everyone with a probing eye that she had been sewn together in a Frankensteinian experiment that had succeeded all too well.

Perhaps she was too rough on herself, she thought. If you didn't use a magnifying glass, her body looked good in the tiny outfit. Yet that thought made her uncomfortable as well.

She would be an object of desire but her flesh was dead, blasted into fragments and reassembled. To parade herself in front of men seemed an act of reverse necrophilia, a dead woman craving sexual attention. And the men who desired her would have no idea what she actually was, a revenant, a body that existed for the purpose of revenge, of making the wrong things right.

She tried to put the thought from her mind. She had to be what she appeared to be, a seductress with a gun. The red-haired wig helped, as did the extra layer of makeup she had put on. She doubted if anyone would have recognized her, even the Crow.

But as quickly as that thought came, she dismissed it. The Crow had known her even as dust. This tawdry disguise would not fool it for a second.

When the phone rang, Amy picked it up. As she had guessed, it was Cyndi calling from Arnie's room. Amy said she would be right up.

Cyndi seemed like a nice girl. It was a shame she had to flaunt her body (and more, Amy suspected) for a bunch of gun nuts. For all her hard-boiled surface, though, the girl seemed naive, immediately accepting Amy's story the night before after Amy found out that she worked as a gun show "model" for a dealer with a string of stores in the Twin Cities area.

Listen, hon, you could do me such a favor . . . See, my boyfriend is flying in tomorrow and we were gonna meet at the gun show, because that's what he's comin' in for mostly, oh, to see me, sure, but that boy's just crazy about guns, so much so that he just ignores me times like this. And I was thinkin' that if he was to see me in a cute little outfit, you know, showin' a lot of skin and all, and holdin' a big old rifle, well, I think that would make him so hot that he'd not only forget about all those guns, but he'd pop the question . . . Oh no, I don't want your boss to hire me or anything like that, I'm just talkin' about takin' your place for a little while, y'know, in the morning? I could make it worth your while too, pay you for the fun of it instead of takin' your money. That way, you get paid twice and don't hafta do anything. Whaddya think?

Cyndi had taken her back to her room and had her strip down, and Amy hadn't had to feign embarrassment. *Oh sure, I'll be okay tomorrow, I won't be shy at all, why, you should see what I wear at the beach. But I guess I feel a little funny lettin' another woman see what I got, I mean, I'm a man's woman, you know what I mean?*

Cyndi had assured her that she was a man's woman too and only wanted to see her "credentials" because as sure as God made little green apples, Arnie would want to see them before Amy (or Arlene, as she called herself) hit the show floor in the morning. Cyndi accepted the hundred dollar offer to play sick so quickly that Amy wished she had offered less but then thought what the hell, it was right out of dead Sonny Armitage's wallet and it still left her with three hundred more.

So now she pulled on her denim slacks and her leather jacket and trotted upstairs to see Arnie. He was about what she had expected, in his late forties, a little paunchy, and with dyed hair that he had carefully spread out to make it look fuller. His face, however, was almost handsome and she bet that he had been a lady-killer in his younger days.

He didn't smile when he saw her, however, and there wasn't the trace of a come-on. He just said, "Okay, let's see what you got," and gestured to the jacket. She was glad that Cyndi was still in the room, encouraging her with a close-mouthed smile.

Amy unzipped the jacket and shrugged it off, then stepped out of her pants. Arnie looked her up and down, then spun his right hand, index finger downward, as though he were stirring batter. "Turn," he said. She did, slowly, until she was facing him again. He gave a businesslike nod. "Okay, you'll be fine. Cyndi, fill her in on the do's and don'ts, then go back to bed. You look like shit."

Cyndi lost her smile after that but she demonstrated with several rifles that Arnie had in his room, showing Amy how to hold them up and turn, how to work the bolt-actions, and how to snap in the magazines of the semiautomatics.

"Do it as loud as you can," Cyndi said. "It gets the guys' attention and they love to see a girl work the guns, it's like phallic or something."

"You mean like we're handling their . . ."

"Yeah," Cyndi said, and giggled. "That's it. Now don't worry about questions. Arnie answers all the questions and makes all the sales."

"Do we ever really load the guns?"

"Uh-uh. That's like against the law or something. But we sell the bullets and stuff from under the table. Look, you got any other questions, Tracy will help you out, she's the other girl, okay?"

Tracy wasn't nearly as friendly as Cyndi. Amy suspected it was because she was older and looked on Amy as more of a rival than Cyndi did. As far as Amy was concerned, Tracy didn't have to worry about a thing. She was a knockout. An inch or two taller than Amy, who was five foot eight in flats, she had a pair of large, high breasts which Amy suspected were surgically enhanced. Her shining black hair was perfect for her dark complexion and her slim waist led down to tight and muscular buttocks and perfect thighs. Her face was thin and exotic and Amy felt pedestrian next to her.

Fine. Let Tracy get the attention, Amy thought. That way she would be free to do what she had to do.

"Whoa," said Junior Feeley softly, "whadda we got here?"

Junior had left Karl back at their booth while he made a little tour of the gun-honeys. With well over two hundred displays in the large meeting room, there had to be a nice selection of pussy.

But as he cruised down the aisles, he realized that he had seen most of them before and when they saw him, they looked away. There wasn't any point in trying any lines with them. They either had experienced Junior's peccadilloes personally or had heard about them in no uncertain terms. It was fresh meat he was looking for. Fresh and dumb.

And he thought he found it over at Arnie Bailey's booth, all the way at the end of the big room. There were two girls working there, wearing tight little shorts and even littler halter tops that turned the place into Titty City. One was a brunette Junior had seen before. Bitch's name was Stacy or Tracy or something, and she had actually pulled a blade on him in a hallway when he had tried to press her up against the wall for a little dry-hump. Mean woman, not worth messing with.

It was the redhead that caught his eye and promised possibilities. She was a little older than most of the models but had a nice build, long and tall, the way Junior liked them, and he thought his fat ass would look pretty good sitting on those tits. Besides, he *loved* redheads, especially if they were natural. This one's hair kind of looked like a wig, but hell, that was okay. In Junior's experience, natural redheads were scarcer than honest Jews or smart niggers.

He decided not to say anything to her right away but to come back and talk to her later. It was almost nine and the doors would open soon, spilling hundreds of gun nuts and potential militiamen into the aisles. Junior knew there was no way that young Karl was going to be able to handle the rush. Big Red would have to wait until later.

Rick Carlisle tried to make himself feel at home in the throng waiting to go into the gun show. He was dressed correctly, anyway, in a worn red wool shirt, green duck pants that were thin at the knees, and low, thick-soled boots with heavy laces. It seemed to be a variation of what every other person there was wearing.

Some of the men waiting outside with him were talking to each other but many stood silently, watching the doors. Older, white-haired hunters gathered in small groups. Some wore jackets with state wildlife patches that dated back decades. They seemed serious and professional, as though expecting to find something to help them retain the aim that aging and shaking hands were spoiling. They reminded Rick of his father's hunting companions.

Rick had nothing against guns. His father had hunted and Rick had too when he was a boy. But he had lost interest as he grew older. He recalled a lot of his dad's gun-toting friends as good, decent men who obeyed the game laws and mostly ate what they killed. He assumed the older hunters here followed that pattern. But he wasn't so sure about the younger ones.

There were a lot of loud young men with shaven heads, Doc Martens, and military surplus coats who, if they had ever taken aim, had probably had humans in their sights rather than deer. More than a few of these skinheads were wearing white power buttons and Rick saw one with an SS patch sewn on his sleeve. The older hunters' conversations seemed genteel compared to the skinheads', which were sprinkled with swear words that brought them several hard looks from their elders.

There was also a contingent of men in their thirties and forties that seemed more political in nature. Most of these men wore full beards or mustaches and had on camouflage clothing and campaign hats. A few wore shoulder patches or caps that identified them as belonging to a militia, and Rick glimpsed a T-shirt beneath a camouflage vest that read *Just Say No to ZOG*. One of the older hunters noticed it too and asked its wearer, a bearded man with a ruddy tan, who ZOG was.

"Zionist occupied government," the man replied in an angry tone.

Jesus, what a crew, Rick thought. Firearms made strange bedfellows, everybody from legal hunters to neo-Nazis to militia nuts, all looking for something that goes bang.

Then the double doors rattled as though someone were unlocking them and at the same time a black shape shot from above the roof, casting a shadow on the men below. Rick, like most of those waiting, jumped at the sudden movement, then saw that it was only a crow, large as a hawk and black as night, that must have been sitting on the roof and been startled from its perch by the rattling of the doors.

A few of the men laughed and aimed imaginary shotguns and pistols at the bird, which was placidly drifting toward the trees across the parking lot. They yelled, "Pow!" and "Blammo!" as their fingers pulled the air triggers and they laughed again.

Then the crow circled and came back toward them, flapping its wings with an easy and enviable economy of movement until it was directly above them, its wings outspread, riding the wind, moving neither forward nor back. It hung magically suspended in space as the sun suddenly vanished behind dark clouds.

The sight was eerie, uncanny, and a silence fell over the crowd. Then a few men laughed uneasily and a young skinhead raised his arms to mimic shooting once more, opening his mouth to imitate a gun's roar. But something in the mien of the crow hovering above them, wings outstretched like arms giving a blessing or a curse, stopped him and he lowered his hands with another edgy laugh.

Then suddenly the doors screeched open and latched into place and the crow swept away out of sight. The crowd, forgetting the crow in their excitement, surged into the building like an amoeba, splitting in a hundred different directions when they got inside the large room.

Rick found a spot from which he could observe a large part of the chaos and decided to home in on the booths that catered to the paramilitary crowd. He had worked up his cover story but he didn't know whether he would have the chance to use it. Maybe everybody here was just interested in selling and buying guns.

As he strolled throughout the room, he was amazed at the number of different ways there were to deal death. There were booths that catered to hunters but he wondered what kind of hunters would go after wildlife with the semiautomatic assault weapons that many of the vendors displayed.

Most of them were obviously designed to kill men, to allow the shooter to fire just as fast as he could pull the trigger. There were stands that sold sniper rifles, assault rifles, short-barrel military shotguns (some with bayonets), and even assault shotguns with round magazines that looked to Rick like pregnant tommy guns.

Rick was also surprised to see a number of scantily clad women behind the tables holding up rifles and pistols and shotguns and parading back and forth with them in the few square feet they had to move. It was one hell of a draw, as the tables with the models had the lion's share of customers. Most of the women were playing their roles to the hilt, giving lascivious looks to all the passersby and bending over to deepen their cleavage whenever a man looked their way. Rick, embarrassed, avoided their glances, keeping his attention focused on the arms sold at the tables and searching for other signs that would, against all odds, lead him to his quarry.

When Amy saw Rick, she froze for a moment. Then knowing that the sudden stillness would only draw attention to her, she continued to do her assigned work, snapping in magazines and detaching them from the weapons she held.

Still, her thoughts fragmented as she performed the automatic actions. What was Rick doing here? He wasn't a hunter. Could he be looking for a pistol to defend the home that he now shared with Nancy, to protect his new family? If so, why didn't he go to a sporting goods store or a gun shop?

And why was he wearing those clothes? They weren't like Rick at all. It almost seemed as though he were in disguise . . .

Then she realized that was exactly the situation. He *was* disguised—just as she was. They were both hunting, acting as bait for the predators that they wanted to make their prey. He also had come here to find those responsible for the bombing.

But things were different with Rick, she thought. He wasn't a hunter, he wasn't up to this. He had never wet his hands with human blood. She had. It was why she was here, why the Crow had brought her back, and no harm could come to her.

It wasn't the same for Rick. Amy knew what these people were capable of. They had shot Wilson Barnes, and the man she had killed in the garage had gutted William Standish like a pig. Even the old woman had been potentially deadly. They wouldn't hesitate to kill Rick in a minute if they thought that he endangered them.

And her shock at seeing him was further intensified by their confrontation through the window the other morning. What would he think if he saw her now?

But he wasn't looking in her direction or at any of the half-clad women scattered here and there in the booths. That was like him, she thought, and smiled. He had always had an embarrassingly puritanical streak. He passed Arnie's booth without a glance at her, his eyes remaining on the guns on the table, and moved down the aisle, toward the front of the room.

"Like lockin' and loadin', sweetie?" said a tall, rangy man who was staring at her chest. "Or was that smile for me?"

"That smile," she said, "is for anyone who purchases a new weapon from Arnie's Arms, sir."

"Fat chance," said the man. "Got my own stand down there. But I don't have any pussy to look at." He laughed and smacked his buddy on the shoulder. Then with one more appraising look at Amy, who felt naked under his eyes, he headed back toward his stand.

It was an oppressive morning of being eyed and ogled. Never before had she felt like such a piece of meat, hung up for all the wolves to admire. The feminine draw worked, however, for Arnie was doing a good business, steadily selling ammo and guns and filling out the endless array of government forms that were required with each purchase.

And while she was examined by the passing crowd, Amy examined them as well, looking at the name tags the dealers wore, reading each one to find a name that she recognized—Rip Withers, Chip Porter, Powder Burns, whoever those bastards were, and especially Junior Feeley. And then after she had swatted them all, she had to find the nest those creatures had crawled out of.

During her five-minute breaks she got ready for them. Arnie had thoughtfully arranged a curtain at the back of the booth that gave one girl a four-by-eight-foot area to sit and relax in while the other drew all the stares. He had stored arms and ammo back there too and Amy had been "lockin' and loadin'" on every break, then replacing the fully loaded weapons back in their small crates.

She had already loaded a 9 mm Weaver Nighthawk and four magazines, giving her a hundred and twenty-five rounds, and a Cobray M11/Nine, a semiautomatic machine pistol that she intended to fire while changing magazines on the Nighthawk. As an afterthought, she loaded an old Army .45 to stick in her belt as backup if one of the others jammed.

All she needed now was Junior Feeley to wander by, and the gun nuts would see some real action.

twenty-three

RICK SLOWED AT ONE OF THE STANDS HALFWAY TO THE DOOR. There were a number of weapons and boxes of ammo on the table but what drew his attention was a small stack of red-covered paperbacks. On the cover a man and a woman were firing guns at an unseen target. It was *The Turner Diaries*, the book that had supposedly helped to inspire Timothy McVeigh and was considered a second Bible to the militia movement.

He picked it up and started to flip through the pages, careful not to look too interested or to look at the people behind the table. "Y'ever read that?" one of the people asked and Rick looked up at him. He was built like a six-and-a-half-foot fireplug, tall and heavy, and wearing a camouflage vest over a green flannel shirt. His name tag read "Clarence Feeley, Jr." with "Dealer" underneath.

"Yes, I did. Some years ago."

"Yeah? How'd you like it?"

Rick smiled. "It is one helluva book. Oh, it's a great story but I liked it more for what it said, you know? About . . . the way things are."

"Changed my life," said Feeley. "How 'bout you, Karl?" he asked the boy sitting next to him. His face was spotless and Rick wondered if he even shaved. His eyes were blue and fringed with long lashes. His nose and mouth were small, almost petite, and he had a little smile in which Rick could see no trace of guile. He looked like a Norman Rockwell teenager crossed with a Giotto angel and he was wearing a small button with a picture of Bill Clinton and the words "Wanted for Treason."

"I liked it a lot," the boy said in a soft, shy voice. His smile widened, just a little.

"Well, I lost my copy a long time ago," Rick said. "I'll take one." He handed Feeley a twenty and accepted the change.

"You a shooter?" Feeley asked him.

"Aw, a little. Don't hunt, though. Mostly interested in self-defense. I really didn't come to the show for the guns, but for stuff like this." He held up the book. "You're the only one selling anything like it though." He started to move away, hoping that Feeley would call him back, and he wasn't disappointed.

"Whaddya mean, stuff like this?" Feeley said.

"Oh, you know," Rick said, turning back, "stuff a little more political. I heard some groups have stands at shows like this, militia and such. Little disappointing, though."

"Well," said Feeley with a smile, "you gotta know where to look. There are sympathetic folks around but you don't wanta be too obvious about it."

"Why?" Rick said. "Because of the goddam government?"

"Part of it."

"Shit, they got their fingers in everything. Every time you turn around, they're telling you what to do and how to do it. Fuckers." He glanced at the boy. "Excuse me, son." The boy shrugged, as though he had heard worse. "They took an awful lot from me," he added softly.

"Yeah?" said Feeley? "Like what?"

Rick fixed him with a hard look. "Why should I tell you?"

"You don't have to tell me *shit*," Feeley flared. "Just making conversation. What, you think I'm a fucking fed or something? Hey, asshole, you don't have to talk to me."

Rick shook his head apologetically. "Sorry. It's just that I gotta be careful." Feeley eyed him suspiciously and Rick snorted a laugh. "There are people'd like to find me."

"You telling me you're wanted?" Feeley said with a smirk of disbelief.

Rick looked around uncomfortably. "Well, I ain't public enemy number one, but, uh, yeah, I'm what you might call a felon, if believing that you got a right to be free in your own country is a crime. I guess it is."

Feeley gestured him closer. "What'd you do?" he asked softly.

"Look, I don't wanta talk about it, not with all these people around. You never know who's who, know what I mean?"

"You wanta grab a beer?" Feeley asked. "Trade you a beer for your story."

Rick smiled as though he had found a comrade. "A fed wouldn't make an offer like that—you're on."

"Watch the place, Karl," Feeley told the boy, then ducked under the table and together they made their way to the bar.

They sat at a back table. There was only a glimpse of the outside but Rick could see that the dark clouds, the ones that had begun to gather when the crow had flown overhead, were now pouring down rain. Feeley ordered a pitcher of beer and Rick began to improvise the way he had planned, using the details from the books he had read on militias and the patriot movement.

"I just wanted to get off the grid, you know? Lost my job to a nigger, you believe that, after six years? And this is when my wife's dying of cancer so we lost the medical coverage too. Just made her go faster. When she died, wasn't any reason for me to hang around anymore so I figured why not start fresh? I was pissed as hell at the way things had happened. It made me see the only thing a body can depend on is himself. But not enough people believe that, they're too busy sucking at the government tit, everybody without the guts to stand up on their own.

"So I said fuck that, tore up my social security card, driver's license, every damn thing I had that connected me to that nigger-loving Jew government. But though I let *them* alone, they wouldn't let *me* alone. Arrested me for driving without an inspection sticker or registration, but by that time I'd read a lot, you know? And I knew how full of bullshit this

government was and I said fuck you, you don't have any juris-
diction over me, and I didn't show up in court. After that,
things got nuts . . ."

Rick spun his tale of a man against the system, of how he
coldcocked the constable who came to arrest him and stole his
car, abandoned it three states away, and made his way to
Minnesota because he had heard there were a lot of militias
there, places with people who thought the same way he did
and into which he could disappear.

"Like a hole in the wall. You know Butch Cassidy and the
Sundance Kid? They had their Hole-in-the-Wall Gang and I
guess that's what I'm looking for." He looked at Feeley strangely
for a moment, then shook his head. "But hell, why am I telling
you all this? Just because you're selling this book," he slapped it
with his palm, "doesn't mean I can trust you."

"Well, fuck you," said Feeley. "You think I'm a traitor to my
race? You think I'm gonna kiss ZOG's sorry ass by turnin' you
in? Fuck that . . . fuck that, uh-uh. You wanta meet people, you
can maybe meet people, but it isn't as simple as all that, oh no.
Now what's your name anyway?"

"I've got no name anymore. I'm just a guy, you know? So I
call myself Guy. Guy Adams, since Adam was the first man and
Yahweh made him. Yahweh made me what I am too. So that's
in honor of Yahweh."

"Okay, Guy Adams, you hang around after the show and
maybe I'll introduce you to some people can help you, okay?"

"Why?"

"Huh?"

"Why would you do that for me? For a stranger?"

"Hey, remember what Jesus said? I was a stranger and you
took me in, right? Besides, you seem like a really pissed-off
guy—hey, *Guy*, get it?—and pissed-off guys make good soldiers."

"You connected?" Rick asked dubiously.

"Am I connected?" Feeley chuckled. "You wait, pal. You
wait and see."

They finished the pitcher, mostly talking about who they
hated most, but Feeley said nothing more about his "connec-

tions." That was all right. Rick could wait. He had gotten his foot in a door. Whether or not it was the right door remained to be seen.

It had been one helluva morning so far, thought Junior Feeley as he rejoined Karl Withers at the table. True, they had hardly sold a damn thing—one secondhand deer rifle, a few boxes of shells, and two books—and it was raining like a sonovabitch outside, but Junior had found one helluva good-looking red-head *and* had turned up a prime candidate for the Sons.

This Guy Adams had new recruit written all over him in the blood of the ZOG oppressors. Junior knew he was going to be just fine and once old Guy got out there to the compound, he wouldn't have to worry about being nailed by ZOG again.

Junior was so delighted at his find that he told Karl all about "Guy Adams" and the kid seemed to be happy at the news, though you could hardly ever tell what he was thinking. Junior couldn't wait to get Karl laid just to see an emotion cross that blandly smiling face of his. It wasn't that the boy was stupid like his Uncle Ray but he just seemed detached some-how, floating above everything in some dream world. Junior hoped that breeding would tell when the war against ZOG began. The kid was a damn good shot if he could ever be both-ered to shoot the federals and the niggers and the other mon-grel troops that the Jews would send against them some fine day.

Then Junior realized that although his capacious belly was now full of beer, he hadn't eaten since breakfast. "Stay put," he said to Karl. "I'll get us some chow."

Junior walked to the snack bar at the front of the room and bought two orders of fries, two cans of Coke, two hamburgers for himself and two for Karl. If the kid only wanted one, Junior would eat the other one. On the way back he decided to side-track to the booth where he had seen the redhead this morning. Might as well make the little lady's acquaintance. It would be rough without old Sonny along but a lot of girls liked the big and burly type.

There were only a few people in front of the girl's stand. Arnie was filling out a form for some skinhead kid who was holding a fat roll of bills, probably trying to pay cash and give a phony ID so that nothing could be traced to him. The brunette, Tracy or Stacy, was nowhere in sight, but Big Red was strutting her stuff nicely for two lamers standing there watching.

Junior could have picked them up and knocked their heads together, they were so damn thin and skanky. But he only stepped between them, pushing them to either side as he held the cardboard tray with his food in his hammy fists. "Hey, you're new here," he said to the redhead. "I never seen you before. And I'm real, real sorry about that."

The redhead kept smiling as she looked at him and his name tag. She was holding a pump shotgun and she racked it and pointed it at him, widening her eyes innocently. All right, he thought, a playful one, though he felt a little stir in his balls as he looked into the shotgun's mouth.

"Whoa," he said. "Be careful there, red." He glanced down at her tight shorts. "If you *are* a redhead."

"Don't worry . . . Junior," she said in a husky voice that sounded somehow familiar. Then she pointed the muzzle toward the ceiling and pulled the trigger, dry-firing it with a sharp click.

"Hey, hey, Arlene," Arnie said, looking up annoyed from his paperwork, "don't fuck around like that, huh? Don't go pointin' shit at the customers, for crissake."

"It's okay, man," said Junior. "It's empty."

"Yeah, well, dry-firin' ain't good for the guns, Junior, you know that."

"Dry-firin' ain't good for *nothin'*," Junior said suggestively, then lowered his voice so only Arlene could hear, while Arnie turned back to his work. "When I shoot, I always shoot with a full load." He grinned. "So whaddya say, are you really a redhead all the way?"

Arlene held up a finger and set the shotgun on the table, then turned and went toward the back curtain of the booth.

Just before she disappeared behind it, she turned and said in a voice that gave Junior a quick ride to Woodville, "You wanta see red, you just wait one minute, Junior."

Shit, Junior thought, what was she gonna do, come out in open crotch panties or something? Or maybe just give him a quick flash of red-haired pussy from behind the curtain? Man, this chick was hot. And she really seemed to dig him too. It almost made him suspicious.

But then she came back out and she wasn't wearing less, she was wearing more, a black leather jacket, and she was holding a gun in each hand, with another one jammed into her shorts.

And she wasn't smiling anymore.

twenty-four

WHEN AMY SAW THE MAN'S NAME TAG, SHE FELT HER TEETH clench. She had noticed him before, when he blatantly checked her out before the place had opened to the public, but he hadn't been wearing his name tag then.

And now here he was, delivered into her hands. Clarence Feeley, Junior. Her jaws ached as she held the smile on her face and played with him, making sure that he would stay. And now here *she* was, ready for him.

He lost his grin, not understanding what she was doing, and she leaned across the table and put her face close to his and said, "I always wanted to meet a Son of a Free America."

His look of shocked surprise told her beyond doubt that she had the right man and she brought up the Nighthawk and fired several shots as quickly as she could pull the trigger. The explosions sounded as one and the tray of food he was holding turned into a thick paste that instantly became one with his flesh.

His stomach split apart under the fusillade and he staggered backwards, arms waving, head jerking. Gouts of blood flew from him like demons escaping hell. His fat ass bumped against the table across the aisle and he flopped down onto the floor in a sitting position. His eyes, still miraculously alive, were looking at her and she knew that he saw her, the bringer of his death.

"You wanted to see red," she said and shot him in the face

with seven rounds so that his eyes pulped and his brains painted everything around him.

"Get her!" somebody yelled, and the roar of another shot punched the air. Something tore into her shoulder and when she looked to her right, she saw the thin dealer who had talked to her earlier. He was standing behind his table several stands away, racking another round into a pump shotgun. He lifted it and fired at her again, catching her full in the chest and knocking her backward so that she toppled into the skinhead behind her.

The kid squealed and rolled away, his hands over his head as if expecting to get kicked. Amy sat back up and glanced at her chest. The halter beneath the open jacket had been shredded by the tightly choked wad of shot, but as she watched, the gaping hole in her chest closed up and she leaped to her feet, firing at the shooter before he could rack another shell. A ribbon of blood streaked from his neck and he fell.

Then all hell broke loose.

Rick Carlisle was standing by Junior Feeley's booth when the shooting started. He had seen that Feeley wasn't there and thought he would use the opportunity to try and make friends with the kid. He had scarcely said three words when the gunfire started.

He jerked his head around but could see only the people between himself and the noise. Many of them tried to scatter but because of the crowded aisles found nowhere to run. Most dropped to the floor, some crouching, some lying prone, heads down.

As the bodies dropped, Rick saw the glow of muzzle flash and then heard a single, louder boom quickly followed by another. Somebody was unloading a shotgun.

Then there was another blast of fire and as more spectators dropped out of harm's way, Rick saw a flash of red hair and a ripped leather jacket. It was a woman, and she had just hit the man with the shotgun, who was falling in a cloud of blood.

Then half a dozen more weapons sounded at once, spraying the woman with bullets. Many of them got past her and Rick saw bystanders fall, some hit in the head, some in the chest, thrashing about where they stood or toppling like trees. Suddenly a string of automatic rifle fire snaked behind him, pocking the walls.

Rick dove over the table for the kid, who was just standing there as if stunned, and hauled him to the floor a fraction of a second before another string of wildfire traced its way across the wall where he had stood. He raised his head from the floor and looked at the surprised boy lying next to him. "Let's stay down," he said, and Karl breathlessly nodded agreement.

It seemed to Amy as if every son of a bitch with a weapon had ripped open cartridge boxes, loaded, and was firing at her. The bullets hurt when they hit but she was able to stay on her feet as shots from one side would push her one way and those from the other side back again.

With the press of panicked bodies moving slowly away from her and the people lying facedown on the floor, she didn't know how the hell she was going to work her way out before her clothes were chewed to bits, and she wondered if there were a point at which her torn flesh would stop healing itself. So far there didn't seem to be.

Then she saw her escape route, as well as a way to better target her fire. The tables ran the entire length of the room and they were empty except for guns, a few cardboard stand-ups, and the bodies of those who had been hit by her attackers' stray gunfire.

She leaped up onto the closest table and ran down the white-tableclothed runway, firing at the bursts of muzzle flash or whenever she saw anyone aiming at her. She was hit frequently but made the shooters pay, firing with pinpoint accuracy and holding her fire whenever unarmed men were in the way.

The shooters weren't as particular and Amy saw more than

a few people go down because they happened to come between her and a bunch of trigger-happy assholes. She would have been content just to blast Junior Feeley and walk out but they had taken that option away from her.

At last she had battled her way to the doors and now she leaped off the end table while the onlookers who hadn't already run out screamed and scattered at the sight of her flying through the air toward them, her tattered black leather fanning out behind her like the feathers of a giant black bird descending to feed upon their souls.

She ran unimpeded out into the parking lot, which had become almost as chaotic as the show inside. A cold and heavy rain was falling and cars, RVs, and pickup trucks were skidding in the water, smashing into each other in their haste to get away from the carnage or to take the wounded to hospitals. Amy darted through the mess, her feet slapping the puddles as she ran toward the back of the building where she had parked the Avanti.

But just as she was about to round the building, she heard someone yell *"Bitch!"* and turned to look.

Only a few yards away a man was standing in the back of a pickup truck aiming a double-barreled shotgun directly at her. She started to bring up the Nighthawk but he fired and both barrels discharged, sending two wads of shot right into her face.

The pain was shocking, beyond life's ability to bear. She felt her eyes implode, her teeth splinter, her mouth and nose and forehead cave in. And in that moment she remembered the pain of the explosion, *all* the pain, the psychic as well as the physical, and she fell back into darkness, hearing the triumphant cry of the shooter, hearing his words like sharp pellets of rain: *Yes! Goddammit yes, I nailed her! Shit if I didn't, fucked her right in the face, right in the goddam—*

And then she opened her eyes, newly made. She raised her reshaped head from the ground and let the rain reannoint it. She thought with her mind, reborn, that this man must die. And she stood up.

The man, his shotgun empty in his hands, only stared, his mouth open, his face trembling, rain running off of it like copious tears. His fingers unclenched and the shotgun fell at his feet, hitting the truck bed with the sound of a deep bell tolling, then instantly dying away.

Amy bounded up onto the truck bed and grabbed the man by his neck with her left hand. With the right, she grasped his face with fingers as strong and wiry as a metal claw, and dug in.

Her index and middle fingers pierced his eyes, her thumb and other two fingers popped through either side of his cheeks like a screwdriver through paper, and she ripped away the flesh—lips, cheeks, nose, and chin—pulling it right off the bone the way the explosion had ripped away her own flesh and that of the children.

And Amy screamed. She screamed for the man she killed, for the memory of her children and her own pain, and she screamed for what she had become.

The raindrops were her tears and they soaked the earth.

twenty-five

No one saw where the woman went after she killed the man in the truck. If they had been panicked before, the sight of her getting up after taking a shotgun blast in the face and then tearing the man's flesh off had driven them over the edge.

A few who had witnessed it remained, however, to tell the police what they had seen, and one man, a grizzled old hunter who had come to the show to get a bargain in .30–06 shells, was apparently the last to see the woman.

"She ran around the back of the building there and that was the last I seen of her."

"Didn't you look to see where she went?" asked an officer.

"Mister, I don't care *where* the hell she went as long as it wasn't around me. And it's gonna be a long time before I come to one of *these* shows again, lemme tell you."

The police interviewed Arnie Bailey, who couldn't tell them a thing about his temporary model except her description, her first name, and the fact that "that's the last fucking time I ever let that bitch Cyndi get her own fucking replacement."

The story made all the network news programs that evening, although the only footage had been that taken after the incident. The show's promoter examined a video that he had shot earlier but the only glimpse of the alleged assailant was from the back and twenty yards away. The only thing anyone could tell was her approximate height and the fact that the red hair was in all likelihood a wig, something that Cyndi attested to later on *Hard Copy*.

The final toll was ten dead and fifteen wounded. The bullets in the wounded were not from the guns that Arnie Bailey claimed were missing from his stock. "I was there," he told the news people, "and believe you me, when she aimed at something, she hit it."

Besides Clarence Feeley, Jr., and Barton Douglas, the man in the parking lot, four other people had been killed with bullets from the Nighthawk and the Cobray. All of them had been shooting at the woman. The other four dead, as well as all the wounded, had been hit by "friendly fire," shooters who were trying to bring down the woman.

The conclusion was that it was a planned killing. The first victim, and the only one the woman had shot without being fired on, was Clarence Feeley, Jr., a thirty-two-year-old unemployed bricklayer who had a series of arrests for sexual offenses, none of which had ever resulted in a conviction. Theorists guessed that the execution had been carried out in retaliation for a sexual attack, either on the woman herself or on a friend, and police were questioning all the women who had ever made complaints against Feeley.

What no one could explain was the impression given by witnesses that the woman had been hit by gunfire innumerable times, including a double-barreled shotgun blast full in the face, and had fled seemingly unharmed. Those who had not been there suspected body armor. Those who saw knew better.

Rick Carlisle had seen. Against all common sense, he had raised his head over the table where he was sheltering with Karl and amid the barrage of bullets that flew over his head saw the woman near the other end of the room, running down the tables, firing as she went. He saw the bullets hit her bare legs, smack into her back, and at one point strike her in the head. Her head had rocked but she had paused for only a heartbeat, then continued to run as if nothing had happened, firing again.

There was something too familiar about the woman and he

knew as soon as he saw her what it was. She looked like Amy, moved like Amy.

She *was* Amy.

The vision in the window, the voice on the radio, and now this. If he had not seen her shot, he might have thought that she had never died, that she had somehow survived and had remained hidden for six months and come back to wreak vengeance on those who had destroyed her dream.

But he *had* seen her shot. She had taken rounds that should have killed her and she kept going, "like that fuckin' pink bunny with the batteries," as one witness told a news team. They had not used the quote.

Rick believed implicitly the story of the shotgun blast in the face. He had seen, and he knew that she was not human. She was something strange and alien and unknown, and she was finding her way to them.

Rick was finding his way too, and he would continue to try and infiltrate them. And now Amy's slaughter had dropped the perfect opportunity right into his lap.

He had saved young Karl's life and the boy knew it. He had seen those bullet holes in the wall right where he had been standing before Rick had pulled him down. And when the shooting was all over and they had seen Clarence Feeley's bloody corpse, Karl turned to Rick and said, "We gotta get out of here. Can't be here when the police come, right? I mean, Junior told me about you, and . . . well, I shouldn't be here either."

Rick nodded. He was a fugitive from justice as far as this kid was concerned, and it seemed there was more to the boy than met the eye. They easily got outside in the melee and Karl led the way to a dark, dusty sedan. "Get in," he said, unlocking it.

"You're going to leave the guns?" Rick asked.

"No time to get them."

They got into the car and Karl drove slowly away, as if trying to avoid attention. In truth, his studied driving was in sharp contrast to the vehicles around them, tearing out of the lot as if trying to get away from hell.

"Thanks," said Karl. "You saved my life. Man, I thought I was done for. I couldn't even move."

"That's all right," said Rick. "My name's Guy. Guy Adams."

He held out his hand and Karl shook it. "I know. Junior told me. I'm Karl Withers."

"Good to meet you, Karl. So . . ." He felt as though he had to make some comment about Feeley. "So Junior? Is that what you call him? So were you related to him?"

Karl shook his head. "He was a friend, that's all, and one of the . . . well, a friend of my dad's. So you want me to take you somewhere?"

"Well, I'd been hoping that maybe Junior was going to hook me up with some people."

"Yeah, he told me."

"Sounds like he told you a lot."

"Yeah, he did." Karl seemed to think for a minute, then he flicked the car's turn signal and pulled into a gas station, parking next to the phone booth that sat in the corner of the lot. "I want to make a call," he said. "You wait here."

Karl talked for a long time but Rick wasn't able to hear anything. When the boy got back in the car, he was smiling. "I got some people for you to meet," he said and pulled back onto the road.

She had done it. She had killed the fat bastard. She hadn't known if she was going to be able to just shoot down a man in cold blood, but she had. It was as if something had taken over her body, turning her pain and loss into red rage. And while she was shooting him, *killing* him, it was the most liberating feeling that her spirit had ever known, as if loosing him from life loosed weights from her own aggrieved soul.

But after he was dead, then she had to kill more. Her response was automatic, animalistic. These men firing their weapons caused her pain and she had to stop them, to get through and away from them, and the simplest way to do that was to kill them.

And that had been the easiest thing in the world, to target their chests with her guns and fire, dropping one after another until she had reached the end of the room. If the stupid fools' bullets had hit others, that was no fault of hers.

But then she had come outside and the man had fired his shotgun at her and the pain had maddened her and she had made him pay. She saw in his face the faces of the men in the car, and something told her that by destroying that face she would be destroying all those faces that had caused the pain of the past. And she had done it.

Standing there in the rain with the dying man's flesh in her hands, she had for a horrifying instant felt as though she had become a monster, felt like old Uncle Abraham stalking the streets of Kishinev for his victims.

And then she had run. And now she was back in David Levinson's garage, sitting in the welcome darkness, the door closed behind her. She tried to focus on her next step, the festival tomorrow, Chip Porter.

The door to the kitchen opened and David Levinson stood framed in the light. He was wearing his uniform and his service revolver hung at his hip. She couldn't see his face but she could hear his voice.

"Ten bodies. You left ten bodies behind you." He turned and walked back into the kitchen, closing the door behind him, leaving her in darkness again.

She could stay there, she thought, or she could go inside, into the light, and face the truth. She got out of the car and went into the kitchen.

Levinson was sitting in the breakfast nook, a cup of coffee in his hand. He was freshly shaven and his hair was neatly styled and she knew he was ready to go out on his shift. His face was expressionless as he looked at her, eyeing the tattered leather and the ripped shorts. "You weren't hurt at all, were you?"

"I was hurt," she said softly. "I was hurt, David."

"And a lot of other people got hurt too, didn't they? I mean, at least if what I just heard from my friend Trotter on the force is true. This Feeley, he was your target, right?" She nodded slightly. "And you killed him."

"Yes."

"And then what happened? You decided you liked it?"

"No! That's not it at all. They started shooting at me."

"Oh really? Just because you blew away an unarmed man, and one of their fellow dealers to boot, in the middle of the show floor? God, that was shallow of them, wasn't it."

"I had to defend myself."

"Against what? Getting temporarily perforated?"

"If I hadn't kept shooting, they would have grabbed me."

"And you could have tossed them off like a bull tossing kittens. But okay, even assuming that you were justified in shooting the people who were shooting at you, innocent bystanders got hurt too, Amy."

"Innocent bystanders," she repeated. "You mean like my kids? Like me? Like my friend Judy?" She sat across from him and looked him hard in the eyes. "I've come back to fight a war, David. And there are no innocent bystanders in a war. I killed the ones trying to kill me, that's all. If their bullets hit *innocent bystanders*, well, the ones who killed those bystanders are dead now at my hands, so I've already avenged their deaths. And if I'm wrong, if it's all my fault, then let the Crow bring them back to avenge themselves on *me*. So help me God or the devil, I'll fight the living *and* the dead if I have to, to set things right again."

Levinson looked at her for a moment as if trying to fathom her depths. "Do you remember how this all started?" he asked her. "With the shedding of innocent blood. Now I know what Junior Feeley was. He was a turd with legs. I think he must have hated women, he did things so nasty to them. And when they made complaints and brought charges against him, by the time the court dates rolled around they always changed their minds, like somebody had convinced them not to testify, and the charges were dropped, the complaints withdrawn. He's been involved with white supremacists and racists ever since he was a punk kid. He's beaten up gays and blacks and Jews and it was always the same story as with the women.

"Amy, you could have killed that fucking slug ten times over, while he was feeding a puppy or making confession or saying his bedtime prayers, and I wouldn't have made a peep.

I'd have said great, kill the prick a few more times while you're at it. But your target was him, nobody else, and as far as I'm concerned, nine other people died for nothing."

"So what are you going to do about it, take me in, officer?"

"I don't think I could, could I?"

"You're damn right you couldn't. If you tried it, David, if you tried to stop me from what I have to do, I'd kill you."

He shook his head slowly. "I don't believe that, Amy."

"All right then, maybe I wouldn't kill you. But the Crow would. The Crow knows what needs to be done." She held out her hands. Just like the last time Levinson had seen them, they were rusty with dried blood. "But the Crow would do it with my hands."

Levinson looked at her hands for a very long time. Then he reached across the table and held them, his fingers curling slowly around hers. "Do what you have to do," he said. "But don't let them make you what they are."

Amy looked down at the pair of strong, heavy hands, knowing that she could easily have crushed them with a grip. "It's too late, David," she said, pulling her hands away from his. "I think I'm already far worse."

twenty-six

RICK CARLISLE HAD NEVER BEFORE BEEN TO THE DALLAS DINER. He had never even been on this road, fifteen miles northwest of Hobie near Petersburg, a one-store, one-street village. He couldn't figure out why it was called the Dallas Diner, since neither Texan decor nor cuisine was evident. It looked just like a hundred other aluminum diners that had survived from the forties and fifties, only in worse shape than most.

He was having a piece of blueberry pie to finish the meal that Karl had bought for him. "Least I can do for saving my life," the boy had told him. "Besides, we're gonna wait here for my dad."

That had been an hour ago. Karl hadn't said much and they had eaten mostly in silence. Rick figured that the boy wasn't too broken up about Junior Feeley's death. His expression seldom changed from the look of benign disinterest he had worn since Rick had first seen him.

His face did not even brighten perceptibly when a dark blue pickup truck pulled into the parking lot. Karl just pointed at the window and said, "There's my dad."

Karl's father came into the diner alone although Rick could see another man waiting in the truck. "Rip Withers," the man said, coming up to the table and shaking Rick's hand, then sliding into the booth next to his son. "My boy tells me you saved his ass," Withers said, peering at Rick from beneath frowning brows. He was a stocky man about six feet tall and was wearing a brown field jacket and a red wool cap with a tan canvas bill. His cheeks were ruddy above a well-trimmed beard.

"I just pushed him down when the shooting started," Rick said.

"He jumped over the table and everything," Karl said with as much animation as Rick guessed he was capable of. "I'da been shot sure."

"I owe you my thanks then," Withers said. "Karl's my only child."

"Well, you're welcome," Rick said, looking away in what he hoped came off as embarrassment.

"Karl tells me you need a little help. You and the government don't exactly see eye to eye, huh?"

"On some things, that's right. There are some people who'd, well, like to talk to me, to put it mildly."

"You're wanted."

"I am. I was telling Junior that I was looking for a group of people who . . . thought the way I do. Place to get away from the ones looking for me, maybe I could help do things that had to be done. Help in the struggle, you know?"

"And your name is . . ."

"Guy Adams. That's my name now."

"What was your name *then?*"

Rick shook his head. "Nope, sorry. I swore before Yahweh I'd never speak that name again nor use it in any way. That was ZOG's name for me. That name is dead and that man is dead. I'm Guy Adams and that's all anybody has to know."

"Well, I'll tell you something, Guy Adams," said Withers. "Somebody that does what you did when that shooting started, somebody that's got that much discipline is either one of two things. First, he's a good, brave, trained soldier who saw a boy in trouble and helped without thought of his own safety. Second, he's a fed. A cop or an FBI man or a company spook or somebody trained in situations like that. Now which one are you, Mr. Adams?"

Rick made his face look as stern as he could, trying to be

Henry Fonda in *The Grapes of Wrath*. Then he stood up. "I'll tell you what I am, Mr. Withers—I'm gone. Thanks for the meal, son. Glad I could help you."

He was out in the parking lot, walking purposefully toward the road back to Hobie before Withers caught up to him. "Hey," Withers said. "Hey, come on, just a minute."

"I don't need this shit," Rick said. "I've eaten this shit since I was old enough to crawl and I don't need any more of it from you, not from somebody who's supposed to know about how I feel . . ."

"Goddam it, all *right!*" He grabbed Rick and spun him around. "Now you listen to me a minute, *Adams!* Do you know what it's like to have several dozen men that I'm responsible for? Do you know how confident I have to be of a person before I take them into our group, show them where we live and work, tell them our plans? I have to believe that person is a *brother,* man! I have to believe beyond the shadow of a doubt that that man is a true patriot, a real son of what will one day be a free America! So don't you give me your 'I'm all insulted' shit when I'm trying to preserve my men's lives!"

By the end of his speech, Withers was breathing hard and Rick found it surprisingly easy to feign sympathy and admiration for the man. Rick was playing a role, yet Withers's passion made it easier for him to make himself believe in the part. He could see how driven the man was and as a result Rick's mumbled apology came out easily and almost sincerely.

"All right then," Withers said, more calmly. "I truly appreciate what you did for my son. And I want to make it up to you. I believe you're a good man and that you're telling me the truth but it's not my decision alone. There are other people I have to talk to. That is, if you're still interested."

Rick nodded. "I am."

"Karl will take you back to Hobie now. Tomorrow over in Eau Claire they've got a White Christian Brotherhood festival. Be there. There'll be a band playing called Shock Troops, though they spell it some weird, dumbass way. The bass guitar player is one of our men. You go up to him and tell him who you are. And he'll either nod his head yes or shake it no, depending on what we decide. If it's no, we don't see you again. If it's yes, he'll take you in the van after the festival's over and bring you to us. But if it *is* yes, then you're one of us. You don't leave the compound. You're a soldier. You got any problem with that?"

"Nope. Got a problem with getting to Eau Claire though. That's about a hundred and fifty miles from here and I've got no car."

"Then I guess we'll see just how resourceful you are, won't we? You got any money?"

Rick shrugged. "About twenty bucks left. I'll manage."

"I'm sure you will. The only thing you can depend on in this country is yourself, my friend."

Rick smiled cynically. "Unless your skin's not white."

"Amen to that. Yahweh watch over you."

"He will. Same to you and your boy."

Withers walked back to Karl, who had been standing a few yards behind his father listening to the conversation, and said a few words to the boy that Rick couldn't hear. Then Withers got into his truck and drove away. Karl smiled and nodded toward the dark sedan.

They drove back to Hobie and Karl asked him where he wanted to be dropped off. "Doesn't matter," Rick said. "Downtown, I guess."

"I really want to thank you again, Guy," Karl said as Rick got out. "You really did risk your life for me and I really appreciate it. If there's ever anything I can do for you, you let me know."

Rick smiled. "You could put in a good word for me with your dad."

"I'll do that. I hope to see you again. Yahweh bless you." He drove away, leaving Rick on the street.

The first thing Rick did was go sit on a bench and think about what to do next. The best thing would be to get a cab to take him back to the Holiday Inn parking lot where he had left his car and go home, get a good night's sleep. He'd leave for Eau Claire early in the morning, parking his car far from the festival and hitching a ride in.

But when he stood up, he noticed a familiar form in the

reflection of a shop window. It was Karl Withers standing across the street a dozen storefronts down. He was walking stealthily and Rick could only assume that he didn't want to be seen. To test his theory, Rick slowly turned toward where Karl stood and from the corner of his eye he saw the boy crouch down behind a parked car.

It was only too obvious to Rick what Rip Withers had told his son: *Follow him. See where he goes. Don't let him see you.* So the kid had pulled around the corner and come back on foot.

Rick thanked God, or Yahweh, he thought sourly, that he had noticed the kid. If he hadn't, in another minute Karl would have seen him get a cab, a strange move for a near penniless drifter. And if the kid had followed him, he would have seen right through Rick's pack of lies as he took him first to his car and then to his wooded, suburban home. Rick would have been lucky if there hadn't been a kill team sent to dispatch him, another lying agent of ZOG.

So instead, he had to do what Guy Adams would have done. Rick started walking slowly toward the seedier side of town, looking for the cleanest cheap hotel he could find. He stopped before each one, just the way anyone, even Guy Adams, would have done, thinking about its appearance, and finally settled on the Excelsior, a hotel that consisted of three shabby rowhouses.

Rick signed the register as Guy Adams, writing down an address in St. Paul, though he doubted the clerk, who didn't ask for identification, cared. The room was eighteen dollars and Rick paid in cash. When he asked for a room that fronted the street, the clerk looked at him oddly but complied.

The room was exactly what Rick had expected. There was a slightly musty bed with clean but gray sheets, an old chest of drawers with a washstand on it, and an open closet with no hangers. A thin white towel and a washcloth whose nap was nearly rubbed off were folded at the foot of the bed. The shared bathroom was down the hall.

But Rick was more interested in what was outside the room than inside. He turned off the light, crossed to the window, and looked down at the darkening street.

Karl Withers was there all right, standing across the street and looking at the Excelsior Hotel uncertainly. He paced back and forth for a while, then seemed to make up his mind, and headed back down the street the way that Rick had come.

Rick smiled. He hoped he had passed the test. But now he had to let Nancy know where he was and where he was going, at least as far as he knew. He walked downstairs and went outside. Karl Withers was nowhere to be seen but Rick walked several blocks just to make sure he was not being followed.

Then he found a pay phone and called Nancy.

twenty-seven

NANCY GRABBED THE PHONE WHEN IT RANG AND WHEN SHE heard Rick's voice she nearly cried with relief. She had tried to talk him out of going to the gun show but he had refused to listen, and when she heard the news stories about the shootings, she had called the police but was told that she would be informed if her husband was among the injured.

She had left Karin with a neighbor and driven to the Holiday Inn but the place was surrounded by police lines and they would let no one in. So she had gone home and waited for the call to tell her that her husband was dead.

And now here he was, alive, and she was so happy to hear him that she couldn't get out a sensible word for several seconds. He assured her, however, that he was all right, although he had been there when the shooting occurred.

"Oh God," she said, "I'm so glad you're okay, so glad. Oh Rick, when are you coming home?"

"I can't for a while."

"What?"

"That's why I called, to let you know. And to tell you not to worry. I think I'm getting close to them—the ones that planted the bomb. The first man who was killed? This Feeley? I think he was in on it. It's this Sons of a Free America that Wilson Barnes mentioned on the radio."

"But how do you know?" Nancy pleaded. "How do you know it was them with the bomb?"

"I . . . just know," he said, and she could tell from his voice that he was holding something back. "Believe me."

"And you're . . . *meeting* with these people? Why can't you call the police, just call the police and tell *them*, let *them* handle it!"

"I can't do that. I'm not close enough yet. But I will be and then I'll know everything and *then* I'll turn them in—all of them."

"Oh Rick, God, please don't do this, it isn't safe."

"I have to. It'll be all right. I'm being careful."

"How can you be careful with these people!" she shouted into the phone. "They're *killers!* They kill children! Why would they hesitate to kill you?"

"I'm sorry, Nancy. I've got to go. I'll be in touch with you when I can but don't be alarmed if you don't hear from me for a couple of days."

"A couple of *days?* Rick, you can't—"

"Good-bye. Give Karin a hug for me." There was a click on the other end, then silence as deep as a cave, as black as death.

Then she cried. She cried so loudly that Karin came out of the rec room in the basement and asked her what was wrong, if she had heard from Daddy yet. The name came hard to the little girl, who had always called him Uncle Rick during their friendship.

"He's all right, honey," Nancy told her, taking her into her arms. "I just talked to him and he's fine and he wanted me to give you a big hug." She wiped away her tears and looked into Karin's face. "He's going to be gone a few more days though. On business."

"Why are you crying, Mom?"

"I just . . . miss him a lot, that's all. I worry when he's gone."

"Don't worry," the girl said, hugging her mother again. "He's okay."

Nancy nodded and smiled. "Sure. Sure he is." Karin went back to her TV show in the basement and Nancy sat for a minute and then put on her coat and went outside into the cold

November evening. She ached inside, both from the fear for what would happen to Rick and for the suspicion that he didn't really love her. What hurt most was when he hadn't told her on the phone.

She knew that it was going to be an uphill battle when the thought of marrying Rick first came into her mind. He was a one-woman man, always had been, and that woman had been Amy. During Nancy's own bushfire of a marriage, it had been Amy's marriage and Amy's husband that she had envied—not coveted, never that, but envied.

And when Amy had died, when Rick was free, it had been only natural that the thought of the two of them getting together had crossed her mind. He seemed so sad, so alone, and she shared in his grief since Amy had been her best friend. And the more time they spent together, the more Nancy realized that she had loved Rick for years, loved him for his thousand kindnesses to her and Karin, for the countless attentions he had paid to Amy, for the fact that he had been a good husband and a good man.

And to see such a man in so much pain made her discard her reservations about propriety and the proper amount of time to mourn a friend and a wife, if anyone still followed such conventions. They drifted toward each other like two boats and when they came together, each made the other stronger.

But her mistake had been to think that they had so much in common when what they had most in common was Amy, whose memory they both loved and whose loss had brought them together; Amy, who Rick still loved and would not give up.

Why else would he endanger himself and their marriage in this way? Didn't it mean anything to him that he had a wife and a daughter now, the child that he had always wanted? Nancy had given him that and could still give him children of his own. But he was willing to throw that away, along with his life, to seek the kind of vengeance that was best left to the law.

He was going to die. Nancy knew it. He was going to die and leave her and Karin alone again. He didn't care. He didn't love her. He loved Amy, a dead woman, and the only thing that would make him happy would be to die too.

Nancy wept, and her tears were cold in the night air.

"Somebody is fucking after us. Somebody has our number." Rip Withers looked at the other men in the room. The council was growing smaller. First Will Standish had turned traitor and had to be disposed of, but Sonny had gotten himself killed in the process. And now some crazy bitch had blown away Junior and nearly taken out Rip's own son.

And who was left? Ray, Yahweh love his poor dumb soul, Powder Burns, Chip Porter, and Ace Ludwig, who had become master-of-arms after Sonny's death.

"It started with that bastard Wilson Barnes," Rip said. "All he did was say our name on the air and now we're dropping like flies."

"And he said it to a fucking woman," Powder said. "Some *chick* made him give us up."

"And some chick shot Junior down too," said Rip. "Weren't you the one, Powder, who said he didn't believe in Wonder Woman? Well, maybe you better start believing. It wouldn't surprise me one bit if this is the same cunt who killed Sonny and Will's mama too."

"You believe that stuff about her getting shot and not getting hurt by it?" Powder asked, less cocky than usual.

"No. I believe there were a bunch of half-assed, panicky shooters in there who were firing at anything that moved, which is why so many damn people got hit. Karl said it was a fucking nuthouse and he never saw her get hit. Assholes just missed her, that's all. You know how people get when they panic. That's why we stress discipline.

"But she was after Junior, there's no doubt about that. He was the first she shot and she killed him hard." The phone rang and Rip snatched it up. "Yeah? He didn't come out . . . How long you wait? . . . Okay, come on back then."

Rip hung up and looked at the others. "Maybe one good

thing came out of this—a guy saved Karl's life." Rip told the others about Guy Adams and his shadowy past and how he had Karl follow the man. "He seems on the level. I told him to go to the festival over in Eau Claire tomorrow. Chip, end of the day, he'll come up to you. You just nod yes and bring him on back. But don't talk about anything important, not about the Sons at all. And make sure you're not being followed—check him for sensors and all that shit, go up his ass if you have to. I trust this guy enough to bring him here and once he's here we'll see how sincere he is. We can use another soldier. So, all agreed on bringing him in?"

The men nodded. "Sure, sure," Powder said. "But what about this bitch? How the hell does she know who we are? Barnes didn't know anybody but you, Rip."

"That's right. And he didn't even know my name. No, I suspect that she got her information from either Will or Sonny."

"Sonny would *never* turn us," Powder said. "He was a straight guy. But Will was a cocksuckin' traitor all the way. It *hadda* be him."

Rip nodded. "He probably gave her a few names before he died. Junior's anyway."

"But who the hell *is* she?" Chip Porter asked. "Some crazy mother, like you said, Rip? Out for revenge or something?"

"No way. No little mother could take Sonny with a knife or shoot Junior and then blast her way out of that show today. This slut's a professional—a one-woman government hit squad. I'm betting she'll have no identity if she's captured or killed. Goddam killing machine, that's all she is. One of Clinton's cunts."

"Hillary herself!" laughed Powder, but no one else joined in. "So what do we do about her?"

"Watch our backs, that's about it. One person working on their own—how *can* we do anything except wait until she comes after one of us again? But if I were you boys, I wouldn't go picking up any strange pussy.

"But I'll tell you what we *can* do—and what I *want* to do." Rip took a dramatic pause while he looked at each man in turn. "We can move the schedule up for the big bang. To next week."

The men looked at each other and some took deep breaths. "Are we ready for that?" Chip asked.

"We can be. Right, Powder?" Powder Burns nodded. "Way I see it," Rip went on, "if they think they're getting to us, they'll expect us to lay low, keep our heads down, not do anything except be concerned over the state of our own hides. And that's the perfect time to strike. We do that fast and hard and it's retaliation for their assassinations and the loss of our men."

"I get you," Ace Ludwig said, and Rip could see the battle lust in his eyes. "They've thrown down the fucking gauntlet so we pick it up and smash them right in the face with it, right?"

"Right."

"When are we looking at?" asked Chip.

Rip looked at Powder. "When can you be ready?"

"Well, this is Saturday . . ." Powder thought for a moment, then nodded his head slowly. "Tuesday."

"Shit, *this* Tuesday?" Chip said.

"Yeah. This Tuesday. I got enough shit, all I gotta do is put it together, but do it right, y'know? Need time to do it right."

"The bird shoot's scheduled for Monday," Ace said. "You wanta cancel it?"

"No, we'll still have it," Rip said. "The men need their fun. We'll tell them about it after the shoot."

Rip had no doubt that they would all be glad to hear it. They all knew the plan, but now at last the day was almost here. It was an ideal target, occupied by most of the major villains that threatened the principles of the Sons of a Free America: an FBI field office, a regional Office for Civil Rights, a Minority Business Development Office, and an Office of Criminal Enforcement for the Bureau of Alcohol, Tobacco, and Firearms.

All in all, Hobie, Minnesota's Floyd B. Olson Federal Building, with its four hundred and fifty government workers, was more than a worthwhile target.

twenty-eight

THE NEXT MORNING THE FRONTIER FAIRGROUNDS PARKING LOT was packed to its four hundred car capacity. People were parking in the adjoining fields and all along the road out front, and Rita and Billy Joe White, organizers of the White Christian Brotherhood festival ("Whites for the Whites" was on their letterhead) were praising their white Christian Lord for the fine turnout.

They had worked long and hard to find a place that would allow them and those like them to gather and share in their beliefs, and the Frontier Fairgrounds had the advantage of being privately owned, so there was no town council or board of supervisors to deny them their God-given rights. The man who owned Frontier just told Billy Joe and Rita that if they paid him the money and promised not to kill anybody, the place was theirs for two days and two nights.

Although it wasn't what Rita would have chosen, the fairground buildings were functional enough, with electric heat, corrugated tin sides and roofs, and good concrete floors. The tin, however, was rusty in spots and must have rusted through in a number of places on the roof, for there were puddles and streams all over the concrete floor. But praise the Lord, the sky had stopped spitting down that cold, devil's rain and it promised to be bright and sunny all day. Folks would just have to step around the puddles, that was all.

Some of the vendors had arrived the night before and some between four and eight the next morning. Most of the early birds brought RVs and slept in them on the grounds, as did many of the attendees.

The first and largest building was the meeting hall. This was where the speakers would give their addresses and where the featured musicians would play in the evening. It seated well over a thousand, and Rita and Billy Joe expected it to be filled much of the day.

The second building was the exhibition room, with all the vendors' displays. Anything could be sold except guns, for which the Whites couldn't get a license. It was just as well, since that big gun show the day before over in Hobie had surely been visited by the devil, and the devil in this case had been a woman.

Rita wasn't surprised though. She had always said that guns and half-naked women were Satan's mix, and that was why whenever Billy Joe went to a gun show, Rita always went with him, to keep him company and out of the hands of those whores who worked in some of the booths. In the hands of the Lord's servants, guns could be a real blessing, but Rita didn't for the life of her understand why they had to have harlots show-ing them off along with their boobies.

But though there were no guns at the festival, there were plenty of books on them, along with lots of books on pure Christianity (none of that liberal, Billy Graham stuff, as Rita said), the dangers of race mixing and faggotry, the *Protocols of the Elders of Zion*, and plenty of tables selling *The Turner Diaries*, Billy Joe's favorite book next to the Bible. Rita had tried to read it but hadn't liked all the violence.

At eight A.M. Rita and Billy Joe were strolling up and down the aisles of the exhibit room, greeting all their friends and a lot of good folks they didn't know but welcomed as brothers and sisters in White Christian Brotherhood. Billy Joe, in keeping with the occasion, had foregone his usual camouflage and was wearing a freshly pressed dark green suit, his only concession to the private militia he headed an olive beret and a necktie with a cross and American flag design. Rita had seen to it that his gray-white beard had been carefully trimmed, along with his nose hairs.

Rita had on a dirndl dress with puffed sleeves, lace trim, and a bodice that she thought was a wee bit too tight but which Billy Joe and every other red-blooded American male never failed to compliment her on. Her hair was the crowning touch, a bouffant that both invited and forbade touching, like a beautiful soufflé so dainty a breath would destroy it. Still, Rita wasn't worried. She had used plenty of hair spray.

Before too long Billy Joe got into a nice conversation with a man selling Nazi memorabilia and books debunking the so-called Holocaust while Rita "just rattled away," as she put it, to a woman and her husband staffing a Ku Klux Klan recruitment booth. The place was full of booths for various militias, church denominations, and white supremacist groups, but there was much more available.

T-shirts, bumper stickers, and mesh caps were in abundance, all of them with anti-government or anti-mongrel sayings and logos. A lot of them had been around forever and had lost their humor for Rita, but one that she hadn't seen before was a T-shirt with a hook-nosed man hanging by his neck from the Nike swoosh. It read, "Just Do It," but NIKE had been replaced by KIKE. Rita had to chuckle. Billy Joe bought one of the shirts but the message wasn't quite subtle enough for Rita's tastes. She wasn't much of a T-shirt wearer anyway. She liked buttons.

There were computer-oriented booths showing how to set up your own website (Rita's nephew ran the site they had—she didn't know a thing about those computers) and a lot of CD and tape booths, selling everything from old-fashioned gospel to white power country to this new skinhead music.

Rita was surprised to see a lot more skinheads than usual, even as early as it was. She didn't like the way they dressed and their music was just awful to listen to, but they were always nice and polite to her and Billy Joe, and an awful lot of full-fledged patriots started out as skinheads. They did get into their fights but it was always with each other or the niggers or the sodomites, so that was all right. Boys would be boys.

A short whoop of feedback made Rita cover her ears and look up at the raised stage at the end of the exhibit building. That was where the lesser-known bands would play throughout the day to entertain the vendors and their customers. Everybody got a ballot with the bands' names so they could vote for who they thought was best, and the winner would get to play a set on the main stage before Wild White West, the nationally known country rock band that would close out the day's festivities.

The first competitor was setting up. Rita saw a banjo and a mandolin and was sorry she'd have to miss it, but it was already eight forty-five and the Sunday morning service next door started in fifteen minutes. Then all of a sudden the whole room seemed to get a little quieter and Rita looked up toward the main entrance to see who had come in.

Most of the women attending were with their husbands or boyfriends, but there were a few unescorted females. They were mostly tough, no-sass country girls, not that there was anything *funny* about them, like that horrible Ellen person on the godless television networks. They would find menfolk to take care of them soon enough, just like the Bible said, while those homos would go to hell sooner or later where they would burn forever with the Jews and the Clintons.

Still, Rita White didn't think she had ever seen a woman like the one who was now walking in alone through the main entrance. She was dressed all in black, almost like a motorcycle rider, and had on glasses that were tinted just enough to hide her eyes. She wasn't a skinhead—she looked a little too old for that—yet she had that swagger that so many of them had.

A lot of eyes turned to follow her as she came in, but she didn't seem to notice. One skinhead, probably ten years younger than the woman, walked up to her and though Rita couldn't hear what they were saying, she got the general idea from the way the boy's smile changed to a frown and his cheeks reddened as he walked away. "Whatever he's sellin'," she told Billy Joe, who had also noticed, "she ain't buyin'."

Well, Rita didn't have the time to watch any more young pups try to impress the mystery lady. It was getting on nine and the Reverend Johnny Harkins's keynote address was something she didn't want to miss. Now there was a man who knew his Bible.

Amy thought that if Dorothy Standish's trailer had been a den where monsters were bred, this was the college where they were trained. What appalled her most was the seeming normality of the people who walked through the narrow aisles and sat behind the tables selling hate. It seemed to her as though she could as easily have been at a craft fair or the Arts on the Square that was held every June in Hobie.

These people were smiling and happy, laughing and waving to each other and hugging when they met and shaking hands like an insurance salesman trying to double your coverage. Some even had their children with them. Boys and girls as young as five or six were wearing T-shirts with stomach-turning words of hate on them, and little caps with white supremacist symbols. A few were even sporting swastikas.

For the most part the children seemed well-behaved, although Amy saw one incident that made her flesh crawl. A mother and father were moving through an aisle but their kindergarten age daughter was lagging behind. The mother took a swipe at the girl, slapping her on the side of the head and knocking her to her knees in one of the puddles of water that dotted the floor.

The girl immediately jumped up and hit her mother in the chest as hard as she could. With that, the mother grabbed the child by her long hair and dragged her toward the father, who seemed embarrassed by the whole thing. The girl burst into tears, her mother released her, and she ran toward the door, the father following, then the mother, shaking her head.

"That's the way," a man called after the mother. "Don't take that from them. Bring them up right." Then he chuckled and turned back to the grinning salesman of survival foods to whom he had been talking.

Jesus. It was no wonder the kid hit back when she had been

taught that hitting was what you did when you got mad. Amy wanted to run outside and show the woman what hitting was really all about, wanted to hit her and her dumb redneck husband so hard that both their necks snapped and their stupid brains smashed open against the pavement.

But she kept her temper. She was here for *her* children, not for these poor little creatures who were destined to grow up and become the beasts their parents were making them. And those like Amy would have to fight their own battles against the hate-filled brutes that were being created. These *parents* weren't fit to bear the name, she thought. They were only monsters that bred more of their own kind.

In Thailand, Amy had read, parents sometimes prostituted their own children, and the government, which seemed to profit from the child-sex tourism trade, tacitly approved. Amy had joined a boycott, vowing not to purchase Thai goods until the government did everything within its power to stop the horrible practice.

But it seemed that Thailand was not the only country where parents turned their children into something unspeakable. If Amy had had anything in her stomach, she could have brought it up then and there.

But she did not. She had neither eaten nor slept since her advent back into the world. She hungered solely for revenge and the only sleep she longed for was that unending rest that would be hers when she had satisfied not only her own soul, but the souls of the children, with the deaths of their killers.

Today she had a chance to feed the fire of vengeance that burned within her until she could finally enter the den itself and find those responsible—Powder Burns, Rip Withers, and whoever else had helped them, supported them, been a son of a warped and twisted "free" America. And then she would let that flame grow until it devoured them and her in one white burst of light.

But today it was Chip Porter's turn. Chip Porter of Shoktrupz. And when she found him, it would be time to rock and roll.

First, however, it was time to pay and pray as Amy learned

when she went to the building where the Sunday service was just starting. She doubted if she would get any leads on the Sons of a Free America from the speakers, but she couldn't cruise the booths all day. Besides, after the gun show, she was damn sick of dealers' booths, and if anyone had been at the fracas yesterday, she didn't want them to see her, even with a different look, in an environment that could jar their memory.

Of course, there was a big difference between a redhead in black leather, shorts, and a halter, and a brunette in denim, even if it was so dark a blue as to appear almost black. Levinson's wife must have outgrown her denim phase too, which was lucky for Amy, who needed to replace her shredded black clothes. She had found a brown blouse to wear under the jacket and felt fairly confident that this outfit would not be chewed to pieces by bullets, not today.

Taking to heart what Levinson had said, Amy had determined that there would be no gunplay here, at least not on her part. Her knife was strapped to her ankle, and she would use it to kill Chip Porter unless she could find a better way.

Then the Reverend Johnny Harkins of the Church of White Christian Brotherhood was introduced by Rita White, the founder of this hate feast. Harkins fit the mold perfectly, with a gravity-defying pompadour whose dark and solid color had come out of a bottle. Amy thought it didn't look as much like hair as it did a shellacked armadillo.

Harkins offered a prayer calling for universal peace, which seemed holy enough, until he added that he would prefer to see that peace achieved by the destruction of all races but the white one and all faiths but the true faith of the Lord. He also prayed for the rapid destruction of homosexuals, fornicators, race traitors, tyrants, which he quickly defined as liberals, and those leaders who would impose any laws other than the biblical laws of Moses.

Then he called for an offering. Needless to say, Amy was not in a giving mood. But not wanting to tip her hand, she dropped a dollar into the plate.

After the good reverend had finished his prayer, he preached a sermon even more spiteful, always being careful, however, not to inspire his listeners to any actual violence, "lest there be persons among us who belong to Satan and not the Lord and who would go to the authorities in the cowardly and Jew-like spirit in which those who hated Jesus bore false witness against him to the authorities of their own time."

Yeah, Amy thought. When it comes to you, pal, put me on the side of Satan. But don't worry, I wouldn't turn you in—I'd hate to miss the pleasure of killing you myself.

The sermon finally ended and the congregation sang a hymn that everyone seemed to know, but which Amy had never heard. The last few lines were:

With thy help we'll take our stand
To make our home a white man's land.
So preserve us in our fight
For all that's holy, true, and white.

Amy could not shake off her feeling of amazement that there were people in the world who could believe these things, who could hate this way, who could use a vital and uplifting concept like faith to drag people down to such a brute level. Amy had been raised a Lutheran and she and Rick had always attended church regularly. But never had she heard the gospel of love used to rationalize hate, and try as she would, Amy could imagine no deeper sin.

It was that certainty of right, she thought, absolute right, that had driven the killers of herself and her children. This was where it started, where it was nourished, and where today it was going to stop for Chip Porter. If the wages of sin were death, today was payday.

After Harkins's rant was finished, a gospel quartet came up. The two men wore white jackets and the two women white dresses, and they sang very white songs that danced completely around the black gospel tradition. The lyrics were in keeping with the occasion, about how we would all stand around the great white throne and give praise to the great white lord. There was another real crowd pleaser whose refrain included the words:

Watching them burn (oh, yes Lord!)
Watching them writhe and twist and turn (oh Lord!)
From our home up in the sky,
We will watch those sinners fry.
As the fires of hell leap high,
We're watching them burn! (Praise the Lord!)

As Amy sat and listened to the songs, the words, the laughter and the praise of some hideous, spiteful god that had never been hers, she began to hate these people. The lessons she had learned about love were forgotten and David Levinson's cautionary words along with them. She had intended to creep up on Chip Porter in some hidden place, behind his van or at the back of the makeshift stage, and tell him who she was and then cut his throat.

But no longer. Now she wanted everyone there to see how these dark wages were paid.

Watching them burn . . . Maybe it was possible.

twenty-nine

IT WAS EARLY AFTERNOON WHEN RICK CARLISLE ARRIVED IN
Eau Claire. He had left the Excelsior Hotel at six in the morning,
unable to sleep for more than a few hours on the lumpy and
odoriferous bed, and had walked to the outskirts of Hobie, where
he started trying to hitch a ride, something he hadn't done since
his college days. He didn't think he was being observed but he
wasn't about to take a chance on retrieving his car.

Hitching seemed harder than it had been when he was
younger. He had to walk several miles before a trucker finally
picked him up who would take him as far as St. Paul. He made
Eau Claire in a series of short hops and every time it took a little longer to get a ride.

But finally he saw the sign for the Frontier Fairgrounds and
asked his driver, an Eau Claire businessman who was coming
back from a visit to Minneapolis, to let him off. The man's
jovial personality changed instantly, dropping several degrees
toward chilliness. "You going to that thing? That festival?"

"Yes, sir."

"You don't seem like the type."

"Well, I just have to meet someone there."

The man nodded as if he thought Rick was lying, and the
sour expression stayed on his face as he drove straight away.
They had had a nice conversation up until then.

Rick paid the five-dollar admission fee at the door and was handed a White Christian Brotherhood button which he was told to wear at all times. "It lets you in this building here and the one next door where all the speeches are," said a gaunt and raw-boned cashier, who Rick thought looked like a misplaced Okie. "And that ballot there lets you vote for the best band that plays in here. Mind the puddles now."

The place made him sick. The ignorance and the hate was palpable in the huge metal barn of a room. Nevertheless, he bought a hot dog, his only meal of the day so far, and sat alone at one of the picnic tables by the snack bar.

At the other end of the room on a raised stage made of wooden and metal risers, a country band was playing and a dozen people were standing around listening. The lyrics were hard to make out over the twangy guitars and when he was able to comprehend a few of them, Rick was glad he couldn't hear more. Christ, he ought to just turn this whole damn bunch in to the police—or to some mental institution.

He read the ballot while he chewed his rubbery hot dog and saw *Shoktrupz* among the alphabetically listed band names. When he finished his rough meal, he returned to the ghost of Tom Joad and asked him if he knew when Shoktrupz was going to play. The man pointed to a handwritten poster on the wall.

Shoktrupz wasn't scheduled to hit the makeshift stage until four o'clock. Shit, that meant three more hours of listening to this crap or going next door for the speeches. Rick sighed and started drifting down the aisles between the tables, trying not to look too closely at what was being sold.

Amy sat patiently listening to everything, letting the music and the prayers and the speeches and the sermons brand her already burned soul, letting their hate feed her own. But at last she could bear no more and had to get a breath of fresh air.

She walked outside and around the back of the building. Behind the fairgrounds were acres of farmland. There under the cloudy sky on the wooden rail fence that divided a field of dry corn stalks from the buildings sat the Crow.

Amy knew it was her Crow. Its feathers were unruffled by the slight breeze that blew coldly through the dead corn, making a sound like whispering children. It watched her dead-on and she walked slowly toward it, afraid that her approach might make it fly away. She did not think that she would scare it, for it did not seem capable of fear.

It seemed, rather, like some divine mystery that would not deign to let mortals, even resurrected ones, approach too closely for fear of letting them see too far beyond the veil, into the mind of . . . what? God? Or something else?

Yet the bird did not fly as she approached and soon only a few feet separated them. "*Is* it God?" she asked softly, but the Crow did not move. "Or is it the devil? What are you? Who sent you? Who gave you the power to give to *me*?"

There was still no response. Amy smiled and said, "'Prophet still, if bird or devil.' But that was Poe's *raven*, wasn't it? Not a crow." She thought for a moment, looking into the deep black beads of the Crow's eyes. "Bird or devil," she repeated. "Or bird . . . *and* devil." She touched her breast and said to the Crow what she had once said to God in prayers: "Use me as you will."

The Crow's beak slowly opened, and Amy could almost hear a word or the beginning of a thought in her head, when suddenly something flew from over her shoulder and brushed the right wing of the Crow. It rose into the air in a rush of black feathers, then whirled and vanished amidst the corn.

Amy jerked her head around and saw, ten yards away, a hatless skinhead in a long military coat. He was tossing a second rock up and down in his hand. "Thought it was gonna peck you," he said with a broken-toothed grin. "And I didn't think that was the kind of pecker a woman like you would want."

She didn't reply but held her face expressionless, with just the hint of a smile for the fool who approached her.

"I saw you leave," the skinhead said, chucking the rock over his shoulder. "Looked like you were gonna take a little walk and I thought maybe you wanted a good strong Aryan man to accompany you." He nodded toward the cornfield where the

Crow had disappeared. "Some of the wildlife can get pretty dangerous."

"I like . . . the wild life," Amy said.

"I thought you might. You don't look like a lot of those other chicks in there, into the whole God thing, keeping it until you're married and all. You look like you're into this whole scene more for the fun of it."

"What kind of fun?" she asked, leaning back on the fence in as sluttish a pose as she could imagine, and tossing her head so that her hair shimmered in the pale light.

"Well, of course there's kicking the shit out of niggers and faggots, which is fun." He laughed almost self-consciously, which puzzled Amy. "But there's also Adam-and-Eve fun. That's in the Bible too. And the Song of Solomon. Like, sex?"

Amy nodded. "I like sex. But boy, you're not gonna find it in there with all those holy rollers, those women wearing white, buttoned up to their necks."

"Yeah, pretty tight-assed. But when I saw you, I thought now there's a woman looks like she accepts her God-given body and knows how to have fun with it, am I right?"

Amy had had enough of this shit. She knew what she was after and how to get it. "So do you wanta talk all day or do you wanta fuck?"

The skinhead's jaw dropped for a moment and then he smiled what he must have thought was his studly smile. "Fucking sounds real good."

Amy nodded toward the field. "I want to do it out there."

"Huh?" He looked surprised. "It's pretty damn wet . . . and *cold*."

"I'll warm you up. And my nipples get *real* hard in the cold. Besides, the corn stalks have dried out, and we can bend them down. Make our own cozy bed." She licked her lips. "I want to hear them rustle and crackle as we do it . . . if you're not afraid of the wildlife."

He snorted a laugh. "Shit, no." Then he looked back toward the building. "But you know, I got a pickup with a cap . . ."

"Forget it," Amy said, starting to walk past him toward the buildings. "If you're not man enough . . ."

He grabbed her arm and whipped her around to face him, and she almost lost it then. But here out in the open wouldn't be good, even if no one was watching. You never knew who'd come through the door. And this asshole was just an appetizer for the main event, just a way for her to vent some of the hatred she felt for these holy monsters and the frustration at not being able to do anything about them.

"I'll show you who's man enough, missy," he said sneering down at her, trying the ape-man thing. *Missy?* Jesus. "Come on."

Keeping hold of her arm, he led her to the fence and helped her climb over into the rows of corn stalks taller than their heads. Before long they had passed from the sight of anyone watching from the buildings.

The ground was muddy but the cold had hardened and dried it in spots. After about fifty yards the skinhead came to a dead stop. "Fuck this corn stuff," he said, "and fuck you." He pulled back the front of his coat and unzipped his fly, taking out his penis. "Now get on your knees and get to work."

Amy looked at the small and shriveled penis peeking through his fingers, then back up at the man's face. "Is it the cold," she asked, "or is that just the way it normally is?"

The skinhead drew back his hand to slap her, but when he swung his arm she grasped the hand as if in a steel vise and squeezed. She was rewarded with the sound of cracking finger bones and a high-pitched squeal.

Instantly she let go and smashed both her palms against the skinhead's mouth. The blow knocked him backward and he fell, Amy riding him to the ground. He struck hard so that thick gobbets of mud flew up on either side of him, missing Amy. She crouched on his stomach, her hands still over his mouth, and pressed down, pushing his shaven head downward into the thick, sodden earth.

His eyes rolled at her but she continued to push, and slowly the mud covered the back of his head, his ears, and was up to his temples when there was a noise over her shoulder of crackling and rustling cornstalks. She looked and there behind her was the Crow, its claws clinging to a cornstalk, swaying in the breeze. But its feathers never moved.

Amy looked back at the prone man and saw that his eyes were staring in horror at the Crow. "It all started," Amy said, "when you threw stones at the birds when you were a little boy. And you've been throwing them ever since."

Then she pushed one final time and the head went slowly under the earth, so that mud filled the hollows of his eyes and seeped into his nostrils, and only Amy's wrists remained above the surface of the ground.

The skinhead's body kicked and spasmed beneath her, but was soon still. And when she pulled her hands out of the mud and stood up, she saw that urine was dribbling pitifully from the man's still-exposed penis. That too soon stopped and the man lay there, his head buried, his body sprawled in the mud.

"A time to sow and a time to reap," said Amy, looking at the Crow. It cawed once, but Amy heard no sense in the sound other than perhaps a cry of triumph colored with a note of regret.

And why regret, she wondered. Regret for what this dead man might once have been? Or regret for Amy, for one who was once so full of love and now lived for vengeance?

"It doesn't matter, does it?" Amy asked the Crow, and the bird rose again, flying back toward the fairgrounds. Yes, it was time to go back there where there was more work to be done. She felt tired, but it was not a physical tiredness as much as a weariness of the spirit. More work to be done. Many to die. Miles to go before she slept the good sleep.

thirty

AMY USED THE END OF THE SKINHEAD'S LONG COAT TO WIPE OFF what little dirt had gotten on her clothing; then she walked back through the corn. There was a faucet outside and she washed the dirt off her hands and wrists. No one came around to the back of the building while she washed and she thought that maybe God was on her side after all. Something was. Maybe it was just the Crow.

She decided not to listen to more speeches. Her ears already felt as though they had been syringed with strychnine. According to the schedule, it would be another half hour before Shoktrupz, Chip Porter's band, would play. She decided to go and watch them set up.

Amy saw Rick within seconds of coming in the door. His back was partially to her but she could see the side of his face. Her immediate response was exaltation and in that instant she knew that it was no use denying that she still loved him.

But a second later she stepped back around a pegboard that one of the vendors had set up to hang his caps and sweatshirts. From that safer viewpoint she suppressed the urge to go to him, and let the logic of the predator take over, asking herself the obvious questions.

Why was he there? It almost seemed as though he were fol-lowing her. Had he somehow gotten a lead on Porter? Or was he just fishing, sniffing for clues, as she had assumed he was yesterday?

But Eau Claire was pretty damned far afield to be searching at random. She had spoken to Levinson of synchronicity and maybe that was the cause here. Maybe something *wanted* them together.

But she dismissed that thought as quickly as it came. No one would want the dead and the living together for any longer than it took to . . . well, to do what she was doing, to put the wrong things right. Maybe he had been brought here for another reason, to help Amy somehow.

She nearly laughed at her own fancies. It was remarkable how she had changed, seeing cosmic significance in what before she would have accepted as coincidence, no matter how bizarre. But that, of course, was before she had been brought back to life from sundered pieces of herself by a large black bird. After such an occurrence, what was impossible?

Amy remained sheltered behind the pegboard, pretending to be interested in the religious books on display in the next stand, until she saw Rick get up and move toward the stage. She stepped into the aisle to watch him and saw that he was greeting a man with hair just a quarter inch away from being a pure skinhead. He had an electric bass strapped around his neck and Amy recognized him as Chip Porter from the picture on his website.

Rick didn't shake hands with him but just went up and said something. Porter nodded his head up and down and smiled, then said a few words to Rick, and gestured toward the wall beyond which was the parking lot. Then Rick said something else and turned to walk back down the aisle toward her.

Amy ducked behind the pegboard, crossed over to the other aisle, and waited until Rick passed. When he did, she followed him until he went outside. Then she counted to a hundred and went through the door.

He was already far down the road, walking toward Eau Claire. Amy could make out an assortment of buildings and lights a mile or so away, maybe a strip mall. That was good. She was glad he was going. She wanted to do this on her own.

Still, she couldn't help wonder what Rick had talked to Porter about. At least it seemed to indicate that he wasn't just fishing. He had somehow contacted one or more of the Sons of a Free America and was closing in just the way she was. She only hoped she could get there first and keep him out of danger.

Now she went back inside and stood at the back of several rows of metal folding chairs that had been set up for people to relax and watch the bands. Most of the skinhead contingent seemed to have gathered for Shoktrupz's set. There were about fifty of the breed, posturing and preening for each other. Amy was the only woman around.

One of them eyed her and came over. She got ready to make a ball-busting crack but the young man only said, "Hey, you seen my buddy Pete around?"

"Pete?"

"Yeah. He said he was gonna go outside and talk to you a while ago."

She chuckled. "Oh, he came outside all right, but I think I kind of put him down. He can't take much teasing, can he?"

Dead Pete's friend looked confused. "Well, uh, no, I guess not. Did he say where he was goin'?"

"Just something about a corn roast. That make any sense?"

The skinhead shook his head again. "Okay, well, thanks. Um, you doin' anything later?"

Amy smiled. "Sorry. I have plans."

The young man nodded, rather politely in contrast to his friend Pete's brusqueness, and went back to the safety of the other skinheads. Amy wondered how long he would look for Pete. She was damn sure they wouldn't go into the muddy cornfield in search of him. No, the first time old Pete would come to light would probably be next spring when a plow turned him over.

Amy turned her attention to the stage. The band was nearly finished setting up. In addition to Porter on bass, there was a lead guitarist, a rhythm guitarist, and a drummer, who had painted the band's name on his bass drum with a lighting bolt providing the final *Z*. So original, Amy thought.

They all had shades on, even though the fluorescent strip lights hanging from the ceiling were far from blinding, and wore metal bands with studs on their wrists. Porter and the lead guitarist had added what looked to Amy like spiked metal dog collars around their necks.

The drummer wore black leather pants and a ripped T-shirt with *White the Power* scrawled across the chest in laundry pen. The lead guitarist's scalp was painted in alternating red and black stripes from front to back like a multitude of Mohawks, and he wore a black leather vest with no shirt underneath, despite the November weather. Maybe his tattoos were insulated, Amy thought.

The rhythm guitarist sported pegged jeans and a sleeveless gray sweatshirt that displayed a massive set of biceps, and Porter had on a denim work shirt heavy with slogan buttons, and a pair of black jeans. The overall look seemed to strike the right chord for their sympathetic audience, who stood or sat, ready to comment favorably on each bit of instrument tuning or thrown away drum riff.

At last the rhythm guitarist stepped to the microphone and said, "We're Shoktrupz, spelled S-H-O-K-T-R-U-P-Z!" The skinheads yelled, applauded, and spelled along. "And we hope you like what you hear. If ya do, vote for us to play in the main room tonight. If ya don't . . ." He took a brief pause. "Then yer a Jew nigger faggot. Hit it!"

There followed twenty minutes of the most cretinous music Amy had ever heard, a combination of garage band, punk, and metal, with the worst qualities of each. Surprisingly, though, the language was fairly circumspect. There were no coarse sexual words used, no *goddams* or *shits* or *Christs* or *asses*.

But there were numerous references to Jews and niggers and faggots, as might have been expected by the spokesman's opening remarks. There was a power ballad about the white man being the

One against the many,
Light against the darkness,
Fire against the icy grip of night . . .

Amy thought she counted night-white-light-fight rhymes ten times in as many minutes.

But the real mind twister was when goon-boy said, "Here's our theme song—'White the Power!'" Then to the screams and cheers of their devotees, they launched into a *rap*, an out-and-out rip-off of Public Enemy's "Fight the Power," in which they chanted, "White's the power . . . white's the power, be free!"

That people who hated blacks so much would use a decade-old black power anthem and art form to express that hate only proved incontrovertibly to Amy that they had shit where their brains ought to be. The idiots would have been more racially pure if they had written an oratorio.

Still, their intended audience ate it up, chanting along, shaking their fists in the air, and pogo-ing up and down, at first disregarding the fact that three times out of four they came down in puddles of standing rainwater and then delighting in the fact. In the midst of this action Amy made her way to the side of the stage and gave a once-over to the band's setup and equipment. She liked what she saw and she hoped the current popularity would bring Shoktrupz to the main stage.

She didn't have much to worry about. After the song was over and the set was done, the skinheads passed around pens and pencils, filling out the ballots and dropping them into the box at the front of the room. "You're gonna *win*, man!" dozens of skinheads assured them.

"Hardly nobody's been votin'," said one skinhead, "and when they do it's in like twos and threes for the ones they just seen. But you guys got a *block*, man!"

By the time Shoktrupz had packed their gear and taken it to their van, only three people were left in the stage area: a teenage brother and sister who sang gospel duets to the accompaniment of the boy's acoustic guitar, and their mother. Amy figured they were no competition.

The ballots would be counted at six. That meant that she had an hour and a half to check out the main stage and go and get what she needed to make Shoktrupz's appearance something to remember.

• • •

Rick Carlisle was sitting in a booth in the Neptune Diner, looking out the window at the road. In front of him was a plate of meat loaf, mashed potatoes, and corn that had cost him $5.95 and that he was devouring hungrily. He was keeping an eye on the road on the off chance that he'd spot either Rip Withers's pickup or the sedan young Karl was driving, though he still hadn't seen anyone tailing him by car or on foot.

Nevertheless, if one of those two vehicles pulled into the Neptune's parking lot, Rick intended to get up, drop a ten on the table, and walk out. If anybody asked, he had had a cup of coffee, all he could afford.

But nobody came or asked and he relaxed, enjoying his meal, watching the occasional car pass by. Once he saw a low, slightly boxy black car flash by, a model that he couldn't recall seeing in years. A professor had used it as an example in one of Rick's design courses. He tried to remember the name and finally came up with it—an Avanti. He was surprised there were any still on the road. That style had to date from the sixties.

So when he saw it returning, traveling in the opposite direction fifteen minutes later, he looked more closely. Though he had only a split second to see the driver of the fast car, a shock went through him as he saw Amy's face in profile.

At first he didn't believe it, then he *knew* it was her, and then he didn't believe it again. By a stretch of the imagination, he could imagine her, if she really had somehow come back, tracing the Sons of a Free America to the White Christian Brotherhood festival, but driving a classic sports car? Couldn't she just *fly* or transport herself somehow?

God, no. This was ridiculous, just ridiculous. It wasn't Amy at all, it *couldn't* be. The voice on the radio, the figure at the window, the woman at the gun show—all these things had to have some rational explanation short of his wife returning from the dead. He had just projected Amy into and onto all of these occurrences because he so much *wanted* her to be alive.

That had to be it. It was easier to think that he was going a little bit insane than it was to really accept the fact that she had somehow been resurrected. He smiled bitterly at his reflection in the window. He had to be careful and keep his sanity intact.

Otherwise he'd be seeing Amy everywhere.

thirty-one

AS PEOPLE GOT SETTLED FOR DR. GARY SKELTON'S SPEECH AND the evening concert, Rita White felt as if she was walking with the Lord. That was what she called it when everything was going right and that was certainly the case today.

Attendance had been grand, the response had been overwhelmingly positive, and all the people were so nice, even those skinhead boys. Rita was mildly disappointed, however, that their band had won the contest and would be playing here in the main building following Dr. Skelton's speech and before the Wild White West's concert. But they had won fair and square. Next festival, she thought, maybe they'd have a panel of judges instead.

"I hope that you and Dr. Skelton won't be too put off by the rock and roll," Rita told Mrs. Skelton, who was sitting next to her in their reserved metal folding chairs in the front row. Dr. Gary Skelton was the most eloquent and persuasive speaker Rita had ever met in the movement. In fact, tonight Billy Joe was going to introduce him by saying that if you gave him an hour, he could have talked Martin Luther Coon into lynching himself.

But Dr. Skelton was also gentlemanly, and Rita didn't know how he was going to like these Storm Troopers, or whatever their name was, with their loud drums and guitars and their yelling their rhymes. It could be a long half hour.

"I only wish," Rita went on, "that one of those nice gospel or country groups would have won."

Mrs. Skelton shook her head to dismiss Rita's concerns. "No, it's quite all right. Like Gary always says, times change, and if you don't get the young people involved, in twenty years we'll all just be a bunch of old dinosaurs everybody will laugh at. That's why I'm glad to see these young men play." Mrs. Skelton looked back at the crowd. "And I'm glad too that so many good parents have brought their children along. It's never too early to learn the truth about the direction the Lord wants us to take."

Suddenly the song "You've Got to Be Carefully Taught" started playing on the P.A. system. "Well," said Mrs. Skelton, "a sign from heaven!" Both women laughed. "That's from a show, isn't it?"

"*South Pacific,*" said Rita. "You know, that would have been really good if it hadn't been for that part about that Navy man falling in love with that South Seas girl."

"Mmm." Mrs. Skelton nodded. "Yellow or brown, a nigger *is* still a nigger and has no business being with a white man." She chuckled. "The ironic thing is that that song was written to criticize people with our views, and I think Rodgers and that Jew Hammerstein would roll over in their graves if they knew that we can take it quite *seriously.*"

"You're right," Rita agreed. "You are so right, it's all true—kids *do* have to be carefully taught while they're still little."

"Mmm, before the system of ZOG gets ahold of them and teaches them the opposite of everything that's right."

"And that's why I say thank the Lord," Rita rattled on, "that nearly all of the parents here home school or send their children to those good little private schools that teach the principles of White Christian Brotherhood."

"They'll be the leaders of tomorrow," Mrs. Skelton said so proudly that it made Rita proud too.

She smiled and looked up at the stage where Billy Joe was fiddling with the lectern, trying to get it to the right height for his introduction. At least he and Dr. Skelton were the same height, tall, fine-looking men.

Behind Billy Joe the skinhead band was getting themselves

ready for their part of the concert. They seemed really excited and happy and Rita thought they would probably be just fine after all since their hearts were in the right place and since Mrs. Skelton thought they were okay.

She looked back over the crowd and was delighted to see that the room was filling up so fast. The seats were all taken or saved with coats, and folks were starting to stand along the sides and in the back. It was going to be a real party, a true celebration of white brotherhood and superiority.

After a few more minutes Billy Joe tapped the mike and called for attention. He thanked everyone for coming and said that since it was so successful they'd have another festival real soon, and everyone cheered. Then he apologized for all the water on the floor and made a little joke about the festival scaring the pee out of all the niggers so watch your step. Rita thought it wasn't in very good taste but the crowd laughed and moaned at the thought of stepping in nigger pee.

Then Billy Joe introduced Dr. Skelton, and to his joke about Martin Luther Coon, he added "or he could talk Bill Clinton into being faithful to Hillary" and that got a good laugh too. No doubt about it, Rita thought proudly, her man knew how to work a crowd.

Then Dr. Skelton came to the microphone and gave a masterful speech that had everyone clapping and shouting *amen!* after nearly every sentence. Rita would have entrusted her sacred soul to that man.

He talked about the shining city on the hill, a pure white Christian America where all men were brothers, a paradise on earth to prepare us for that paradise in heaven, a country governed by the Mosaic laws given by the Lord, where adulterers and homosexuals and witches would be stoned to death, "and that pretty much takes care of the current administration," he added in one of his few jokes.

When he was finished, after calling for all of them to keep their faith strong and fight for what was right by whatever means necessary, he sat down beside his wife to thunderous applause and a standing ovation that lasted five minutes, during which he got up and bowed several times.

At last Billy Joe got back up on the stage and quieted down the crowd. "And now," he said, "we get into the musical portion of our evening's festivities! A little later we've got the greatest country band anywhere on the face of the earth, Wild White West!" The crowd went crazy and Billy Joe waited them out. "But first we've got a real treat for you youngsters, the winner of our band contest today, a young white power group from, well, these boys don't like to say where they're from, for fear that the forces of ZOG will hunt 'em down and steal their *git-tar* strings! But they're here for us tonight. Are you ready to rock and roll?"

The crowd, even the older members, roared and Billy Joe shouted into the mike, "Then give a loud White Christian Brotherhood welcome to Shock Troopers!"

The band hit the stage like Hitler taking Poland. They slammed out a series of power chords that rattled the tin walls and roof, and Chip Porter felt his dick grow hard with the thrill of playing to so many people. There had to be nearly fifteen hundred in here tonight.

With the first notes, their fellow skinheads mobbed the area directly beneath the stage, some of them dragging along girls they had met during the day, turning the eight feet between the first row of chairs and the stage into a mosh pit. Some leaned on the front of the stage, moving their shaven heads up and down in rhythm while others stood bouncing, grinning, and laughing. Chip had to laugh too. From where he stood the rhythmically moving bald heads looked like a bunch of bobbing ass cheeks.

Billy started singing then, launching into "Sailors on a Sea of Blood" with more raw guts than Chip had ever heard before. The amps sounded diamond sharp, with none of those shrieking highs or gutbucket lows that you got from cheap, modern solid-state crap. Uh-uh, these were *tube* amps, man, old-fashioned shitkickers from the days of yore. Shoktrupz's music was today all the way, but the sound technology was motherfucking *roots*.

And also motherfucking cheap. Billy's dad had used these amps back in the sixties when they were the only Ku Klux Klan–associated country-western band north of Tennessee. Chip had played with the amps and tweaked them into near perfection so that they could afford their axes, and it was damn well worth every hour he had sweated and slaved over them. If there was one thing their fans loved, it was their *sound*. And now, tonight, they were the big deal, with no keeping the volume down for the dainty-eared shits in the vendors building. Now they could let it rip, and they did.

> *We ain't gonna rest till we smash 'em in the mud,*
> *We're sailors on a sea of blood! . . .*
> *We'll stand alone against the flood! . . .*
> *We'll buy our freedom with our blood!*

The first number finished with a flourish of faux gunfire from Kurt's tom-tom and the others went down on their knees, White Christian soldiers sacrificing their lives for the cause.

Then, with a huge four count—POW! POW! POW! POW!—they rose with each beat until they were on their feet again and slashed their way into "White Blood, Black Blood," snarling out the lyrics:

> *White blood, black blood, they ain't the same!*
> *To us it's a crusade, to them it's a game!*
> *True blood, Jew blood, they ain't the same.*
> *We're true believers—they'll die in our flames!*

Chip didn't think they had ever sounded so good. Billy's voice was like an angel's coming down from heaven, totally pissed off, sword in hand, ready to kill. Kurt's drums were pounding and sizzling at the same time, fire and cannons, and Sandy's lead guitar was saying everything that they couldn't get into their lyrics.

Chip felt newborn. He had seen good crowds before but nothing where it had all come together like this. Even the old farts seemed to be digging them. Hell, most of them were standing up—the whole damn house on its feet. Little kids were scooting down the side aisles and pressing forward and the skinheads were letting them in, even putting some of them up on their shoulders to grab their shiny domes and get the best seats in the house.

The babes were loving it too and Chip figured he could pretty well have his pick. He really had his eye on that more mature-looking chick in black or dark blue who had checked out their first gig at four. She was working her way through the crowd, sliding around toward the side of the stage, probably wanted to be there when they finished. Helluva good-looking woman, and that dark getup she had on looked cool, a little dangerous.

He looked away from her, getting his attention back to the music. It was such a trip, maybe the start of a whole new thing for him and the guys. Yeah, maybe the Sons would have to take a back seat to Shoktrupz. He'd hang in on this big bang coming up, but after that, well, maybe he'd just hit the trail with Kurt, Billy, and Sandy, head on out to L.A., and see what happened.

Hell, you worked for the cause in the best way you could, and why should he tinker around with computers for Rip Withers when he could be tearing up the halls and bringing hundreds, thousands, maybe someday even *millions* of kids into the camp of white power?

Chip closed his eyes and let the music take him, whirling him into his dreams.

Oh my, Rita White thought, standing and trying to look over the heads of the young people. They were getting rowdy now, jumping up and down in the puddles near the front of the stage so that the water splashed onto her stockings and, worst of all, onto Dr. and Mrs. Skelton too.

Rita looked at Mrs. Skelton apologetically but she only gave a long-suffering smile and rolled her eyes slightly as if to say these are the things we just have to put up with. Dr. Skelton was graciously watching the stage and nodding his head in time to the music. Billy Joe, next to Rita, leaned over to her and shouted above the racket, "These boys are all right . . . Good words, *good* words . . ."

The group must have been on their fourth or fifth song now and Rita glanced at her watch to see how much longer they had to play. She hoped that all these young people in front would sit down when Wild White West started since they were scheduled to play for an hour and Rita knew she couldn't stay on her feet all that time, especially with these sweaty teenagers all around her.

The band finished their number and Rita thought that maybe they would stop now, but they started another. The boy playing bass and the lead singer stepped up to their microphones again and started singing in what Rita thought was supposed to be harmony. It was some song about fire in the hole, whatever that meant, and two of the boys kept chanting *Fire, fire, fire* over and over while the singer sang the verse. Rita thought it was about hell but she wasn't sure.

Then suddenly something sparked behind the stage, ten times as bright as someone taking a flash picture, and the speakers screeched for a second and then, with what sounded like a huge pop, died.

So did Shoktrupz.

There was a smell of ozone, and the three boys at the front of the stage started to tremble. Their eyes rolled up in their heads and the guitars dropped from their hands, but still hung around their necks.

Then smoke started to come from their clothing, and the guitar player's long hair began to smolder, then quickly burst into flame. Rita tried to scream but realized she could not, that a feeling of intense vibration, which prevented it, was rolling up her body.

She could feel the vibration in her heart as though it were beating faster than it ever had before, as though it were *humming* and she could do nothing to slow it down, could do nothing at all except stand there and feel sweat burst out all over her. And then Rita's heart muscles fibrillated and before she even realized that she was being electrocuted, she was dead.

When her body fell to the floor the current continued to run through it, more strongly now that Rita's flesh was in direct contact with the water on the floor. Billy Joe stood beside her for a while longer, but then he too fell right on top of Rita without even knowing it. The Skeltons joined them, as did nearly everyone standing in front of the stage and sitting in the first couple of rows.

Others further back felt the tremors of the shock but were far enough away that they could react and flee. Chairs were overturned, the slow and the weak were pushed out of the way and trampled by the strong.

But the skinheads, the children on their shoulders, the girls who had been dancing and laughing, the older people standing up to see over the heads of the revelers, those still sitting on their metal chairs, the hearts of all trip-hammered, staggered, stopped.

What have I done? thought Amy. What the hell have I done?

She had wanted to kill Chip Porter, of course, and figured it would be no great loss if the other members of the band from hell died too. So she had gone into a Wal-Mart a few miles up the road and bought a roll of copper wire and a small wire cutter.

Then while everyone else was watching Shoktrupz play, Amy had gone behind the stage and connected lengths of wire to the legs of the metal risers on which the band was standing, twisting them all together with still more wire. Then she disconnected the grounds from the amplifiers and used the wire cutters to scrape away the insulation from the amps' power lines.

She wrapped an end of the copper wire around a cold water tap in a janitor's sink, then took two more strands of the wiry Gordian knot and hooked them around the exposed hot wires of the amps, twisted them, and finally let them make contact.

The shock nearly knocked her on her ass. She staggered back into the wall and immediately felt the concrete floor vibrating with electricity. The sound from the stage died and was replaced by screams and the sound of metal chairs clattering to the floor.

Then Amy realized with a start of horror that the electricity had not been limited to the stage alone. The concrete floor, damp everywhere and dotted with puddles, was acting like the wet sponge the executioner placed on the shaved head of the condemned as he sat in the electric chair. The current was flashing down the risers' metal legs onto the wet floor, a grid of death.

From behind the risers Amy could see the band members lying where they had fallen, still twitching with the electrical current. Smoke was rising from their bodies and little flames still licked at the few locks of hair that remained on the lead guitarist's scalp.

And beyond them in the packed audience were mounds of bodies and some people still standing, shivering with the shock that was still climbing up and passing through their flesh.

Amy turned, ran to the wires, and grasped them, ignoring the amperage flowing through her as it attempted in vain to fibrillate her already dead heart. It fought her but she clung to it, her muscles trembling as she untwisted the copper wires and jerked them away from the hot wires connecting the amps to the outlet. The electricity that had literally filled the room ceased so that only its ozone ghost remained to welcome into the beyond those ghosts newly made.

Then she walked around the side of the stage and looked at what she had done.

Returning from his meal, Rick Carlisle saw dozens of people running out the door of the main fairgrounds building. Some were shouting angrily while others were screaming. The street lights brightened and darkened in cycles and he ran until he reached the door, hoping that whatever happened had not happened to the bass player who was supposed to take him to the Sons of a Free America.

He quickly found out from the people fleeing the building that his contact was dead. Still, he pressed against the throng until he managed to get inside, where he found panic and confusion. But whatever the danger had been, it was now past.

People were dead, dozens of them lying over toppled chairs, their faces in puddles of water. He saw the members of Shoktrupz sprawled on the stage, their faces frozen in a death rictus, eyes wide, lips pulled back from their grimacing teeth. The sickness he felt increased as he made out the smaller forms of some children, but he went down the aisle toward them in the dim hope that he could be of some help.

A woman was holding a little girl in her arms, her head bowed, pressing against the girl's chest as if trying to breathe life back into her. The woman seemed to be crying, and even before she looked up at him with tearless eyes, he knew who it was.

"Amy," he said.

If she could do so much, if she was so strong, so powerful, so invulnerable, then why couldn't she bring this little thing back to life? She could feel the tears start to form but they wouldn't come, and then she heard someone call her name, and she looked up and saw Rick.

He looked surprised to see her but not amazed or stunned or terrified. And most incredibly of all to her, he didn't ask her what she was doing there or why was she alive. He asked, very simply and almost numbly, "What happened?"

But before Amy could answer, a young woman pushed her way through the people who were still congregating inside. She looked as though she were in shock, and she stared at Amy and the little girl, then knelt down and held out her arms. Amy put the girl into them, and the mother, tears streaming down her face, embraced her daughter while Rick and Amy watched. Then she stood up and staggered up the aisle to her dark future.

Amy looked back at Rick, who was again staring at her. He

took a step closer and his arms started to come up toward her but she stepped back. "No," she said. "Don't."

"What is it?" Rick spoke as if he were in a dream. "What is happening?"

"I'm killing children," she said softly, even before she knew the words were coming. "Oh, Rick . . ." Her words drifted out like prayers. "I'm killing children."

thirty-two

THEY HEARD THE SIRENS AS THEY WENT OUTSIDE TOGETHER. Ambulances, fire trucks, police cars descended on the fairgrounds like flies streaming to a roadkill rabbit. The firemen went inside first, then quickly beckoned the medics, who ran inside with their stretchers. Someone detached the power from the entire building, and from the doorways the glow of emergency lights appeared, making the figures coming out with their burdens appear white and ghostly.

Rick and Amy walked away from the building and into the parking lot, where they sat in the Avanti. "I saw you in this car earlier," Rick said. "And I saw you at the gun show. And it was you outside my window, wasn't it?"

"Yes, it was me," Amy said, looking through the windshield.

"How did you . . . survive?"

She paused before answering. "I didn't."

For some reason, the answer didn't surprise him. He supposed he already knew.

Then Amy told him everything, how the Crow had brought her back from the dead, how David Levinson had discovered her and told her the story of his Uncle Abraham. She told Rick about questioning Wilson Barnes, about following Will Standish and killing Sonny Armitage and Standish's mother, and about finding Junior Feeley and shooting him down.

"I saw you yesterday," Rick said. "I was there looking for these people too. You got shot but you weren't hurt."

"No." She still refused to look at him. "And I just got God knows how much electricity through my body—enough to . . . kill all those people in there—and I just walked away from it." She shook her head. "I didn't mean for that to happen. I just wanted to get him and his band."

"Chip Porter," Rick said, and was rewarded with her turning to look at him at last. Her eyes seemed haunted, but there was an intensity in them that bored into him.

"How do you know him?" she asked.

"I was supposed to meet him. He was going to take me to the Sons of a Free America. They think I'm one of them, that I believe like they do and I'll join them."

She looked at him in disbelief, then pounded the steering wheel in frustration. "*Jesus*, I can't believe this—I've been tracking these bastards down and you just stumble right into them."

He nodded. "Yeah, a lot of it was luck. I happened to save a kid's life yesterday during the shoot-out. I think he's their leader's son."

"What's his name?" Amy demanded. "Burns? Withers?"

"Withers. I don't know any Burns. The father of the kid is Rip Withers."

"Do you know where they are?"

Rick felt as though he were being pushed against the door by the force of her questions, and had the uncomfortable feeling that she would go right through him to get to the people she sought. "No. Porter was going to take me."

"God *damn* it! Goddammit! If I'd only have known . . ." The breath hissed out of her and the sound somehow relieved Rick. At least, he thought, she breathed.

Then silence sat with them in the car, while outside people scurried and ran and wept and screamed. It all seemed unreal to Rick, as though they were on a calm island in the midst of a terrible storm. "Amy," he said at last, "I don't know what to say . . . I never expected to see you again. I got . . . Nancy and I, we—"

"I know. It's all right. I'm glad. I didn't want you to be alone."

"But you're *here* now . . . You're *back* and I—"

"*No.* I'm not back, Rick, not for good. I'm here to do what I came back to do."

"Which is?"

"To make them pay for what they did . . . To put the wrong things right . . . But I don't know, I don't know . . ."

He knew what she meant. What had happened tonight seemed wrong, very wrong. "I'm sorry, Amy. I'm sorry for . . . everything. What happened to you, and the children, and to-night . . ."

Rick just shook his head. Words couldn't begin to contain what he felt, what he wanted to say, so he tried to turn to the task. "They have a place somewhere, I'm sure of it—a camp, a headquarters, something. And there are a lot of them. Porter was going to take me there, but maybe I can still get there. And you can follow."

"How?"

"They know I'm here and they'll soon hear about this . . . accident. Maybe they'll send someone else for me. Now Withers said that Porter had a van here that he'd take me back in, probably what they hauled their equipment in, so some-body should be by to pick that up. I could just . . . wait, hang around the parking lot. And when they come for me, you can follow."

She looked at him for a long time, then said, "Why do you want to do this? Why did you start this in the first place, track-ing them down?"

"The same reason you did, I guess. So I could rest. And now I have more of a reason—because I want you to be able to rest too, Amy." He felt his face begin to quiver, and tears filled his eyes. "Oh God, I love you. I never stopped loving you. And if you can't be back with me, if you can't stay, then I want you to be happy and at peace."

"I don't know if I ever will be, Rick, or if I'll just . . . snuff out like a candle when this is all over. But know that I love you too. I always will, no matter what happens to me, because I don't think that love can ever really die."

He took her hand then and she didn't pull away. But it felt cold, as though no blood warmed it, and she squeezed his hand gently and then withdrew hers. "Let's find that van," she said.

It was parked close to the building, a dark gray panel van with Minnesota plates. A cheaply produced Shoktrupz bumper sticker adorned it, and on the other side of the bumper were three small Day-Glo letters, *SFA*.

"Convenient," said Rick.

"Stupid," said Amy. "A secret militia that this idiot couldn't resist bragging about. It's a wonder they haven't accidentally blown themselves up a long time ago. You wait here and I'll watch from the car. It could be a long time. What if the police question you?"

"I'll just tell them the truth. I'm waiting for my ride. Besides, I think they've got enough on their hands right now."

It was true. Bystanders and news crews had appeared, as they always could be counted on to do at a disaster. Along with clearing out the bodies and directing the traffic of medics, firemen, reporters, and survivors, the cops were going to have plenty to do.

"All right then," said Amy. "But I want you to promise me something. After you lead me there, I may not come in right away. I don't know what I'll need. After all, I can't fly. And if it's too close to dawn, I won't come in until the next night. I want to do this in darkness. But when . . . *something* happens that makes you know I've arrived, I want you to stay out of it. Hide somewhere, keep yourself safe, don't try to help me anymore. Remember, Rick, they can't hurt me. They've already hurt me enough. And when it's over, get away. Don't tell anyone what happened. No one will believe you, not even Nancy.

"And finally, take good care of her and of Karin. Will you promise me that?"

Rick nodded. "Yes. I promise."

She looked at him for a moment longer and then turned and walked back toward her car. He watched her go, wanting to run after her, embrace her, take her away from there, go somewhere together where there was sunshine and warmth and *make* her live, will her with his love to be fully alive again. In a world where the dead could return, how could such a simple thing be impossible?

But it was. He knew it as surely as he knew that this would all end in more blood.

Ace Ludwig steered his black Chevy east on Route 94 heading for Eau Claire while Ray Withers kept hitting the scan button on the radio. They listened to station after station, trying to catch more news about the accident at the White Christian Brotherhood festival. When the first stories came on the air, Ace had thought Rip was going to go ballistic.

"It's that fucking bitch again!" he had roared. "That fucking government hit squad! They were after Chip this time—*shit!* Those *bastards!*"

Ace thought it was a hell of a conclusion to draw on the basis of the news story, which was simply that during a rock concert at a "white supremacist gathering" near Eau Claire, what was apparently an electrical malfunction had caused serious injury to both the band that had been performing and audience members, though the extent of the injuries was not yet known.

But that had been enough for Rip. He had ordered Ace and Ray to get down to the Frontier Fairgrounds right away and see if Chip was still alive. If he wasn't, they were supposed to bring back the van and try and find this Guy Adams that Rip had such a hard-on for. "And you make fucking well sure that nobody follows you. Anybody tries, lose 'em, and let me know. And once you pick up Adams, don't let him out of your sight."

"You don't trust him?"

"It's not him I'm necessarily worried about. Just do what I say."

So he and Ray had hit the road. The radio reports had come in in bits and pieces, but by the time they reached the fairgrounds they had learned that a group named Shoktrupz had been performing when the electrical mishap had sent power from the stage onto the floor. Dozens of people had been electrocuted, some fatally, particularly those in the immediate vicinity of the stage. The last report stated that all the band members had been killed.

"So long, Chip," said Ray as the announcer finished the story, but Ace was damned if he could hear anything but sincerity in Ray's tone. The guy wasn't smart enough to joke.

The area of the fairgrounds was a real zoo all right. It looked like the Martians had landed, what with all the remote TV trucks and their antennas and blinking red lights along with the blinking red lights of a fire engine, several emergency medical vehicles, and more police cars than Ace had ever seen in one place or ever wanted to see again.

He parked the car along the side of the road, and he and Ray walked into the parking lot near the back of the main building. There was already a police line around the building itself, but Ace quickly found the van parked nearby. Sitting on the asphalt, leaning against the driver's door, a man in his thirties was sleeping, head to one side. He looked like the Adams guy that Rip had described.

"Hey," Ace said, touching the man's leg with his shoe. The man opened his eyes drowsily and licked his lips. "What's your name?"

"Guy . . ." he started but his voice cracked and he cleared his throat. "Guy Adams. Who're you?"

"We're here instead of the man you were supposed to meet. You know who that was?"

"Yeah, Chip Porter." Adams got to his feet. "He one of the dead ones?" he asked, nodding toward the building.

"Appears so."

"So . . . you gonna take me to Mr. Withers?"

"*Colonel* Withers," Ray said.

Ace waved a hand, telling Ray to be quiet. He got the message and looked down at the ground. "Maybe. You see what happened in there?"

Adams shook his head. "I was outside getting some air. Pretty loud band."

"Not anymore." Ace tossed a pair of keys to Ray. "Ray, you drive the van back. Go ahead, you can leave now." Ray got in the van and pulled it out of the lot onto the road, heading for 94. Ace gestured for Adams to follow him and together they walked out of the lot and down the road to Ace's Chevy.

God, at last. Amy turned the key in the Avanti's ignition but didn't turn on the lights. She wouldn't do that until she got out on the road. Now she let out the clutch and the car slipped forward out of the parking space toward the road. The Crow, which had been standing on the hood of her car all that time, rose and flew slowly ahead of her. When she reached the road, Rick and the other man were a hundred yards away, their backs to her.

She had seen the van pull away and had nearly followed it, but made herself be patient and wait for Rick's contact. She had no idea where the van would go, but from what Rick had said, she felt certain that whoever met him would take him to the Sons of a Free America.

They had been waiting for six hours until the two men came, and in that time, sitting alone in the dark car, her only companion the silent and inscrutable black bird, Amy had battled with her guilt. Part of her said that it didn't matter, that the Crow had brought her back for one purpose alone, and what was imperative was that she accomplish that purpose no matter how many people died in the process.

But the part of Amy that had held the dead girl could not accept that. She had killed in cold blood, and though she had not intended harm to anyone other than the killer she sought and his blood brothers in hate, many were dead nonetheless.

The two sides of her had struggled for hours as she tried to rationalize her actions, then spat in the face of those rationalizations. By the time the vigil and the debate were over neither side had won, and she doubted if a victory would be forthcoming.

But now she had action to occupy her thoughts, again playing the game of follow the leader without letting the leader know he was followed. Down the road she saw Rick and the stranger climb into a dark Chevy and watched as it drove onto the road and moved quickly away. Still, she bided her time before she turned on her lights and slipped into its wake. The two red tail lights were far ahead, but she expected the car to head back toward Minnesota and was not disappointed when it got on 94 West.

She followed it for two and a half hours, hanging back as far as she could. Although she had been concerned about keeping it in sight through the Twin Cities area, she had no problem since they passed through at three in the morning. The problem came when they got off the four-lane.

If the driver was heading for Hobie or beyond, she figured she had been spotted. He could have stayed on that road nearly all the way to Hobie, but instead he got off on a two-lane state road. She followed, trying to hang back even further than before. Still, it was difficult. She couldn't drive without headlights.

The road became more twisting, and for minutes at a time she saw no lights ahead of her. Finally, after several miles she came out onto a length of straight road to discover that the Chevy had vanished. It had either put on a tremendous burst of speed or it had taken a smaller side road or pulled into a driveway and backtracked once she had gone past.

She whipped the car around and headed back the way she had come, but realized that the Chevy could have been miles ahead of her by now. She slapped the wheel in frustration but was startled by a sudden streak of darkness that appeared at the top of her windshield and shot out ahead of her.

It was the Crow and it hung just beneath the top of her headlights' beam, its pounding wings an invitation to follow.

Of course, Amy thought with a burst of relief as she stepped on the gas pedal. The bird, high above the trees, had seen where the Chevy had gone and could keep it within eyesight, flying high overhead and returning to Amy before she reached the places where the roads met and split. The Crow would be her guide.

And it happened as she had hoped. The bird would soar out of sight for a minute or two while she continued to drive straight ahead. Then it would drop back into her headlights' beams, banking to show her where to turn. The dark cicerone who had guided her from the land of the dead now led her to the place and the goal through which she would return to that shadowed land.

The Crow led. She trusted and followed.

The trail brought her back to the four-lane road, back toward Hobie, and past it, northwest, toward the heavy forests and the hills. She never saw the car again, but she saw the Crow, and it was all that she needed.

thirty-three

JUST AS DAWN WAS STARTING TO TOUCH THE RIM OF THE eastern sky, the Crow alighted. They were in back roads passing through thick woods, and had just come up a hill when the bird stopped, perching on a dead branch of an oak tree whose leaves autumn had nearly denuded. To Amy's right a dirt road led back into the forest, wide enough for only one car at a time.

Amy wondered if she should drive in on it, but decided that if the Crow had intended for her to do that, it would have flown in, leading the way. No, this was where she was supposed to stop.

She pulled the car off the road in among some trees where it would not be seen and climbed out. It was growing lighter every minute and she had nothing with her, so this would be a reconnaissance trip, to make sure she had found the right place, to gauge the strength of whoever and whatever was at the end of the dirt road, and to see what she would need to combat it.

Tirelessly she jogged along the lane, the Crow flying just ahead of her. After fifteen minutes along a fairly straight road, she came upon a sign that read:

WHITE OAK HUNTING CAMP
MEMBERS ONLY
TRESPASSERS WILL BE PROSECUTED

Prosecute away, thought Amy as she continued running. The road began to twist now and she thought what an ideal location this would be for a militia group. A long, straight, narrow road that prohibited access and allowed the defenders to fire at any invaders, including the government, then a series of twists and turns that made it easy to set ambushes. As far as tanks went, the road was too narrow, and the trees were old growth, perfect guardians against military encroachment. What was next?

She found out when she rounded a curve and saw the glint of metal ahead. She got off the path and ran through the brush instead. It was slower but it assured that no guard or watcher would see her approach.

Finally she saw a chain link fence several yards in front of her. It was ten feet high and topped with razor wire. Whatever this place was, it wasn't a hunting camp. Staying in the cover of the brush, Amy started to circumnavigate the compound, heading to her left.

The place was huge, she quickly discovered from the nearly flat arc of the fence surrounding it. It must have taken up a couple dozen acres, and to put a chain link fence, not to mention razor wire, around it all must have cost in the tens of thousands.

Finding no gate, she went back the way she had come and finally discovered the gate at the end of the dirt road. It too was narrow and fringed with heavy trees on either side. She could see the buildings from where she stood and was relieved to find among several other parked vehicles the dark Chevy in which Rick had been driven away, as well as the van the other man had taken. Rick was here then. The Crow had guided her well.

The buildings sat in a large open area and were utilitarian, barracks-style structures painted a gray-green that blended into the trees. The roof shingles were dark green.

There were three large buildings and several smaller cabins. Beyond the back of the open area, tucked among the trees, was a round-roofed building partly dug into the earth like a bunker.

A shooting range was on the right, with targets at one end and benches at the other where guns could be sighted in. Next to the gate was a twenty-foot-high tower reached by a ladder. Its height was far less than the trees around it, but it would provide an effective platform for firing on any people or vehicles that came near the gate.

Amy could see a man standing in the guard tower. He was looking through the trees but she knew he could not pick out her dark form in the heavy brush. Even though most of the leaves had fallen, the trees grew so thickly together that they provided plenty of cover. The greater danger was that he might hear her footfalls in the dead leaves, so she trod carefully, looking for bare ground or patches of moss.

No one was stirring in the camp, and Amy decided to exercise her patience and wait until they rose, to try and see how many of them there were. An hour after dawn they began to come out of one of the larger buildings and head toward another one, probably for breakfast, Amy thought. She counted twenty-three before she saw Rick appear with the man who had driven him there that morning. Two others were with them, a boy in his late teens and a man in his forties who carried himself with a bearing that told Amy he was a leader, if not *the* leader.

These were the men, then, the ones who had killed her, Judy, and the children, this *militia*, a group of cowards who hid from the world and showed how tough they were by blowing up babies. Amy wanted to storm the fence and attack them with her bare hands. But she didn't know how great her physical strength really was. She would have taken on any three of them, but two dozen was a different story. They might be able to overcome her by sheer numbers.

And if she were captured, what then? They wouldn't be able to kill her but they could imprison her, maybe forever. She wasn't Superman, she couldn't smash her way through walls, but she didn't think she would ever starve or die of illness or exposure. She wasn't sure just *what* the hell would happen but she couldn't afford to take the chance.

No, she would return by night and take them in the darkness, the same darkness that had hidden them and their crimes. She would come equipped with enough firepower to end it all.

No innocent bystanders would be harmed, not out here. And when it was over, she could rest. They all could rest.

For Amy knew that somehow the spirits of the children were with her. From the moment she had arisen from the dust, from the time she had asked them to be with her and inspire her, they had never left. Their souls were in just as much torment as her own, if not more, for they were helpless to do anything but suffer while she at least could take action.

And it was time to act and stop thinking about it. She trod carefully away from the fence until she could no longer be seen or heard by anyone in the compound, and then she ran back toward her car, paralleling the dirt road.

She arrived back at David Levinson's house in Hobie at nine in the morning. Levinson was sitting on the couch in the living room, wearing a warm pile bathrobe over his pajamas. A nearly empty bottle of single-malt scotch sat on the coffee table. He was holding a rocks glass with ice cubes that had melted to pale beads. He looked at her with heavy-lidded eyes and poured himself another drink.

"Nice work," he said. Though his voice was soft, it held an edge. "That was you, wasn't it? That thing in Eau Claire?"

She held his gaze and nodded. "That was me."

"Well." He took a deep breath and sat back, resting his arms on the back of the couch, still holding the drink in his right hand. He nodded toward the coffee table. "Have a drink. You earned it." Levinson took a sip of the scotch and smiled. "Nineteen people dead, Amy. Four of them were children. That's a higher body count than the gun show, and the best part is they were all your kills, no friendly fire necessary."

She didn't say anything, but kept watching him. She was damned if she was going to look away.

"And I have to tell you . . . that I'm so proud to be a part of this. To give aid and comfort to . . . what do you call a child killer anyway? I'm a cop, I ought to know that. There's fratricide—that's killing your fraternity brother, matricide, which is smothering somebody with a mattress. There's patricide . . . So what is this? Kidicide?"

"You're drunk."

"Yes ma'am, I'm afraid I am," he said, shaking his head loosely, as if it were on a spring. "But not enough, because I'm still pissed. If I was drunk enough, I wouldn't still feel this pissed. And you know who I'm pissed at?"

"Me."

"Yeah." He half smiled, half leered at her. "Because you didn't give a damn who you hurt, didja? You didn't hear a fuckin' thing I said after the gun show fiasco, didja?"

"Go to hell, David. You didn't see these people, I did." All her practice at rationalizing paid off now. "They were monsters, every single one of them. And they were turning their kids into monsters too! Another ten years and they'd be ready to burn you because you're a Jew!"

"And who the hell let *you* predict the future!" Levinson roared, springing to his feet, staggering and bumping the coffee table so that the scotch bottle tipped over and spilled. "Yeah, maybe they would have—but maybe they *wouldn't*! Maybe they'd have met some teacher or some preacher or even some *Jew* who'da straightened them out! Jesus Christ, Amy, they weren't doomed! They were only seven, eight years old, for crissake! You got your own fuckin' battles to fight, not ones that won't take place for another decade . . ."

"I'm telling you, everyone there was mad, insane. Those children were . . . *preconditioned*, David. They would have become just like the adults there."

"And *so fucking what?*" Levinson said heavily. "What if they had, Amy? This is America, you have the *right* to grow up to be a total racist idiot."

"What about the old Hitler question, David?" Amy said. "You go back in time with a gun in your hand and see Hitler as an eight year old, are you going to pull that trigger? Or are you going to give me that bullshit about talking to him and making him see what was right to do with his life?"

"No, I wouldn't do that, I wouldn't talk to him, and I wouldn't shoot him either. I wouldn't do a goddam thing, Amy, because people like that aren't unique—the devil doesn't make one in a century. They're made in *mass*, and they're made by *history*.

"You wanta know what would happen if somebody had plugged Hitler when he was cute little Adolf?" Levinson went on, his words slurred. "There wouldn'ta been any Hitler, no. But sure as shit there woulda been somebody *else*—maybe Kurt Von Fuckmeister—who woulda come along and made the Jews the villains anyway, and maybe old Fuckmeister was even *smarter* than Adolf, maybe so much smarter that he went slower and cagier, built a war machine five times better than Hitler's, put his boys to work on an A-bomb earlier than we did, invaded Poland in 1945, and then dropped the big one on London. Roosevelt surrenders. Fuckmeister conquers the world. Heil Fuckmeister!

"Six million dead? Shit. Chicken feed. *Sixty* million . . . six *hundred* million—those are Fuckmeister numbers! And that's all your fault, Amy. It's all your fault for blowin' that eight-year-old kid's brains out." Levinson fell back onto the couch and the air went out of him.

"Lady, you got your own battle to fight. Don't you pretend to fight anybody else's but yours. People hurt you, they hurt your children, so go hurt them. Kill 'em, make 'em pay. *But you can't kill everybody who agrees with them*. And don't you *dare* brush away your crimes by saying that because of what you've done that's one less battle that'll have to be fought someday."

He smiled grimly and went on. "Way I look at it, you've given every fuckin' wacko right-wing extremist in this country a whole stellar pantheon of martyrs. Look how much mileage they got out of the old lie that medieval Jews killed Christian children and threw their bodies in latrines. They'll be painting *these* people on their chapel ceilings."

thirty-four

AMY COULDN'T LOOK AT LEVINSON ANYMORE. SHE HAD LOOKED away a long time ago. "I didn't mean for it to happen," she said softly in the brooding silence. "I tried to kill the ones on stage, but not anyone else."

"That makes *me* feel better," said Levinson. "Not a whole lot, Amy, just a little. But I don't think it's gonna do much for the survivors." He shook his head as though he were trying to clear it.

"See," he went on more slowly, "the sorrow and the pity of all this is that you came back because they killed your children and now you wind up killing theirs. Strikes me that the kids themselves didn't have a whole lot to say about any of it." He gave a bitter laugh. "You know that old chestnut from Nietzsche? I used to read a lotta horror novels, and for a while there every other one you picked up had that quote that if you fought monsters—"

"You had to be careful not to become a monster yourself."

"You read 'em too, huh?" Levinson continued dreamily. "And if you look too long into an abyss . . ."

"The abyss will look back into you," Amy finished.

"When I was in Detroit," he said, "I looked into the abyss too long. That was why I came here. I wanted things to be better. I wanted to live in a perfect town with a perfect wife

257

in a perfect marriage." He closed his eyes. "And now that old abyss seems to be yawning again. Close it, Amy. Do what you have to do and close it for good. No more innocents dead, no more angels taken from earth to heaven too soon." He opened his eyes and looked up at her. "Swear to me. Swear on their souls."

Amy knelt next to where he sat and put her hand over his, trying to ignore the small shudder that went through him at the touch. "I swear to you. On their souls. No more innocents will die. *On their souls.*" Then she stood up, paced to the far wall, and turned. "I have them now, David. I know where they are. All together. I'm going back and I'm going to end it."

"No innocents."

She shook her head. "No children, no women. Soldiers. At least that's what they'd call themselves."

"I don't suppose you'd consider turning this information over to the police and let them deal with it."

"No, I wouldn't. I wouldn't even consider it," she said without a trace of a smile. She wanted him to know there was no joking about this, no compromise.

"What if I wouldn't give you the Avanti?"

"I'd take it. Or I'd steal another. You know that nothing is going to stop me. So why don't you help me?"

Levinson sighed. "Before I make my decision, I think I'd better have some coffee."

He ground beans and put them in the coffee maker while she sat at the breakfast table. After he turned the machine on, he walked to the door to the garage, opened it, and turned on the light. "You got some mud on it," he said.

"It was raining."

He walked around the car and came back into the kitchen. "No scratches. Thank you."

"You're welcome. I'll try and take as good care of it on this last trip."

"Wouldn't want me to take you there, then I could bring it back safe and sound."

She smiled. "No, I don't think so. I'll put a letter in the mail, let you know where to find it."

He took a pad of paper and a pen out of a drawer and handed them to her. Then he got an envelope and put a stamp on it. "Mail it today, I'll get it tomorrow. Will that be time enough?"

"By tomorrow," she said, "everything will be finished." She tore off the top few sheets of paper and put them on the hard surface of the table. "I wasn't born yesterday, David. I know the old impression trick."

He got a cup of coffee while she wrote. She described how to get to the road leading into the compound and told about the thick grove of trees where she would leave the car:

> *Even if the authorities descend on the place afterward, no one should find it. I'll cover it with brush, so you might have a problem yourself. But look hard. Remember, you're a cop.*
>
> *Thank you, David, for everything, and for knowing about what I am and how I came here. I'm sorry things worked out so badly for so many people. I didn't want these things to happen, but they did. I didn't want any of it to happen, from the very beginning, but it did. Sometimes I think no one gives a damn what we want, but then I remember how I returned. Someone, something was listening, and that knowledge makes me feel not quite so alone.*

She signed her first name, then folded the paper in thirds, slipped it in the envelope, addressed it, and put it in her pocket.

"If you want to help me," she said, "and get this over fast, there are a few things I'm going to need."

"Such as?"

"Ammo. I put the guns in your basement. I've got a Weaver Nighthawk, nine millimeter, and a Cobray M11/Nine. A couple hundred rounds for each should do it."

Levinson nodded. "Enough for a small army, huh?"

"Exactly. Also, I want some camouflage clothing. Dark. And tight—I don't want to get caught on the vegetation. Doesn't have to be warm. I don't feel the cold anyway. And camouflage paint too, for my skin." She thought for a moment. "Bring me white too, just a small tin of white."

"Jesus, I ought to write this down," Levinson said, reaching for the pad and pen. "Getting to be quite a list." He listed the items she had asked for. "Anything else?"

"Yes. Wire cutters, heavy gauge."

"I've got some. This other stuff I'll have to go out for. Some reason you can't do your own shopping?"

She shrugged. "You're a cop, you can get the ammo easy. Besides, for all I know, they might be seeking a woman of my description not only for the gun show, but for the Eau Claire . . ." She searched for a word.

"Fuckup," Levinson said.

She nodded. "So I'd prefer not to go out again until . . . it's time."

"I don't think you have to worry about the gun club thing. No one reported seeing the Avanti. As for Eau Claire, I don't know. That's another state and we don't have access to their records—or their thoughts—without a good reason. But odds are they're not going to be looking seriously around here, no reason to. Still, I'll do the shopping. You save your strength." Then he winced. "You know what I mean."

"Yeah, I know."

She went down into the basement then, not because she needed to learn any more from Levinson's files or computer, but because she sought the darkness. It seemed the right place for her now. It would happen in darkness tonight, at the very end, with the guns and the knife and whatever else she found to kill them with.

She sat in the darkness for a long time, seeking a calm, a peace, something on which to center and something to drive her, a core of iron that would sustain and strengthen her when the dark came down. She thought about the children first of all, about their smiling faces that would never smile again, the laughter that would never be heard, lives that would never be lived, generations vanished in a heartbeat.

She thought about Judy Croft, her joy in the presence of the children, her patience and humor and understanding blotted out in an instant.

She thought about her own life, her own love, Rick, and

how he was risking everything to lead her to the killers and bring them to the dark justice only she and the Crow could mete out. She prayed that he would survive and return to the family he had wanted for so long.

The thought of Rick in Nancy's arms pained her for a moment, but she pushed that pain down, made it part of the greater pain that drove her, rendered it faceless. She knew that he had to love again, and prayed to whatever was there that he would live so that he could.

When that first prayer came, she tried to focus on the deity in which she had always believed. But when she tried to picture him, the kindly, white-robed, white-bearded Judeo-Christian God to whom she had prayed for all her brief life seemed to move and shift in her mind, darkening, its robes and hair and beard fading to black, their textures blending until she saw the Crow sitting like an ancient statue, many times larger than its present form, its ebony eyes looking down at her.

And in them she read a vast indifference. They were black, devoid of emotion, glistening with reflected light and nothing more.

But how could that be? The creature, be it god, demon, or avatar, had brought her back from the dead. Why would it do that if cosmic indifference was its raison d'être?

No, it had brought her back out of some other emotion. If not out of love for her, as she had always expected from God, then perhaps it was out of respect for *her* own love and how that love had been betrayed by those who had killed her and the children. And it had brought her back so that she could put the wrong things right.

But how did it expect her to do that? Expectations, yes— perhaps she could find its motive in its expectations . . .

She realized, with a chill even colder than her flesh, what she had always known:

It expected death.

It expected lives.

Would God have done that? Would her gentle Christ have brought her back to kill, to put her in a position where she would take the lives of children, no matter how predestined toward evil?

No, surely not. But then, if not an agent of God, what was the Crow? Though Amy had believed in God, she had never believed in the devil or demons or any other manifestation of evil other than what dwelled in the hearts and minds of men and women. But now she wasn't so sure.

Still, if the Crow were evil, wouldn't it have wanted evil men, such as the Sons of a Free America, to live and thrive? Why would it have brought her back to kill them?

Perhaps then it was something between good and evil, a more primitive deity from an earlier time, surviving through the eons, a force that demanded justice and used the unjustly killed to achieve its ends, not a devil, but a dark and angry god in its own right.

And a hungry one.

Though she would never truly know, she would let that be her answer then. It was as good as any other. And if Amy was somehow damned for what she had done so far, then so be it. She would go ahead. She could not be damned twice.

She would feed the dark creature that was the Crow, feed it the justice it demanded and that she desired more than love, more than life, more than the eternal rest she hoped would be her reward.

PART THREE

Ah, love let us be true
To one another! for the world, which seems
To lie before us like a land of dreams,
So various, so beautiful, so new,
Hath really neither joy, nor love, nor light,
Nor certitude, nor peace, nor help for pain;
And we are here as on a darkling plain
Swept with confused alarms of struggle and flight,
Where ignorant armies clash by night.

—Matthew Arnold, "Dover Beach"

thirty-five

"AS SOON AS YOU STEP ON IT, YOU HEAR A CLICK AND THEN IF YOU know what that click means, you just stand there, not knowing what the hell to do. If you *don't* know what it means, or what's more likely, you don't even hear it, you just keep walking. And as soon as you lift up your foot, boom. Your legs disappear into a big red cloud, your dick and your balls get slammed up inside your guts, and you die pretty fucking fast. If you're lucky. Most of the men know where they are by now, but there are some that can't remember, like Ray. He's my brother and a sweet guy and I love him, but he doesn't have a lot upstairs. So if you can't remember where they are, avoid the perimeter. Not much reason to walk around there anyway."

Rip Withers was giving Rick Carlisle the grand tour of the compound of the Sons of a Free America, of which he would become a member that night. When they had arrived early in the morning, Withers had been there to greet him. He had not been a happy man because of the loss of Chip Porter, his computer and electronics expert, but he had been genial enough to Rick.

Withers had shown him to the barracks building where the men lived and slept, given him a towel, washcloth, and toilet articles, and shown him a bunk. Rick was able to get two hours sleep before the rest of the men started getting up, and when he joined them, Withers took him under his wing for the tour, starting with the gate, the fence, and the land mines.

Then he showed Rick the various rooms in the barracks, including the activity room, with a television, a VCR, and an assortment of videos. There were also several hundred books on shelves, most of them concerning American history, military arms, and politics. Rick recognized none of the authors or the publishers. There was also a pool table, a ping-pong table, and several card tables.

The mess hall, where they had breakfast and where Rick was introduced to the men as a new recruit named Guy Adams, was large enough to seat a hundred, although Withers told Rick they had twenty people living there full-time, which increased to thirty on weekends. "Some of the men still hold down jobs, have families. But everybody's here today, staying over for the shoot, and . . . something else."

"The shoot?"

Withers led the way to a large storeroom at the back of the mess building. When he opened the door, Rick heard the sounds of birds, some singing, some making more raucous sounds. Several large cages held an assortment of wild birds, everything from pigeons to crows to small sparrows.

"We do this every few months," Withers said. "Got the idea from that pigeon shoot in Pennsylvania. But we're equal opportunity shooters. We put up nets and traps for a week beforehand and put whatever we catch in here. Then tonight we let them go and take turns bringing them down. Some of them get away to fly another day, especially the little ones—they dart around a lot, make harder targets. But the doves and the crows, they don't have much of a chance with our shooters. These men are good. How are you, Guy?"

"I hate to say it," said Rick, "but I haven't held a gun since I hunted as a boy."

"No service time?"

"I tried to enlist in the Marines but they wouldn't take me. Look." Rick kicked off his right shoe and peeled off his sock. "Little toe turns under. They saw that and said good-bye fast."

"Well, don't worry about it. You'll learn to shoot here."

The third large building was an indoor drill area and pistol range. There were also thick mats on the floor. "This is where we practice hand-to-hand. A lot of the men are skilled in martial arts. Any background?"

Rick shook his head. "The spirit's willing but the flesh needs some training."

"You'll get it. Now let me show you something *really* interesting."

Withers led the way toward the back of the open area, where a structure sat half buried in the earth. It had an arching roof of corrugated metal and the end was brick. Cement steps led down to a door.

"This is what we call the powder magazine," Withers said. "A little old-fashioned name. You might just as soon call it the armory, I guess, but the older name gives us a sense of tradition. This is where we store our weapons, ammo, explosives . . ."

"Explosives?" Rick said.

Withers smiled. "You bet. And here comes the master now."

Rick turned and saw a loose-limbed man with greasy black hair and a dirty pea coat coming toward them. His face was crisscrossed with scars, some pale, others red. "Hey, new guy," the man said, and nodded to Withers.

"This is Ronald Burns," Withers said, "but we all call him Powder. You can see why."

"I put a lot of myself in my work," Burns said with a smirk, holding up his left hand, which was missing the ends of his little and ring fingers.

"How's it cooking?" Withers asked.

Burns nodded happily. "I'll be done another couple hours. We can load it up tonight after the shoot, take it in by dawn's early light." He looked at Rick and frowned. "This guy isn't with *Sixty Minutes,* is he?" Withers laughed and so did Rick. In another few seconds so did Burns. "Well, you came at just the right time for fireworks, man. You told him yet?" he asked Withers, who shook his head no. "Your party," Burns said, and walked down the stairs to the powder magazine, opened the door, and went inside.

"You don't lock that?" Rick asked.

"We don't need any locks here. We're all brothers. If we start thinking we can't trust a brother, well, he doesn't last very long. See, once you come in here, you don't go out for two months. By then we can pretty well tell who's a true Son and who isn't."

"And what if you decide somebody isn't?"

Withers pointed beyond the powder magazine to another stairway leading down that Rick hadn't noticed before. The earth was slightly humped above it. "That is the only cell we have here in the camp. If someone proves to be a traitor, we imprison him there. Then we have a trial. And then we have an execution."

"That ever happened?"

"Guy, way back in those trees . . ." he pointed, "there's a real mossy spot. And under that moss is real soft dirt. And four feet down in that dirt there are three men. Now we thought they were good, white Christian warriors like yourself. But they weren't. They were Judases. They would have sold us out as quickly as Judas sold out Jesus. Two came in together and one came in alone. I don't know whether the two knew the other one. I don't care much. They disappeared and nothing ever happened as a result. No sheriffs or feds or anybody ever came looking for them."

"So . . . what did they do?" Rick's balls were crawling and he hoped his anxiety didn't show.

"Not much, really. Maybe another militia would have let it slide. But we couldn't. We're more *serious* than most other militias. Now I don't want to tell you what it was because I don't want you to constantly be on your guard." He grinned. "There's no point in getting paranoid after all. Besides, I don't think you'll be doing anything like those other men. I really feel that I can trust you, Guy. Or at least I'll be able to after we talk about something."

Oh shit, Rick thought. "What's that?"

"Last night, Ace said that you had a little visitor on the way here. Somebody was following you."

"That's right. But Ace lost him. I don't know why anybody would be following me. Maybe they were following Ace."

"Maybe they were. So you don't know who it was?"

"No, I don't. If I did, I'd tell you."

Rip was quiet for a moment and then he nodded. "Okay. Okay. Well, let me hook you up with some of the men right now—give you some firearms instruction, whaddya say?"

"How do you know he isn't the guy who's been knocking us off, Rip?"

"It was a woman, Ace," said Rip Withers. They were sitting in Rip's cabin, along with Ray and Powder, who had been called from the powder magazine for the meeting to discuss Chip's demise and the advent of Guy Adams. "A woman killed Junior and definitely had something to do with Wilson Barnes spilling the beans."

"What if it was two of them?" Ace went on. "What if they're government people working together? I mean, ain't it a real coincidence that he was at the gun show where Junior bought it *and* at the White Christian Brotherhood thing?"

"Hell, no—*I* told him to go there, Ace. I wanted to see if he could get there and I wanted some time so Karl could tail him, see if his story was straight, see if he met anybody—and he didn't. He said he was dirt poor and he went to a flophouse. He didn't know anybody was watching him."

"I still don't like him. I drove nearly three hours with him last night, Rip—you didn't. You spend three hours alone in the dark with a guy, you get a feel for him and this guy don't feel right. Besides, I swear I seen him somewhere before."

"Well, when you figure out where, you tell me."

"Dammit, Rip, I just don't think this is the time to bring somebody in, with what's going down tomorrow and—"

"He saved my son's life!" Rip exploded. "Why the fuck would he risk his own neck to do that if he was out to kill us? I *owe* him, Ace! Now we'll keep an eye on him, we won't let him alone." A thought hit him. "Tell you what. We'll let him in on what's happening tomorrow. If he's really with us, he won't do a thing. But if he's not, he'll either try to get out and warn people or he'll try and fuck it up by messing with the bomb. We'll just watch him, stop him if he tries anything, and the next twenty-four hours will tell the tale. Agreed?"

It made sense to everyone there, and Rip sent Ace to assign two men to watching Guy Adams around the clock. When he got back, it was time to talk about what had happened to Chip Porter.

"The main thing is, whether Adams had anything to do with it or not, someone is carrying out a vendetta against us. We know it was a woman who got Barnes to squeal on the air. Then somebody killed Sonny, then Junior, and now Chip's dead. You know how Chip was, he never would've let an electrical fuckup like that happen. Would he, Powder?"

Powder shook his head. "Definitely not the Chipman. He knew his wiring front and assbackwards. His stuff was old, so he had to take more care with it, but he always did. Whatever went down wasn't his fault."

"And if you noticed," Rip said, "they're not calling it an accident. Nobody's said yet that it was an act of sabotage but that sure sounds like that's what they're setting us up for."

"Well, why would they tell us that?" asked Ray.

"What?"

Ray spoke slowly as if trying to choose every word. "Why would they . . . the liberal press . . . say it was sabotage? I mean, if these government people did it, wouldn't the government want it to look like an accident? So why won't they *say* it's an accident?"

"I don't know, Ray," Rip said impatiently. His brother seldom spoke but when he did Rip always hated it. When it was just the two of them, fine, but these meetings were official and he didn't need Ray's thoughts wandering. "But that doesn't matter. What matters is finding out who's responsible and how they've been tracking down and fucking *eliminating* us. They got three of us so far and damn near got Karl.

"Now we're going to strike back *big* with this bomb but that's not going to stop this. We've got to find this bitch and whoever's working with her and terminate their asses for good."

"So how, Rip?" asked Powder. "I mean, it ain't like we got a surveillance or intelligence section or anything."

"No, but maybe this piece of shit will come to us. I think that whoever was following Ace and Guy Adams last night was the same person who wired up Chip to die. It'd be too big a coincidence otherwise. And if they were smart enough to track us down one by one, they'll eventually be smart enough to find this place."

"And bring the feds," said Ace.

"Not necessarily. If this was the feds they'd have taken one of the men for questioning before they killed them."

"That's right," said Powder. "But with Sonny and Junior and Chip, it was out-and-out assassination—they didn't try to interrogate them before they snuffed them."

"And that's what I don't quite get," said Rip. "It's like they're not out to arrest us but to pick us off one by one. Well, lots of fucking luck, sweetheart. Next time we leave this place, it'll be tomorrow with the bomb, and we'll be leaving in a van and two cars with four soldiers in each, and all of us will be armed to the teeth. So if this cunt and whoever else is with her want to get us, it's going to have to be today. She's going to have to bring Mohammed to the mountain. I want double guards tonight and nobody better fuck around. We've come too far to blow it now, especially when we're really going to *blow* it tomorrow. Got me?"

Rick hoped that Amy would come tonight and end it all. He felt unclean among these men, as though their madness had rubbed off on him in the hours in which he shared their lives and their twisted dreams.

Some of them had actually talked about what they had done so far—the executions, as they termed it, of Wilson Barnes and William Standish and, far worse to hear about, the explosion at the day-care center, Amy's center. A man named Ed Conover was chatting with him about it while he showed Rick how to load and fire an automatic rifle.

"Oh yeah, it was bad news, y'know, 'cause we were trying to get that Jew-loving senator, but it turned out all right because of a couple different reasons . . . Okay, that's it, just push that magazine up in there, uh-huh . . . Well, yeah, it was too bad those kids got killed and all, but we hadn't planned for that to happen. Still, first of all, it let them know, the federals, I mean, that we weren't anything to mess with. Told 'em straight off that we had the technology and the know-how to get the explosives in where their big boys were, y'know? . . . All right, now just yank that slide back there . . . No, no, don't be so dainty, give it a good yank, it won't break . . . *There* ya go . . . And in the second place, Barnes—Satan take his black soul—did us at least one last favor when he said that patriots never woulda done anything as bad as blowing up a bunch of little kids, but the government already had at Waco so this was just one of *their* tricks to make the militia folks look bad. And you'd be surprised at how many people bought it.

"Okay, you're locked and loaded, pal. Now let's head on over to the range and—"

"Set for bear, huh?" Rip Withers said, interrupting. "I'll take him over to the range, Ed." Withers loaded a weapon in a tenth of the time Rick had taken. "Let's go, Guy."

They walked out of the building and toward the firing range. "Ed telling you about our 'explosive situation'?" Withers said, and chuckled. "That's nothing compared to what we got next. You came just in time, Guy. We already got our delivery crew picked but you'll be able to share in the glory."

"What, uh, what do you mean?"

"I mean the Olson building in Hobie—where all the government offices are. We got a real sweet treat going in there tomorrow. All the plastic explosive that we've been stockpiling for the past year, minus, of course, what we used for the day-care place. None of this fertilizer-and-petroleum crap. It's going to make Oklahoma City look like a cherry bomb. There won't be *anything* left standing afterwards."

"Tomorrow?" Rick asked. He could feel his heart pounding.

"Tomorrow morning we head out. Powder's finished putting it together. Stored in the magazine. Though, boy, if it'd go off I think we'd all turn into Jell-O." He laughed as he sat down at one of the shooters' benches. "Okay, let's practice firing at those targets right there . . ."

As he aimed at the black circle, Rick thought about what in the hell he could do. He could quickly turn on Withers and kill him and then try and make it to the powder magazine. But there were several other shooters on the range and he couldn't hope to shoot them all before they gunned him down.

And even if he could get inside the magazine, what then? Could he blow the whole damn thing up and himself with it before they got to him?

Probably not. Rick didn't know a thing about explosives. No, any quick attempt at sabotage would end up with him dead and nothing accomplished. At least the powder magazine wasn't locked. Maybe he could slip away and figure out some way to dismantle the device or get to a phone, although he hadn't seen any.

And maybe, just maybe, Amy would get here in time to do something to stop this plan.

thirty-six

Night had fallen at last, and Amy Carlisle looked at herself in the mirror. The camouflage was perfect. She would blend seamlessly into the night, and the fit was tight enough that she wouldn't get hung up on any branches. If thorns tore her flesh, it made no difference. The pain would pass and she would heal as quickly as the wounds appeared.

Levinson had bought everything she had requested and more. The boots she wore were masterpieces of engineering, lightweight but with sturdy soles with which she could move through the forest like a wraith. He had gotten her a combat belt for her knife and a second knife as well. "In case you leave the first one sticking in a tree or the ground or an insane extremist," he told her.

He had also bought extra magazines for both weapons which could be slipped into the belt. When a magazine was empty, all she had to do was pop it out and slam in another one. "This must have cost you quite a bit," she told him as he sat on the bed, watching her.

"It just came out of my extermination budget." He shook his head. "God, that sounds awful. That was the phrase the Nazis used about the Jews—extermination."

"The Jews were innocent. These people are guilty."

Levinson took out three small tins from a paper bag. "You still want the paint?" he asked.

Amy nodded and took them. She tied back her hair, then opened the green and the brown and began to rub thin layers over her face, mixing the two until her skin was the color of mud. It dried quickly and then she opened the white. "I want to blend into the darkness," she said. "And yet I want them to see *something*. I think I want them to see their deaths coming."

She dipped a finger into the clown white and drew a thin line that outlined her lips. At the corners of her mouth, she brought the white line upward an inch on either side like a ghostly smile. Then she outlined her eyes as well and looked closely into the mirror. She shook her head. Something was still missing.

Then she knew what it was. She dipped her finger into the white and made one more line under each eye, straight down, like a pale falling tear.

"I'm ready," she said, and turned to Levinson.

The man shuddered and Amy knew that her face contained all she had hoped it would. It was a face that would inspire terror, a face of the dead that was one with the night, yet would shine out of the darkness like an angry star ready to burn away all those who tried to stop it.

"Yeah," he said. "I think you're ready." Then he smiled. "I just hope you don't get stopped by an officer."

"I'll just tell him I'm a little late for a Halloween party," Amy said, and smiled back, though from the look on Levinson's face, it probably would have been better if she hadn't.

He walked her to the car and they put the weapons and the heavy-gauge wire cutter into the trunk. Amy got behind the wheel and looked at Levinson. "I probably won't see you again. Thank you, David. I don't know what else to say."

"I don't either, Amy. I really don't. It has been . . . a unique experience."

"We never really talked about it," Amy said, "but are you religious?"

"I know where the local temple is but I haven't been there since I moved here. I'm afraid I'm pretty well one of those lapsed Jews." Levinson smiled. "But what I've gone through lately has made me wonder. I may be *re*lapsed."

"In any case," she said, "will you do me one more favor?"

"If I can."

"Will you pray for me? In your temple? Pray for my soul, wherever and whatever it is. And for the souls of those who died. The innocents."

She didn't say whether she meant those who died with her or those she had killed, but it didn't seem to matter to Levinson. "I will," he said. "I promise. For *all* of them."

That was good enough. She knew what he meant and that he had known what *she* meant. "Thank you. Good-bye, David."

The garage door opened and she backed out, then drove into the night, toward her purpose, toward the end of it all.

She drove well under the speed limit so that no policeman would stop her on the way. On the outskirts of Hobie she dropped the letter to Levinson in a mailbox and then left the lights of the city behind, threading the black Avanti through the twisting back roads and the dark forests.

The Crow flew before her, dropping in and out of her beams. Though she did not need it to guide her, she was glad it was there. "'Prophet still, if bird or devil,'" she whispered, and followed.

When she reached the dirt road back to the compound, she drove the Avanti off the road and among the trees, fifty yards into a small clearing next to a patch of brambles. She ripped out brush and broke off branches to hide the car from sight, then took out the weapons and the wire cutter, loaded her combat belt with the filled magazines, and walked back to the dirt road.

The full moon made it easy for her to find her way. Its light fell through the nearly leafless trees onto the forest floor, making a pale path before her. It was even brighter on the dirt road itself. The night was windy and she thought that would help to cover the sound of her footfalls on the dry leaves. With luck, they would not know she was there until she was standing beside them, her knives in their backs.

Ace Ludwig was pissed. He *knew* he had seen this Guy character somewhere before. If he could just remember . . .

Ace didn't buy this fugitive-from-justice shit at all. The dude was too *clean*, almost as if he had done himself up to look shabby, like he was in a fucking movie or something. And when Ace had talked to him in the car on the way back to the compound, he had given all the right answers but there was something weird about the whole thing. The *words* were right but it was like he really didn't believe what he was saying.

If the guy was a fed, they could be fucked royally, even though Ace had lost the tail who had climbed on his ass somewhere on the interstate. But if he *was* a fed, how the hell would Ace have ever seen him before? Through the afternoon Ace had gone through the file of photos they had of feds whose covers had been busted, and there wasn't anybody who looked like this Guy Adams.

Shit. Maybe somebody he had been in the service with? No, the guy was too damn young to have been in the Nam and so fucking dumb when it came to guns that Ace knew he had never been through basic. Hell, he had probably never even been in a fight in his whole life. Looked like too much of a yuppie for that.

His hands were soft too. No matter what he'd told Rip, this was not a working man. Guy Adams was a desk jockey with a pretty wife, two cars in the garage, a deck, a couple kids in an expensive day-care . . .

Then Ace froze. That was it. Day care.

He walked into the rec area and started flipping through the videotapes Rip had made of the news stories about the bombing, and started shoving them in the machine. After twenty minutes of searching he found it and went looking for Rip.

It was dark by now but the flood lights illuminated the compound as brightly as if it had been day. Near the shooting range several of the men were positioning the cages for the bird shoot.

The search lights outside the enclosure were on too, lighting the dirt road coming up to the gate. They weren't usually on but Rip wasn't taking any chances of a last-minute covert attack by the feds. Anything was possible.

Ace found Rip in the mess hall, talking with some of the men over a cup of coffee. He leaned down and spoke into his ear. "Where's Adams?"

"I don't know," Rip said. "But don't worry, he's being watched."

"Good thing. I got something to show you about our new friend." He stood up and led the way back to the rec hall. Powder and Ray came with them. "Check this out," Ace said, and hit the play button on the VCR.

A reporter stood in front of the smoking rubble of the Making Friends Child Care Center. It was night not long after the explosion. The reporter was saying how everybody inside had probably been killed, and then she turned and said, "I believe this is the husband of one of the victims. Sir? Sir, would you mind telling us how you're—"

Then a man in a dark jacket appeared behind the reporter, crossing the screen with a woman. He looked toward the camera for less than a second and looked away so quickly that his brightly lit face was distorted by motion blur before it disappeared. But Ace hit the remote's review button and the image backtracked, then froze on the man's face. "Look familiar?" Ace asked.

There was no doubt in any of their minds that the man looking at the camera was Guy Adams. Ace let it play out. "I guess he has no comment," the reporter said, turning back toward the camera. "That, we believe, was Richard Carlisle, the husband of the owner of the center, believed to have died in the blast."

Ace turned off the machine and looked at Rip. The man's already florid countenance was reddening even further and Ace could see his jaw muscles clench as he leaped to his feet.

"That fuck! That lousy *fuck!* Find him, we gotta find him *now!*" Rip led the way outside but when they burst through the door they saw the man they now knew to be Carlisle and the two men assigned to watch him coming from the direction of the powder magazine. The two men were holding pistols to Carlisle's head.

"What?" Rip asked impatiently. "What'd he do?"

"Nothin', I hope," said the one man. "He went into the magazine and when we followed him he was messing around with the bomb."

"*Shit!*" Powder Burns barked, and sprinted across the area toward the magazine.

Rip walked up to Carlisle and looked him in the eye. "Richard Carlisle, huh?"

Carlisle smiled. Ace had to give him points for that. That took guts. Or maybe the guy was just stupid. "My friends call me Rick," he said. "You can call me Richard."

Rip backhanded him with a shot that staggered him. He fell back a few steps but didn't fall down. Ace gave him some more points for that too. It was one hell of a wallop. "You slimy *prick*," Rip said. "You fucking traitorous *shit!*"

The other men were starting to gather now. Ace saw Karl come trotting up, looking worried. Rip looked at the boy, then at the other men. "We got a real treat here, men—an out-and-out sonovabitch *spy!*"

Karl walked uncomfortably up to Rip. Ace could tell the kid didn't want to say a word but felt that he had to. "Dad . . . he, well, he saved my life . . ."

"He saved your life to get in *here*, you dumbass! It was a setup—he was with the *bitch!*" He looked back at Carlisle with murderous eyes. "All right, let's take this piece of Jew-loving, nigger-loving crap to the cell and have a little talk with him."

Just then Powder Burns came back, looking pale and tired. "It's okay," he said. "He just pulled a couple wires, tried to screw up the timer or something, but didn't have time to do anything."

"He shouldn't have had time to do *shit*," Rip complained, snarling at the two men who had been guarding Carlisle. "Is it all right?" he asked Powder.

"Yeah, I wired it right back up. Never any danger."

"I want extra sentries tonight," Rip ordered. "Not just at the gate but four more to cover the perimeter. Karl, you're one of them—go to the north end. Powder, assign the rest. Come on, bring him," he said, pointed to Carlisle, and stalked toward the cell half buried in the earth of the forest.

• • •

Rick's only chance now was Amy. If she didn't come he was dead, and he was probably dead anyway. At least then maybe he would be with her again someday, after this whole thing was finished. He had tried to dismantle the bomb but had no idea of what he was doing. The main danger was that it might go off, and if it did, that would have been all right too.

But no such luck. And now he was being taken to the cell Rip Withers had shown him earlier. And torture chamber? Rick wondered. He didn't know how Withers could resist.

As it turned out, he was right. They tied him to a wooden chair with leather straps and put another strap around his head so that they could move it, exposing his throat or either side of his head. There were four of them in the cell, Rick, Powder, Withers, and Ace, who had joined them after assigning the sentries. All were armed with guns in holsters, but it was a knife that Withers held in front of Rick's face.

Rick tried to keep smiling but he was scared shitless. He hoped that whatever happened he wouldn't piss himself, but was afraid he probably would. Wasn't there some involuntary reaction to extreme pain or terror? He knew that if he died, he would lose it all, bladder, bowels, the works, but by then he wouldn't care much. Let these bastards deal with the mess.

"See this knife?" Withers said. Before Rick could respond, Withers had stuck it in the hollow of his ear and jerked the blade sideways, slicing the flesh and the cartilage.

Rick couldn't help but give out a yelp, but the shame made him grit his teeth immediately. Flop sweat started to bead his skin and he could feel blood trickling down his ear lobe and dripping off onto his shoulder.

"It won't bleed much," Withers said. "Just wanted you to know that I'm serious. If you don't tell me what I want to know, I will disfigure you, I will cripple you, I will kill you. You are worse than the enemy, you are a spy and a traitor. You are less than *meat* to me. You're going to die and you can make it

281

easy—*relatively* easy—or you can make it hard. Now the first thing I want to know is, who are you with?"

That was an easy one. "My partner." Partners in life, partners in death.

"Not the feds? Not the police?"

"They don't know I exist. Like I said, it's just me and my partner."

"All right—who *is* the bitch?"

Rick paused. "Yo mama," he smirked.

It was a stupid thing to say and Rick knew that it would only bring more pain. But maybe he would get lucky and this asshole redneck shithead would get so pissed he'd kill him right off. But the main reason Rick said it was that he was pissed. He hated this man and what he had done.

Apparently Withers had interrogated prisoners before. He didn't get mad, not raging mad anyway. His nostrils widened and his teeth showed and he moved the knife to the other ear and sliced again.

This time Rick was ready for it. A grunt came from deep in his throat, but goddammit, it was a *manly* grunt. Fuck this wanker anyway. Let him cut, Rick had lots of skin. And with both ears slashed, the drips had evened out. He was bleeding in stereo.

"I don't like it when you get smart with me, *Richard*," Withers said. "Not a bit. I'm not amused and neither are my friends. Now I can cut your ears to make you look like a dog. I can slice your chest to give you hanging tits. And I can make a woman out of you in other ways too. You get my meaning?"

"I believe so," Rick said, breathing heavily.

"All right. Now I want to know who the woman is. The woman who killed Junior at the gun show, the woman who got Wilson Barnes to spill his guts."

"You know what else she did?" Rick asked. It had just occurred to him that he might as well tell this nutcase the truth, that it would scare the shit out of him and, most of all, that Amy would probably want him to know. It might also have the advantage of saving him from more torture. "She killed the guys on the stage—all of them. You had any other of your storm troopers killed in action lately?"

Withers looked serious as hell. "Yeah. A man in a parking garage and the mother of one of our men—in her trailer."

"Tell me," Rick said, smiling. "How'd they buy it?"

"The one was stabbed. The old lady's neck was broken and her trailer set on fire."

"Sounds like my partner's M.O.," Rick said, and chuckled. He wondered if he were going a little crazy. "She likes to leave things messy."

Withers grabbed the leather strap and yanked Rick's head back, exposing his throat. Rick felt the edge of the knife against it. "Who is she? Who the fuck *is* she?"

"You don't know?" Rick said roughly, his throat taut. "You ought to. After all, you killed her."

"What?" The knife moved away from his windpipe and the strap was released. His head slumped down and he looked back up at Withers, who was staring at him, confused. "What do you mean, I killed her?"

"My wife. Amy . . . Amy Carlisle."

Withers stared a moment longer. Then a smile bent one side of his mouth and he barked a phlegmy laugh, one that was afraid to be heard. "What are you talking about? She's *dead*."

"That's right. But she's *back*."

For a long moment Rip Withers looked terrified. Then his face became set with resolve and he lifted the knife so that it was less than an inch from Rick's right eye. "You're a fucking liar and liars lose things that are important to them."

"I'm *not* a liar," Rick said with as much fire as he could. "Your own son saw her get shot and keep walking. She fried your guitar player, took the juice herself, then walked away from it. You can't kill her, Withers." He smiled in the eye of the knife. "To paraphrase that tape Rush Limbaugh always plays for laughs, She's here, she's a feminist, she's *in your face*. But this time nobody's laughing."

Withers swallowed hard and the knife came slowly away from Rick's eye. When he spoke, his voice shook just enough for Rick to hear. "I don't care who the hell she is. If she comes here, she's going to die. If she tries to stop us, she's going to die."

"That'll be tricky. Like I said, she's already dead."

"And *you're* gonna *join* her!" Withers said as he stood up. "Right after the shoot, the one who gets the most kills gets to finish you, you little faggot! There's gonna be one more grave under the moss by morning!"

"There'll be a lot of dead people by morning, Withers."

"Get somebody to guard this motherfucker," Rip said to Ace, and spun on his heels and left the cell followed by Powder and Ray. He couldn't stay in the same room with this liberal piece of shit for another second. He was afraid Carlisle would push him too far and he'd kill him. No, he wanted him to live on for a while, to think about dying, about getting shot down in front of the people he hated most in this world.

Well, the feeling was fucking mutual. Rip hated these yuppie, government-loving lefties just as much as they hated him and probably more. There wasn't any answer, there was no compromise, there was no possible way for two ideologies so different to coexist in the same country. Congress was pulling itself apart and bipartisanship was a fucking joke. War was the only answer, war and extermination or banishment of whoever lost, and Rip didn't intend it to be his side.

"What do you think, Rip?" Powder asked. "About what he said."

He whirled around and put his face right into Powder's. "What do I *think*? I think okay, let Amy Carlisle come back from the dead. If she can hold a gun, we can shoot her and we can shoot her again and again and again until we blow her into so many pieces the cunt'll *never* be able to pull herself together!"

Ray looked down for a moment, the thoughts slowly falling into place, then looked back up. "But we already did that."

284

Rip's teeth clenched. Words failed him. He was angry and anxious and scared, about the spy, about the woman, and about the bombing the following day. There was just too much to think and worry about.

So he decided not to think at all. He would kill something instead. "Hey!" he shouted in mock joviality to the men standing around the cages near the range. "Who wants to shoot some birds!"

thirty-seven

Amy was careful to put at least fifty yards between herself and the compound fence. The open area had been lit up like Steven Spielberg was expecting the mother ship to land and the light filtered into the surrounding forest, letting her see while remaining unseen.

She had decided the best place to enter would be at the opposite end from the gate. There was no reason for the Sons to think that anyone had discovered their location and if the bastards were as inept at security as they seemed to be at everything else, she should have no problem getting in.

And once she got in, the best way to handle things would be to do what she had done on the outside. Take them one or a few at a time. Even the gun show had been a close call. She had been assaulted with so much firepower that she had feared falling beneath it several times. If she had, and if they had been able to get chains on her or imprison her, she would have failed.

She might fail now against the sheer firepower of several dozen armed men. Best to come upon them like a white-eyed plague, one at a time, until none were left.

Amy wondered how Rick was doing. His mission had been braver than hers. She remembered Scrooge's protest to the spirit from *A Christmas Carol*: "I am a mortal, and liable to fall." He was indeed, and she wished that she could stop thinking and worrying about him so much.

She wished she could stop loving him so much.

She had told herself over and over that he and she were now on different shores of creation, though they had been face to face. That was why she had not fallen into his arms, not clung to him as though she would let nothing, not even death, pull them apart again. It was not fair to him. It was not even fair that she had let herself be seen by him. She should have remained a memory.

And yet, wasn't it somehow reassuring for the living to know that there was indeed something after death? That they might be reunited again?

Amy. And Rick.

And Nancy.

It stuck in her heart like a barb. If she had been passed over to wherever the peaceful spirits go when they die, she could have looked down and seen Rick and Nancy together and felt not only love for both of them, as she did now, but fulfillment, knowing that the one she loved was no longer alone. And wasn't that what love was all about? Not wanting the loved one to die so that they could join you, but wanting them to live happily and live loved.

It was not resentment she felt, but sorrow, and she had fought it as best she could. In a little while she wouldn't have to fight it anymore.

As she walked beyond the throw of the powerful lights, she moved nearer to the fence so that she could keep it in sight. Once she saw something moving on the other side and at first assumed it was a deer. But when she froze and looked more closely, she could see that it moved with the unmistakable gait of a man walking slowly and carefully.

So there were extra sentries out tonight. She would have to be more careful then.

When she heard the first of the gunshots, she dropped to a crouch, even though the shot did not sound near to her. Another shot followed, then more, and she realized that they were coming from the brightly lit area near the buildings.

Perhaps Levinson and other policemen had followed her and she was hearing a gun battle.

But no, the shots were coming at too long intervals. They must be training or having a competition. At any rate, more than just the sentries were up and about and armed, and her caution increased even more.

At last she reached the place where the fence started to curve to the east, and she trod gently across the fallen leaves until she reached the ten-foot-high chain link fence. The razor wire at its top shone brightly in the moonlight. Though she thought about simply climbing over it, it would be too easy to get entangled in it. Her clothes, if not her flesh, would be torn to shreds. So she took the wire cutters and started snipping away at an open spot where the brush did not come right up to the fence.

The powerful tool cut the individual strands like dead twigs and in a short time she had made a hole big enough to climb through. She left the cutters behind. Her weapons were all she would need now.

Once within the fence she listened intently, but heard only the wind and the sound of the guns to the south. Her gaze searched between the trees but she saw no movement.

Amy could have headed straight south toward the buildings, through the trees in the center of the fenced area. But she reasoned that if she kept to the perimeter, she would come across the sentries and could take them individually. They would be looking outside the fence, not inside. So she began to follow the fence line, staying several feet from it, working her way south. Both weapons were slung over her shoulders so that her hands were free. She didn't want to draw attention to her presence yet, and the knife would be quiet.

Amy saw the first sentry after walking two hundred yards. He was a tall, heavy man, holding an assault rifle at port arms as he walked unconcerned through the trees toward her. As she had assumed, he was looking outside the fence for danger. Drawing her knife, she stepped behind a tree and waited for him to come closer.

It was almost too easy. His back was to her as he passed and she had to take only one step to reach him. Wrapping her left arm around his head so that the inside of her elbow pressed into the hollows of his eyes, she drew his head back and, with the knife in her right hand, scored the blade across his throat.

She didn't even feel the blood splash. She only felt the man spasm until she released him, and he fell straight down on his face, across the weapon he was holding.

Amy kicked him over easily. His finger hadn't even been in the trigger guard. Amy wiped her knife on the dead leaves, slipped it back into its sheath, and took the dead man's weapon. She didn't know the name of it but it looked deadly, and she decided to start her shooting with it and toss it away when it was empty. It would save her a change of magazines.

Shots continued to be fired from the other end of the compound as she dragged the dead man into the brush and kept moving south. She was about fifty yards away from where she had killed the sentry, when she stepped on something other than the loamy forest soil.

Before she had time to question what it was, the world burst into flame around her and an intense pain ripped at her body. She could feel her feet and legs torn apart and what seemed like fists of fire slamming into her torso, shredding her bowels like they were paper. She flew, her flesh ravaged, into the night sky, seeing her blood arc from her, the drops glowing like bits of jellied napalm, then, as the flame died, like glistening rubies in the moonlight. She fell, landing heavily on her back, her sundered face looking upward at the moon through the skeletal branches of trees.

Her throbbing brain knew that it was a mine. She had stepped on a mine and though she had not even heard it, it had exploded beneath her, the concussion stunning her and the blast smashing her to pieces.

Then her eyes saw, alighting on a branch so that its dark shape eclipsed the moon, the Crow. It seemed to look down at her, though its eyes were shadowed, and she knew that her mission was not over. She did not question. She did not lift her head and look down at her body to see if she was capable of rising. She simply sat up and got to her feet.

Her clothing hung from her in shreds but it covered her flesh, which was knit together again as though the mine had never been. The guns she had been carrying on her back had been wrenched from her by the mine's force, but when she picked them up, they seemed functional. They were made to take punishment, she guessed, although the weapon she had been holding had taken the full impact of the concussion and was twisted beyond use. She was glad to see that her knife still had its edge.

A rustle sounded overhead and she looked up to see the Crow flying south again, toward the sound of guns and the lights. Amy started walking.

thirty-eight

POWDER BURNS LOOKED UP IN ALARM. "YOU HEAR THAT?" HE asked Rip Withers, who was standing next to him, watching the shooting.

"What?"

"Sounded like something up in the north—a shot or explosion or something."

"Ah, you heard an echo, that's all," said Rip.

Powder thought about it. The sound had come right on the tail end of a shotgun blast. Maybe Rip was right and it *had* been an echo. But man, it had that *crump* quality to it, and the more Powder tried to recreate the sound in his head the more certain he became that it wasn't a shot, but one of his antipersonnel mines going off.

Hell, it happened now and then, but it had always been a deer that had made an unlucky step. A lot of the men were worried about it, though, and with sentries in the north, where they weren't used to patrolling, anything was possible, though they were told over and over not to go within ten feet of the fence.

Powder tried to get his mind off of it by watching the men shooting. There was a certain beauty to it, the bird being released and darting into the air lit by the bright lights, then the sound of the shot and the bird either flying away while the other men hooted at their comrade's lack of marksmanship or, as happened nine times out of ten, the bird exploding in a supernova of blood and feathers.

Now Ed Conover took his stance and yelled, "Go!" A dove shot into the sky, zigged and zagged for two seconds, and then Ed blew it apart with one shell.

As Powder watched the bird dissolve in the air, he thought about what his mines could do, and then he remembered that Karl Withers was up there, walking around the perimeter, within yards of those mines. Karl Withers, Rip's one and only son, one of the nicest if not the brightest kids Powder had ever known, and it was that not-so-bright aspect that now alarmed Powder. What if the kid had blundered into a mine. Odds are he hadn't, but oh shit, what if he had?

What the hell, it wouldn't hurt to check. He could get up and back in a half hour or so. He'd take a flashlight and whistle the Horst Wessel song all the way so that the sentries would know he was coming. Might as well take a pistol too, just in case.

Phil Riley knew damn well what that sound was, though he was a lot closer to it than Powder Burns had been. Somebody or something had stepped on a mine, and the hair on Phil's belly curled even more at the thought. He hoped to hell it wasn't one of his brothers, as he trotted toward where the sound had been.

Phil wasn't scared of the mines. Although he didn't know where all of them were located, he knew just how close he could come to the fence before he risked getting his nuts blown off. But some of his brothers were a little more careless than he was.

After all, it came with the territory. If you were an outlaw in the eyes of the Jew government, it tended to make you a little reckless. You knew you stood a good chance of dying before you reached a ripe old age so you tended to value your life a little less than you otherwise might have.

But not Phil. If Phil was going to die, he wanted to do it for a reason, for a cause. He wanted to go down taking as many Jews and niggers with him as possible. He wanted to make the bastards pay. The damn ZOG government took all his money in taxes for those raggedy-ass coloreds who didn't do shit except sell drugs to each other. Even now, in the cool night air, the thought made Phil Riley's blood boil. He wished he had a nigger to kill, one of those so-called poor, raggedy ones.

He walked more slowly as he approached the place where the noise had come from. And then he saw it in the moonlight. There was a small crater in the earth where he was certain that a mine had exploded, but there was no body anywhere. Now what the shit was *this* all about?

Phil leaned his gun against a tree and stepped gingerly toward the crater. No use in taking any chances, though Powder probably hadn't put his mines that close together. Phil knelt, looking at the crater, searching for any signs of flesh or blood when he heard leaves crackle behind him. He turned and standing between him and his gun was his worst nightmare.

The figure was dark. Its skin appeared black in the moonlight and rags hung from its thin frame. Its face was dark except for the eyes, two white circles with darkness at their core, and the mouth, a pale, painted smile. It looked like a blackface minstrel gone insane. And it had a big knife in its hand.

Phil couldn't even speak. His mouth moved but no words came out. Finally his mind cleared just long enough for him to reach for his survival knife and yank it from its sheath. The black figure still didn't move.

Phil lunged at it with his knife and tried to scream, "Die, nigger!" But the words came out choked and pinched. Still, the knife entered the raggedy nigger's guts and Phil ripped to the side and stepped back.

The nigger didn't move. It only smiled, and now he could see its white teeth rimmed by the white mouth. Then it spoke, in a woman's voice. "It's not nice to call names." The nigger's arm shot out and skewered him, sticking the knife in the same place where he had stabbed it. *"Redneck,"* it said, and slashed to the side, the same way Phil had done.

The effect on Phil was far more impressive. He put his hand

to his side to try and stop his guts from sliding out over his belt, but it didn't work very well. Then he plopped down on his ass, trying with both hands to shove back into himself the warm loops that flooded over his hands and forearms like wriggling snakes. But goddammit, he couldn't *do* it, it wouldn't *work* and he didn't want to have to die this way, for nothing, and to have it done to him by a *nigger*, by some blackface *coon*, was more than he could bear.

So he died.

Amy wiped the knife on the leaves again. This was getting to be a habit. Maybe she should just leave it wet with their blood so it would slide into the next one more easily. She took the dead man's weapon, a good replacement for the one that the mine had destroyed, and started running lightly across the leaves.

She hadn't gone twenty yards before she saw another shape moving toward her from the south. Good, she thought. Another one. Line them up and knock them down.

Amy slipped behind a thick tree and waited. The shape came walking up, and when she glanced around the tree at it, she saw his face. It was only a boy, no older than seventeen or eighteen. His young skin looked smooth in the moonlight, his eyes were wide and frightened. The gun he was holding looked big and bulky in his hands. He appeared to be no taller than Amy and she guessed he might have weighed less.

He looked innocent. Young and guileless and innocent. There was no other word for it. And what had she promised Levinson? That no more innocents would die.

That was what had started all this, wasn't it? The slaughter of innocents had brought her back and the death of one more misguided child would not help to put the wrong things right. It would only make things worse, *perpetuate* the wrongs. No. It had to stop sometime.

But what could she do? The boy had a gun and if he fired it, it might arouse the others. Her plan to take them slowly had worked so far and there was no reason to change it now.

Then she would stop him from firing the gun without hurting him.

Let's see how innocent he really is, Amy thought, as she set down her guns. She staggered out from cover only a few yards from the boy, keeping her head down so he would not see her painted face, and moaning, "Help . . . please, help me . . ."

He *was* an innocent and came to her immediately, lowering his gun. When he was close enough, she wrenched it from his hands, then flung it away and raised her knife to his throat. "I don't want to hurt you," she said, "but I will. I've killed two men already."

The words panicked him and he staggered backward, turned, and ran. She was after him in an instant and leaped on him from behind, bearing him to the soft floor of the forest. He trembled beneath her and tried to roll over, turning his head so that his face came into contact with hers, cheek against cheek, flesh against flesh . . .

And images, more vivid than the most intense dreams, flooded from his mind into hers, and she knew his name, knew his father, saw his soul, what had made him what he was—

The raging, florid face of a man towering over him, fists, palms, open hands, fingers as hard as sticks. *Be a man, dammit, be a man, don't let those niggers push you around.*

The hands, those big hands coming down like thunder and lightning, pushing him away. *Daddy, stop, stop, don't hit her!*

A woman crying, tears falling down her cheeks, a bloody lip, bruised eyes. *Seen you looking at that ugly black stud, that fucking gorilla, you bitch, you whore, you nigger-loving cunt!*

Playing in the yard and Daddy, Daddy coming out yelling, *Get out of my yard, you damn Jewboy,* and saying, *He's my friend,* and Daddy's hands and *Jews aren't your friends, leeches running the fucking country, niggers, goddam niggers and Jews, that school's full of 'em!*

Jews, goddam Jews, all their fault, and the faggots and the niggers and the spics and the chinks and the gooks . . .

. . . and the and the and the . . .

Be a man Be a man I'll teach you to be a man!

Daddy's hands, Daddy's hands, Daddy's hands.

And then peace, a place of stillness, Mommy's arms and her voice, soft as a kiss as she cried and told him:

He's not yours, not yours, don't ever tell him, but he's not yours . . .

And then a name, the name of his real father, the name his mother told him to forget but that he never could . . .

Amy tasted it all, the bitterness of the boy's life, of secrets and hate and the venom that was fed to him every day until he gave up, succumbed to the poison, and let his soul die. It was easier that way.

She rolled away from the boy as though further contact would poison her as well. He lay there on his side and slowly his knees drew up, his shoulders hunched, and he started to cry in a way that would have brought a sneer to his father's face.

"It's all right," she said. "It's all right. I'm not going to hurt you." Then she moved him next to a tree whose trunk was a foot across and bound him there, as gently as she could, with the mesh and leather slings of her weapons so that he hugged the tree. She put a ball of torn cloth in his mouth and wound another strip of cloth around his head to secure it, making sure that he could breathe through his nose.

"When it's over," she said, "I'll come back for you." Then she started moving south again.

She was running over the dead leaves when suddenly the Crow appeared in front of her, fluttering down and standing on the forest floor as if to bar her way. She stopped and the Crow walked slowly in a circle. Then she understood, unslung her weapons and set them down, took out her knife and crouched in front of the bird as it rose into the sky again.

Amy used the knife like a pick, pressing it gently into the soil beneath the dead leaves until she heard a *tick* and felt the knife point hit a solid surface. It was another mine, and she prodded until she knew exactly where its edges were, then began to dig it out. She wasn't sure what she was going to do with it, but could picture herself tossing it like a Frisbee into the midst of the Sons of a Free America, and the image nearly made her laugh.

She had just straightened up, holding the mine, one hand on the carrying handle, the other on the base plate, when she heard a voice behind her. "Just hold it right there . . . Turn around slow."

She did as ordered and was rewarded with the sight of the widening eyes behind a pair of wire-rimmed glasses. The eyes and the glasses belonged to a long, lanky, scar-faced man whose greasy hair curled out from under his military cap. He looked, Amy thought, like the character Tom Courtenay had played in *Doctor Zhivago*.

"Greetings, Comrade Strelnikov," she said, holding the mine in front of her so that the pressure plate faced the man. "Or would you prefer Pasha?"

He started to back up but she followed, slowly closing the ten-foot gap between them. "Wait a minute!" he said. "Now just take it easy! If that thing goes off, it'll kill us both!"

"Are you so sure of that?" Amy asked with a light tone that belied the gravity of the situation. She didn't want to experience an exploding mine again but she had no real fear of it, and if she could bluff this skinny cracker out of his gun, it would be well worth the risk.

"Yeah, yeah," the man babbled. "I am *fucking* sure of that. I know my devices, okay, lady?"

"*Your* devices . . . ?" A thought crossed Amy's mind. "You planted this?" She walked closer.

The man tried to back up further but bumped against a tree. The contact made him jump. "Yeah," he said breathlessly. "Yeah, it's mine . . ." He looked about frantically for a means of escape.

"You're the bomb man," Amy said slowly. "The one who put the bomb into the center." The man didn't respond. He was too busy looking for an out. Then it hit her. "Powder . . . *gun-powder* . . ." She looked more closely at the scars on his frightened face. "You're Powder Burns."

He neither admitted nor denied it, but started to slide his back around the side of the tree.

"No," Amy said, walking right up to him and making him freeze where he stood, his gun uselessly at his side. "Don't leave. I know some people who want to meet you, Powder. They want to welcome you home . . ."

She pressed herself against him then, the mine between them, and for the third time in her life and death and life, the world exploded.

This time she saw the results on someone other than herself. The charge blasted away Powder Burns's chest, leaving a downturned arc of shoulders from which ripped muscle hung like red streamers. For an instant Amy looked at the head that topped that arc, a face clawed away by shrapnel, which had driven the man's glasses into his eyes and deep into his brain. Then that face fell along with the shoulders, slapping the ground wetly, and Amy fell with it, ruined and shattered once more.

And once more, miraculously, she was healed. To her surprise, the damage was not as great as it had been the first time. The charge had been directed outward, toward Burns, and she had suffered the recoil, which was enough to make a crater in the earth and kill any living being. But as she reminded herself, she had the advantage of already being dead.

She picked up her weapons and began to walk, moving deeper into the forest. She had had enough of mines, and the sound of the last one, unmuffled by the ground, had surely been heard by the rest of the compound. Now they knew. Someone was inside and killing.

thirty-nine

IT WAS DAVID LEVINSON'S NIGHT OFF BUT HE WASN'T RELAXING. He was scanning the police bands and listening for any news that he could connect to Amy Carlisle or a militia group. Fires in the woods, unexplained gunshots, explosions, you name it, he would have gone to the scene in a minute.

But it was a quiet night in and around Hobie. There was nothing out of the ordinary at all and that fact was driving him crazy. He wanted more than anything to help Amy Carlisle end this. He had been her accessory, helping her to break the law more than once, and even contributing to the deaths of innocent people, and he knew he would take that sin with him to his grave, where he would have to answer to . . . something.

Before this had all happened, Levinson believed that dead was dead. His forebears' Sheol was just that, the underworld, the place beneath the ground where bodies rotted and vanished, given enough time. But now he knew there was something more, some other place from which Amy had returned to do what she had to do.

He wanted to help her because he wanted to see justice served. But there was another reason too. As absurd and impossible and even blasphemous as it seemed, he was a little bit in love with the woman.

Jesus Christ, Levinson, he told himself, talk about going

after the inaccessible. He might as well have had a crush on Marilyn Monroe. This woman wasn't just beyond him, she was on a whole different plane of being.

And maybe that was why he was fascinated by her. It was impossible, hence, it was safe. No commitment necessary. But still, she was here on his plane for now and he just wished that there was something he could do besides sit around and wait to help clean up the fireworks or, he thought grimly, hear about nothing at all.

He considered pouring a good stiff one but decided not to, in case something did come through on the scanner and he had to move fast. Instead he put a video in the VCR. It was a copy of the tape that an attendee had made at the gun show, the one from which the brief footage of Amy had been excised. He watched it primarily to see her, just get a glimpse of her from the back.

Yes, there she was. He could tell from the way she moved. He saw her for two seconds and then the camera moved away. He rewound it and watched again, then let it play on, thinking about her, barely seeing what was happening, at least not until Rick Carlisle crossed from right to left and out of sight.

Levinson grabbed the remote and backed it up. Yes, it was Carlisle. No doubt about it. What the hell was *he* doing there?

And then the thought occurred to him that maybe there were *two* vigilantes out there, one dead and one alive.

He looked up Carlisle's number and dialed it. If he professed an interest in guns, which Levinson doubted, all well and good. But if not, or if he denied having been there . . . well, Levinson would cross that bridge when he came to it.

A woman answered and when Levinson identified himself as *Officer* Levinson, he heard an audible gasp. Before he could say anything else, the woman asked, "Is he all right? Did you find Rick?"

Oh *shit*, Levinson thought, but only said, "I'm sorry, ma'am, who are you, please?"

"I'm Nancy, his wife. Do you know where he is?"

"No, I don't, ma'am, but I think we'd better have a little talk. May I come over to your house?"

After he assured her that he did not know where Rick was or *how* he was, she agreed and he got in his Blazer and headed to the address she gave him. He took along his service revolver, as well as a Winchester 1300 Defender pump shotgun with a seven-shot magazine that he slid under the seat. He didn't think he'd need it for the new Mrs. Carlisle, but God only knew what *Mr.* Carlisle might have gotten himself into.

forty

WHEN THE SECOND MINE WENT OFF, THE ONE THAT KILLED Powder Burns, Tom Danvers had just missed a pigeon which Ace Ludwig had then drawn on with his pistol and downed with two shots, just as it was about to disappear in the trees. People were teasing Danvers and congratulating Ace, and Rip Withers was thinking that he should bawl the man out since nobody was supposed to shoot at another man's target, when they heard the sound. It was much louder than the mines they had heard go off before.

"What the shit?" Rip said, looking around for Powder Burns and thinking that maybe Powder had been right and that it *was* a mine they had heard earlier. But Powder was nowhere to be seen. Oh fuck, and *Karl* was out there on guard duty.

"*Ace,*" he barked. "Get some men out there and see what's going on—and don't get yourself blown up!" Ace nodded and picked half a dozen men, the cream of the Sons' crop.

Ace didn't complain about being taken away from the shoot. He had gotten a perfect ten out of ten, a score reached by no one else so far and not likely to be surpassed. No, it looked like Ace was going to have the pleasure of blowing away the liberal pigfucker tied up in the cell. He was sure Ace would make it entertaining.

Rip just hoped that it hadn't been Karl who had stepped on

one of Powder's mines. He had thought about leading the party himself but was afraid of what he might find. If anything had happened to Karl, Rip would tear Powder apart.

Then he remembered what was going down the next day and decided that he would tear Powder apart later. Better yet, maybe he'd leave him tied up and gagged in the van so that he could feel the results of his handiwork.

Aw, fuck it, Rip thought. It probably wasn't Karl at all. Like everybody else, he had been told a hundred times not to go within ten feet of the fence. It was probably just a deer again, maybe that first time too, if it really had been a mine. Everybody was just too edgy, knowing what was coming tomorrow.

It was just a deer and Karl was fine and he wouldn't do a damn thing to Powder and tomorrow night they would all laugh and clap each other on the back and dance on hundreds of ZOG graves.

She heard them coming through the trees. If they were supposed to be stealthy, they needed a lot more training.

They were moving in a line, five or six across, by the sound of them, and Amy flitted through the trees, taking the knife from her sheath, moving to where the man on the right would pass her, and positioning herself behind a tree. She heard a slight rustle above her and imagined the Crow settling onto a nearby limb, her companion, her collaborator, her avatar.

When the man passed, she stepped out behind him, wrapped her arm around his head, and slashed across his throat. But unlike her other victims, this man had his finger on the trigger and jerked it spasmodically, sending a burst of automatic fire ahead of him, biting the bark off trees and filling the woods with a roar of exploding gunpowder.

Ace Ludwig had been well trained by the government he hated. As soon as he heard the first shot, he instantly fell prone, shouting *"Down!"* to the rest of the squad. The shots were on the right flank, where Tannahill had been. Then the gunfire stopped and in the moonlight Ace saw Tannahill falling and a shadowy figure slipping away from him behind the cover of the trees.

"Fire three!" he shouted to Andy Brett, meaning for Brett to fire three shots and warn the main party. Then Ace got up and ran into the trees after whoever had downed Tannahill. Behind him, he was dismayed to hear a near fusillade of shots. He turned around and yelled, "*One* of you, dammit!" then plunged into the brush after the intruder again.

He saw the shape dodge in and out from behind the trees but had no clear shot, so he ran faster in pursuit. He was closing in, and finally had enough of a sight picture so that he slammed his weapon up against a tree and waited for movement.

It came, higher than he had expected. For a moment he thought that maybe the attacker had climbed a tree, but before that thought had formed, he was already firing a string of shots at the black blur of motion. Ace heard the bullets smack wood and his heart leaped at the softer sound of them tearing into something wet and yielding.

He stopped firing. In the sudden silence there was a cry, a human cry that seemed to come from beyond the tree where he had seen the movement. Then he heard something fluttering and falling. From the sound it made when it struck the dead leaves, he thought that if it was a person, it was a damn small one.

When he reached the dying thing, the moon was bright enough to show him what he had shot. "Shit," he said when he saw it. "A fucking *crow.*"

The bird had been hit twice as far as Ace could see. One bullet had nearly chopped off a wing so that it hung by a thread of bone, and another had struck between belly and breast, leaving a large red hole. He thought he could see its heart beating, black in the moonlight.

"Fuck you," he growled, and stepped on its head, smashing it into the mat of dead leaves.

"Ace?" It was Andy Brett, gingerly coming up beside him. "What was it?"

"Just a nigger bird. A damn crow. But it's dead now. How's Tannahill?"

Brett shook his head. "Somebody cut his throat. He's dead."

"*Fuck!*" The others were coming now. Ace counted four with Brett. That meant Tannahill was the only one down. But where were the sentries? "Somebody's in here," Ace said, looking to all sides. "Somebody's killing our people and they're heading toward the camp."

He led the way south toward the buildings and the bright lights.

When Amy heard the shots, she thought she had been hit. There was a terrible pain in her right arm that made her drop the weapon she had taken from the dead man, and a jolt to her stomach that was like a fiery punch. It drove her to her knees and toppled her over and there was so much pain that she could only lie there wishing she were dead. But worse was to come.

Pressure suddenly seemed to build up in her skull as though her brain were expanding against the bone, and the only way to relieve it would be if her head burst open. The pressure increased. Her eyes felt as if they were being pushed out of their sockets, her ears were throbbing with the blood that pulsed behind the thin drums, demanding exit.

Then her head burst open and she entered the darkness.

When she awoke, she had no idea how much time had passed. Only a dull ache remained from the killing pain in her head. Her stomach felt as though it had taken a hard blow and her arm was stiff and sore.

There was something else too, some change that she couldn't name. She felt different, maybe weaker. Yes, that was it. She was tired, so very, very tired. She should try to end this, end it so that she could rest.

She heard something coming toward her from the north and pushed herself to her feet. The dead man's gun was on the ground and she picked it up, but was surprised at how much heavier it seemed. Then she started to run.

She *was* more tired. She was stumbling over roots, tripping in brush. The whole forest was like a covert ally of her pursuers, determined to slow her down.

Amy breathed a curse and pushed on. The lights of the camp glowed through the trees, and she shifted the gun in her hands so that the muzzle was pointing ahead, toward all those Sons of a Free America who she would soon put to rest in American soil. It had come to that now, just a firefight, her against them all. But her bullets would kill while theirs would only pass through. They would hurt her, but she had already been through enough pain for an eternity of hells. She could bear more.

Now she could see the buildings through the trees, see something moving, men walking, looking toward where she hid. Behind her, footsteps crushed the dead leaves as her hunters closed in.

It was time. She burst from the shelter of the woods, aimed at the men ahead of her and pulled the trigger, downing two of them. But they responded quickly, bringing up their guns and firing back. Suddenly something struck her arm and her weapon dropped to the ground. She stood there for a moment, hands empty, scarcely knowing what had happened, as more bullets whizzed past her.

Then the shots stopped, though she didn't know why. All she knew was the fire in her arm and the blood that was running down what was left of her sleeve. Something moved behind her but she had no strength to turn and see what it was.

Then her head burst into a ball of pain and everything flickered. And as she fell to the ground, these words ran through her mind:

I am a mortal, and liable to fall . . .

forty-one

NANCY CARLISLE WAS NEAR PANIC WHEN LEVINSON ARRIVED AT the home she shared with Rick. After he calmed her down, she told him all about Rick's obsession with finding Amy's killers, and that in his last call to her two days before, he had told her that he had gotten in contact with the Sons of a Free America.

"All right, Mrs. Carlisle," Levinson said, "I think you need to come down to headquarters and give us a statement. We've got to start looking for your husband as soon as possible."

"Do you think he's in danger?" she asked, her voice shaking.

"I think it's very possible, yes. The sooner we find him the better."

It made sense to Levinson. This was the way to do it. He would get the entire force looking, call in the feds and find not only Rick Carlisle but hopefully the bastards he was tracing, the very ones that Amy was on her way to confront right now. Maybe the police could only mop up after she was done, but at least it gave Levinson something to do besides sit on his ass and wait.

Levinson, Nancy Carlisle, and her daughter, Karin, headed for the police station in Levinson's Blazer, pausing to drop the girl off at a friend's house several blocks away. Levinson watched as Nancy kissed Karin good-bye at the friend's front door and felt a dull ache as he thought about the life that might have been his.

Their route took them by the empty lot where the day-care center had been. As always, it looked tragic and barren under the street lights that stood on each corner. Levinson turned and looked at the thick layer of dust that covered the site, and then without thinking, he slammed on the brakes.

Nancy, startled, asked, "What is it? What's wrong?"

Levinson thought he said *look*, but he only pointed to the blasted rubble until Nancy saw it too.

The dust was moving, although the wind had died down and no longer rattled the few dead leaves that still held fast to the trees. The pale dust and ash that had been the Making Friends Child Care Center and the people who had died there were gathering into what looked like individual waves that flowed together until a number of mounds had formed. The mounds rose and lengthened into rounded cylinders, with smaller mounds on top. They were, Levinson saw, taking the shapes of birds.

There were ten of them, and as Levinson and Nancy watched, their color darkened from ashy gray to a black so deep that they would have become lost in the night had it not been for the sheen of the feathers in the street lights' glow.

Then the birds spread their wings, and even through the closed windows, Levinson could hear a sound like dry paper being torn as the newly born creatures moved for the first time. They rose as one, their broad wings beating the night air, and flew north.

Without a word, Levinson began to follow them, and Nancy Carlisle made no protest.

"Wake up, you fucking bitch!"

The slap across the face brought Amy Carlisle back to consciousness. She felt cold, colder than she ever had since returning from her death. Her arm ached unbearably and when she tried to move it, to ease it into a more comfortable position, she discovered that her arms were bound behind her.

She blinked several times and saw that she was tied to a chair. Three men she did not know were standing before her. The one who had slapped her was breathing heavily. His teeth were clenched and his hands were balled into fists. He was wearing a gun belt from which hung a holstered .45; a sheathed knife hung on his left hip.

The other two men were dressed in camouflage like the first. One of the men was holding an assault rifle. There was a thin smile under his dark mustache. The third man was clean shaven and slightly resembled the first. His face seemed blank and Amy suspected he was mildly retarded.

"Awake, huh?" the first man said. "Look around, bitch, see anybody you know?"

Amy turned her head. Sitting next to her, tied in the same way, was Rick. Before she even knew she was doing it, she said his name. "Rick . . . oh God."

"Rick, huh?" said the first man. "Well, Ricky, it seems you know our little friend here. Why don't you introduce us?"

Rick looked terrible. Both of his ears had been cut, and dried blood coated his neck. His face was bruised in several places and one eye was blackened. Still, he smiled at her. "You already know her," he said. "But for formality's sake, this is Ace Ludwig, Ray Withers, and his charming brother, Rip."

Rip Withers. The first name that William Standish had given her. Here he was right in front of her and she couldn't do a thing about it.

"And what's the cunt's name?" Rip Withers asked.

Rick kept smiling, but this time he smiled at Rip Withers. "Like I said, you know her. You killed her. This is my wife. Amy."

Rip Withers looked as if Rick were crazy, but then his face cleared. "I get it," he said. "I get it now. They never found your body, but that wasn't because you were blown up, it was because you were never in there to start with. You must've left before the shit hit the fan and played dead ever since, huh?"

"No," Amy said. "I died. And I came back. For you." She strained against the ropes but they held her fast as her arms throbbed with pain. She felt as if all her strength had gone, as if she were a different creature entirely from the one the Crow had brought back.

"Well, you had a good run, lady," Rip said. "But it ends here. Now you tell me, where the hell is my son?"

"Who?"

"Don't fuck with me! My boy was out there on sentry duty! My son, Karl! Did you hurt him?" The knife came out of the sheath, and Withers brandished it in front of her. "You tell me or I swear before Yahweh I'll cut your tits off and make Ricky here eat them!"

"Your son's alive," she said. "I tied him up."

"Now you know you're going to die," Withers said. "But if you hurt him, you're going to die slow." He turned to the man with the rifle. "Ace, I don't want a whole squad trooping through the trees, in case she brought some friends along. You're quieter in the woods than anybody we've got. Go find Karl, okay?"

"What if I find some of her friends?" Ace asked.

"Go ahead and kill 'em."

"All *right*," Ace said. "I'd like to nail something tonight besides a goddam crow," and he slipped out the door.

That was it then, Amy thought. The Crow was dead. That was why her strength was gone, why she had been wounded in the arm and lost consciousness.

What would happen now? Would she die for a second time at the hands of this madman? If so, she would make sure that he would never forget her, that if she could not kill him, she could at least make him live in pain.

"All right, whore," Withers said. "Now tell me who else knows you're here."

"General Custer, the Sixth Fleet, the Terminator, Superman—" She had been about to continue with Nancy Drew and Jackie Chan, but Withers hit her with a vicious backhand that rocked her head and caused more pain to shiver through her wounded arm.

"Haven't you learned not to fuck with me yet?" he said, waggling his knife in front of her nose. "I can promise you a world of hurt, bitch."

"You know," Amy said, looking fiercely into Withers's eyes, "your son was a whole lot nicer than you. Doesn't that ever make you wonder?"

His eyes narrowed. "What are you talking about?"

"If he's really your kid? I mean, the way you treated your wife, don't you think it was likely that she sought . . . *comfort* from someone else? Someone nicer, more gentle? Someone who was always there at family gatherings and picnics and holidays?"

"Shut up," Rip said. "You just shut the hell up . . ."

But Amy knew that he wanted to hear more in spite of himself, so she kept talking to Rip Withers but turned her glare toward his brother, Ray, using the information that she had derived from her psychic link with the boy in the woods. "Personally, I think Karl looks and acts a whole lot more like his *real* dad than you, Rip. What do *you* think, Ray? Proud of your boy?"

Ray Withers looked confused and frightened and on the verge of tears, and Amy knew from his reaction that Karl's mother had told the boy the truth about his parentage. Rip was glancing from Amy to Ray and back again, and when his shocked face came to rest on Ray, Amy knew that the shot of pain she had just injected into his soul would gnaw at him as long as he lived.

"Ray?" Rip said, sounding angry and scared and so very close to losing control. "Tell this whore she's full of shit . . ."

It sounded like a plea but it found no pity in Amy. "You know it's true, Rip . . . It's why Karl was never as sharp as you. Why he wasn't as quick with his hands or his mind and why he never will be. Because he isn't even yours. He's Ray's. He's your dumb brother's boy. But your brother wasn't so dumb that he turned down some sweet, sweet lovin' when it was offered."

"Ray?" Rip said again. "You tell me that she's lying . . . you just tell me that and it'll all be all right." He gripped his brother's arm and swung him around to look into his teary eyes, his quivering face. Ray shook his head as if he didn't know what to do or say, and Amy guessed he didn't.

"Ray," Rip went on, and he sounded more dangerous now.

"Did you fuck Elizabeth? You tell me that you didn't . . . You tell me the *truth*, Ray!"

"He can't tell you both," Amy said softly, feeling like the serpent in the garden. "Which do you want?"

"I . . . I . . ." Ray was saying and Amy felt sorry for him, but not sorry enough to try and stop what she had started even if she could have. "I . . ."

"You *what?*" Rip demanded, and Ray responded with two words that told everything.

"I'm sorry . . ."

Rip stared at him for what seemed like a long time. Then motion sprang from the stillness and Rip brought up his right hand, the one that held the knife, straight into Ray's belly and wrapped his left arm around his brother.

Ray gasped, his eyes wet and wide, and as his breath began to come in soft little puffs, he looked in disbelief at his cuckolded brother and put his hands lightly on Rip's shoulders. "I'm . . . sorry . . ." he said like a child. "I . . ."

But what he intended to say next was never heard. His big body slumped in his brother's arms and Rip lowered it to the floor as the knife slid out.

"Did I hit a sore spot?" Amy asked gently. Though her strength was only mortal again, the flame of retribution burned strongly within her and she gloried at the pain she had caused her captor, the murderer of her children. As for poor, stupid Ray, she looked on him as just a dumb but deadly weapon aimed by maniacs. He was a dog with rabies, worthy of pity but meriting death.

Rip Withers stood up slowly, and the face he presented was one that should have been seen only in nightmares. "You . . . *fucking* . . . BITCH!" he said, the air hissing in and out through his clenched teeth. He held the bloody knife in front of him and seemed ready to plunge it into her face at any second. If she wanted to continue to live in this strange half-life of hers, she would have to respond quickly.

"You're what I expected," she said scornfully, showing no fear, for she felt none. "You're not a soldier, you're a sadist. You should be ashamed to call this a militia when you're nothing but a bunch of loonies. Just look at yourself. There's nothing military about you or your whole operation. Now you'll probably stab us too, won't you? Or will you torture us first to make you feel better." She laughed derisively, then stressed each word: *"You . . . sick . . . fuck."*

The speech had the desired effect. Rip Withers's face looked no less hateful, but some of the madness had withdrawn from it. "We're not sick," he said. "And we're not sadists—we're patriots!"

"Then why did you kill your brother?" Amy asked flatly.

"He was a *traitor!*" Rip strove to keep his temper. "He betrayed *me*, he would have betrayed the *Sons* sooner or later. He had to die. And so do you." He stood stiffly, a warrior again or so, Amy thought, he wanted them to believe.

"You think we're insane, but we're not—*you're* the ones who are crazy, to defend ZOG, a government that wants nothing more than to trample you and every other non-Jew citizen, unless you're one of the mongrel races they use as their soldiers against us. The time for outright war is coming fast—the first real blow will be struck tomorrow."

"How?" Amy asked.

Rick answered the question, probably tired of Rip Withers's speech. "They've got a bomb in their bunker that's going to blow up half of Hobie tomorrow morning."

"That's right," Withers said. "Centered at the ZOG government building. Too bad you won't see it. But you're two of ZOG's soldiers who will never raise up arms against true patriots again. You're going to die now, and you'll die as any spy would, by firing squad."

"What about the contest?" Rick asked. "I thought the winner was supposed to have first crack at me."

"That policy has just been changed," said Withers. *"Everyone* will have a crack at you—both of you." He opened the cell door and called out, "Prepare for firing squad detail! Jackson and Anders, bring the prisoners to the firing range!"

Two of the militia members appeared at the door with their guns. When they saw Ray Withers lying there, they looked with uncertainty at Rip but he looked back firmly. "Another traitor," he said in a tone that allowed for no questions. "Take the prisoners."

The two men undid the leather straps that were holding Amy and Rick to the chairs, but left their hands bound behind their backs. Then they grasped them by the right arms, but Amy winced and her guard took her by her left, unharmed shoulder. Withers led the way.

The entire open area was still brightly lit. Amy saw that the bodies of the two men she had shot had been zipped into body bags. They lay against one of the buildings and several of the men stood around them. Others sat on the shooting benches, their weapons across their knees, or returned from the barracks where they had gone to get their rifles for the firing squad. When Amy and Rick appeared, all the men looked at them with the same expression of undisguised hatred.

No wonder, she thought. They were spies and she, for one, had caused the deaths of several of their comrades. It didn't even enter their minds that they had caused the deaths of the children she had loved; and if what Rick said was true, they would cause the deaths of dozens, maybe even hundreds more tomorrow.

Oh God, Amy thought, when would it stop? If only she could have finished her work, just killed them all in a hail of gunfire, then it would have been over.

Yes, until the next group went too far, until another militia chose to become terrorists for whatever cause they celebrated. She knew that she couldn't end all the madness in the world, but at least she could have put a stop to the particular madness that had killed her babies.

She could have, that is, if the Crow had not been killed. Was there any way out, she wondered. When the avatar of death dies itself, how can the dead put the wrong things right? And if not, what happened to the dead who failed?

It looked like she was going to find out.

forty-two

RIP WITHERS LED AMY AND RICK AND THEIR GUARDS TO THE shooting range, but did not take them out to the end where the targets were placed. Instead he stopped only twenty yards out and turned to them.

"So," he said, "we're not going to tie you to stakes. You can stand here and meet the bullets. If you fall down before we fire, we'll just shoot at you on the ground. Your chances for a clean kill will be better if you stay on your feet. That's about it, except that I know you'll both burn in hell and I'll look forward to looking down from heaven and seeing that someday."

Withers turned his back on them and walked toward the rest of the men, the two guards in his wake. "Line up for firing squad duty!" he cried, and the men scurried to obey.

Rick turned to Amy and smiled. "I guess this is it."

"For now," she said. "I have no idea what's coming afterward."

"Maybe we'll both come back."

"No," she said, watching the men form their ranks in two rows. The front row knelt, the back row stood. There were over twenty of them. "I don't think I'll ever come back again. The fact that I got *one* chance to put things right was miracle enough."

"You're right," Rick said thoughtfully. "That *was* a miracle.

319

But maybe the miracles aren't over yet, Amy. Believe." He smiled at her while the men prepared their rifles for firing. "I love you, Amy. I've never stopped loving you. I'm glad I'm with you now. I wished a thousand times that I had been with you then."

"Don't wish that. Don't ever wish for death. Life is too precious."

"Not when the one that makes it that way is gone."

She faced front, looking toward their executioners. She would not tell him that she loved him. She could not. He was still Nancy's husband despite the skewed realities that the Crow had caused. "I'm glad I'm with you now" was as much as she could say.

Still, she felt a dull fury that it should end this way, that these men should win and should wreak more havoc tomorrow, letting slip their dogs of war, a dirty, filthy war, waged in hate and fought in cowardice.

Rip Withers walked to the end of their ranks and barked out his order, "Prepare to fire!"

Amy looked up at the dark sky, far above the reach of their lights, and wished, prayed, hoped, *demanded* something to drop down from it, one giant black bird from the blackness to devour them all, one great Crow to put the wrong things right for good. Not all the wrong things, but the wrong things created by those wrong people who were all encompassed by a chain link fence on this small plot of earth.

Oh yes, now was the time for justice. Now, if ever, was the time for the Crow.

Her prayer was answered. She heard them before she saw them. At first it sounded like the distant cries of children at play. She could see the militiamen stiffen as one, their rifles to their shoulders, and the barrels slowly dropping toward the ground as the sounds grew louder.

Yes, she thought, they *were* the cries of children, the shrill laughter of Brenda Tran, Pete Grissom's teasing catcalls, the subdued giggles of DeMarole White as she clapped her hands over her mouth in a paroxysm of mirth. But as they grew louder, they changed, becoming the keening cry of birds, the raucous cawing of a murder of crows that grew louder and more demanding, insisting on being heard.

At last she saw them, set like black pearls against the topaz of the moon. They flew in a single line, straight across, unlike the delta formations of migrating geese. But their unity was unmistakable and, to Amy, their purpose certain.

They descended in the same line in which they flew, directly between Amy and Rick and the line of militiamen. When they landed, every one of them was facing the two ranks of riflemen.

Amy counted ten of them. Ten crows, one for each of the children who had died. Her heart leaped in excitement, but a cold fear crept along her flesh.

Then as she and Rick and the self-proclaimed soldiers watched, the crows began to grow and shift and change shape, lengthening here, broadening there, until with a chill of horror Amy saw her children, the toddlers, even the babies, all in a row between her and the soldiers,

She pictured them falling under the bullets as they had fallen beneath the bomb, and started to run toward them to shield their little bodies with her own. But they remained children only for a moment, just long enough for Amy to run up to them and see their faces.

They were faces filled with loss, children's faces laden with the adult knowledge that they would never grow up, never grow old, never see their own children run and play. They were faces of tragedy on features of childlike delicacy, and all the more terrible for it.

But those faces changed as Amy and the killers watched, became more adult and rose upward as the bodies beneath them grew. They were aging before Amy's eyes, living in seconds those years that no longer lay ahead, until there were ten young men and women, fully grown, possessing all the strength that loving upbringing would have given them, ten strong bodies, nude without sensuality, creations, not of life, but of some life beyond death, of some dark, feathered justice that refused to let things end with two bound corpses lying in their own blood on a cold field of dishonor.

They did not look at Amy. They walked past her, walked with purposeful and silent steps toward the two rows of soldiers. They walked with their heads high, their hands clenched into fists, and their eyes, alive for this night only, filled with righteous anger.

"Fire!" Rip Withers cried, but his voice cracked in fear. "Shoot! Shoot them!"

The riflemen aimed at the approaching figures and fired their weapons. The bullets tore through the flesh but did no harm, and in seconds the young men and women had closed in on their killers. The guards in the gate tower came down to help repel the invaders, but their weapons had no greater impact than did their comrades'.

Guns were wrenched from fearful, weakened hands and thrown far away. The soldiers fell to their knees as supernaturally strong fists pounded down on them. Some tried to run, but their pursuers, fast as the wind, pulled them down and wrapped wiry fingers around their throats.

In the midst of the attack Rip Withers stood, frozen in disbelief and shock, until a young man with Asian features and golden skin gripped his neck and began to choke him. And in the raging face of that young man, Amy saw the soft eyes of Charlie Tran, come back from the dead to avenge where she had failed.

"No!" Amy screamed, and was amazed to see the faces of all the young men and women look up at her. Their fists, ready to deliver death blows, paused in mid-air. Their fingers, digging into the flesh of thick necks, relaxed, letting air flow into windpipes, blood rush back to dying brains.

"Stop!" Amy said. "You can't do this, this is *my* battle. You can't stain your souls with these . . . fools' deaths! I'm the one who came back for justice, not you. Their deaths should be on *my* soul."

She looked at all of them, her eyes pleading. "I didn't come back to see you made killers—I came back for *love* of you. Please, don't do this. Give me your strength. Let me be your justice again . . ."

One by one, the ten children, grown to adulthood as they

would never be in reality, straightened up, letting their adversaries fall to the ground, coughing and choking, shaking battered heads, nursing their wounds. Not a one seemed ready to fight again, after this attack by the invincible undead.

The ten figures now completely ignored the men on the ground. Instead they came walking slowly toward Amy, and she saw the eyes of a child shining from the face of every one.

When they reached her, they surrounded her, their arms on each other's shoulders, their heads close enough to hers that she could smell their breath, sweet and ethereal, like the purest incense.

She felt a love so overwhelming and so deep that it made her giddy. And she thought again of Scrooge, reborn, saying that he was "as giddy as a drunken man," and so she was, reborn too, giddy and happy and filled with joy and love at the presence of those she had never thought to see again in this world or the next. She felt there could be no higher state. She felt enfolded by love.

Then the youths began to vanish, and at first Amy thought that they were fading away. But she saw instead that they were turning to dust, pale dust that fell like snow to the ground and gathered in peaceful, rounded mounds at her feet. Her children. Her sweet children.

> Golden lads and girls all must,
> As chimney-sweepers, come to dust.

She didn't know what it was from but the words came to her as their requiem.

But there was no amen. Instead there was a cry from above, and when she looked, she saw, perched atop a round-roofed building half buried in the ground, the Crow.

The Crow. Alive. If that were so, then . . .

She strained at the leather bonds that held her wrists together and felt them come apart like paper. The strength was hers again. Her love for her children, and their love for her, had replenished her, and brought back the Crow.

forty-three

AMY LOST NO TIME IN FREEING RICK AND THEN PICKED UP THE nearest weapon, an assault rifle with enough firepower for her to mow down all twenty of the broken and battered men slowly picking themselves off the ground. Rick found a gun too, which he held on the defeated soldiers while he gathered any weapons close at hand.

Amy joined him in his work, and when they had piled all the guns together, she heard a sound of an engine from beyond the gate. In another few seconds she saw the lights of a vehicle approaching the compound on the only access road.

"Watch them," she told Rick, gesturing to the feeble remnants of the Sons of a Free America. Amy ran to the gate in time to see David Levinson climb out of his Blazer, a pump shotgun in his hand, ready for combat.

When he saw an armed Amy, he lowered his weapon, and his jaw. "What the hell," he said, as Amy opened the gate for him.

"How did you get here?" she asked.

"We followed the crows. But what—"

"We?" Amy's question was answered when the passenger door opened and Nancy stepped tentatively out. Their gaze met, and she saw first surprise, then joy, then shock quickly pass over her friend's face. Nancy turned white, and seemed to stagger.

Then the sound of shots split the night's regained silence. At first Amy thought that Nancy had been hit, but then she realized that the bullet had hit *her*, entered her back and exited her stomach. She barely felt a twinge of pain.

Amy whirled, heard another burst of shots, and then saw the boy, Karl Withers, running from the forest, unarmed, looking back over his shoulder, yelling at someone to stop, stop shooting.

But whoever it was didn't listen. A bullet from the next burst caught Karl. Amy saw blood splatter from his left leg and the boy went down. Another burst spat up the dirt near him, and then everyone was running.

Amy dashed toward the trees from where the shots had come and heard Levinson's footsteps pounding behind her. To her left Rick raced toward the boy, firing blindly into the woods as he ran. Then he knelt, covered Karl with his body, and tried to pick him up.

Another burst shook the night, and Rick stiffened, then fell over onto the boy. Amy shrieked in rage and started to fire into the woods but stopped as something huge and black entered her sight. The Crow flew like an arrow behind a stand of trees, screaming its harsh cry, and Amy saw Ace Ludwig stagger sideways into the open as the Crow rushed by him.

Amy and Levinson fired as one. Amy's burst punched Ace in the stomach and Levinson's shotgun blast hit him in the neck. Either one would have killed him, but the result of Levinson's fire was more dramatic. The wad of shot severed the neck and the spine, and ripped off Ace Ludwig's head.

Immediately Amy swung the muzzle of her gun toward the rest of the militia, but they didn't move. Only Rip Withers was slowly walking toward where Karl and Rick lay. And it was to Rick that Amy was now running, still training her weapon on the deflated corps of madmen.

Karl had crawled out from under Rick and was ignoring his own wounded leg in his concern over the man who had tried to save him once more. It was all clear to Amy. The boy had broken his bonds and escaped, witnessed what had happened, and run from cover, trying to tell Ace to stop shooting, that it was all over. But Ace hadn't listened or, as was more likely, had looked on Karl Withers as a—

"*Traitor!*" It was Rip Withers who was yelling, moving toward the boy and Rick. "You traitor *bastard!*" he moaned, and there were tears in his eyes.

"That's far enough," Levinson said, pointing the muzzle of the shotgun at Withers. The man stopped, breathing heavily—his son, his army, his dream all gone.

Nancy and Amy arrived at Rick's side at the same time. He was beyond speech. Blood was frothing at his lips, and Amy knew he had only a few moments left to live. She nodded at Nancy, who, as if having received permission, knelt at Rick's side. Amy remained standing, looking down at them.

Nancy cradled her husband in her arms, oblivious of the blood that ran from the exit wound in his back. Rick turned his head slightly to look at her. A small smile bent the corners of his lips, and Nancy, tears rolling from her eyes, kissed his forehead, then his bloody lips.

His head rolled slowly back so that he was looking at Amy, but whether he had done it on purpose or whether it had been merely a gift of gravity, she could not tell.

Whatever the reason, the smile had fled his face, and in another moment life had left it as well. His lifeless eyes looked into Amy's, and she could read nothing there, not love, not the promise that they would meet again. They were merely dead eyes, as taciturn and enigmatic as the dead have always been.

Nancy's whole body shook with her loss, and she looked up at Amy, not knowing what had happened or how or why, knowing only that she would never really understand. Still, she strove to ask. "What . . . happened? What . . . have you . . . done?"

"I came back," Amy said, "to put the wrong things right." She looked back at Rick's face, and at the boy who had proven himself not yet beyond redemption, the son of her killer, who Rick had tried to save at the cost of his own life. "But it was Rick who did it." She shook her head. "All I can do is end it now."

She looked at Levinson, who had hoisted an assault rifle

from the pile and stood covering the crowd with it and his shot-gun. "David," she said, and he glanced at her. "Take Nancy and the boy out of here. Go get help."

"What about . . ." Levinson gestured to the men sitting on the ground or standing, their shoulders hunched in defeat. Their eyes, however, still burned with anger.

She walked up to him so that the others couldn't hear. "We'll lock them in that bunker," she said, gesturing to the half-buried building.

"What's in it?" he asked her.

"Nothing to worry about. I'll stay with them." She stepped toward the men and raised her voice. "Listen to me! We're going to imprison you for now. Then Officer Levinson will bring back more—"

Maybe it was the thought of imprisonment, or maybe it was being defeated by a Jew, but one of the men made a dash for the pile of weapons. Amy had anticipated such a move, and shot him in the chest before he had even gotten halfway. He fell without a sound.

"That's not something anyone wants to try again," Amy said calmly. "Now get moving. We're going to that bunker."

"Ma'am," said Karl Withers, as Nancy was helping him to his feet. "There's guns in there, and—"

"I know what's in there. There's not going to be any prob-lem. I intend to be the chaperon for these gentlemen until the authorities come." She jerked the muzzle of her gun in the direction of the bunker and the men started walking. "Anyone makes a break for it," Amy said, "he's dead before he runs five steps. So make your moves wisely."

Amy noticed they were murmuring among themselves, and she was sure that the idea had gone through several of their nar-row minds that they could get arms inside and turn the tables on the bitch with the gun. They did, however, think enough of her prowess that none of them tried to escape. Instant death was a strong persuader.

While Amy and Levinson herded the militiamen to the bunker, Nancy helped Karl as he limped through the gate to the Blazer. Amy preceded the men down the steps.

The inside of the building was far larger than its exterior suggested. A variety of firearms stood in racks along one wall and cases of bullets were piled against the other. Further back were wooden cases labeled GRENADES and near them were bins neatly loaded with dynamite sticks. There were also a number of glass jars filled with a gray putty, as well as packets of something sealed in paper.

But what Amy was really looking for was on a table near the entrance, next to the racks of rifles. She made sure that none of the militiamen went near it as she guided them over to the side of the building with the bullets. Let them have all the ammo they want, she thought. It was useless without the guns.

"Keep moving, gentlemen . . . that's it. Sit on those cases if you like. I'm sure you're all pretty tired. Just don't make any move for the weapons, please."

"Amy," Levinson said softly to her. "You're staying in here with them?"

"That's right." She kept watching the men. They looked edgy and dangerous. Rip Withers was standing, like most of the other men whose legs hadn't been injured in the attack. "But none of us are coming out." She glanced at him and saw he was looking at her with concern, and maybe a little fear. "Don't worry, though, they won't feel a thing." She pointed to a key that hung on a nail over the inside of the door. "Odds are that's to this building. Lock it from the outside. Now. And get Nancy and that kid far away, as fast as you can. Thanks, David." She smiled. "You're a *mensch*."

Levinson tried to smile but something in his throat wouldn't let him. "And she speaks Yiddish too," he said huskily. "My dream girl. Shame we had to meet like this . . ."

He turned, grabbed the key, and went up the few stairs in a flash, slamming the door behind him. Amy heard the key turn, and at last beheld the situation she had been waiting for.

She waited for as long as she could. She pictured Levinson running across the clearing and out the gate, helping Nancy get the boy in the truck, if she hadn't already. He would fumble for his keys for a moment or so, then start the truck, panicking if it didn't turn over right away. But it would start. Then he would turn around carefully, avoiding getting stuck, and drive out the dirt road as fast as he could, expecting every second to hear something behind him.

There. That was time enough. He was safe now.

L'chaim, David Levinson. To life.

And now to death. The men were beginning to move. They could nurse their broken arms and twisted ankles and smashed noses only so long. It was inevitable that they would try to overpower her, even though some of them would have to be sacrificed to her bullets. Then they would break down the door and flee before the Jew returned with the feds. That was how they lived and how they thought. So she would have to entertain them.

Moving so decisively that they could only stand and watch, she walked past them, keeping her weapon and her eyes trained on them. She stopped at a carton of grenades, put her fingers under the wooden lid, and yanked upward. The nails shrieked out of the wood and the men gazed in wonder at what would have taken any of them a crowbar to accomplish.

The grenades were nestled like eggs in a nest of excelsior, and Amy plucked one out. She pressed the safety lever with her left hand, hooked her right index finger through the pull ring, and yanked out the safety pin. It was live now. All she had to do was to let it go and no one could call it back.

"Now," she said, turning back to the wide-eyed men. "If any of you were wondering just how I was planning to maintain discipline . . ." She held up the grenade in her left hand and her rifle in her right. "Behold. And don't bother to run for the door. It's locked." She strolled slowly back toward the front of the room and stopped by the table with the box.

"I'm sick of this," she said, unaccountably weary. She felt like sleeping for a very long time. She wanted to sleep in Rick's arms and then wake to see their children around her, but she didn't know if that would ever happen. She hoped it would.

"I died because of you," she told the men in the round-roofed room. "And I'm here because of you. I bring you justice. But I pray for mercy on your souls." She looked down at the grenade in her hands.

"Because if you're damned, then so am I."

Amy looked down into the large wooden box that held Powder Burns's final bomb. Then she released the safety lever of the grenade and jammed it into the multicolored jungle of wires and switches that sat hugging the bomb's payload, a hundred and fifty one-pound blocks of C–4 explosive.

There was only time left for the men to scream and for Amy to close her eyes, hoping that the darkness would remain.

Levinson saw the flash before he heard the sound, and he heard the sound before he felt the shock.

It sounded as though the entire forest was exploding behind him, and felt as though the ground were a giant quilt that someone had suddenly decided to shake out. He slammed on the brakes until the shock wave passed, but even a good half mile away, debris showered down like hail on the Blazer's roof. He wondered if there was anything left of the area within the fence.

Nancy Carlisle's trembling slowed and she said, "Amy . . . she's . . ."

"Yes, she's gone. They're all gone now." He looked at the boy. "All your friends."

There were tears in the boy's eyes. "They weren't my friends. None of them . . . *none* of them . . ."

It was a long road this boy was going to have to walk. Levinson hoped he could make it.

As they drove toward Hobie and its general hospital, passing the police cars that were coming the other way, Levinson told Nancy the story, as much as he knew of it. When he was finished, she was quiet for a while. Then she said, "I can't believe it. Amy couldn't have been dead in the first place. She and Rick . . . they planned this somehow." Her voice became thick with sorrow and humiliation. "I don't think . . . Rick ever loved me."

"What I've said is true," Levinson answered, "and I think that he did love you, as much as he could. But he loved Amy too."

"He's *with* her now," Nancy said, and he heard the grief and the anger and what he hoped might be love in the woman's voice.

He didn't answer, but he thought, I hope so. God, Crow, whatever makes these decisions, please let it be so.

forty-four

THE NEXT MORNING JUST BEFORE DAWN DAVID LEVINSON WAS climbing into his Blazer parked outside the police station. Karl Withers was safely in the hospital, Nancy Carlisle was sleeping a sedated sleep, and Levinson had told his superiors and several federal agents much less than everything he knew.

The tale had taken hours to spin. He had told them that, to the best of his knowledge, Amy Carlisle had survived the explosion, probably wandered away afterward, having lost her memory, and upon regaining it had contacted her husband, now remarried. The two of them, without the new wife's knowledge, had then begun to hunt down the bombers, and ended their quest by dying in the explosion at the terrorists' compound.

The yarn probably had more holes than a pound of sliced Swiss but what seemed to be the linchpin was sturdy enough: the same gang of armed extremists who blew up a day-care center, then killed Wilson Barnes, William Standish, and his mother, had been blown up themselves by another bomb that they had built.

In Levinson's opus, Amy or Rick Carlisle may have been responsible for the killings of Sonny Armitage and Junior Feeley. However, a more likely scenario for the electrocution deaths in Eau Claire may have been a vendetta waged by the leaders of the terrorists against those whom they suspected of being traitors, in this case Chip Porter, though God only knew why.

So they were not only responsible for the deaths of those they insanely considered their enemies, they had also brought about the deaths of those sympathetic to their cause. The feds liked that idea a whole lot, and Levinson suspected it would stick in spite of any evidence to the contrary.

Well, he had done what he could to keep Amy Carlisle's memory as sacred as possible. He started his car and headed home, thinking that he would ask Trotter to help him go back for the Avanti. Trotter would ask no questions.

The former site of the Making Friends Child Care Center was not on Levinson's way home, but he wanted to drive by nonetheless, just to see if anything had changed. He was not disappointed.

Dawn was breaking as he pulled the Blazer up to the curb and got out. It was cold, but just the sight of the sun's rays pouring across the horizon made Levinson feel warmer.

Physically, the place had not changed. Or had it? There was something that had not been there before, some added piece, and it took him a moment to figure out what it was.

There were seedlings, three of them, that had pushed their way through the dust and the ashes, small trees growing from seeds the wind had brought and lodged in this spot. Less than a foot high, they stood in a rough triangle, several feet apart from each other.

As Levinson walked closer, he saw something that he was at a loss to explain. In November, on the cusp of winter and with the temperature close to freezing, the seedlings were sprouting small buds of green. Several tiny flowers had also grown and were blooming in the dust of the triangle the young trees made.

There were ten of them, their delicate petals all of different colors. They were moored in the dust and the ash, beauty born of destruction. Ten flowers.

Ten children lost.

Three trees.

Judy Croft. Amy Carlisle.

And her husband?

With Rick Carlisle's sacrifice, he had done as much as any of them. He had earned his place. He should have a tree.

Jesus, listen to yourself, Levinson thought. Signs in trees and flowers. Hell, it was coincidence, that was all.

But flowers and buds in November? In Minnesota?

He shook his head. Maybe now that the culprits were identified and after all the legal hassles were over, someone could do what nature had already started and make this a garden—a *memorial* garden, with some playground equipment, so that you could hear little kids laughing here again.

He looked up at the brightening sky, hoping to see a crow soaring dramatically out of the dawn. But instead, a few sparrows flew down, landed on the sidewalk, and began pecking at crumbs or pebbles.

Levinson chuckled and shook his head at his expectations. Always wanting more. Hadn't he seen enough miracles for one lifetime?

He watched the sparrows until they flew away. And then, keeping his promise to Amy Carlisle, he went to temple for the first time in many years. There he said Kaddish, not only for her, but for those who died with her, and those who died because of her.

He who maketh peace in his high places,
May he make peace for us.

CHET WILLIAMSON has contributed to Crow lore as the author of the novelization of the film, *The Crow: City of Angels* (Boulevard Books) and the short story, "The Blood Red Sea," in the anthology, *The Crow: Shattered Lives and Broken Dreams*, edited by James O'Barr and Edward E. Kramer (Del Ray). His other recent titles include *The Searchers*, a new paranormal fiction series from Avon Books, and *Second Chance*.

Over eighty of his short stories have appeared in *The New Yorker*, *Playboy*, *Esquire*, *The Magazine of Fantasy and Science Fiction*, and in many other magazines and anthologies. He has been a final nominee for the World Fantasy Award, the Mystery Writers of America's Edgar Award, and the Horror Writers' Association's Stoker Award.

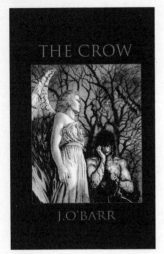

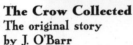

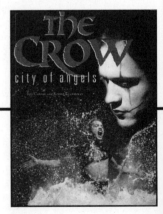

VENGEANCE COMES ON WINGS IN THE NIGHT.

THE CROW

In the realm of The Crow the innocent must die so that justice can triumph. Hovering in the twilight world between the fading light and the hungry dark, he guides those tortured souls who fight for revenge *and* love, those willing to go all the way—and beyond.

Join the hunt in these original novels by today's masters of terror. . . .

Quoth the Crow
by David Bischoff
ISBN 0-06-105825-4
$13.00/$18.50 (Can.)
The grave is the doorway to truth when a writer sets out for vengeance on the human carrion who savagely murdered him and brutally violated his wife.

The Lazarus Heart
by Poppy Z. Brite
ISBN 0-06-105824-6
$13.00/$18.50 (Can.)
Wrongly convicted of murder and then killed in Louisiana's prison system, a shadowy avenger stalks the gothic netherworld of New Orleans, seeking in death the justice that proved so elusive in life.

Clash by Night
by Chet Williamson
ISBN 0-06-105826-2
$13.00/$19.00 (Can.)
A dedicated teacher cut down by a hate-crazed militia's bomb sets off on a search-and-destroy mission of her own, accompanied by a black-winged avenger.

At bookstores now, or call
1-800-242-7737 to order direct.

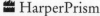 HarperPrism
A Division of HarperCollins*Publishers*
www.harperprism.com